CHILDREN OF ATLANTIS:
KEEPERS OF THE CRYSTAL SKULL

Dear Susan,

Wishing you many blessings on your journey

Bob

Other titles by Dr. Robert Maldonado

The Calling of the Heart—A Journey in Self-Healing

CHILDREN OF ATLANTIS: KEEPERS OF THE CRYSTAL SKULL

ROBERT R. MALDONADO PHD.

ISBN: 1506191509
ISBN 13: 9781506191508

*In memory of the "disappeared"
and victims of Argentina's "Dirty War"*

ACKNOWLEDGEMENTS

I owe a huge debt of gratitude to many friends who gave so generously of their support, advice and help during the writing of this book. Most important, my love and gratitude to my wife Ellen, for her love, insights and editing recommendations. She was always upbeat, positive and encouraging, never doubting that the book needed to be written.

My editor, Alisha was brilliant throughout and gave fantastic editorial support through numerous iterations.

My friends, John Woods, Judy Bishop, Kent Rush and Linda Herndon, who gave for their time and keen insights on improving the manuscript. I cannot thank them enough. I am also grateful to Mahala Church for her creative writing classes and helping me to better understand the writing and editing process.

To Patricia Cori and fellow travelers to Machu Pichu, Lake Titicaca and Amantani island for inspiring me to write this novel.

To Patricia Hayes and the faculty at Delphi University for the soul portrait reading and Entura Art classes. They were wonderful. Thank you.

Finally, to all my colleagues and friends on the spiritual path for showing me the way.

TABLE OF CONTENTS

INTRODUCTION

In 2012, I received a Soul portrait and reading from a gifted psychic artist who channeled the energies of my spiritual guides and images of my energy field. The technique known as Entura Art enables the artist to enter the auric field of a person and channel the energy through color and motion on paper. Beautiful colors and shapes form mirroring the energy field and revealing new insights and information. Many of the scenes in this book and my past lives emerged through this technique taught by Ms. Patricia Hayes, founder and President of Delphi University and Spiritual Center, in McCaysville, Georgia.

My portrait revealed a past life as a high priest during the final cataclysmic destruction of Atlantis, the ancient island-continent that mysteriously disappeared approximately 10,000 years ago. During that life I had led a small contingent of survivors on a migration to South America, settling in the Lake Titicaca region of Peru.

As a high priest, I had been engaged in a life or death struggle in opposition to the threatening Temple of the Sun; a religious order made up of loyal descendants of the Sons of Belial vying for manipulation and enslavement of the Atlantean population to suit their plans for a New World Order.

I was so intrigued with this information that I felt I had to examine the meaning of this mysterious past life in my current one. I knew very little about Atlantis and I had many questions. I reasoned that exploring where I have been and where I come from afforded me an opportunity to better realize who I am and where I just might be able to go. What unfolded was a fascinating journey of self-discovery and exploration culminating in the writing of this book.

The story of the Lost Continent of Atlantis is one of the most exciting mysteries of history, the subject of extensive archeological research as well as popular legend. Atlantis was a magnificent, idyllic world, the stuff of our wildest dreams; an advanced culture in the style of our modern western civilization. It occupied a large land mass between Europe and America, now submerged beneath the Atlantic Ocean. To this day, no one has been able to say with certainty where it was. Nonetheless, many experts believe it influenced ancient civilizations from Egypt to pre-Columbian America.

For thousands of years, this society tried to see if its people could live in a physical body and still keep their connection with God, their creator. Throughout its history, its citizens endured many crises and catastrophic disasters. Each time the cities were destroyed, it became clear that their core values of love, community, and oneness, had been perverted and supplanted by greed, lust for power and materialism moving them further from Source. Yet, in the midst of the shift back and forth, an Atlantean "Golden Era" emerged. Over a period of roughly 1,500 years, the people re-discovered their pure natures and oneness with the creator enjoying some incredible spiritual, psychic, and technological powers. During its "Golden Age", Atlantis rose to world prominence and heights of intelligence and prosperity rarely seen on Earth.

Yet even this greatest of civilizations could not withstand a prolonged attack, and it slowly rotted from within. Driven by the selfish, manipulative, mystic order known as the Temple of the Sun, Atlantis was torn again by conflict and succumbed to the temptations of the ego: the unbridled hunger for power, influence, and empire. As these negative elements exerted themselves, the Law of One began to fade.

The great struggle with the Temple of the Sun continued for hundreds of years. Throughout, the generations of the Law of One served as beacons of light. Illuminating the path of unselfish love, they helped the lost find their way home to their spiritual heritage of oneness, harmony, and freedom.

A small cadre of priests of the Law of One rebelled against the Temple of the Sun. They were a small group of believers chosen to be guardians of the wisdom of Atlantis for future generations. This is a story of their struggle and sacrifice.

Today, some of the same events that affected Atlantis are being played out as we move through a time of accelerated evolution into a new Golden Age of Aquarius. One of my goals in this book is to bring a new awareness around the energies at work in the final hours of Atlantis because it directly relates to the duality of the earth field reality we presently inhabit. It manifests in the inner and outer struggles that we face as human beings. I believe that ultimately, the struggle is an inward one and, the key question we must ask is whether or not we can accept and integrate ALL our polar aspects—the good and bad, the light and darkness and strive for more balance and self-acceptance. Do we have the insight and courage to own our own dark side—the shadow to be whole? Can we celebrate the process of our inner transformation with love and honesty and accept that we are truly amazing "star beings" undergoing an "earth" experience in our spiritual growth? Can we really accept and become the magnificence of who we really are? I believe that the answers to these can be learned from the Atlantean experience.

I ask that you read this book with an open heart and mind. I realized as I wrote it that some of it may appear fanciful - subjects like our shadow and darker natures, crystal skulls, energy healing, reincarnation and past lives, dark entities, soul rescue, automatic writing, the horrors of torture, and the enigmatic draw of life purpose are rarely treated in this manner. If you are drawn to this story, then perhaps you too come from the last generation of Atlantis and are now on your own a voyage of self-discovery to help raise the consciousness of humanity and the planet. Welcome aboard!

Although this book is fiction, sadly, the plight of the "disappeared" from the years of the oppressive military junta during the "Dirty War" (1976-1983) in Argentina is not. It was not my original intent, but somehow the tragedy of the "disappeared" found its way into the narrative. Perhaps it is a message for us to pay attention to this drama in our times and its lessons in the context of the Atlantean drama. I was careful to present this accurately but with respect and compassion for the voices of the victims and their families. I felt that they wanted to be heard, their souls clamoring for a voice. There were also many special moments where I was compelled to do deep meditation work and connect with some of the discarnate souls still on the earth plane from that time period, to help them move into the light. I do not take this responsibility lightly and offered whatever assistance I could.

Finally, in October 2011, I traveled with an international group to Lake Titicaca in Peru. It is a beautiful place and I was struck by the generous hospitality and friendship of the local people, the original descendants of the Incas. I was enthralled and blessed by many memorable experiences during my visit.

Robert Maldonado, February, 2015

PRINCIPLE CAST OF CHARACTERS

PRESENT TIME

Dr. Andres Paredes—Senior Archeologist, Department of Archeology and Anthropology of Bolivia, La Paz, Bolivia.

Oscar Mendoza—Paredes assistant, Department of Archeology and Anthropology of Bolivia, La Paz, Bolivia

Don Julio Carasco—Bolivian shaman and mentor to Paredes.

Dr. Lorenzo Epis--Professor of ancient cultures from the University of Bologna, Italy.

Dr. Edmond Grasser-- Professor emeritus of ancient archeology from UCLA, expedition team chief.

Naval Captain Julian Becerra Marti—retired Argentine naval officer implicated in torture and atrocities committed by military junta during the "Dirty War" in Argentina 1976-1983.

Naval Lieutenant Francisco Paredes—Andres Paredes step-father and former Argentine naval officer.

Elizabeth Paredes—Andres Paredes step-mother.

Sarah Inez Escobedo—Paredes biological mother.

Dr. Enrico Busam—Astronomer, National Aeronautics and Space Agency (NASA) Jet Propulsion Center, California Institute of Technology.

Dr. Shan Simrah-- Astronomer, National Aeronautics and Space Agency (NASA) Jet Propulsion Center, California Institute of Technology.

Captain Enrico Bedoya—police chief, La Paz, Bolivia

ATLANTIS TIME

Alkur—priest & healer of the Law of One. A leader of survivors who fled the destruction of Atlantis to Lake Titicaca. Former officer in the Kings Elite Imperial Palace Guard.

Akaus—a princess who uses her talent in music in the Law of One to pacify conditions between humans and their environment. Friend of Alkur and sound specialist; travels to Lake Titicaca. She develops "music" to counter Sons of Belial sounds. She soothes Alkur's soul.

Amillius—high priest at the Temple of the Sun in the city of Poseidon who rose to prominence as leader of the Belial Illuminati. He displayed great talents of ambition, deception, and manipulation. He found a great avenue of experience in politics and furtherance of his ultimate goals for himself and Atlantis. He became obsessed by his lust for materialism and power. Became ruler of Atlantis.

Ampero—Alkur's wife. Priestess of the Law of One.

Am-ee-lee—a high ranking librarian who was afraid that conflict would undermine civilization; organized and dispatched several missions to transfer vital religious, scientific and historical records for safekeeping around the globe. Alkur's trusted confidant who helped secure skull from Temple of Thoth; travels to Lake Titicaca.

Asa-masa-me—priestess in Law of One religion; language expert and specialist in ancient indigenous practices. Helped with translations and good will ambassador with natives. Travels to Lake Titicaca.

Ax-Tos—humble physician and priest in the Law of One. Argued against the materialist Sons of Belial. Performs medical miracles. Close friend of Alkur who survives and travels to Lake Titicaca.

Caphala—warrior, friend and former member of Kings Guards, travels with Alkur to Lake Titicaca.

Elchi--Atlantean navigator. An expert on transportation/teleportation and movement technologies. Travels with Alkur to Lake Titicaca.

Ellm—Alkur's father. A former head priest of the Law of One who rose up against Sons of Belial in rebellion. A leader and martyr. Escaped the destruction of Atlantis only to be captured and executed later in a far away land.

Hulos—Indian chieftain's daughter; name means "running water." Rescued by Alkur at Lake Titicaca and later becomes his wife.

Ilax—"princess of fire" in the Law of One; Priestess and shaman; lost her power when she took the wrong side. Advisor to Alkur—travels to Lake Titicaca. She represents the divine feminine who trains Alkur in the "force" of love.

Rariru—native chief--instrumental in blending newly arrived Atlanteans into prehistoric Peruvian society; instituted worship of the sun and solar forces; later became Inti-Rai-Mi, the most important Andean Sun god ceremony.

Saail—defrocked priest who used the temples of Law of One for "sin"; traitor who turned to Sons of Belial in active rebellion against his former flock. Father of Salkuzzar who becomes evil ruler in Lake Titicaca.

Salkuzzar—High priest in Temple of the Sun; architect of plan to destroy Temple of the Law of One and to bring Atlantis under his control.

Zonar--High priest in Law of One; betrayed and conspired against his order and joined Belial Illuminati.

PART 1: BEGINNINGS

For it is related in our records how once upon a time your
State stayed the course of a mighty host, which, starting
from a distant point in the Atlantic Ocean, was insolently
advancing to attack the whole of Europe, and Asia to boot.
For the ocean there was at that time navigable; for in front of
the mouth which you Greeks call, as you say, 'the pillars of
Heracles,' there lay an island which was larger than Libya
and Asia together; and it was possible for the travelers of
that time to cross from it to the other islands, and from the
islands to the whole of the continent over against them which
encompasses that veritable ocean. For all that we have here,
lying within the mouth of which we speak, is evidently a haven
having a narrow entrance; but that yonder is a real ocean,
and the land surrounding it may most rightly be called, in
the fullest and truest sense, a continent. Now in this island
of Atlantis there existed a confederation of kings, of great
and marvelous power, which held sway over all the island,
and many other islands also and parts of the continent...

PLATO'S TIMAEUS

*A hero ventures forth from the world of common day
into a region of supernatural wonder: fabulous forces
are there encountered and a decisive victory is own:
the hero comes back from this mysterious adventure
with the power to bestow boons on his fellow man.*

JOSEPH CAMPBELL

PROLOGUE

What I describe here may seem unbelievable, yet it happened. I made a choice that changed everything and found myself facing the gravest dangers of my life.

I am an archeologist. I was born in Argentina during the "Dirty War", where the repressive military regime kidnapped, imprisoned, tortured and killed tens of thousands. My family escaped to Bolivia.

I've always been a quiet, academic sort of guy, not the sort to rush to the spotlight for glory, fame or fortune, just an ordinary guy. History, ancient history fascinates me. When I can, I'm an avid reader, scuba diver and hiker. I love to watch futbol, especially Club Bolivar, although they've been doing poorly lately. I also meditate. It started when a college girlfriend dragged me to a class; lost the girlfriend, but kept the practice. Although not married, I've been in a couple of long-term relationships that teetered on the marital brink. I love my work.

But now, somehow, I've fallen, no – been thrust in to a completely strange, but true, adventure. It all began when I made the discovery of an ancient crystal skull in a cave at the bottom of Lake Titicaca. What happened next I cannot explain: that the skull would have mysterious powers and induce trance states which somehow compelled me to write about a past life in ancient Atlantis.

I am on a quest armed with a new purpose; to walk in service to the planet using the energies of unconditional love channeled through the crystal skull to open ancient energy portals and strengthen a new crystalline grid, for the ascension of the earth and humanity.

I now know what I am up against, and they know who I am, too. Forces of darkness are after me. They do not want the change. My task is clear. One day the light will triumph, must triumph. I fear for all humanity if the dark succeeds.

This journal, really an extract of notes I've kept, is meant for others should my quest prove fatal. At least someone will understand; someone who will continue the fight.

This is my story...

Chapter 1

JUNE 6, 2013
AMAZON JUNGLE

I'm in a remote and unforgiving part of the Peruvian Amazon near the ancient Inca city of Vilcabamba where I conducted a ceremony yesterday to open an ancestral portal, closed for thousands of years.

The ceremony was held in a cave, tucked back in the hillside. Afterwards, with tired smiles, we retired back to our camp, happy and pleased with the outcome. Stories and jokes, missing for the past few days, came back as we relaxed and even the native helpers were laughing and at ease for a change. But the cave never left my mind.

Legend has it that the cave was the place where the Incas, fleeing from the Spanish, hid their Empire's treasures. The treasures were never seen again. The native legend says that the cave is the burial site of a tall, red haired, fair skinned man, believed to be a culture bearer, and their leader. The story is that he arrived by ship, leading survivors from a catastrophe in their homeland, faraway in the East. Could this be a Spanish explorer or what the natives call the White Barbarians or Atlantean survivors, I wondered? Sometimes there are little nuggets of truth in the old legends.

It's unreal here, we feel like we've being transported back into some timeless dimension devoid of civilization. My small party of six, mostly native helpers and guides, are at the mercy of the suffocating heat and humidity. By the third day of our trek in, we were miserable and exhausted. We got lost for a while. Then two of my friends slipped on the bank and were swept up by the fast running river and, although we quickly pulled them out, both were injured by the logs and branches that lurk beneath water. One of the natives is ill from snakebite; but thanks to the local curadero or medicine man, he'll recover.

We're still hobbling along. But after the monsoon-like rains typical of this area and an attack by Indians armed with poison–tipped arrows we're lucky to be alive. And, it's not over. Our translator says that our native workers are unhappy with the pay and hazards; we may have trouble with them.

But I didn't start this journal to complain about our hardships. I started it to tell the world about our discoveries.

We will be leaving soon on our way back to Cuzco. I pulled my dirty boots back over my swollen feet and left the group who were all still sleeping in the tents, to explore. I could not sleep. It was the cave. I had this strange feeling of being called to it once again.

I didn't see anyone on the trail. Back in the cave, I flashed my torchlight around for a better view. Then I saw it. A door, made of a reddish native wood, fit neatly into the rock to the left. I hadn't noticed it before. I pushed, then pulled it, but it wouldn't budge. I tried again and it suddenly gave way with a shudder, releasing pieces of rock and dust. I shoved it open slowly and peered into the darkness. The damp, musty odor of decay hit my palate and filled my throat. I pulled my bandana up to cover my nose and mouth.

The opening behind the door was about two meters high and a meter and one half wide; the edges were irregular. The damp earth was alive with the frantic writhing of worms, centipedes and other insects exposed suddenly to the light. As my eyes adjusted to the dark, I could see a long, narrow tunnel-like cavern ahead.

Taking a deep breath, I stepped into the passageway careful not to brush against the walls. I hesitated for a moment, a small warning that ahead lurked something that was better left undisturbed. But the dark drew me in. My flashlight scattered shadows off the jagged walls and I could make out the size and shape of the cavern. It was small, about 12 meters long and perhaps three meters tall, clearly fashioned by men rather than by nature alone.

Moving ahead, the footing was loose, the dirt less firm beneath me. Suddenly, I lost my balance as my right leg dropped into a small hole and I fell forward. Pointing the light, I saw that I was in a shallow hole. As I lay there I noticed that I was lying on a piece of yellowed cloth, covered in dirt. As I brushed the dirt away and pulled back the cloth I noticed a human skeleton, its bones carefully wrapped in the cloth, eroded by time but intact. I was in a shallow dug-out grave. Someone took the trouble to lay this person out neatly, respectfully. Lying next to it were dusty gold and silver cups and flasks encrusted with rubies, emeralds, diamonds and unknown stones.

I was already sure that this was a major find and then I saw the quartz dagger by the skeleton's feet. Jesus what a treasure, I thought. The discovery of this burial alone, in fact against all odds of time and nature, would have put this expedition on the map, but the dagger was unlike anything I've ever seen.

Even in the dim light, it was beautiful. It appeared ceremonial, made of bronze, gold, silver, or copper. I wasn't sure. It was three hand lengths long and the handle was made of a green-blueish stone, perhaps lapis, and embedded in it were an assortment of colorful stones and crystals.

I pulled my eyes from the treasures and crouched down to examine the skeleton, careful not to disturb anything. The right frontal area of the cranium appeared crushed perhaps from a blunt impact, maybe a sword or rock. There was more evidence of violence on the right hand, a missing little finger, and several broken ribs. It was a common practice in the days of the Incas for elaborate burials to prepare their royalty for the next life. This person must have been very important.

Then something shifted within me. As I stared at the skeleton, I had the odd sensation of being in the presence of someone extraordinary, of knowing him, of being at home here. It was if I was looking at myself.

If you're going to understand anything that follows I feel like I need to tell you how we found ourselves here in the Amazon in the first place. I've reconstructed the following from notes that I kept in my datebook.

Chapter 2

MARCH 10, 2012
LAKE TITICACA, BOLIVIA

Fifteen months ago the team saw on the pulsating monitor screens the outlines of an ancient city.

"There it is! Fantastic." I shouted and slapped my trusted assistant Oscar Mendoza on the back. We grinned at each other. There was high fiving, and whoops around the boat cabin.

The pictures that the ROV (Remotely Operated Vehicle) sent back showed what appeared to be a sunken temple, flanked by lop-sided buildings. It must be a temple; the structure still had some large steps raising it above the other plainer enclosures. Debris from the lake water floated through the pictures.

"Yes, yes – this is it!" Carlos, one of the divers, was excited by the find. Then he joined the huddle staring at the screens.

Even though it was settled in the lakebed, the symmetrically organized stone buildings looked set out like a town, a tumble-down town, but still we could discern roads and clearings. As the ROV's light panned the area, we saw huge granite blocks lying in regular rectangles, circles and pyramids. Most were two to five meters long and appeared smooth and obviously engineered by experts. The pictures revealed distinct targets for exploration along the survey lines.

"This is incredible" Oscar said in an exuberant voice with a huge smile, a change from his normal reserve. "We showed them."

Despite three earlier unsuccessful attempts, international grants and government support had finally made this expedition possible. It had certainly helped to have the backing of two of the world's most renowned experts on ancient Inca and Tiahuanaco civilizations: Dr. Lorenzo Epis, professor of ancient cultures from the University of Bologna, Italy and Dr. Edmond Grasser, professor emeritus of ancient archeology from UCLA. Dr. Grasser was acting as the expedition team chief. Their interest validated the enterprise that scientists had disparaged as a wild goose chase.

Our research vessel, "Inti," was specially equipped for this assignment. It had high–precision side scan sonar and radar, satellite-integrated seafloor positioning systems, and a multi-beam swath bathymetry system. All these systems were integral to displaying and mapping a three-dimensional picture of the lost city we sought. I leaned over the shoulders of Drs. Epis and Grasser as we all watched the images.

Dr. Epis, excitedly remarked, "You can even see the ancient road leading to the temple. The clarity is amazing. Can you zoom in? Right there. Good." Dr. Grasser was elated, too absorbed in the images to comment. The technician quickly adjusted the controls.

As the camera image focused, there was a collective gasp of astonishment. Right by the temple wall, we saw, plain as day, a tunnel leading under the building. That it could survive hundreds of years under water was impossible. I moved closer to the monitor, "A cave!"

I asked our technician Enrico "Zoom in closer."

As the optics focused some more I could see it more distinctly. "It looks like the legend was right after all" whispered Grasser.

Dr. Epis was jubilant. "I have seen enough. Let's dive. We need to survey the area and get some markers out so we can plan the exploration. Let's get the building map started."

Still focused intently on the monitor, I remember saying, "Wait. I think we need to check out this cave."

Epis looked up in surprise. Glasser watched the monitor without comment; he gave no indication that he had even heard my suggestion.

"Andres, you know it's not in the plan. We have already discussed our approach for this expedition. It's no time to chase mythology." Epis turned to the dive locker.

He was right, I thought. It was not in the plan. It was risky and a distraction from the primary objective to explore the temple and its surroundings.

"But...can't you see that we have a valuable opportunity here?" I insisted. "This will capture the imagination of people and could be important."

Epis stared at me, features stiffening, then, he walked away shaking his head. He was not used to anyone challenging his views. Perhaps I was out of line. I didn't want to sour our working relationship.

Glasser finally raised his head from the monitor. He stood up looking at me with concern, and then put his hand on my shoulder. "Andres, you know he's on the hook for the overall success of this. Lorenzo is afraid the money will run out before we've discovered anything that will justify continued financial support. I know how important the cave is to you. But Lorenzo's right. We'll get to the cave in due..."

"But..." I interrupted, stopped and nodded acquiescence. At least Glasser understood. I grabbed my gear and went out on deck with the others.

The air that morning was soft with a mist slowly disappearing as the sun rose over the placid lake. At 12,464 feet above sea level, Lake Titicaca sits on the borders of Bolivia and Peru. It is the highest navigable lake in the world. The first inhabitants called Titicaca their Lago Sagrado or "holy lake." There's something to that I thought; every time I visited, I was struck by its beauty and was changed somehow. On that day, I was proud and eager to be in her warm embrace again. After twenty five years with the Institute, the morning's find was the most important discovery of my career.

The Inti lay anchored on the calm waters. It was going to be a long day as we assembled on the fantail for final equipment checks and to review the dive and safety plans. For the first dive, my team was to follow the route that the ROV had taken and map the site. Time permitting, we could collect surface artifacts for later examination at the Institute. Dr. Epis stressed the importance of documenting everything and following the plan and dive protocol.

I was curious about the cave - drawn to it. I could not get it out of my mind. My focus in archeology has been the nexus of myth and physical materials. I was fascinated with Inca power places in particular the Andean archaeo-astronomical connections and how they tie to their legends. For centuries, locals have told stories of an ancient cave beneath the lake where humans were sacrificed to the Gods. It was said that 200 children were sacrificed in one day there.

It may have been the exchange with Dr. Epis, but I had a nervous twitch in my stomach that dampened the excitement of the dive. Something did not feel right.

Once in the frigid waters, I descended along the anchor line and watched the other teams swim out to their assigned areas. The southern side of the temple lay straight ahead. Near a large column, the one we had seen on the camera feed lay the cave opening.

When we swam by the city I was mesmerized by what was unfolding before us. It was beautifully preserved in the water. What happened to the people who lived here, thousands of years ago? Who were they and what can we learn from them? My academic training took over as we mapped, measured and diagramed the area.

After two dives and the mid-day meal, we finished the survey a little ahead of schedule. With oxygen remaining in my tank, I decided to take a few minutes and explore the cave. Over the radio, I asked for volunteers since this was not part of the day's plan. Perhaps it was stubbornness but I pressed on anyway.

Three guys from my team wanted to come. Luckily, we still had nylon rope to serve as a safety line should we become lost. Although I had done some caving during my time in the Andes, looking for relics, I knew underwater cave exploration was entirely different and much more dangerous. I had a sudden tightness, perhaps a primeval fear of the unknown. But a sense of urgency and excitement took over. I was not about to let this opportunity pass.

At the cave entrance we checked our gear, remaining oxygen and the headlamps. I saw three thumbs up. We were ready. The water was clear as we glided single file past the entrance. Ahead we could see that the walls constricting slightly. After about 100 meters, the cave walls narrowed unnervingly and the visibility abruptly dropped as our fins disturbed the sediment on the bottom.

"Keep close together," I called on the radio.

The current was becoming stronger. As we made a turn, the passage grew smaller still. I felt the top of my oxygen tank rub the ceiling. It was tight and dark. Then it hit me. I was afraid of confined spaces, and I was getting stuck. As the darkness and sediment engulfed us, I doubted my decision to do this. My heart raced and my breathing grew rapid, the onset of panic. I remember thinking This is really stupid, Andres. You may not make it.

I may be reckless sometimes but I knew never to endanger my team and I knew I had to face my fear head on. "I'm going on alone from here. You all stay back by the entry. It's too risky for everyone" I transmitted to the others.

I got some argument from Carlos, one of the more experienced divers, but reluctantly, they agreed and slowly backed away. I knew I was breaking a fundamental rule of cave diving – going alone.

Just a few meters ahead, the cave widened and I could see a faint, shimmering light. I strained to see through the suspended silt. The visibility was low but as the water cleared, I realized I was heading into an underwater room, a concert hall size room really. With air.

I surfaced and slowly removed my mask. I was able to prop my arms up on a rock protrusion resting my legs. The air in there was thick and musky, yet breathable.

For a moment, I thought, Oh God, I've got narcosis and I'm hallucinating. The cavern walls were covered with thousands of crystals embedded in white, red and black stones. The iridescent glow of the colors seemed to melt on the walls of the cavern. I have no idea where the light originated – totally unlike anything I had ever seen before. The cavern glowed pink and gold. It must have been a sacred ceremonial chamber, I thought. I was thrilled and couldn't wait to tell the others.

I knew that this discovery would be unprecedented. I tried to radio in to tell the team what I found but heard only static.

"Inti, Inti, Paredes, come in, over." No answer. The cave blocked all transmissions. I needed to get back to my friends. I pulled up the camera that dangled from my dive belt and quickly took some pictures.

Then, I saw something odd floating on the far side of the cavern, a black raft-like thing. Check it out; it will only take a minute. I pulled my mask back on and swam the 30 meters or so over to it. What had looked benign, I realized to my horror, was a diver in a black wetsuit floating face down.

With effort, I rolled him over. His white swollen face, eyes and mouth were agape, frozen in sheer terror. He looked as if he had died from fright. He must have been dead for some time, the skin was sloughing off. His gauge showed oxygen still in his tanks. I saw no signs of injury or identity tags. What happened? Who is this guy?

My euphoria with the cavern was dampened if not gone. I scanned for any other unusual signs or hazards. Nothing. I toyed with the idea of pulling him behind me out of the cave but decided I couldn't do it alone. I needed to get back to the Inti.

As I turned away, a shiny object on rock shelf tucked behind a rock column caught my eye. I swam closer and could see that it was a human skull. The legends about the temple mentioned skulls, but the skull certainly didn't come from any human. It was crystalline and radiated a violet-translucent color. The closer I got to it, the harder it was for me to focus my eyes. The skull seemed to fade in and out of my vision, as if it did not want to be found. How strange. A low-frequency buzzing sound with a distinct tone and rhythm bounced off the cavern walls.

I couldn't help but wonder if the dead diver was after this skull.

I closed in on it and carefully planted my foot on an ornamental shelf protruding from the wall. To keep my balance, I very slowly reached for the skull; I didn't want to drop it in the water. I moved carefully until I grabbed it. I had to shake it loose from the dirt; it may have been there for centuries.

"Yes!" I shouted.

As soon as I held it, a sharp pulse of energy shot through my hand and in between my eyes. It scared me; I was transfixed. My eyes closed and for a split moment I saw a vision of me, entering the cavern and then unable to get out. I felt like imminent doom. I carefully put the skull in the watertight artifact bag.

Then, I realized I no longer had the nylon rope.

"Shit, shit" I remember blurting to myself. How am I going to get back? I quickly swam around the cavern desperately trying to locate the rope; it should have floated. It was gone. My air supply was getting low. I tried the radio again and got no reply. Not a good sign.

For a moment, I was a kid of eight again, playing by the river. I had slipped over a waterfall and plunged directly below the pounding water. Stuck in the undercurrents, I couldn't surface. Out of air, I panicked and made a mental plea for help. Immediately, a soft voice told me to be calm and that everything was going to be alright. Somehow I broke free of the water and hungrily gulped the air, bruised and shaken but alive. Now, I'm back in that place. I unconsciously shook my head to clear my thoughts.

I glanced at the skull in the bag and a trance-like calmness overtook me. Sounds crazy, but I knew I had to keep the skull in front of me as I swam out. It would guide me through the cave's black passages and back to the entrance. Like the soft voice at the waterfall, I trusted this thought. It was the only way to make it out alive.

I gripped the skull firmly and hoped for the best. With one hand I adjusted my mask and mouthpiece and slipped beneath the water heading to where I thought the passage out would be. Enveloped in the darkness I lost all sense of direction or distance. But as I hovered on the edge of panic, the skull grew brighter, like a giant floodlight illuminating the path ahead. This was my first glimpse of what I would come to realize was the unique power of this incredible object.

Peering through the silt, there was the nylon rope and further ahead, the entrance to the cave. My air was nearly gone; I'd have to surface fast. I was betting that decompression wouldn't be a problem. Ahead I could dimly see Carlos and the others, waiting for me.

I surfaced near the ship, suddenly exhilarated. Triumphant and relieved. The sunlight was glorious. I had survived and had a trophy from the cave. Despite being a bit giddy, I couldn't figure out how to explain to the others what I saw and experienced with the skull. They'd think I was nuts. I put the skull back in my bag; its glow was gone.

What could I tell the group? I kept thinking about the dead diver. That face. Someone was surely missing this guy. I should have taken a picture.

The others were grinning in relief when they saw me. Carlos, already on the metal ladder, turned shaking his head, "Jesus Christ, Andreas, we were worried ..." I grinned, but found I was so completely drained of energy that I couldn't pull myself from the water. The team dragged me aboard.

I heaved myself up on a bench. Panting, I managed to pull the crystal skull from the bag. Everyone stared at the skull, then back to me. Then I started to recount what had happened.

Dr. Glasser joined the group. He tried to hide a smile, and in a half-serious tone added, "We were afraid that you were the legend's latest victim." Carlos took my arm to help me up. Dr. Glasser was saying to the group, "It's been a productive day ..."

"I've never seen anything quite like this" I couldn't help interrupting. In the daylight, the skull glowed. Dr. Glasser came closer to examine my find, after his first glance; I could see he was intrigued. Then Dr. Epis emerged from the cabin, visibly irritated. I figured he'd calm down once he saw my prize and realized that I was alright.

"Andres, you deviated from the plan and almost ran out of air. What if you had been caught underwater? You were alone. You endangered the entire expedition with this foolishness. Totally irresponsible, Andres!" Dr. Epis looked stern; his voice was angry.

He's right, I thought. I came close to being a bad statistic. I was lucky. I'll never be able to tell him how close it was.

Dr. Epis then noticed that I held something. "What's that?" curiosity overcoming his annoyance.

"It looks like a crystal skull." I said, turning it toward Dr. Epis so he could get a clearer view.

Both Epis and Glaser edged closer; Glaser pulled out his pocket magnifying glass for a quick once over. "I don't see any inscriptions but there may be linear grooves. We'll have to get a better look. It's a very unusual crystal material."

Dr. Epis looked at me, "Get some photographs and log it in Andres. Can you document exactly where it was found?"

I told him that I'd take care of the paperwork, but that I needed to tell them all the whole story of what had happened. I was now eager to tell my story. I set the skull carefully on a towel on the bench for all to see.

Suddenly, a rasping growl came from the skull. Everyone jumped back; those on the bench edged quickly away.

My legs weakened. The last thing I saw before blacking out was two men on shore dressed in black suits. From the boat, it looked like they were packing up camera equipment and stowing it in the trunk of a black sedan. One was elderly with a distinctive mustache. I faded out as the van sped away.

Chapter 3

MARCH 11, 2012
DEPARTMENT OF ARCHEOLOGY
AND ANTHROPOLOGY OF BOLIVIA

I slept for ten hours, and when I woke up the next day the team doctor pronounced me healthy and fit to return to work. They chalked the collapse up to sheer exhaustion and the unusual sounds to an odd breeze whistling through the skull. The Inti was in port while the initial survey results were analyzed.

Dr. Epis met me in the passageway by the doctor's office. After asking how I was, his only comment was, "since you found it, why don't you start the skull study." He patted my shoulder as he walked on by, clearly pleased with the find. He had already inventoried and photographed the skull.

I was delighted. I knew that somehow the skull had triggered my blackout. Then, there was the image of the two men. What was that all about? I wondered. I was eager to examine it; there must be some electro-magnetic components or something within it. After all, it had glowed in the water.

"Oscar, this discovery will keep us busy for some time," I told my assistant as we settled in for work that morning.

He nodded in agreement, "Coffee first?" I smiled and turned toward him, cup in hand, "Of course."

He reached for the coffee pot which we kept going in the office then turned back to his review of the survey photos. Oscar was always the practical one.

I shook my head and turned back to the artifact that lay on my desk. I traced the skull's grooves, taking notes on a yellow lined pad. Although I was convinced the skull had some emanations that affected me, I was oddly reluctant to voice that to Oscar. At least until we found a cause. I hadn't told anyone of my experience in the cave. What caused the strange sensations between my eyes? How did the skull light up and lead me to safety? I had more questions than answers.

We'd almost done processing the pictures from the survey trip.

I wondered aloud how it was made. I was talking to myself mostly. "There aren't any obvious scratches indicating it was carved with metal tools. It looks like a solid quartz crystal." That's an unusual material for the ancient Inca and Tiahuanaco craftsmen to work with, I thought.

Oscar rose from his desk and leaned over my shoulder, "Perhaps from another civilization?"

I thought that Oscar had a point. It was definitely worth considering. The ancient Andean cultures had some amazing technologies; I've learned not to underestimate them.

My preliminary internet searches revealed that skull carvings had been found in ancient temples in Tibet, Peru, and Mexico. It was a common motif with an abundance of folklore surrounding them. Museums and private collections held a number of skulls.

No, I thought, there is something more at work here. This one's different. It's strange energy for one thing. Maybe it was used for healing and prophecy, maybe by shamans. It's a starting point.

"What are these markings on top here? Can you see them?" I asked. Oscar has a good eye for patterns and a remarkable ability to recall similar designs once seen. That's one of the reasons I like having Oscar around.

He moved closer, "Yes, I see... very symmetrical and look ... almost like hieroglyphics or dioramas of daily life. The Sumerian and Mayans both incorporated decorations like that." He nodded; satisfied we're getting on track.

"Right... perhaps it's connected to our Andean cultures but I don't see a clear resemblance yet. And how did they do it? It's really expert craftsmanship."

We both stared at it for few moments, silently pondering the question. It was time for science and modern equipment to take over.

"Artisans of the 19th century had tools that could carve a skull like this, but this looks older. Okay, let's see what she looks like under the microscope." Oscar left to retrieve some reference books on Mayan art.

The microscope showed a very fine series of indentations along the skull's surface. It looked like it had been worked using a precision diamond cutting tool or laser which was impossible even a few hundred years ago. How was it created? And by whom, and how did it get into that cave at the lake's bottom? Could this predate the known Andean civilizations? Perhaps carbon-dating could trace its age and origin.

I fiddled with my reading glasses looking out the window at people gathering in the plaza for the holiday celebration. It was the celebration of Pakar Waray an ancient Inca tradition celebrating the blooming of flowers and earth ripening. It was a beautiful time to be in Bolivia.

All along the cities boulevards and the outlying communities were beautiful flower arrangements honoring the Earth Mother Pachamama and gratitude for her earth bounty. The ceremonies were about to start; the festivities would last the entire week. Oscar's extended family came down from the mountains for the party. It was his big reunion each year.

With that in mind, I waved a good-bye to him as he dropped a stack of books by my desk and told him to enjoy the rest of the day. Oscar grabbed his light jacket and saying, "Manana patron. See you tomorrow boss" and was gone.

It was later that afternoon when I dropped my pencil and bending down to retrieve it saw the symbols. Etched in the crystal under the occipital ridge behind and above the skull's base were four symbols of different shapes and sizes. The magnifier gave a better look – I was surprised. We had all missed them before.

What I saw was something I'd never seen before. I've sketched them here:

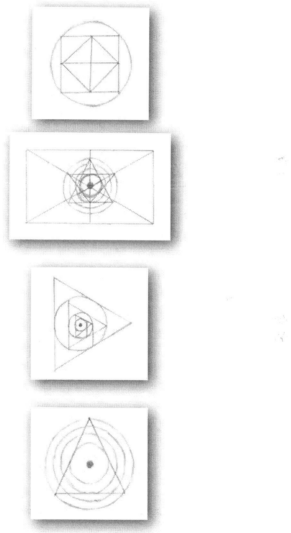

Was this a new language or code? My excitement grew. I checked it again and again. Sure enough, moving from left to right, the symbols became more intricate and complex. I grew excited.

It was late, but I couldn't let go yet. I picked up the tape recorder to dictate my findings for transcription later. I retold my experiences in the underwater cave, discovering the skull and the observations with the symbols and finding the dead diver. It had been two days and I had not told anyone about him. I knew that eventually it had to be reported.

I was dead tired and ready to call it a night and head home. Concluding the recording, I slowly turned the skull between my hands and traced each one of the symbols with my finger on its smooth surface. The designs grew large in my mind; I could see myself move through each pattern. Waves of color and vibrations washed over me. Each design produced distinct sensations, all pleasant.

I closed my eyes and entered into a deep meditative trance that felt much deeper than my past meditations. A soft, yet powerful vibration coursed throughout my body, mostly in my spinal column, on my forehead, sacrum and heart areas as if all my energy centers were being realigned. My breathing slowed. Opening my eyes slightly, I saw the skull lighting the room with brilliant colors.

Suddenly, I saw images, not clear at first, but they appeared to be priests and priestesses, men and women from another era. Their features weren't familiar to me. Then it shifted and I saw scenes from my own life: glimpses of family, friends, schools, adventures and tragedies. It was instantaneous and like I was seeing a life review or preview; a tapestry of all my experiences, good and bad. It was so rich and vivid as if living it all for the first time. There was no judgment, only a feeling of peace that defied understanding, and love and gratitude towards myself and all life. I cannot explain it.

And then the slow, deliberate rhythm of my breath and the vibrations of the symbols slowly began to fade. As I came back out of the trance I realized I needed to get some sleep. But instead of grabbing my jacket to go home, I stretched out on the office sofa, closed my eyes and drifted away.

Chapter 4

MARCH 12, 2012
DEPARTMENT OF ARCHEOLOGY
AND ANTHROPOLOGY OF BOLIVIA

I woke up the next day and my desk clock read 9 a.m. I must have slept for 12 hours. Damn, I could use a shower and change of clothes. I felt rested, but different and was not sure why. Oh yeah, I had dreams of my father. I hadn't done that for years. I remembered wishing he was here to share these discoveries with me.

What happened last night? I can't say with certainty. But the images were so vivid they stuck with me even in the morning. I felt this flow of information coming through me and with it a compulsion to write. It was something I had to do.

I reached for my pen and my journal.

I wrote "ATLANTIS" and then began the book that would change everything for me.

Chapter 5

ATLANTIS

It's a beautiful night and the air crisp and clear, the snowcapped mount Atlas looming in the distance, silhouetted under a full moon. Alkur, a young boy of seven or eight, cowers among the crowd anxiously awaiting the signal to join the ceremonial circle. He is overwhelmed by a sense of being in the presence of something supernatural, something bigger than his experience or comprehension.

All those gathered here are followers of the Law of One, meeting secretly to escape more torment from the Temple of the Sun. Still, the memories were strong of earlier times, when they gathered in their temples to worship in love, harmony and peace. At least tonight they are together once again.

The traditional fire ceremony is about to begin. Alkur watches the head priest dressed in his white garment and deep purple sash adorned with gold necklace and bracelets and a gold headband of the high Alta priesthood, preparing the circle.

The circle, made of precious stones, is shaped like the star system Pleiades to honor and welcome the inter-dimensional star-seed energy of their ancestors.

The priest slowly follows the circle smudging himself and the others with fragrant sage; the smoke cleanses negative energies and expands their energy fields. Finally, he lifts both hands skyward offering sage to the gods. The sacred fire is lit, and they enter the circle.

He then opens the ceremony by calling for blessings, from the Creator above, Earth Mother below and the indwelling spirit. He acknowledges the spirits of the directions by facing first east, then clockwise to the other cardinal points of the sacred wheel. He blows his breath upon the sage, holds it out in offering, saying:

"As we gather here, in communion with each other we honor ourselves and our ancestors, the star beings from the galaxies. Through the sacred fire we find the spirit of our culture; it nourishes each one of us. We are all brothers and sisters united in Oneness. During our time together let us love each other and with respect to mother earth, our divine mother and father sky."

On signal, the drumming commences. The collective beating reverberates through the circle and out across the fields. The otherworldly rhythm synchronizes to the earth's natural harmonics. As the drumming intensifies, etheric forces enter the circle. The flames grow taller and brighter as sudden wisps of wind-driven dust twirl around the fire. Then, the priest holds up his hand and the drummers stop.

The fire is ready to receive the prayers. The priest approaches the fire first. Soon, each person moves in and stands or kneels before it in a sacred connection, a timeless exchange of humility, love and reverence. Some prayers are spoken. Others bring small tokens or scrolls with images of things to be forgotten and forgiven; these are thrown into the fire.

Alkur watches his parents kneeling before the fire, holding hands. He is overcome with a strange sensation that this is the last time he'll see them, a premonition of something terrible that is about to happen. The long hugs and loving words from his father and mother before their journey had felt like a final farewell. He had kept it to himself, too embarrassed to say anything about his fear. His father always told him to be brave.

Suddenly, Alkur turns at the loud noise in his rear. He watches in horror as a large band of masked men on horseback charge out of the shadows towards the circle. The dark shapes ride straight into the people, their razor-sharp swords and spears indiscriminately slashing and hacking.

Thrown into panic, the crowd scatters fleeing for their lives. The horsemen wheel, trampling and slaughtering the terrified men, women and children. Some closest to the fire fall into the flames, their horrible screams piercing the thin air. Black shapes on horseback chase down the remnants, pressing home the attack. There is no mercy, no escape.

Alkur stands motionless watching. Abruptly, he bolts, running as fast as he can to the rocks across the open field, desperate to get away. Not far behind him, others are also fleeing the carnage. Scared and out of breath, he throws himself between the boulders, his hands clenched in fear. He knows they'll find him.

Daring to look up, Alkur sees a tall dark shape giving orders to the men to finish off the wounded. The man ignores their desperate pleading. Alkur recognizes his voice; he has heard that distinct accent before. It sounds like Salkuzzar; the high priest from the Temple of the Sun. Alkur rises to his knees and, peering over the rough stone, stares intently. It is him. Alkur feels cold evil in the air.

In the distance, the dead and wounded are being heaved onto the fire. Horrible shrieks echo. Trembling, he covers his ears and stares in shock at the unfolding violence and the smell of death.

Some of the men were on foot now, hunting for survivors. He closes his eyes and lies still against the rocks. He holds his breath. He can hear their footsteps approaching and their spears swishing through the tall grass, then the anguished cries of the discovered.

Salkuzzar's commands rise above the ground. "Kill them all. Don't let any escape. Show no mercy. Their gods cannot save them now,"

Alkur, frightened, hugs the dirt in his tight crevice. A technique, taught by his father, pops into his head. They had practiced it to become invisible, but Alkur has never performed it under pressure. He thinks: now or never. His eyes close and he sees his power animal, the hawk, rise from the lower world. A warm protective energy surrounds him as he shape-shifts into a hawk. He soars above and away from the carnage and with his sharp vision sees the dark shapes disappear into the darkness. He hears the scattered and chaotic remnants of a triumphant celebration in the distance. He glides back to earth and drifts off into a deep sleep.

Hours later, Alkur lies huddled on the grass remembering the bits of strange dreams from his sleep. In the dream, he had been floating up into a column of bright white light.

Tall iridescent beings radiating unconditional love and compassion greet him. They glow in the light and then congratulatory applause breaks out. He sees other figures walk past him into the vortex of light and the applause of thousands of clapping souls grows louder as they pass by.

The image of his mother and father, love etched on their faces and holding hands, pass before him. He tries to reach out to them and then dreamlike he is unexpectedly looking through the column of light into the fire of that horrible night. White and red streamers swirl around the fire and into the sky. He would have never imagined this —the murdered souls returning through the light vortex to Spirit and being welcomed back by their respective soul groups. It is a grand celebration as they are congratulated for a job well done, a mission successfully completed in the divine plan of Oneness.

Alkur realizes he had been shown a momentary glimpse of higher dimensions. It was a gift, the experience of one's multidimensionality, divinity and the Oneness with all.

All of a sudden he feels older. He is alone in the field. An adult awareness that his life had changed irreparably drops over him. All his family, his dreams and their future just snuffed out. As the sun rises, his despair is complete.

Chapter 6

ATLANTIS

The sky stretched out before them in a painter's palate of blue and pink brushstrokes. Alkur and his father laugh and shout as their horses chase the darting light; his father chides him to keep up. Ellm was a charismatic man; and his gentle strength was never lost on Alkur, who always leaned in, ready to maneuver and pull ahead, continuing the game. Those were the good days, filled with the joy of just being alive and with his father.

There was one time they climbed Mount Atlas and a ferocious storm came screaming in; they barely made it down alive. They competed in sword and wrestling matches, Alkur learning the moves from a master.

But the best memories, those closest to his heart, were of their intimate discussions in the Temple of One reading the sacred texts. One of his favorite passages was:

"The Law says there is no separation from God. We are all parts of the whole and each of our actions affects every creature. All life is a sacred gift worthy of respect. The earth is a living thing and we are the earth's keepers. The Law of One is about freedom, the freedom to let our inner light shine through. We bring our unique selves to the world and allow others to do the same."

Alkur, whose birth name means "the awakened one," is at 26 a tall, well-built man of hazel eyes and long black hair. As head of the security detail responsible for protecting Amillius, the king, and his family, he is growing alarmed by the ongoing unrest in Atlantis. Months before, regime opponents had nearly succeeded in assassinating Amillius. It was his timely and courageous actions that had saved the king that day.

Amillius had been the high priest of the Temple of the Sun and when the government collapsed, he seized power. Salkuzzar, the new head priest and a man of great charm and enormous ambition had succeeded him. He believed in control, intimidation and fear. So far, that tactic has met with mixed results.

These distant memories fall away as he wakes from his memories with a hand on his shoulder. Startled, he turns to see Salius, the king's senior adviser.

Without wasting time on greetings, Salius says simply "Alkur, the king has asked to see you."

Alkur is surprised. He hasn't been summoned by Amillius since the attempt on the king's life. Alkur follows Salius as he briskly walks to the private entrance leading to the king's chamber. The underground passageway is lined with elaborate statues, expeditionary flags and trophies from Atlantis's many military conquests.

As Alkur approaches the chamber he sees the large imposing statues of the Atlantean god Poseidon riding atop his ocean nymphs in exalted glory. Salius knocks on the open door, then walks away leaving Alkur. King Amillius turns and motions for him to enter.

"Please, come in."

Alkur steps forward, stops and bows.

"Alkur, at your service, Excellency."

"Alkur, it's good to see you. Your reputation, indeed your diligence, recommends you. Sadly, I can't say the same for most of my staff; they are useless and given to talk of conspiracies and the opposition," he says with a half-smile. "But you are different, I think, and understand the benefits of loyalty." King Amillius grows serious. "I have an important task for you."

"Yes, Excellency." Alkur is curious, but his face reveals nothing.

"Salkuzzar will be visiting me this evening for a private meeting and he will want to stay overnight in the palace guest quarters. I don't know what he wants from me now."

Amillius stares at the wall, walking and shaking his head. "Salkuzzar is a ruthless, blood-sucking creature, who will not stop till he appoints himself king! Even the gods cringe at the prospect!"

Alkur is startled that the king would share such confidences, but silently agrees with his assessments.

Amillius pauses, then smiling at Alkur, "I need you to not only ensure his safety, but maybe mine as well. I expect he will come alone. You will escort him wherever he goes. Do what he asks but report to me, and only me, afterwards if anything seems unusual. If he is up to no good I need to know it, anything. Understand?"

Alkur uncomfortable says, "Yes, Excellency."

Amillius sighs, "I realize I am asking for something a little beyond your normal duties. But I trust you, and assigning someone from my staff would raise suspicions."

"Your Excellency, does your staff know?"

"That's for me to deal with." Amillius turns toward his table and picks up a scroll. For him the interview is over.

"Yes, of course, Excellency."

"Good. That is all." The king does not look up again, just raises a hand in dismissal.

Alkur bows and walks out uneasy with this turn of events, but also sees the opportunity. This is his chance. His body tenses as he remembers Salkuzzar slaughtering his parents, the murder of innocents, and the heinous cover-up of the incident as a factional dispute within the order. Worse, he can't erase the vivid images of the hundreds of burned and dismembered corpses left to scattered on the plain to rot, and torn by wild animals. Surely Amillius must have known the truth, he thinks. There would be no justice for his loss.

Alkur remembers his vow to avenge, to bring justice, to those who killed his parents. The years after their deaths had been a desperate time for him as he was unable to forgive, to release his anger and hatred towards Salkuzaar and the Temple of the Sun; and deal with his loneliness and hopelessness for the future.

Alkur strides quickly through the palace. Walking helps him think. His preferred option is to confront Salkuzzar and kill him. But even with perfect planning and impeccable timing, the odds were great that he would be arrested and executed. Or, he could ask Amillius for justice against Salkuzzar; Amillius trusts him. But without any evidence or witnesses, it would be Alkur's word against Salkuzzar's, who would certainly deny it. Maybe Amillius would grab the accusation as a chance to imprison Salkuzzar and cut short his ambitions. No, Alkur reasons, this will not work. Regardless, he would be a marked man pursued by Salkuzzar's henchmen. His wife could be targeted. Then again, he could create an "accident" whereupon Salkuzzar dies in his sleep. This felt cowardly. He considered doing nothing but quickly ruled it out.

Alkur decides that confronting and killing Salkuzzar would give him the greatest satisfaction. He would fulfill his vow. It energized him. Salkuzzar must die. He thinks—the hell with the consequences.

It is early evening when Salkuzzar's carriage arrives at the palace. Alkur steps forward to assist him down shadowed by four other Guards.

"Good evening, Excellency. I am Alkur. I will be your personal escort during this visit."

Salkuzzar pauses and looks at him intently. Alkur gazes at his eyes and can feel a shiver as if a cold darkness has enveloped him. Salkuzzar nods and walks by without saying a word. At the Kings quarters Amillius rises to greet Salkuzzar. Alkur discretely retreats and positions himself by the entrance within hearing distance.

Alkur stands silently, alone with his thoughts. He knows that he must patiently wait till Salkuzzar is in his quarters for the evening, and once asleep carry out his plan.

The meeting with Amillius lasts some time. Eventually, the door opens and he hears the king say, "Alkur will escort you to your quarters. I will see you in the morning. Rest well, my friend."

Salkuzzar bows, "Thank you for your hospitality, Excellency."

Amillius exchanges glances with Alkur; the King looks relieved as a trace of a smile crosses his face. The King nods goodbye.

Alkur leads Salkuzzar to the guest quarters in a far wing of the palace. Crossing the large courtyard, Alkur cannot help but notice the starlit sky and the full moon reflected in the small pond and statues. On such a night, his parents died.

"This is your room, Excellency."

Salkuzzar looks in and then turns to face Alkur,

"Do I know you?"

Alkur, completely taken by surprise, barely hesitates.

"I think not, Excellency."

"Are you sure we have not met before?"

Alkur unsettled replies, "I am sure we have not, Excellency... Is that all?"

"Yes, for now."

Alkur bows and walks away with a nauseated feeling that his worst fears have materialized and Salkuzzar has recognized him. How could he know me? If Salkuzzar knows his identity – and his desire for revenge – he'll be on guard throughout the night. This changes everything.

Alkur positions himself by Salkuzzar's room. He waits, fidgeting with his belt then pacing silently in the corridor. Finally, he decides to peer in. A dimly lit lamp discloses some of the room's layout. He regrets not studying the room earlier. He decides to check on Salkuzzar. He knocks and pushes the door fully open.

"Excuse me, Excellency. Will you need anything this evening?"

Salkuzzar is sitting contemplating the wine cup in his hand. He unhurriedly looks up at Alkur.

"How convenient for us to meet again. The king left me with plenty of wine. Perhaps you would like a cup."

Salkuzzar is drunk. Empty flasks are strewn on the floor around him.

Salkuzzar peers intently at Alkur. "So tell me, how is it that the king assigned you and not Carnius or Sagius or his usual staff to watch over me?" he sarcastically intones. "Were they dismissed?" He laughs out loud. "Instead I get a lowly Guard." He sneers and looks back at the cup.

Alkur watches, carefully keeping contempt off his face. He wants to choke the bastard right then, but holds back.

"What's the matter, you agree with me? Something is odd here."

Alkur stares at him and does not answer.

"I have touched a nerve, I remember you now," Salkuzzar blurts out. Alkur freezes; his throat tightens. But he remains still.

Salkuzzar shifts in his chair while taking a long swig from the cup. In a slurring voice, he mutters, "I don't know what they were thinking— having a secret ceremony-- feeling safe with their God. He could not save them that night. They were all doomed, every single one of them, and their stupid children, the next generation of the defeated. That's what they are, defeated!" Salkuzzar holds his gaze too long; the impact is chilling.

Alkur is furious, his body tense. Now that Salkuzzar remembers, this is the time to tear him to pieces, to get it over with, damn the consequences. Get a hold of yourself, Alkur.

"How did you do it?" Salkuzzar is looking at him with a blurry interest on his face.

Alkur warily, "Do what?"

"Escape, of course. I noticed you. You have your father's instincts, his drive, ambition, stubbornness, his walk, his features, it's written all over you."

"How do you know my father?"

Salkuzzar almost laughs, viewing Alkur with disdain. "You are Ellm's son. I knew your father. I too come from a long line of priests. My father was Saail; once a high priest in the Law of One. They defrocked and expelled him. He then joined the Temple of the Sun and exacted his own retribution. He led the Temple against his former flock." Salkuzzar grins.

Alkur freezes hearing his father's name. Vaguely, he remembers his father saying something about Saail and his banishment. Saail was never fully accepted back by the Temple of the Sun and disappeared from Atlantis.

Salkuzzar's face grows grim; he is lost in the past. "The infidels of the Law of One destroyed my father. He never recovered from the shame and humiliation. Worse, he abandoned us. I was turned over to a half-way home for abandoned children." Salkuzaar is silent for a moment as he looks at the cup.

Looking up at Alkur, he says clearly "I had a rough going so to speak. Do you know what it is like to grow up without parents?"

Yes, ugly bastard, you should know—you took mine, Alkur thinks.

After a long pause Salkuzzar continues, "I got tough the hard way. I escaped and joined a gang. We started with petty crime and went on from there, rather successfully. Then, I was captured, imprisoned and told to clean up my act. Eventually, the Temple of the Sun accepted me as an initiate. It saved my life."

You want me to feel sorry for you, you bastard! Alkur says to himself.

Alkur keeps his face calm and professional. He doesn't want to give Salkuzzar the satisfaction of seeing his anger and confusion. He feels disgusted. He wants to get away.

"Is that all, Excellency?"

"I am sure we will be meeting again, soon."

Alkur bows and leaves as he sees him turn back to his wine. He is mad as hell but knows that anger works against him. He steadies himself but can't fully contain it as he paces back and forth in the darkness. Such contempt, the bastard. Who does he think he is! He feels his body shaking with anger.

Hours go by. Unable to contain himself any longer Alkur extracts his sword from the scabbard and glides silently into the room. He almost expects to see Salkuzzar slumped over in his chair asleep. The room is dark, lit only by moonlight through a slit in the drapes. He looks around to make sure he is alone. He is.

Edging closer to Salkuzzar's chair, he inadvertently kicks one of the wine bottles. It rattles across the floor tile. He freezes. Minutes later, he hears the light snoring from the side alcove. He approaches and in the shadows sees Salkuzzar's limp body curled in a fetal position on the bed. Alkur is hit with the smell of alcohol and the stench of evil. He tightens his body, and with both hands grabs the hilt of the sword and raises it over his head. He will drive it right into his temple and kill him and with it earn the satisfaction of fulfilling his dream for justice that has eluded all these years.

He hesitates, stops. His body trembles and starts to shake uncontrollably. He slowly lowers his arms. He quickly raises his arms up again to strike but can't do it. It's as if some invisible force inside was blocking him. His grip slips as sword lowers to the floor. Silently, tears fill his eyes. Quietly, he turns away and walks to the chair. He sits down and placing his head in his hands begins to weep.

Chapter 7

MARCH 13, 2012
DEPARTMENT OF ARCHEOLOGY
AND ANTHROPOLOGY OF BOLIVIA

I looked around at the stacks of yellow handwritten pages that had slipped to the floor. I had no idea where all that came from. Alkur lost his folks; he was just a kid. At least he knew what happened, and had tried to avenge his father's murder.

That's when the memories came flooding back.

I was struck with a vision of my mother bursting into my room, her tone was low but urgent, "Andres, come with me now, quickly." She held out her hand to pull me.

I was very young then. Her worried, frightened look said something bad was about to happen. When I hesitated, she grabbed me by the arm but said nothing as she hurried us to a safe room next to the bedroom closet.

I yelped, more in surprise than pain. She kept whispering, "Cayate Andres! Los Patotas." "Be quiet, it's the Patotas."

The Patotas were the dreaded Argentine secret police. They were coming to arrest my father. At the time the word Patotas was synonymous with death. I did not understand that then.

Moments later, we heard men pounding on the door followed by a hush and then the crash of broken timber. We heard them moving from room to room, ransacking our home. Mother was quietly praying that they would go away and not find us. Seeing my mother afraid, terrified me.

All this happened back in 1979, three years into the Junta's reign and Argentina's "Dirty War." We lived in Belgrano then, a pleasant suburb forty minutes from central Buenos Aires. My father was in the Navy and many of his colleagues and their families lived nearby.

Later, when I was in my twenties I learned that just down the road from our home was the Junta's most notorious clandestine interrogation center, the Escuela Superior de Mecanica de la Armada (Superior School of Naval Mechanics) known as ESMA.

Years later, my mother told me that she had seen a four-door green Ford Falcon in front of our house. The car, a standard issue vehicle for the police and military, was a symbol of terror. Junta supporters would cruise in their Falcon's through the city, the car packed with armed men, hunting for dissenters. Some were kidnapped off the streets. Others were arrested in their homes and businesses. Most of the "disappeared" were never heard from again.

I never saw my father again. The purge had begun and with it a nightmare for my family and my country. Occasionally, the word "desparecidos" (the disappeared ones) arises like a mantra in my meditations. It feels like the lost souls reminding me to never forget what happened to them.

I shook my head to clear the mental slate. What I need now, I thought, is a long shower and healthy dose of today – enough of this cosmic crap, mysterious symbols and memories. I called Carlos and Fernando and we agreed to meet at the Café San Antonio, our local spot for good drinks, thick steaks and cool jazz.

I felt good when I got home a little after midnight. Still humming the tune "El Lago Sagrado," I kicked off my shoes and slumped on to the sofa. There is nothing like trading stories and jokes with friends to put things in perspective. And I resolved to tell Drs. Epis and Glasser about the dead diver so we could call the police. It was the right thing to do.

Flipping on the television to see the sports scores, an announcer was reporting the breaking news, "Police report a local fisherman found a diver's body floating near Amantani Island on Lake Titicaca. He has been identified as Dr. Francisco Guerra. Professor Guerra was a prominent anthropologist and expert on ancient cultures from Universidad Mayor de San Andres in La Paz. The cause of death is yet to be determined. He was reported missing by his wife two weeks ago. Police report no evidence of foul play". They suspected he drowned.

I froze and leaned forward, riveted. I knew Dr. Guerra from my work at the Institute; I had mentored many of his students and we had attended several conferences together. He must have been my cave diver and, if so, what was he doing there? I had heard that Dr. Guerra suffered from asthma. I could not fathom him relying on scuba gear for breathing.

I had the feeling that something sinister was at work.

Chapter 8

MARCH 14, 2012
AVENIDA MERCEDES, APT # 61,
LA PAZ, BOLIVIA

I'd slept in a little, had just finished breakfast and poured another cup of coffee. I picked up the morning paper, flipped it over and just below the fold on the front page, the headline read:

**"Tiawanaku 2012 Expedition Discovers
Temple under Lake Titicaca"**

I was shocked. At the inception of the project we had made an agreement to say absolutely nothing until the preliminary analysis was done. We wanted to have a fully documented report available before making any sort of announcement. This article was a total breach of the hush-hush pact governing our activities. We had been sworn to secrecy. I knew the Ministry would not be pleased either. Who leaked this?

The more I read, the more alarmed I became. The inside page had a picture of the Inti, our research vessel, on the lake. It wasn't one of our file photos. I knew that the published photo must have been taken with a high resolution camera from another boat or the shoreline. It was a wide-angle shot taken in the early morning, about the time of our dive.

I knew that the Institute had not arranged for off-ship photography due to budgetary constraints. Who took it and, more importantly, how did they know we would be diving that morning? I studied the photo closely. It appeared recent and professionally done. Jesus, I thought, any looter with a boat and dive gear will be out there looking for easy pickings. I felt sick.

I immediately called Dr. Epis to find out the Institute's position on this release. Perhaps the leadership had decided to go ahead and get some publicity in hopes of more funding. Maybe it was something I just hadn't heard.

When he finally picked up, I knew his frustrated voice quickly denied any involvement. "We need to get ahead of this and shut it off Andres. We're not ready. Our financial backers were promised an early look at any discoveries – they're pretty upset right now." Dr. Epis was already working with the public affairs folks to quash the story. He had Dr. Glasser working on getting some sort of security out there to protect the dive site. I decided to do some investigating myself.

I called the El Diario and asked to speak with the reporter who filed the story. A very nice gentleman, Pablo Guzman, told me that it was the most important story he had written in years. He was obviously very excited and pleased at the interest.

Without revealing who I was, I asked Senor Guzman how he got the story and picture. There was a long pause at the other end. Then, he said, "Senor, you know we cannot reveal our sources..." Out of frustration I cut him off "OK, understand, then how did you get the photo?" He said, "That was sheer luck. I couldn't find a decent photo of the Inti in the archives or internet. And a picture just grabs the reader, so my editor wanted one. Then, quite unexpectedly a man came to the paper and handed a picture to the reception desk."

"Had you asked libraries or the shipping interests for a picture? How did he know to bring that particular one?" This just sounded a little bizarre.

"No, it's odd. My inquiries had not revealed anything.

"Who brought it?" This was clearly the most urgent question to ask.

The gentleman paused, and then almost sheepishly said "I don't know. The receptionist sent him to my office because he asked specifically for me. I never got his name. I was surprised, and maybe I should have followed up, but mostly, I was relieved to get it."

"I wonder how he knew... What did he look like?" I prodded.

With a reporter's knack for recalling detail, he immediately provided a description. "The gentleman was of medium build, older, maybe in his 70s, with a full salt and pepper mustache. He stood erect and walked quickly, not slumped and slow like some older people. Maybe former military. He wore a dark trench coat with a crisp white shirt. His accent wasn't from here you know Bolivian – maybe from Argentina or Paraguay. No se!"

That's all he remembered. The man had asked Guzman to get the picture in the paper without even referring to the upcoming article. He had handed him the picture and an envelope then just left, walked away quickly, didn't look back.

He paused, and then added, "The strangest thing is that the envelope was filled with cash. It was that important to him to get the picture in the public eye. You know, we don't operate that way. He just walked away. I walked out after him, but he had disappeared."

I thanked him for his time and reiterated my interest in his article, trying somehow to dislodge the source. But he saw this coming and didn't reveal any clues. If I were him, I would have done the same. But I was hooked on one detail. It sounds like Pablo met the guy I saw on the shore they day I brought up the skull.

This was beginning to get very strange.

Chapter 9

MARCH 15, 2012
AVENIDA MERCEDES, APT # 61,
LA PAZ, BOLIVIA

It was a weird 24 hours in general. First, the article appeared, followed by a gaggle of inquiries and rumors being spun in print, social media and television about buried treasures. They even found the old myth of the cave.

The Institute was in full public relations damage control mode trying to soothe the investors and minimize the story. Oscar and I were pressed into drafting vague statements about the expedition using very academic jargon clearly designed to camouflage rather than explain our activities. It was busy. And I admit I'm amazed at how effective the P.R. song and dance can be in shaping coverage.

But during my commute and even when we went out for lunch, I couldn't shake the feeling that I was being followed. I didn't see anyone unusual, but the suspicion persisted. I kept looking around for an older man with a graying mustache.

It had taken me years to feel settled after my father disappeared and my mother and I moved to Bolivia. I hated having that familiar uneasiness again.

Last night, memories flooded back again. After that day hiding in the closet, I never saw my father again. There were tales that he had betrayed the junta. Others said he had been reined in and taken away so he wouldn't cause any more trouble, becoming himself a "desparecido." Living in that neighborhood of military families, rumors were thick.

None of it ever made sense to me. My father was a naval officer for God's sake. One of them! We didn't care what was said about him, we just wanted to know what happened. Was he still alive?

There is a horrible void when you simply don't know, when a loved one is suddenly gone from your life with no explanation. It leaves an abiding, questioning grief. Time grows a new skin over the wound, but it's always there just under the surface. The families of the "desaparecidos" endured, no, still endure this pain.

My mother never said anything about his disappearance. Her quiet, stoic demeanor suggested denial. Since she never showed any emotion, I could only speculate about her feelings. At first I asked and she would just look away and change the subject. So I stopped asking.

One day, out of the blue, she asked me what I thought had happened to my father. Her eyes were opaque, showing nothing, just asking what I believed. I told her what I thought had happened, that he had disappeared like the others and that I missed him. Somehow I felt she knew more but was not telling me everything.

She just smiled, and then quietly changed the subject. She said that as a young boy I had this gift of being very "psiquico" or psychic. I would make up stories about fabulous places complete with fantastic images of crystal towers and caves. I'd recount in great detail the priestly rituals and wild adventures and a place called Atlantis. What an imagination, she thought.

I knew they met while she was in prison, a protestor against the junta back in 1976. Papa was posted at the EMSA. Growing up, I knew little more.

There were moments later when I felt my father's presence in my life. I sensed he was at my college graduation, congratulating me. I remember my mother saying, "Your father would be very proud of you."

She was convinced that my father had been with us during our flight from Buenos Aires to our new home in Bolivia. After leaving the safety of the Bolivian embassy, while at the Buenos Aires airport the immigration officer randomly selected her for "extra" questioning prior to boarding. She said that Papa whispered the words that she needed to say so we could board the out-bound flight. It was risky. Many people were arrested at the airport when they tried to flee Argentina.

I believe he was at my mother's funeral. It was a traditional Catholic ceremony, and as the priest gave his blessing over the casket I heard in the wind, a clear voice from behind me softly whispering, "Andres, I am with you always." I have never forgotten those words.

I was heartbroken at her death but sort of relieved that my parents would be reunited in the afterlife. I believe that.

I've never forgotten my father's story.

Chapter 10

MARCH 16, 2012
DEPARTMENT OF ARCHEOLOGY
AND ANTHROPOLOGY OF BOLIVIA

Today was so busy, exciting and, well, really fun. It's not often that Oscar and I get to tackle something as unusual, and we believe important, as the crystal skull. I don't care what others think – I've experienced beauty and an energy that's unique with the skull. Even Oscar, solid, staid Oscar was animated all day.

Dr. Epis came by in the afternoon to check on things. He's clearly pleased with the find and our preliminary assessments. I thought for a moment that he was going to claim the skull for his own research – but he didn't. He said the financial backers were thrilled and eager to support more dives. Maybe that's one benefit from the newspaper coverage. One can tell just by the glow on Dr. Epis' face that he's already thinking about the anthropological possibilities and re-writing cultural history.

One small peculiar thing happened, though. I've been unable to forget it. I was on my usual bus coming to work, in my usual seat, half-way back on the left, reading the morning paper. An elderly man got on at the Calle Antofagasta stop. He looked around, spotted me and the empty seat by me and headed my way.

About seventy perhaps, he wore traditional Andean attire, a wool shawl and sombrero, his right cheek bulging with, I suspect, a wad of coca leaves. As he sat down, he smiled tentatively, his face crinkling around the eyes and mouth. He had a long prominent nose, high cheekbones and forehead and the dark eyes of his Incan ancestors. He looked a bit uncomfortable as if out of his element in the city. I folded my paper in half again to give him more room.

He nervously glanced at me again. I put the paper away. For the next few minutes we were caught up in our own thoughts. Then he opened a bag and offered me some coca leaves. I rarely did that, but I thanked him and reached in, crushing some leaves between my fingers before placing them behind my tongue. "Para la altura," he said smiling referring, I guess, to La Paz's elevation of 11,975 feet. The bitter taste was pleasant, not overwhelming. He seemed pleased by my receptivity.

Moments later, he blurted out in Spanish, "Las energias oscuras nos rodean pero nosotros vemos su sombra. The dark energies surround us but we can see their shadow." He looked at me intently, nodding slowly as if conveying an important message.

What did that mean? I wondered. But I nodded in agreement, and then looked out the window.

No sooner had he spoken than I heard the screech of the brakes as the bus rolled to a stop. The old man patted my leg indicating goodbye, got up and handed me a small card. On it was a picture of a lake, probably Titicaca, an address and a phone number written below:

Senor Don Julio Carasco
1448 Avenida Guillaume, La Paz

He bobbed his head several times as if telling me to call him. I replied silently with a quick nod of my own.

As he stepped down the aisle, I stared at the card then tucked it into my pocket. I felt exhilarated by the strangeness of it as if I was being given a message of sorts.

Chapter 11

ATLANTIS

The encounter with Salkuzzar left lasting impressions on Alkur and he decided it was time to leave the king's guard. Following his parent's death, he had been withdrawn and quiet. The King's Guard had been the family he did not have and a way to grow up, become an expert in war and gain respect from others. His failure to avenge his parent's death had ignited a slow and quiet search to understand where he belonged in the world.

Alkur's excellent reputation and the ongoing unrest in Atlantis made his martial skills in high demand and landed him odd security jobs with local dignitaries and wealthy merchants although not bringing him the peace and tranquility he longed for. Then one night, in a dream he saw the image of his father standing before him in the inner sanctuary of the Temple of the Law of One. Ellm told Alkur that his calling was to serve his Order. It was to be his destiny.

Alkur, remembering the dream enters the sacred interior chambers within the magnificent Temple of Poseidon. As a child, his father, then a high priest, would often bring him to the sanctuary in the inner recces of the temple. Its delicate beauty and masterful design had awed him, even as a child.

The Temple of Poseidon is the most extraordinary spiritual feature of Atlantis. Made of immense white and silver stones from the kingdom's 12 regions, its exterior walls are carved in white marble and laced with geometric designs of gold, silver and orichalcum, sprinkled with crystals. The black, red and white stones of the interior chamber make it shimmer in the sunlight. The ivory ceiling dome enhanced with gold, silver, and orichalcum brightens the walls, pillars and floors.

The main room, the Chamber of Knowledge, is dominated by a gigantic statue of Poseidon standing on a chariot and driving six winged horses. Statues of graceful sea nymphs riding dolphins surround it. During the day, light flows in through high narrow slits creating a sense of peace and harmony. Next door is the Great Initiation room where novices who aspire to become High Priests and Priestesses are trained.

Alkur, now a priest of the Law of One, enjoys mentoring the new initiates during their training. He's comfortable with his new vocation; it feels like a path to better understand himself and others. His father had been right, he thinks.

On this day, Alkur watches from the back as the candidates take their assigned places on the white marble floor. They are a disciplined and dedicated bunch, with a lot to contribute to the high vibrational energy of Atlantis. Like spiritual explorers, each one is handpicked after a rigorous selection period. For example, they must demonstrate complete control of their bodies and energy fields, including the abilities to heal, to levitate, show mind control, and do soul retrievals. Many fail; those that succeed have completed a life-changing rite of passage.

The students are silent and ready for the day's lesson. Each one has a personal crystal for healing and self-empowerment. They close their eyes and begin meditating, holding the crystals in their palms. Alkur crosses the room to join them. They attune their energies to each other and set the intention for the tasks ahead. This phase of training emphasizes the importance of stillness, meditation and visualization to tune in with their spirit guides and experience oneness with Source.

Clapping his hands, Alkur signals the start of class. The students, on cue, acknowledge him and clap in unison. Alkur has already pre-programmed their crystals with the information he wants to impart today.

"Today we will practice using crystals to clear the energy field. Place the crystal on the space between your eyes, for today's lesson. When you're done, rub the crystal gently between your palms until it feels slightly sticky. Then close your eyes and set an intention to heal a part of you that needs to be healed."

One by one the students comply.

"Now using the crystal, do a complete body-scan of your energy centers and field. What do you notice?"

Alkur gives them a few moments to do this.

"The goal is to speed up the cells rate while holding the intention of a perfectly balanced and healed body."

Alkur continues,

"One of the unique properties of crystals is that they reflect and amplify energies based on one's intention and will absorb the negative energies to be cleared and transmuted. This temple, like your body, is made from silica. It magnifies all of your thoughts both positive and negative. It's important to be aware of all of your thoughts at all times."

Suddenly, Alkur notices a student rise and move to the back of the room. He did not know the student. Moving is not unusual; he often encouraged students to move around if they needed to. However, this time it feels different. What's going on here, he wonders. He senses an immediate change in the class demeanor. The room's energy has shifted. The students are losing their focus and beginning to talk. Some appear to argue. There is a strange heaviness lingering in the air.

Something is not right, he thinks.

Alkur stares at the student who is standing and peering intently at him. Alkur can see that he is agitated.

"You...I ask that you, standing... return to your place" Alkur directs.

The student doesn't move and continues to stare. Alkur telepathically tunes into the student's energy, but is repulsed, by a sudden and strong energetic pulse. It hits him like a powerful body blow, knocks him off balance, and leaves him confused and annoyed.

The class is now in disarray with fear and confusion etched on the students faces. Alkur senses some dark force at work. He realizes that this is a deliberate attack and the student's energy is still getting through, with alarming intensity.

Alkur grasps that he needs to immediately change his response, so instead of meeting it head-on, he counters the attack by blending and deflecting the energy. He takes a deep breath, shifts to a more oblique stance to minimize his body's exposure, and then closing his eyes, energetically pulls the student's center towards and past himself.

Telepathically, he directs his class to immediately synchronize their energy fields and to meditate about light and love through their heart centers. Then he asks them to surround themselves with an energy vortex of white light as protection against the invading dark thought forms.

I hope this works, he thinks.

He notices a noticeable shift in room as its energy quiets. They have dampened, but not ended, the attack. Alkur then instructs the students to invoke the Violet Flame, a light energy so pure and intense that fears and negativity just dissolve. Again, the vibration shifts in the room, but the student counter-attacks, increasing his energy output even more.

Alkur realizes that it is not working, and understands at once that he needs help. He concentrates and turns his focus within, seeking the right technique. He is guided to invoke the spirits of the light and love from the Archangels of Atlantis and other interdimensional light beings to neutralize the force with compassion and peace.

A much stronger energy shift makes his entire body vibrate. The students are vibrating in unison with him. Now, the dark energy begins to slowly dissipate. Alkur watches the dark aura around the student dissolve. He then instinctively sends warm gold energy flowing between them, grounding the student even further. Reaching into his memory,

he finds the right technique: he visualizes a golden ball of energy surrounding, then filling, the student. Alkur is confident the healing response is working.

Relieved and grateful, he slowly approaches the student who is now
sitting motionless, looking at the floor.

"Who are you?" Alkur asks. His calm voice projects peace, giving no
sign of his earlier anxiety.

"My name is Carn."

Alkur's face grows stern, his voice steady. "Carn, how dare you come
into this space and disrupt my class. What were you attempting to do
here today?"

Carn appears irritated by the question. He quickly looks up and
stares intently at Alkur. Is that a challenge or disdain in his eyes, Alkur
wonders?

"Answer the question."

Carn remains silent and tense. He drops his eyes to the floor.

"Did you not think that you would be found out. Why? Who sent
you?"

Carn blurts out "You are over your head!" No doubt now, that is
defiance.

Alkur is surprised, almost shocked, by what he hears. Carn is working against the Order, certainly betraying the code.

"I suggest you rethink your loyalty, if you can call it that, and
think about what you are doing here." As Carn remains silent, Alkur
continues, "Right, that's all for now. I don't expect to find you here
tomorrow."

Carn nods, rises and quickly walks away.

Alkur turns to face the class who are looking at him, speechless and
with relief etched in their eyes. Alkur smiles,

"Good work. That will be all for today."

That evening, a frustrated Alkur shares his concerns with his wife,
Ampero. They've been married for over 10 years, having met after he
left the guards. She had been raised to the Law of One priesthood

by her father, a senior member. She understood the conflict with the Temple of the Sun.

As they finish dinner, Alkur revisits his frustration with the day. Pushing his plate away, Alkur gives Ampero a look of almost bewilderment. "I don't understand. One of the students attacked me and the class, today. It was unreal. The darkness was palpable. I really wasn't sure whether I could counter it. I can't get over how deliberate the attack was."

Alkur pauses, while Ampero keeps her gaze quietly on her unsettled husband, then continues, "He really wanted me to be afraid of his power. It was a challenge—a duel. When I confronted him, he was arrogant and dismissive. He showed nothing but contempt and disrespect. The audacity! He knew what he was doing. Why? What is this all about?" He shakes his head, his fist clenched.

Ampero, looking at him intently says, "But, he is only a student."

"Yes, of course, I was made to think this, but I know better Ampero. We have seen this pattern before."

"Salkuzzar?"

Alkur's quiet; his eyes search her face, wondering whether to share his real fear. "Yes, I suspect so, Ampero. Who but the Temple of the Sun knows how to deal in the black arts? This is not an isolated incident. I've heard rumors of other, similar attacks; meetings disrupted while newcomers question, even disparage our teachings. I'm afraid somehow Salkuzzar and the Belial Illuminati are sending infiltrators to ... I don't know what."

Ampero winces, it's worse than she feared. With concern shadowing her eyes, she slowly says, "I wonder what Zonar knows about this. He knows the history -- this has happened before – the Temple subverting our priesthood trying to gain control."

Alkur nods. "Yes, you're right. I'll talk to Zonar." His face clears a little, his thoughts stepping back to the bigger picture. "The surest way to foment unrest and incite confusion is within the ranks of new initiates. They're vulnerable and susceptible. And it did happen before – years ago the initiates rebelled. But why now?" Alkur didn't really expect an answer.

Ampero listens in silence. She sees Alkur's frustration and isn't sure how best to help. The sun has set, the glow is fading from the sky.

"Alkur, don't jump to the worst case yet -- you have no proof of a conspiracy. At most, it's a strong hunch based on what one student did. There may be another explanation – something other than the Temple of the Sun."

Alkur nods in agreement. She has a point – maybe it's not so dire.

Ampero continues, "I know the classroom today was difficult and I certainly can't explain it." She pauses, then turning to light the candles, continues, "Have you considered the possibility you have attracted this."

Alkur looks at her puzzled, "Do you mean the attack?"

"Yes" Ampero continues in a serious tone. She turns again to look at Alkur. The candlelight flickers in the graying room. "Since you left the Guards, and the desire to avenge the wrongs dealt to you you've really learned to step back and understand your own darker emotions, like anger. You are becoming more aware of your many selves. But, as your light grows and you are more aware of your spiritual self, you also become more visible to the dark forces. They're watchful and will bombard your weak areas to stop your light from growing."

"Are you saying I caused the attack? My anger and fear allowed the attack?" Alkur's incredulous. He looks at her in surprise.

Ampero simply says "It's a possibility." Noticing his reaction, she quickly continues, "I'm not criticizing – I only want you to consider it. The whole episode may be an invitation to examine yourself. See what you're putting out energetically and what you're attracting." She turns to light the candles on the wall.

Alkur closes his eyes, acknowledging his shadow aspects. He knows he's reacting badly to Ampero's suggestion. He's never quite understood how to deal with anger, fear and rage when they spring up inside -- or how the dark forces stir in his mental and emotional states, draining strength. He is trying not to overreact yet he recognizes the darkness within himself. He feels a simmering anger of being betrayed. He has this feeling a lot lately. Alkur shakes his head reminding himself to keep his vibration high. He can't be swallowed by negativity and despair.

Ampero is right. Zonar, the high priest is the leader of the Thoth tribe, and is well respected for his wit, counsel, leadership, psychic powers and knowledge of occult and dark energies. Zonar's parents and family had survived the second cataclysmic event of Atlantis by migrating to a faraway land where Zonar was raised before coming back to Atlantis. The hitch was that Alkur just didn't quite trust Zonar. Something bothered him about Zonar, a small warning. Dissent in the ranks of the priesthood was not viewed favorably, and it could be punishable by excommunication in serious cases. Alkur didn't want to risk being perceived as an alarmist. Nevertheless, he needs to clear his conscience and trust his wife's advice.

I will meet with him, Alkur decides. He rises to join Ampero by the fire.

Summoned by Salkuzzar, Carn is riding his horse at full gallop through the streets of Atlantis. At the Temple of the Sun, he dismounts, and enters. Salkuzzar voices his displeasure with Carn's actions, a heated exchange takes place and Carn abruptly leaves the temple.

The next day a young woman walking her daughter through the street behind the temple comes upon a body of a young man, his throat slashed.

Chapter 12

ATLANTIS

Alkur arrives at the temple of Thoth. What was a clear plan last night, well, today seems more complicated. He had reflected, as he often does, on his good fortune in having Ampero as this side. He awoke uneasy with the personal and professional risk he was taking confiding in the high priest, but she had brought him back to center with her clear wisdom.

Alkur had been one of Zonar's favorite students. He was eager to learn, with a highly disciplined, yet questioning mind. Zonar knew that Alkur could be obstinate, sometimes even confrontational, but he respected him for speaking his mind. For he saw a bit of his own younger self in Alkur.

At the sanctuary door, Zonar greets Alkur with the traditional handshake and embrace and motions him to a cushioned pillow on the marble floor. Zonar is a tall man, with thick gray hair, heavy black eyebrows and piercing black eyes. He's always carried himself as a younger man, but today, his age is beginning to show.

Zonar smiles, "It's good to see you Alkur. It's been too long. How are you and Ampero?" His words are friendly but the voice sounds hollow and scripted.

"Thank you for asking Excellency. Everything is fine; as always, Ampero sends her best regards."

"Wonderful. I'm happy for you both. What brings you today and how may I help?" Zonar looks strained, his eyes are tired.

"Thank you Excellency. I will get right to the point. I'm seeing a very strange and dark energy at work in my class of initiates. It is not something I have seen before. It feels as if this energy is deliberately intrusive and meant to disrupt and instill uncertainty and chaos."

Zonar looks down at Alkur with a trace of surprise and disappointment on his face. "Alkur, it is not like you to make vague, unsubstantiated complaints. What is really going on here?"

Alkur remonstrates, eager to explain the substance of his concern. "One of my students unleashed a vicious attack in my class yesterday. The class was really disturbed. Fortunately, we were able to neutralize it. I'm afraid that some of our flock are being misled and perhaps have fallen under the influence of some unseen dark force or energy." He raises his hand, saying "I know, I know, this is only one example, and it's my experience. But I've heard others talk quietly about similar incidents. For some reason, these episodes aren't being discussed or addressed."

Zonar listens skeptically, concern growing on his face. "I don't see where you're going with this. Are you suggesting someone or something is behind this attack? And that the temple leadership is complicit as well?" Zonar's voice rises slightly as though personally affronted.

Alkur, seeing that he has antagonized Zonar, steadily replies, "No, not that our high priesthood is involved, but yes, my class was deliberately targeted and attacked. I thought you should know."

Zonar suddenly shifts his stance as he leans forward,

"Who do you think is behind this?" Zonar's eyebrows lower as he studies Alkur's face.

"I don't know." Alkur breathes deeply then says, "To be fully candid, I suspect Salkuzzar, Excellency." His voice is clear and steady.

Zonar's eyebrows rise in disbelief. "I know you mistrust the Temple of the Sun's doctrine and teachings, and that..."

"But, excellency..."

"Let me finish, you hold them responsible for the death of your parents. But you have no evidence – just prejudice." He looks at Alkur as though he were a petulant, complaining child.

Alkur's voice grows emphatic. "Excellency, what I know firsthand is knowledge, not prejudice, that the Temple of the Sun abuses their powers for their own crass benefit. Their denigration of our beliefs and values has already brought separation, doubt, and suspicion into our community. Where we once had peace and cooperation, now its conflict, disharmony and backstabbing, perhaps even at the highest levels. One would have to be blind not to see it."

Alkur pauses briefly, wondering if he's gone too far, but them hammers his point home speaking purposefully, "We were once a united brotherhood under Source, guided by the Intergalactic Council. Now we're divided and mistrustful. I believe that the Temple of the Sun will do anything to gain control of the populace, including subverting our priesthood and planting their 'operatives' to achieve their malevolent schemes. We've seen this game played out before; it may be happening again. Their schemes to infiltrate our energy fields may rob us our innate psychic and spiritual gifts."

His voice gains speed, speaking more emphatically before Zonar stops him. "The classroom incident is just one example. They say they have a direct line to Source, but their real goal is to control, intimidate and enrich themselves. This energy weakens the auric field and vibrational matrix of Atlantis. Its egotist wave has been unleashed and is contaminating our connection to the earth and the divine and ..."

Zonar abruptly raises his hand for Alkur to stop and angrily intones, "Enough. I won't be lectured on what you perceive to be some evil conspiracy. I thought the time in the Guards and with Order had put some sense into you. If what you say is true, we'd see a lot more manifestations. And you have nothing to trace any disturbance back to the Temple of the Sun. It could be some disgruntled student upset with something. One example is just not proof of a massive conspiracy."

He has a point. All other instances are just rumors, Alkur thinks. Maybe he has blown this way out of proportion. But, a high priest of Zonar's stature should be concerned; after all he is the enforcer of doctrine. Or maybe, he is expecting too much from Zonar.

Alkur realizes that he already knew, instinctively, that Zonar would pursue this line of reasoning. That's the true nature of his unease with Zonar; that he deflects or ignores any concern that upsets his own worldview. Zonar is the consummate, loyal bureaucrat, not open to other ideas. He'd never recognize an existential threat to the Order, or worse admit it. Alkur tempers his tone; Zonar is visibly agitated, and annoyed.

"Excellency, surely you can see where I am coming from on this matter."

Zonar abruptly stands. "Alkur, I appreciate your coming. I will share your concerns at the next Council meeting. In the meantime, I am ordering you to remain quiet regarding your thoughts and feelings on this matter. We must not unnecessarily over react and sow confusion. I am confident there is some explanation for this classroom incident. I thank you for bringing this matter to me. I will see you out now."

Alkur is momentarily caught off guard by Zonar's reaction and the abrupt dismissal. He rises, bows and follows Zonar to the temple's entrance. As he leaves the temple, he is still shocked by their conversation. How did it end so badly? He feels let down, empty really, betrayed by Zonar. A thought pops into his head. Zonar's hiding something. It does not feel right.

Alkur then realizes that Zonar's offer to take it to the Council was whitewash. What could the Council to do anyway? They are pawns of the Temple of the Sun. He knew since the last government's collapse, that the Council regularly promoted the Temple's agenda. A flash of unease hits his stomach. What if they bring up his name at the Council? What would be the consequences for him, his career and standing in the community? What will Ampero think? Maybe it was a mistake to be so open with Zonar.

Back at the sanctuary, Zonar paces back and forth nervously, oblivious to the serene surroundings. He slowly walks to the window overlooking the courtyard of the temple, and stares at the statue of Thoth, the guardian of his tribe. It's time he met with Salkuzzar.

Chapter 13

ATLANTIS

The dark sky and heavy atmosphere threatens rain as Zonar summons his carriage. It is late and he is careful not to be seen. His mind feels sluggish; it must be the uncertainty, he reasons. His meeting with Alkur left him nervous.

As the carriage arrives at the Temple of the Sun he notices its elaborate decorations and how different it is from the other temples throughout Atlantis. The exterior walls are covered with strange figures and motifs; its ornamental stones proclaim protectiveness and exclusivity. He is not looking forward to his meeting with Salkuzzar.

Zonar walks through the temple's side entrance into a dimly lit corridor, past guards who watch him shiftily. It gives him the creeps. He feels engulfed by some ominous and dense energy. He's never noticed that before.

Directly ahead, he sees Salkuzzar atop a raised throne intently reading a manuscript. His black and yellow ornamental robes attest to his unique powers; the large protruding headdress suggests a connection with the divine. He is an imposing figure and, from his elevated throne, he towers over visitors below.

Zonar walks up to the throne and makes a shallow bow. "Good day, Excellency."

Salkuzzar, surprised looks down and with a smirk says, "Zonar, my dear friend, what brings you here? Is everything all right at the Order?"

"I am afraid not, Excellency." Zonar hates looking up at him. He deliberately looks to the side.

"I see. Tell me... what brings you."

Zonar turns back and says, "This morning, one of my priests came to me with suspicions about unrest among the initiates. Somehow, he has figured out that the initiates are being used to instigate rebellion within the kingdom. He believes that you and the Temple of the Sun are behind this plan.

"And what did you say to him?" Salkuzzar remains expressionless.

"I assured him that I would look into it and, if appropriate, bring this accusation to the Council. I wanted to put him off taking any action of his own. I came tonight to let you know. "

"I see."

"What if he reveals the plan?"

Salkuzzar leans back in his throne and asks, "What evidence did this priest provide for his story?"

"A new initiate in his classroom was caught using some dark energies to disrupt the lesson. The teacher neutralized it, but it raised suspicions that something wrong, something threatening was underway."

Salkuzzar in a thoughtful voice starts to say, ""I see..."

Zonar interrupts, irritated, "You never told me that the plan involved initiates."

Salkuzzar slowly steps down from his throne and closing on Zonar says in a matter of fact tone, "Of course it does. We have to make sure that they are brought in. The only way to do this is to place my own trusted ones in their classrooms."

Zonar, troubled, says "You should have told me. I am in charge of the Order. Does this mean there are others?"

"Yes. These are dedicated loyalists to the cause. I personally chose them."

Zonar protests, "Why was I not told? You said..."

Salkuzzar looks directly at Zonar. Can this man really be so foolish and easily led he thinks? In a condescending voice, Salkuzzar says, "Let's not kid ourselves, the initiates are our future. We must have their support for our plan to succeed. Last time, during the second cataclysmic event, the rebellion almost failed because the Temple didn't have the initiates on board. We can't make the same mistake again. Besides they're a good source of information. You understand don't you?" The last sentence was almost an appeal.

Zonar, not quite mollified, says "It didn't work -- the energy was neutralized by the priest and the class. I'm worried. The plan has been..."

Salkuzzar steps back slightly, and interrupts. "Who is this priest?"

"His name is Alkur. He was one of my best students. I knew his father."

"I have heard his name before, it's familiar. He probably looks to you as a mentor. Perhaps you could help him understand the importance of loyalty to you and your Order."

Zonar is uncomfortable at the prospect of another meeting with Alkur on this subject. And, although he can stand by and let the Temple act, he doesn't want an active role himself. He bites his lips and says tersely, "But what if he does not go along?"

Salkuzzar looks at him obliquely, "Then you will know what to do."

Zonar lifts his eyes to Salkuzzar's. His reluctance to act is etched on his face.

Salkuzzar, now impatient with his weak ally, forcefully says, "Zonar, you are either with me or not. This is our opportunity to rid the land of the Law of One once and for all. The time has arrived. Together we will make this land great and to bring riches and glory to her and ourselves. When we have won, you will become the high priest of the entire Northern region, and rule over half the Atlantean kingdom, unless you have second thoughts in which case..."

Zonar sighed. He knew this exalted power position would make him a successor to Salkuzzar and the most important member of the ruling Council. He would control the armed forces – and as such, would have their loyalty.

"I am grateful, of course, Excellency."

"I am confident all is well in your very capable hands."

Zonar, in a hesitating voice, "I will see what I can do, Excellency"

"I know I can count on you." Salkuzzar nods, smiling.

Zonar bows, turns and walks out. Salkuzzar watches, considering.

Back in his carriage, Zonar thinks about the task ahead. He must appear to believe Alkur, bring him into his confidence. He must ensure Alkur's silence and convince him that steps are being taken. Yet, he could not reveal his own complicity with Salkuzzar's plan.

Back in the temple, Salkuzzar motions one of his aides to him. The large tall man dressed in black and carrying a small dagger at his hip approaches Salkuzzar. "I want you to bring me information about this priest Alkur. Report back to me. Do not harm him."

The man nods, bows and leaves.

Chapter 14

ATLANTIS

Alkur is restless as sleep refuses to come. He hears Ampero breathing lightly, lost to her own dreams. He tries to move gently so that he doesn't wake her up. Since his meeting with Zonar he kept replaying their conversation through his mind trying to find where it went so wrong and what he should have said.

Eventually, he dozes off and dreams he is being pursued by a grotesque, malevolent creature. He desperately tries to get away, but the creature quickly closes on him. With a swipe of its huge paw he is knocked to the ground. Stunned, weak, and covered in blood he crawls away, finally managing to get up. He runs gasping for breath but the creature knocks him down again. Lying there, he sees the horror approaching, its fiery red eyes, teeth dripping blood, the enormous head and hairy arms. With a horrible roar, the creature mounts him tearing his flesh starting at the feet. He is being dismembered and eaten alive. He screams, paralyzed with fear.

Alkur jolts awake, breathing hard. He frantically touches his legs. They are still there and he is alive. He sighs with relief; it was only a dream. He is hot, clammy and covered in sweat. Ampero, awake now, reaches over to touch him. Sleepily, rising up on her elbow, she whispers, "Are you alright? What happened?"

"Just a bad dream, that's all." Alkur sinks back into his pillow, not wanting to sleep right away just in case the monster is waiting.

In the darkness Ampero sighs. "Are you sure? Let me know if you would like to talk about it." Alkur nods, softly grunts and leans over to gently kiss her forehead. She settles back down and is almost instantly asleep again.

In preparing for the priesthood, he had been taught to evaluate dreams and visions. What disturbs him is how vivid and frightening the nightmare was. He can't shake it off. He decides to step back from the horror of the dream to ask, what did the encounter with the creature mean?

Wide awake, he decides to meditate to uncover the dream's message. The message he receives is that the dream is a warning about his shadow-self, the dark side of his nature. Atlantis is in conflict, these are dangerous times and the darker energies are becoming more prevalent affecting his energy field. He must be vigilant and will have to face his unconscious fears by becoming aware of them and his reactions to events in his life. To do this he has to keep his vibration high and to ask for help to ward off future attacks.

But he receives another crucial insight, that only pure, unconditional love can stop the creature. Alkur ponders this, then with his imagination puts himself back in the dream and tries to feel love and compassion for the creature. At first he fails, and there is fear and revulsion. He tries again, focusing on the love within his own heart. He finds it. He looks into the creature's eyes with love and total acceptance and the beast slowly fades away. This time he awakens feeling calm, peaceful and grateful.

Later that night, Alkur dreams of his spirit guide Ilax. She has accompanied him though all his past physical lifetimes on earth. Now, she warns him of the imminent destruction of Atlantis. She tells him that he will survive to journey to another land to safeguard the secrets of his tribe. He has been chosen to be one of the "wisdom keepers" of the 12 tribes of Atlantis. He is told that in a designated time, the wisdom keepers will join with other light beings to reopen portals of consciousness to move the earth, Gaia, into the higher dimensions. He will come back in a future incarnation to reunite the 12 ushering in a new era for mankind's ascension.

Alkur awakens with a headache and a heavy sense of doom. The dream with Ilax makes no sense and he feels confused and inadequate for the task ahead of him. Readying himself for the day's lessons, Alkur feels confused and distracted. The inner zeal he had for teaching begins to ebb as a different and uncertain future enters the corners of his mind. I hate dreams like that, he thinks.

Chapter 15

ATLANTIS

The scorching sun simmers high in the pale blue sky as Alkur walks toward the entrance to the temple of Thoth. Legend said Thoth himself had once lived there. His tribe's spiritual home, the temple rests on a prominent hill overlooking the city and harbor. In the distance he can see the coconut palms lining the beaches and the aquamarine waters of Atlantis. It is one of his favorite spots, conducive to contemplation, nestled by an ancient forest of evergreens, immense ebony trees and masses of laurels surrounded by sweet smelling brightly colored flowers. Alkur can see the birds flying everywhere—busy gulls, albatross, and high flying sea hawks. It is a magnificent sight to behold, he thinks.

Alkur thought that being buried on its heights must be as close to heaven as one can get. He came here when he needed direction or insights into major decisions. He always left feeling better, as if his burdens had been lifted.

Alkur enters the pyramid shaped temple through a small doorway. Once inside he is surrounded by enormous crystal stalactites that hang from the ceiling reflecting light. The architect must have been listening to God to create such a peaceful, meditative room, Alkur mused. In the center, is a large basin with hundreds of crystals surrounding one large quartz crystal which glows with a fiery white flame.

A separate sacred chamber holds the crystal skull of Thoth. Passed down from the ancients, the skull holds the great secrets of previous generations. During the golden times there were twelve skulls, one from each region of Atlantis, representing each tribe's wisdom. Every tribe safeguarded its skull within their temple complex. The skulls had been programmed by the Intergalactic Council so the people, using their intuition and thoughts, could access ancient and interstellar mysteries like the origins of humanity, knowledge of spiritual laws and planetary ancestral roots. The skulls also held sacred symbols used to heal or raise one's energy vibration and were accessed by one's level of consciousness.

Alkur enters the chamber and sits quietly to gather his thoughts. Today, he whispers, I need guidance and clarity. How should I deal with the continuing abuses of the Temple of the Sun? Alkur pauses, he knows he is being drawn into an ancient conflict and the powerful emotion this creates still frightens him. He closes his eyes hoping for a connection with spirit. But, anger and frustration with his inability to do anything about the darkness keep his heart closed. For the first time, peace at the temple eludes him. He feels betrayed by Zonar and by his own weakness and uncertainty.

Alkur leaves feeling restless and unsure of what to do next. He walks home along a path he has taken many times before. It follows a walled alleyway past a forest and then borders a small cluster of homes scattered along the route. The heat has finally let up and there is a cool breeze from the ocean. It is a beautiful day and Alkur relaxes to enjoy the fresh air, the freedom and the walk.

Rounding a corner, he senses a presence following him. He turns his head to look back and through the shadow of the temple walls notices the profile of a tall man in a black cape and hat. Alkur had not seen him before and this is usually a deserted pathway. Alkur picks up the pace slightly wondering who the stranger might be. Not one to run away from danger and curious he suddenly turns to face the man. But he is gone. Alkur thinks nothing of this until, a little while later, as he approaches his home he sees the man again standing by the entrance to his home. Alkur is startled and on alert. How did he get past me? He stops and then cautiously approaches while peering intently at the man. The stranger's face is hidden and he appears enveloped in a blanket of dark energy. Alkur stops a few yards away and watches carefully. Unsure of his next step, Alkur closes his eyes and connects with Ilax, his spiritual guide.

"What should I do?"

He stands waiting for what feels like an eternity, then, Ilax responds, "Talk with him and show no fear."

"You want me to do what…?" Alkur mentally says feeling incredulous.

"Talk with him. Show no fear, I am with you Alkur."

"Right…"

Alkur slowly moves forward and stops a few feet from the hooded figure. With only a trace of hesitation in his voice he asks, "Who are you and what do you want?"

There is a long period of silence; there is no answer from the man motionless in front of him. Alkur cannot distinguish the face under the dark hat.

"Who are you?" Alkur commands, his voice firm and steady. "What do you want?"

Again, there is complete silence. Then, as Alkur is about ready to push past him into his yard, Alkur hears a raspy, deep voice. "What are you doing?" says the stranger.

Alkur is taken aback by the question. He senses this dark energy can sense his fear and read his thoughts. There is something in the voice, in the words make him hesitate, not knowing how to answer.

He feels Ilax speaking through him. The words just flow effortlessly, "I represent the light. I am bringing light into the world. It is the darkness that serves the light."

There is a moment of silence as if the man is digesting Alkurs words. "You are over your head, Alkur."

Angry, Alkur asks "How do you know my name?"

The man stares at him and does not answer. Then he turns and walks away.

Alkur is bewildered, his chest feels tight, yet relieved that the stranger is gone. He has no idea what that transaction was about. He asks Ilax, "What just happened?"

She responds as a quiet breeze in his head, "The forces of darkness always resist and fight the light. But in the end they both work for the soul's evolution. Everything has a higher purpose Alkur. The darkness always serves the light."

"The Temple of the Sun...Salkuzzar? He said, 'I was over my head'. What did he mean by this?"

She responds, "courageously confronting the darkness and our darker nature threatens it and unleashes a response to force you to back away, to disengage. The darkness fears a challenge to its perceived supremacy. Don't worry, you'll understand."

Alkur stands by the gate and tries to comprehend what has just happened to him. His spiritual training had spoken about the perpetual tension between dark and light but he had never seen it manifested this way. Turning to his home, he can't help but notice an unusual darkness in the sky, yet he can also glimpse a small ray of light sunlight penetrating it. He smiles.

Chapter 16

ATLANTIS

Alkur is awakened early by an urgent summons to see Zonar. The messenger, a boy of ten or eleven, shifts his weight impatiently as Alkur reads the short note. The boy doesn't leave until he sees Alkur ready to follow him out the door. Then the boy runs ahead.

As Alkur enters the temple chamber, he sees Zonar, pacing back and forth glancing at the door. He bows reverently announcing his presence.

"You called, Excellency."

Zonar, with a flat unemotional tone, says "Yes."

He stops pacing, straightens up and facing Alkur says, "Alkur, I will get right to the point. With regards to the matter we spoke of earlier, I have consulted the Council. It is a Council matter now. I have been assured, and can pass that assurance to you, that there is no rebellious activity being taken by the Temple of the Sun. The high priest Salkuzzar is in full compliance with the Council's orders." Zonar stops. He's rather pleased he made the statement with such unimpeachable authority in his voice.

Alkur, disbelieving, allows the words to sink in. He can feel the duplicity in the room. He is not being told the truth; he fears a cover-up. Either that or Zonar is a fool.

Alkur almost stammers in his frustration, "But, your Excellency I can't believe..."

Zonar, angry on cue, cuts him off. "I must warn you Alkur, your future in this order is in jeopardy if you do not heed my words. Take this as a warning from a friend and your teacher."

"Excellency, I was just trying to bring this matter to your attention, to..."

"You have, and there is no more to say about the matter. Is this clear?"

Alkur can see that this is going nowhere. He thinks, I must speak my truth here, now. Alkur feels himself losing it, his disdain and respect for Zonar shriveling. He senses that Zonar is hiding something. He feels the energy drain away and that he has lost a former friend and teacher. Worse, Alkur has pushed Zonar to the point where Zonar no longer listens.

Alkur steadies himself. He walks up to Zonar and looks him in the eyes, speaking quietly and firmly.

"Do you expect me, your former student, to accept this? I am afraid it will compromise my beliefs and threaten our way of life if I don't speak my truth. Excellency, I have always been loyal to you and the Order and appreciate all of your support for me throughout the years. But, don't you see what is happening?" Then it slips out, "Who's side are you on anyway?"

Zonar feels a flash of regret for this turn of events. But, his tone grows imperious, "How dare you question my loyalty. You're making a huge mistake here Alkur. You are out of order."

Alkur angrily blurts out, "You're the one making a grave mistake excellency. My entire life has been out of order since my parents died. You have no idea what this is like. This entire Order we call the Law of One and the principles and values it stands for is collapsing in front of us. Can't you see this? I see the same dark energies, the same contempt and deception by the Temple of the Sun at work in Atlantis and nothing being done about it. Nothing. That is the disorder I am speaking about. Are you and I just going to watch this unfold and not do anything ...?"

"Enough!" Zonar barks.

Alkur tries to regain his composure. He realizes he has shown his lower self and is ashamed. Yet he feels some exhilaration getting it off his chest. He is silent for a moment, and then in a monotone says, "I am sorry Excellency. I don't know what overcame me."

Zonar is also collecting his thoughts. His eyes narrow slightly as he watches Alkur. "Do you understand what I have said to you, Alkur?"

Alkur nods. He can't think of anything more to say that could sway Zonar. Zonar continues "Good, it's important for us to understand each other. I am deeply sorry for what happened to your parents. We must not forget but also must move on with life. You must stop seeing conspiracy where none exists. That is all for now."

Alkur stumbles out of the chamber. His anger had surprised him but Zonar had surprised him, too. He is watched carefully by the Guards as he departs.

At home Ampero quickly sees Alkur's changed demeanor, it is as if the life force has suddenly drained from him. He looks physically and mentally tired, his empty eyes staring into a void.

"How did it go with Zonar? She asks already knowing the answer. Alkur looks at her and says,

"I am scared Ampero, for us and our way of life." He turns and walks away, dejected, at a loss for words. Ampero watches him go. Some time alone may be the most healing thing for him now, she thinks.

That afternoon, Alkur returns to teach his class at the temple. This time he first scans the room for anything unusual. The previous days had worn on him and he's tired. He wastes no time.

"Gentlemen, as you all know, we are often challenged by life. Each day, we face difficulties and setbacks, particularly as we seek spiritual growth. All of us have hit stumbling blocks. Life provides us with the experiences that we need to grow, to develop spiritually. Remember that we are spirits having an earth experience. Our souls develop as we shape our understanding and responses to life's challenges. These are the lessons we each must learn. This is the path our souls have chosen for us in this life."

For a moment Alkur reflects on his own life and continues, "How many of you have ever faced a crisis of conscience?"

Some students raise their hands, some trade glances wondering where Alkur's talk is going.

"Do you know what I am saying here? Crises occur when we confront challenges to our beliefs. It may be about who we are individually or our role in the larger community. The lines between right and wrong are not always distinct and clear. Sometimes they are ambiguous; call them grey. I'm glad to know that most of you have already faced and resolved such situations. Why am I bringing this up now?" Alkur looks around the room seeing only questioning and perplexed faces.

"Generations ago, our forefathers faced the evil of the Sons of Belial. This conflict led to the first and second cataclysmic destructions of Atlantis. We failed to coexist in Oneness and instead allowed distrust, separation, greed and manipulation into our hearts. The life force of the Law of One dried up and our Order was nearly lost as the Sons of Belial grew to dominate Atlantis."

Alkur paused to see if the class was following him. They all knew this history. He proceeded, "We were able to re-establish our community as our presence here together proves. But I'm afraid the same awful subversion is happening again. There are some in Atlantis who are working to destroy the Law of One, again."

There is a restless churn in the classroom. Some are silent, staring at him; some are murmuring to their neighbors. The pause lengthens then a student calls out, "How do you know this?" At the same time, another asks, "What do we do?"

Alkur responds carefully. They need to know, but he doesn't want to alarm them yet. It seems very important to him that they frame the challenge in a spiritually healing way, not as willful egos. "Most of you witnessed the energy attack in this very classroom. That negative energy is symptomatic of what we are facing." There were a few affirming nods as students remembered.

"The forces of darkness must be seen for what they are and their power neutralized. If a robber comes to your house and breaks in to steal your things, wouldn't you resist? Why would we let evil take away our harmony and our peaceful ways?"

A usually quiet student breaks in, "But by resisting, aren't we adding to the problem and becoming like the darkness itself?"

Alkur hesitates to answer. The student is showing true understanding and Alkur wants to validate that. "That is an excellent point and worthy of discussion. Resistance is a tricky issue and one which relies on conscience to discern. That may appear to be the case, but doing nothing may be worse. Acquiescence may be capitulation and compromise. It requires courage, conviction, and staying in touch with your essential truths to be a spiritual warrior. Inevitably, the path you choose to follow, right or wrong, is the path that speaks to your truth and what you feel is just, right and necessary." He looks around the room. There are varying degrees of understanding on their faces.

Alkur himself struggles to understand what he has just said. He doesn't doubt that resistance is the right answer – he just doesn't know what form that will take. At some unconscious level he knows he has to be the change he seeks. More than talk, he needed to act; to do something.

After a few moments he knew what to do. He would penetrate the Belial Illuminati. They are the secret elite behind the Temple of the Sun. He must know their plan.

Chapter 17

ATLANTIS

Alkur walks briskly through the darkening street. Since his confrontation with Zonar he knew something was not adding up, the puzzle pieces were spinning in his head. He suspected that more than the usual corruption was underway and he was now in the middle of it.

He knows it's risky but he has to see for himself what the Belial Illuminati were up to. They controlled the Atlantean government, through a network of favors, intimidation and blackmail, for their own ends. Wealth and power – they just couldn't get enough of it. He feared the Illuminati's plans.

Their secret meetings were usually held in rundown, inconspicuous and well hidden parts of the city. Back when he was a Guard, he had stumbled onto this pattern. A small payment to an old informant had bought the location for tonight's gathering, a ramshackle, abandoned meat warehouse near the main pier where trading ships unloaded their cargos.

Alkur cautiously approaches the warehouse. He can see men pacing about in preparation for the arrival of some important official. This must be it, he thinks. He stops, waits for a safe moment, and then slides behind a small wall jutting from the building.

The sound of a carriage stopping, then footsteps and a slamming door, announce the arrival of a small group. Alkur watches them being quickly led through a previously unseen door.

The men he saw earlier are now fanning out to secure the surrounding area. One rather stocky man approaches Alkur's position. He freezes, holding his breath as the man walks right past him. I have to move, he thinks.

With the men walking away from him, Alkur quickly trots towards the entrance and enters the doorway. Alkur slowly climbs the stone stairs leading to a smallish balcony and a large carved wooden door. He stops and listens, then pushes the door open and enters a dark room. It's too dark to discern its shape or size.

Alkur hears some muffled talking in an adjacent room. He thinks he must be close to the meeting place. As he tiptoes through the darkness, he stumbles on the uneven floor and bumps into a stack of wooden boxes. They don't fall but Alkur freezes, listening for any sound. That was close, he thinks.

Suddenly, he is pulled backwards, a vice-like grip locked around his neck. He instinctively tucks his chin, grips the assailants arm with both hands and drops to his knees, rolling onto to his right side. The dark shape flies off his back onto the floor and Alkur twists so the body is now under him, pinned and struggling. A hard blow to his left temple slams Alkur backwards. Now, he is pinned to the ground and with an arm choking his neck, can't breathe. Blackness edges around his eyes and he starts to lose consciousness. Out of breath and summoning all the energy he has left Alkur strikes the assailant knocking him sideways. There is a muffled cry and Alkur staggers to his feet in time to get another glancing blow to his head. The dark shape lunges again, only this time Alkur centered senses the direction of attack. He parries the strike with his right hand, captures the man's head with his left, pivots and turns, dropping him as his right arm strikes him under the chin. The blow's force sends the man flying backwards into the boxes and then to the ground. Alkur lunges at the man pinning him.

In the darkness he can barely make out the man's face. He looks into his eyes and suddenly recognizes the man. "Perilius...is that you?" Alkur says quietly with a look of complete surprise on his face.

The man utters surprised, "Alkur!"

Alkur stands and offering his arm helps Perilius from the ground. They stare at each other expressionless, bewildered looks on both their faces. Perilius served with Alkur in the Kings Guard and, like Alkur, had been one of the king's finest noncommissioned officers. They had been through a lot together, parting ways only when Alkur resigned from military service.

They hear talking outside the room now and they both look at the door. Perilius shakes Alkur's hand and in low tones says, "You haven't lost your touch after all these years, my friend."

"You are not so bad yourself. What are you doing here Perilius?" as he helps him up.

"I should be asking you the same. After you left the King's Guard, I was assigned as his emissary to the Temple of the Sun. When I left the service I continued as a representative for the Temple attending all their meetings and ceremonies. You are not supposed to be here, and if found out... I can't ensure your safety here, Alkur."

"Thanks for the warning. I could always count on you, but why did you attack me?"

"I thought you were an intruder—we have had them before and you are lucky. The last one we caught was not so fortunate." Perilius looks away and glances to the closed door. Perilius tells Alkur, "I have to go now. They are expecting me. If I were you, I would leave. What are you doing here anyway?"

Alkur smiles and tells him, "I am curious."

Perilius smiles in turn, warmth for his old comrade in his eyes. "You could have chosen a better place to visit. You have not changed much; same old Alkur. Take care, my reckless friend."

Perilius straightens his uniform then quietly walks back out through the door.

Alkur heads towards a glimmer of light at the end of the room where he finds a dark passageway. Soundlessly, he decides to explore it.

Chapter 18

ATLANTIS

The meeting room is dark and damp, yet spacious with chairs arranged in a circular fashion around a large empty table. Light from the glimmering candles cast shadows on the walls giving the room a haunted appearance.

The members of the Belial Illuminati sit quietly awaiting Salkuzzar's arrival. In the back, Zonar sits in a dark corner uncomfortable and fiddling nervously with his tunic, not sure why he was invited.

Alkur strolls quickly down the dark hallway. He is in luck. No one is guarding the room's entrance. He quietly slips into a small closet behind ceremonial curtains, trying to remain invisible. A slit in the drapery gives him a partial view of the room.

Suddenly, the back doors are thrown open and Salkuzzar enters. He is dressed in lavish ornamental robes followed by two very large and intimidating body guards. In unison, all the members rise and bow.

Salkuzzar looks sternly at the group then motions for them to sit. Everyone's eyes are glued on him, some shift uncomfortably in their chairs. A blanket of anticipation, tension and fear settles in the air. As he looks at them, Salkuzzar emanates an electric sense of power and mastery. His secret ambitions are clear and he revels in it all. As he settles at the head of the table, he smiles and looks at Zonar.

"Gentlemen, welcome. Thank you for being here. Make no mistake; we are embarking on a journey together to bring this kingdom the glory that is rightfully hers. We will change the history of Atlantis and usher in a new era of wealth, power and opportunity. The Temple of the Sun is leading this new beginning of growth, progress and expansion." Salkuzzar pauses, looking around the room.

The members smile, relax in their seats and applaud loudly. Salkuzzar raises his hand and they fall silent again.

"Belial and our ancestors rejected the teachings of the Law of One. He was right; it is an outdated system and should be purged. Intellect, technology, and proper use of power will give us dominion over the earth and it's our destiny. Our heroes Poseidon and the Sun deity RA led the way. Progress is about power and force leading to conquest and wealth and Atlantis a global empire. You, the Belial Illuminati will realize the vision of our forefathers. One day, our empire will extend to celestial and other worlds. We cannot be stopped. The technology to program the crystal skulls will make possible our true desires." The room erupts in applause.

Salkuzzar waits patiently then states, emphatically, "We must have all the crystal skulls. It is essential for our plan to succeed. We will soon be implementing our plan to obtain them."

In the closet, Alkur almost chokes. He scans the crowd and sees Zonar. His worse fears have been confirmed. The bastard, I knew it, he thinks. The skulls were in their plans after all!

Salkuzzar starts orating again, "Amillius, our king is passive; a soft leader in the face of rebellion. This is our opportunity to rid the land of the Law of One once and for all. With your assent and my guidance, a small cadre has started infiltrating the Law of One. Others will follow. We will indoctrinate their new generation of students. Those who resist will be purged, including their families. Make no mistake—they will not go down without a fight. The military is on our side and already have their instructions. We are prepared and always a step ahead.

The room grows quiet, uncomfortable glances are shared. Salkuzzar looks again at Zonar.

"I have asked Zonar from the Law of One to join us today. He has assured me the Order is unaware of our plans and will be unable to react in time to stop us. However, he tells me that there is one teacher at the Order, I believe his name is Alkur, may become an obstacle to our plan. Zonar has assured me he will be dealt with." Zonar, fidgeting with his tunic, looks at Salkuzzar, his face hooded by shadows.

Alkur is chilled when his name is mentioned. What does he mean by 'dealt with' and 'purging?' He realizes that he is grave danger. Alkur has heard enough. He slowly moves towards the door using the curtains and darkness to conceal his movements. Then he notices Perilius guarding the door. He stops.

An elderly man stands, "Your excellency, where does his majesty the king sit on this?"

"I have already spoken with the king. Amillius has assured me he does not want to get involved in disputes between religious orders. I take that to mean we can move forward as planned."

"If there are no more questions, that will be all for now. You all have your assignments and know what to do. We will meet again, soon." With a wave, Salkuzzar dismisses the group. Once nearly everyone has left the room, Salkuzzar summons Zonar.

"What can you tell me about this priest, Alkur?"

"I have spoken with him your excellency. He will not be a problem."

"I hope for your sake you are right. Our next phase begins soon."

After what seems like an eternity, Alkur is left alone. He soundlessly slips away, not noticing the tall muffled figure hidden in the shadows who has been watching him the entire time.

Chapter 19

ATLANTIS

Alkur slowly guides his horse along a grassy trail in the early morning light. The previous night he had slept fitfully; Ampero had grown concerned when he told her what had happened during the Illuminati meeting. Finally falling into a deep slumber, his spirit guide and friend Ilax summoned him in a dream to her earth dwelling, she called it. He didn't know why but she said it was important.

He'd never travelled here before. In the dream Ilax told him that once he reached the mountain pass the trail would veer to the right and up to a small knoll with large trees to a clearing. At the clearing he was to follow a small trail that would become visible only after he passed a large boulder, she called her 'looking rock'. She told him to stay on the trail until it ended at a large natural amphitheater of rocks and trees. He would find her in the cave off to the right.

Passing the oddly shaped field, Alkur dismounts, ties his horse near a grassy spot with a creek, and walks towards the entrance in the rock. A distinct pulsation thrums through his body, just like the vibration he feels around the temple skull. It's a powerful energy radiating security, peace, and acceptance.

Alkur pauses just inside the entry of the cave to let his eyes adjust to the dark. Walking forward, he finds himself in an enormous cavern filled with crystals of different sizes and shapes. Winding off of the main room are a series of passageways that twist out of sight. Alkur is amazed at what he sees: crystal generators, healing crystals, wands, a tetrahedron-like device adorned with large crystals, a ceremonial altar and sacred ornaments. A pleasing melody of low and high pitch tones gently sounds. It's beautiful.

Ilax turns from the crystal music generator and with a smile on her face reaches for him with both arms outstretched, saying "Alkur, it is so good to see you and thank you for coming."

Alkur holds her hands and smiles. Ilax wears a dark brown robe and red tunic adorned with small crystals; a dark blue shawl on her head doesn't hide her beautiful face and sparkling green eyes. He looks into her eyes so full of humor and love. She is more radiant than he ever imagined in his dreams. At a soul level, Alkur has always been attracted to her. After all she has been his spiritual guide in many other lifetimes. But now he is with her in the flesh for the first time. He is transfixed, by Ilax and his surroundings.

"I can see you now, for the first time in a human body!"

"Like yourself I have been on this planet many times before; we are old souls Alkur. I have chosen to return at this time in this form now to serve as your guide on your journey. You will understand this later. Did you have any trouble finding me?"

He answers, "Your directions were perfect, although I would not want to do the journey at night." Looking around, he says, "This place is amazing. How did you find, or create it?" He drops her hands and moves to more closely inspect the crystal wall.

"It's a little of both, but we have plenty of time to explore my home later. Right now, I need to make sure you're comfortable. Would you like some food or drink? Please sit down and relax. How is Ampero?"

Alkur finds a small chair to sit on and continues to look around him. "Ampero is just fine, thank you. Like me, she is concerned about some strange happenings lately. Ilax, why did you summon me? Why am I seeing you for the first time?" Alkur words are earnest, he really wants to understand. He realizes that she fits this unusual place perfectly. No one else would.

Ilax, looking intently at Alkur avoids the direct answer and says, "You may not know it but I was once a priestess in the Law of One, an expert in crystal technology. As you can see I am still tinkering away at it." She waves at the cavern and looks around.

Alkur looks at her surprised, "You said once. What happened?" He had always thought that Ilax, as his spirit guide, joined him during his priesthood training, that somehow she was part of the Law of One.

Ilax stopped for a moment, then said quietly "I fell short, deceived myself, and went to the dark side. I worked with the Sons of Belial during the last uprising, a choice I deeply regret." Sadness had pushed the smile from her face. "The Universe doesn't make mistakes, Alkur. As punishment, I was banished by Thoth and the Intergalactic Council and directed to serve my sentence in a cave. It kept me out of the way so I could not do any more damage. So here I am!"

She shrugged her shoulders and the smile returned. "My exile was really a gift. I reconnected with mother earth, Gaia, and was nurtured and healed. Later, I was given new assignments, small ones at first to gauge my trustworthiness. In one, I got to strengthen the earth's magnetic grid at the sacred sites around Atlantis. Afterwards, I was told that I had paid my karmic debts and could again rejoin the Law of One. I tell you this now Alkur so that you know that our journey is to serve the light. It's what we do."

Alkur had been listening carefully to this tale of confession and redemption. He's glad for her. "I'm pleased you called me. I need your wisdom and support."

She shifts to move slightly closer to him. Her tone changes also from just relating a narrative to something more urgent. "Alkur, I called you here because you have a huge responsibility to fulfill your destiny."

"Destiny?" Alkur had relaxed back in the comfy chair, almost sleepy. At that last word, he looked almost reluctant to take on any more responsibility or burden.

Ilax laughs at his chagrin, but continues. "Yes, destiny. It runs in your family. Your father, well, he was a gentle man of integrity and wisdom, and always loyal to the Law of One. He volunteered in this lifetime to infiltrate the Temple of the Sun and to learn about their intentions and plans. You were just a child. He knew it was risky but he chose to finish the work of previous lifetimes. In one, he had led survivors of an early Atlantean destruction to a new land. You come from a distinguished line of priests who have spent their lives trying to defeat the corruption, and the control of the Dark Priesthood."

Alkur takes Ilax's words in looking solemnly at the floor. Memories of his father stream back and tears fill his eyes. "I felt that he was doing something important."

Alkur contemplates her words. At some level, things were beginning to fall into place, his anger and visceral hatred for the Temple of the Sun and longing to set things right again. As part of being a priest, seeking a higher vibration, he had chafed at his inability to let the hatred go. At some level he must have known he would be destined to be on this path, to follow in his father's footsteps.

Ilax continues, "They agreed to come back as your parents to help you with your life work."

Alkur slowly nods his head and looks at her. He remembers an old recurring dream where he watched his parents rise through a vortex of light the night of the massacre. He had assumed they were murdered.

Ilax stops. She thinks he looks so young for the journey that lay ahead. With sympathy in her voice, she says "Alkur, you have your father's energy. I can see him in you. You know, you can contact him at any time for reassurance and guidance." Alkur nods again. Contacting ancestors was a common Law of One practice; he had tried before but never really got a clear message.

Ilax continues, "Now let me tell you why you're here." Alkur looks at her ready to listen. The truth about his parents' life had provided some comfort. As Ilax said, the Universe doesn't make mistakes.

"Thoth, through the Intergalactic Council wants you to safeguard the wisdom of our culture, protect it for future generations. The cycle is repeating and the forces of darkness are again exerting themselves in Atlantis. The Temple of the Sun ignores their connection with Source and is instead obsessed with power. You saw this in the classroom. Others remain asleep to what is unfolding, but not for long."

Alkur interrupts, "I'm not the right one to do this. I'm not prepared to protect our knowledge. There are others more adept and advanced in the Order. Besides, how would I do it?"

Ilax gently continues, not bothered at all by the interruption. "I understand it seems enormous, but I'm here to help prepare you to use your gifts and the power of the light within to counter the Temple of the Sun. Notice, the emphasis is 'within.' You must learn to embody the energies. It is not force against force, the way the Guard's trained you. Instead, it is all about love, Alkur, and becoming love and removing the obstacles to love that keep you from living your life's purpose. Love is the most powerful energy in the Universe. It's a new way of being for you."

She pauses for dramatic emphasis. "Think this over. Ampero must know. The choice is yours."

Alkur looks at her questioningly. "Yes, I'll think about it. Of course, you haven't given me a clear picture of what that future is. But I'll talk with Ampero."

Ilax only says "You cannot escape your destiny forever, Alkur." She tries to lighten the conversation, "But don't worry about it. Things always unfold the way they are meant to. Come see the rest of my home and some of the crystal creations I've been working on."

She rises and waits for Alkur to follow her through one of the passageways. Hours later, Alkur and Ilax perform a small fire ceremony asking for blessings from Gaia and for guidance and strength for the path forward. Alkur heads home thinking about his coming talk with Ampero.

Chapter 20

ATLANTIS

Alkur's horse gallops furiously in the night along the narrow gravel road. He holds on tightly scanning from side to side watching the dark shapes, rapidly closing on him. He desperately swings the reins back and forth and the horse responds, moving faster in the darkness.

The men lay in hiding at the trail's bend as he was about to enter a main road to the city. Sensing danger Alkur had galloped at full speed past them catching his pursuers off guard.

Suddenly, he sees something ahead but it's hard to discern with the horse charging through the night. He makes out the outline of a ghostly apparition, a woman, in the distance. She fades in and out as he approaches. Then he sees her clearly, at the side of the road with a lantern or something glowing in her hands. Then, she's gone again. He slows and can see a hint of a glow coming from a faraway cluster of trees in the distance. His pursuers are closing fast.

Instinctively, he knows he must follow the light. He guides the horse off the main road through a grassy field filled with small trees and shrubbery. Looking back, he sees that his pursuers didn't catch his detour. They disappear from view.

He thinks that was too close!

ROBERT R. MALDONADO PHD.

Alkur continues towards the light, cautiously skirting an open area. The glow is brighter now and then he sees Ilax standing by an old oak. Propped in her right arm is a crystal skull glowing with an iridescent bright light.

She looks at him as though nothing was wrong, as though there was no ambush or pursuers. She smiles, "Welcome to my special place, my home away from home. I love it here, these beautiful trees offer me peace and protection. On a clear day you may not notice this place, especially from the road, it has a natural camouflage." Her voice tails off as Alkur dismounts.

Catching his breath he turns to Ilax. "What happened back there? And why are you here." He is almost brusque. He needs to recover from the close escape.

"I saw them as you were leaving; it was too late to warn you but I knew you would follow the main road." Glancing down at skull, she says "It glowed and guided me here." Ilax continues, "The skull tuned into your fear and gave you another option, honoring your free will, of course. The horse felt it too and trusted it. I'm glad you are safe."

Alkur is looking at her skeptically. He remembers Salkuzzar's proclamation and realizes, aloud, "They were after me. They must be Salkuzzar's assassins."

Ilax nods affirmatively, "Alkur, yes, the purge has begun. Throughout Atlantis, they are rounding up and imprisoning followers of the Law of One. You're in grave danger."

Alkur knows this already. He fears the worst. He looks down at Ilax and with a tinge of panic in his voice, barks, "Ampero, I've got to get Ampero. She too is in danger. I must go." He grabs the reins and saddle horn, quickly mounts and looks toward the road.

Ilax steps next to him and placing her hands on his thigh, says "Alkur, stay here with me. You'll be safe. It is too dangerous now. Ampero knows what she must do. She will understand."

Alkur, impatient and incredulous at the thought of leaving Ampero in trouble, just shouts, "I must go. Thank you." She nods and steps back. He turns the horse and gallops into the night praying that's he's not too late. His mind is already calculating the fastest route staying off the main road.

It's still dark when Alkur finds his way to his neighborhood. There is an eerie silence in the streets. It's as if the entire population is hiding, tense and fearful. He sees a flicker of light ahead and a burning pyre with a whitish-grey smoke rising in the air. A smell reaches him, the smell of something dead and rotting, fetid, burning flesh. For a moment Alkur is in a lost world — a child running away while mayhem and death dance around him. It's gone as quickly as it came.

He turns into the alley by his home, and right away sees the smoke. In the dawn, it slowly drifts upwards. He quickly dismounts and stumbling over debris, enters what used to be his home.

It is black from the fire, gutted, and burned down, everything gone. Alkur is sick to his stomach from the smell. His eyes burn. He covers his nose with his hand and slowly moves through the wreckage. Tripping over a partial timber, he calls out, "Ampero, Ampero!" There's no response as he shoves charred pieces away.

There is only silence and the muted crack of burning embers nearby. He slowly makes his way through the blackened rooms. Books, furniture and objects are strewn about, covered in ash and bright wood embers. He reaches the bedroom, and with his heart thumping, he sees Ampero lying motionless on the dark floor. "No!" the cry escapes him as tears track through the dirt on his face. Her feet are black and twisted under the debris, her arms on her torso as if trying to shield herself. She's gone; the spark of life is gone. He falls to his knees before her, and with both his hands softly holds her face. He pulls her towards him, shaking and moaning in his agony, grieving the loss of the love of his life, the senseless loss.

The sounds of a man wailing pierce the silence.

Chapter 21

ATLANTIS

It's early morning as Ilax kneels before the small altar adorned with precious crystals and candles. Her daily ritual involved being in sacred communion with the earth feeling its energies to replenish herself and to express her gratitude for its blessings.

She is barefoot with gold anklets; her long white robe shows off the gold and crystal necklaces. She sways back and forth in a slow seductive rhythm. As the energy surges through her body, she drops closer to the earth, her hands clutching the ground. Slowly, she rotates her pelvis upwards, downwards in repeated and deliberate thrusting motions. As she moves her long black hair sways back and forth sweeping the ground. She feels the divine feminine pulse. The Mother energy vibrates in her sensual trance-like movements. She arches her back and releases a soft orgasmic moan. She whispers, 'Oh my God, I love you', the energy coursing through her body as she shakes uncontrollably in multiple etheric orgasms. She soon relaxes and lies motionless on the floor, spent and satisfied and slowly begins to rise.

Afterwards, as she walks down to the well she sees a figure approaching on horseback. Ilax watches as the horse crests the hill and begins to cross the clearing. She recognizes Alkur. Something looks terribly wrong. He is slumped over, head bowed, hands barely holding onto the reins. Something dreadful has happened to him or Ampero.

The horse slowly stops. Ilax runs the short distance over to them, looking up at Alkur with a concerned look. Alkur, tears in his swollen red eyes and a sad, defeated look on his face appears to have not slept in days. He stares at the ground then straight ahead, empty and speechless. Laid across the horse is Ampero's lifeless body covered in a blanket.

In a flat monotone voice he says, "They killed her, she is gone now, forever."

Ilax shocked, bows her head taking in what she has heard. Gentle Ampero, she thinks, she leaves an empty space in our hearts. The glorious morning is gone lost to sorrow. Ilax wipes the tears from her eyes without words. She extends her arms to Alkur. He glances solemnly at her for an instant and slides down from the horse. She embraces him saying, "I'm so sorry" then turns to help him carry Ampero's body to the cave.

Its late afternoon and Ilax and Alkur stand in a field of lilies atop a small knoll overlooking a valley of trees stretching towards the blue horizon. In front of them is Ampero's gravesite. Ampero would have approved of this beautiful, serene setting. Her body had been wrapped in purple silk garments and covered with crystals and precious stones before being placed in the ground. A large stone marked its location adorned with flowers and herbs. Ilax and Alkur notice a flock of white doves assembled on a nearby tree looking down in silence. And then quiet unexpectedly the birds take off, but not before overflying them in a graceful formation as if acknowledging her and escorting her spirit to the heavens.

Chapter 22

ATLANTIS

That evening they sit huddled together by the fire in silence. Alkur in a large blanket stares expressionless at the fire. Both are lost in their own worlds. Ilax is the first to break the quiet, and gazing at the fire says, "You know you have come back for a reason Alkur."

Alkur still with his eyes on the flames just shakes his head. "I don't know." He shudders then continues, "Without Ampero ... I just need to think." His voice stumbles.

Ilax says, "Alkur, you're at a crossroads; your world has changed." He looks so lost; she doesn't know whether to go on. "Ampero's death is part of it. I wish I could bring her back to you. I know how much she loved you and you her; yours was a very special relationship." Alkur closes his eyes – whether blocking the thoughts or letting them roll by quietly – Ilax doesn't know.

She places her hand over his. He can feel her compassion, gentleness, and strength but he's too beaten to reply. Alkur rouses himself slightly. He knows she is right. He has come back because it is the only way he can move forward. He can't get the thought out of his head that somehow he attracted all of this pain into their lives. His anger and selfishness caused Ampero's death. He should have been there for her, protected her. He begins to sob softly and Ilax gently wraps her arms around him.

Alkur sleeps uneasily through the long night. Then, while in a semi-sleep state, he's awakened by soft, pulsating sounds coming from deep within the cave. He rises to investigate.

Entering a side cavern, he's met with flickering multicolored lights and the most beautiful sounds he has ever heard. They resonate within, catching his heart, filling him with peace, joy and happiness. The music beckons him forward, welcoming him into a dimension beyond time and space. The walls also vibrate with the sounds making them appear like slow moving waves of color. Small orbs of multicolor energy float by. The sounds and color make his entire body sway spontaneously with a natural rhythm. An incredible peace and serenity envelop him.

Suddenly, he feels warm hands on his shoulders and turns to see Ilax. The shimmering colors reflect on her soft countenance and her luminous eyes. Alkur's heart momentarily jumps. He wants to hold her in his arms, to stroke her hair, to kiss her but holds back. He is not sure why. She smiles and takes his hand. They leave the cavern without a word.

Back in the main cave, Ilax explains. "The experience you had with the sounds and colors, they came from the crystal skull. It creates a field of light that carries encoded healing symbols to restore one's energy field and centers." Alkur nods, "It certainly works. I was drowning in sadness and then when I went into the cavern… I can't really comprehend what happened."

Ilax says, "That's its power and its message to the world. The skull teaches us how to heal the darker energies and bring love into our lives. It's a gift."

She pauses, and then says "There was a time where we could see spiritual energy in our temples. We could tune into the music and see energy balls, even visions if so inclined. You could look into the crystals and commune with angels and other evolved inter-dimensional beings."

Alkur surprised asks, "What happened?"

"We closed our hearts and went over to the darkness."

Alkur looks at her and says, "I know of my tribe's skull but not about its powers. I've been a priest and did not know the depth of this mystery."

Sitting back down a tapestried cushion, Ilax nods and says, "The Atlantean skulls hold the wisdom, healing and higher consciousness we need to evolve. In the wrong hands, they could be used to control the world, possibly destroy the earth, with the violence rippling into the galaxy. To prevent the dark forces from gaining such power, the Intergalactic Council assigned a "Keeper of the Crystals" for each tribal skull. Their task is to safeguard their wisdom and, if necessary, hide the skull away to keep it out of the hands of evil, such as the Temple of the Sun. They would abuse its powers. But if the skulls are safe, the darkness can be defeated through the rise of the earth's consciousness and unconditional love. The skulls will manifest the universal energy we all have and can neutralize the discordant energies of the Temple of the Sun."

Alkur's eyes glow with anticipation. "This is just what we need to push back against the purge and restore our community. We can bring the skull out and confront the Temple of the Sun, head on."

Ilax shrugged, shaking her head slightly. "Perhaps, but that is using love as a weapon, it's a perversion of love."

She went on, oblivious to Alkur's disappointment, "During the golden era, everyone was a healer and could channel pure spiritual healing energy using symbols and sounds. You're attuned to these energies now Alkur, the ones you felt earlier. That knowledge is within you."

"The skull is the key to this system. That's why it is so powerful. It can predict future events, heal, or gift a person with psychic abilities. It can be programmed to raise the body's vibration. But the gift of this healing system must wait until humanity is ready."

"The Sons of Belial and the Temple of the Sun want the skulls badly because when the twelve tribal skulls are reunited, a 13th skill will materialize. That skull will open contact with other dimensions including the darker frequencies of other worlds. It has implications way beyond Atlantis and earth. For example, it is the only hope that the Annunaki warriors of Nebiru have to escape from their exile. They would eventually find a way to access skulls and manipulate the priesthood to re-code skulls to perpetuate their domination of the world."

Alkur puzzled asks, "What 13th skull? And who are the Annunaki?"

Ilax patiently replies, "In consultation with the Intergalactic Council the Atlantean priests created a master crystal containing all the wisdom of the 12 tribes. It appears whenever all 12 skulls are brought together. The 12 skulls are now on Atlantis but the Council has deemed it too dangerous for the 13th to materialize. It is in a safe location until the planet's consciousness rises."

Alkur, just beginning to understand the scope of these revelations, asks again "Who are the Annunaki?"

"Atlanteans trace their lineage from the stars, Alkur. Thousands of earth years ago our priests had observed that a huge cataclysm occurred in the solar system of Sothis, Satais, and Anu forcing the star Satais to collapse. The monumental chain reaction shook the entire Sirian star system and hit our constellation as well. Nebiru, the most remote planet in Anu's orbit, was knocked from its rotational path and sent careening through space. It was grabbed by the Earth's sun and drawn into its solar system, but then ricocheted back into space."

"Nebiru is a homeless planet desperately searching for a new home. The Annunaki inhabit her and travel throughout the universe looking for energy primarily from minerals and ores. The Annunaki ships have appeared in Earth's solar system for over 450,000 years; they return about every 3,600 years. They know that Earth has the greatest potential to provide them with natural resources they no longer get from Nebiru. They are takers, the cosmic lower self parasites that draw from astral bodies to satisfy their need for power and control over their own existence. The more fear they engender, the more they suck energy to feed themselves."

ILax pauses momentarily and continues, "Nebiriun shuttle ships eventually landed in Atlantis. The ships were invisible but the warriors

appeared as interdimensional beings of light bringing messages and
offerings and gifts such as advanced crystal and sound technology.
They presented themselves to the High Priests as gods from the heavens bringing gifts from the heavens. The trusting Atlanteans accepted
all this."

"But these aliens infected the Atlantean priest's hearts with deceit
and trickery that fueled their restlessness and created disharmony. A
Death Shadow Ray generator was created bringing forth a subtle frequency that lowers the energetic vibration of the people, making them
vulnerable to manipulation.

The Law of One community was skeptical of these beings. But they
couldn't hold out against the new technologies. The Temple of the Sun
began to covet and hold power, small efforts at first but then exploding
into empire and conflict. A wealthy elite began to enslave the people;
that's how evil operates, through greed, deceit and selfishness."

Ilax grimly continued with the saga. "By this time, the Atlanteans
had learned to illuminate the continent with crystal powered generators. They created air and sea going vessels, tapped solar energies, and
began to harness the collective mind. The Belial Illuminati allied with
the aliens plotted to gain control over the Council. The Annunaki left,
as they must, but had already seeded their evil. The Belial, hungry for
more power, plotted to reprogram the 12 skulls. Their aim was to bring
back the Atlantis of before except now under their control. The Law of
One supported, still supports, peace and love in a higher frequency existence as well Alkur. You know the rest of the story."

Alkur is trying to comprehend what she is saying. This is what
Salkuzzar is really after. To piece it together, he reiterates the main
points.

"So, the Belial Illuminati's real purpose is to control Atlantis through
the 12 skulls?"

"Yes, they must have all 12 skulls for their plan to work. Your father's
job was to prevent this from happening. The Temple of the Sun came
close to succeeding."

"So, this is Salkuzzar's plan?"

"People like Salkuzzar serve the Annunaki, which is why they have such power. They feed his vanity, and he stirs up food for them. They will return."

"So, I have been chosen to take the Thoth tribe skull away from Atlantis thereby preventing the 13th skull from every materializing."

"That's right. Without the 12 the 13th will not materialize. There is always a risk that the Council will be corrupted somehow and the 13th skull brought out of hiding."

"Why me?" Alkur's brows lower over his eyes. He has changed just in the past day; he is sterner, grave.

"Why not?" She looks at him smiling now. More seriously she says, "To answer you, I can only say that the divine is in you. Your higher self-soul incarnated into this lifetime by choice and with the commitment to do this now. It is part of your soul's memory. All of your life experiences have served to prepare you for this task. I and others you will meet are all part of this divine plan for humanity."

"Including tragedies?" Alkur face contracts for just a moment re-membering the loss of Ampero.

"Yes, sometimes. You may still decide not to do this. You always have the choice, of course. But the opportunity may not present itself again. And that would be a lost opportunity not only for the development of your soul but also for humanity. It is both personal and collective."

Ilax earnestly continues. "It is important for you to understand. To be entrusted with your bigger destiny you will have to commit to clear-ing and balancing your own energies, to face your demons and release what no longer belongs. It is a journey of self-discovery and transforma-tion. You'll learn to embrace the light within, and you'll see and under-stand your lower darker self as you clear old programming, release of the blocked energy, and learn a new approach to living. Your heart will awaken and you'll learn to discern and silence your ego-driven self. In time, you'll be able to accept and integrate the good and bad, the light and darkness and celebrate and change our world."

Alkur just looks on, half-understanding. He was gearing up for a fight with evil, to save his country, make a difference and now hears he must change himself first.

She allows her words to sink in. "In time you'll process your darkness, not by condemning it or running away, but by loving and accepting it. Then, nothing can touch you. The flip in perception will power you and enable you to access other things. Love and accept the dark and leave the combative war energy behind. Embrace softness and forgiveness. By doing so you liberate yourself."

Alkur looks at her and says, "I've lived my life with integrity and courage. Yet, I'm in constant fear and dreading the future. I've been betrayed so many times and the pattern keeps repeating itself: the murder of my parents and now the loss of Ampero and the purging of the Law of One." An odd expression of bewilderment and determination crosses Alkur's face. "What's going on? Everything inside me says that to move forward I must confront and defeat the aggression and hope my soul will rest once this is done."

Ilax knows that he is on the threshold of self-discovery. It just takes time. "You have the wisdom to see the truth within. It's right to honor the feelings that surfaced. Just remember that when you judge something as bad, it is an invitation to bring awareness to it. You can release what no longer serves you while acknowledging all of yourself including your anger, guilt, the parts you hate and other sad energies. Part of you wants to fix things, control and act; it's ready to lash out. Yet there is also that part of us, the divine higher self, that already knows what we need. It's your truth. It will quietly guide you; its power is based in love. That's the big secret. We all have the power of love within us."

Chapter 23

ATLANTIS

The next morning, Alkur's training begins. Walking through the cavern, he is half listening as Ilax starts talking about the skulls. While studying some of the unusual colors her voice interrupts, "The skull is a multidimensional representation of us in crystalline form. We access it through meditation and the use of special crystals."

Ilax stops in front of a small podium, picks up a crystal and hands it to Alkur, "Place it on your third eye. I've found that these ellestial crystals can take one deep within the self, to your innermost truth including revealing the shadow parts of our nature, the dark realms we hide or are unwilling to face."

Alkur closes his eyes holding the crystal to his brow. It's cool against his skin, but uncomfortable feelings bubble up as lower self thoughts emerge. Alkur pulls the crystal away, handing it back to Ilax with a grimace. She just laughs lightly and then says, "Alkur, the 12 wisdom layers are encoded within you at birth. The lower self, the shadow and its low vibration, blocks that knowledge. You just felt it; sadly, many in Atlantis live in that negative energy."

Alkur nods, and says "I used to deal with those people daily as part of the Guards. There are fewer in the Order, I thought, but now I'm not so sure. There seems to be ugliness everywhere if you scratch the surface." He hesitates to tell Ilax about Zonar's deception. Whether from loyalty or because he didn't want to change the subject already, he didn't know.

Ilax isn't paying attention. She's wrapped up trying to convey the layers of knowledge. "The first layer is the "Tree of Life." Atlantean science has shown that all the cells in our bodies retain the memories of our current and past lives. The second layer acknowledges our purpose and direction in life and that we are sentient beings in the image of the Creator. The third layer activates the chemistry and potential to do what our consciousness requires as we complete our life mission…"

Alkur finds this recitation interesting, sort of, but not relevant to the issue at hand. The issue is protecting the skulls and the demise of the Temple. He's impatient with Ilax's presentation but tries not to show it. They stroll while she talks. For the most part she is watching the floor seemingly oblivious to him. Alkur's attention focuses on the crystalline tools set around the cavern. What are these for, he wonders, and how was the lighting in this cavern done?

Ilax's voice breaks through his thoughts. He hears her saying "… the tenth responds to compassion with grace, understanding and spiritual awareness." Finally, he hears, "The last one is the God within that radiates our life force." Ilax turns back to him, pleased with her explanations. Alkur smiles, saying "Thank you. I may not remember all the details, but I've got the basics down." He hopes this exposition is over.

She grins with pleasure and goes on to say, "Alkur, you must consciously activate the layers during your daily meditation. All your psychic and spiritual gifts, including healing power, come from these 12 wisdom strands. Let's go eat; all this talking has made me hungry. And I've got fresh fruit and some meat prepared."

Afterwards, Ilax talks about Atlantean healing. "It's an ancient, proven system of healing symbols, crystals and the skull. Alkur, love energy is the key; it awakens the harmonic frequencies and Oneness consciousness. When you ask the skull for anything you must first be in a state of love and harmony for it to work. This can be very difficult and a challenge in the dense earth field we inhabit."

Ilax places a large crystal skull in front of them. In a soft, measured tone she says, "Sit comfortably and feel relaxed." Alkur shifts a little, stretches his arms and rolls his head before settling down. "Begin with deep breaths and try to relax a little bit more after each exhalation." She pauses for a few minutes.

"Now shift your awareness to your heart area. With each breath feel the energy of love expand throughout your body. Be aware that the love energy is spreading to every cell in your body. Feel it and stay with this for a moment."

She continues. "Now, allow the energy to grow beyond the physical body to the surrounding areas. Allow this field of love to permeate within and around us. You may begin to feel the frequency of this energy mirror the heartbeat of Mother Earth as you connect with her. Be with that connection and then focus your attention on expanding the energy to Father Sky and throughout the universe. Find harmony with them through the same heartbeat. Be still in this for now."

After a few minutes, "Now take a deep breath, and bring your awareness back to this place, feel yourself grounded, and open your eyes. This will take practice, so do it regularly."

They remain silent for a few minutes. Although he had extensive training with the Order on the oneness consciousness, Alkur is more aware now of the unity underlying everything than ever before. He smiles at Ilax, saying "That was more powerful and deeply felt than most of our priesthood rituals. It's simpler, too."

Ilax replies, "Well, sometimes we make it all more complicated."

For the final lesson of the day, Ilax guides Alkur through the Atlantean 12 energy center meditation and explains the healing protocols. "Our system of healing uses an eight-pointed star which represents the divine connection between body and spirit." She goes on to recite and demonstrate the steps to follow:

"First, create a healing space and burn incense or light a candle to cleanse the atmosphere. Then set the intention of love energy within and around you. The meditation we did earlier is a good start. As you feel called, invoke the Angels of Atlantis, Thoth, ancestors, gods, and guides and ask for the energies of love, light, and healing to flow through you. You'll feel a golden light beam move through your spine connecting Mother Earth and Father Sky. Breathe this energy through your being 8 times.

Then, with the skull balance your 12 energy centers. You do this by placing your hands on the heart area and saying HAA three times aloud. This connects with your own heart sound. Out loud, say RA-MA-TI-MA three times to attune you to the skull energies. It means everything is blessed; everything blessed is sacred. Following your guidance, use any of these four major healing symbols."

"Using the Atlantean symbol AKMA-LA is an extremely powerful way to deeply cleanse the aura. It means Light of God and will protect and defend against negative energies. The symbol AKMA-RA-LA is very effective for current problems as well as diagnosing and treating people and animals. It means light and harmony of God. It's also good for treating those with negative entities since it sends the entities into the light. AK-RA-NA is the symbol of distance healing. It brings the joy and love that attends spiritual growth oneness consciousness. And then AK-EL-KIBA is used to access the entire energy field for diagnosis and treatment."

Alkur pays close attention. This is the practical learning he sought. In many ways it reminded him of the military, learning tactics and techniques that can be applied as necessary. Alkur pulls the skull in front of him to practice. He slowly moves through the steps that Ilax described, pausing occasionally to make sure he had made the needed connections. He begins chanting and asks the divine about his greatest need. In a deep trance-like state he recognizes the unsettling emotions of anger and frustration. The skull was projecting his shadow self back into his consciousness. He is surprised with its effectiveness.

Alkur rises out of the meditation. Ilax has gone and he is alone in the cavern. He realizes that he has a long healing journey ahead of him. He sits for a while, and then stumbles out into the daylight, taking in the afternoon sunshine.

Chapter 24

ATLANTIS

For Alkur, the past few days had been a series of challenges posed by Ilax. They focused on self-discipline and building the ability to recognize negativity and set it aside. This was not the training he had envisioned for his mission but he was constantly surprised by its versatility and power.

Today, the air is moist after a brief rain. The grass is slick and the veining of the gray and black boulders are accentuated by the wetness as Ilax heads down a narrow trail in the woods. Alkur follows silently crossing the pine needle matting underfoot.

Ilax stops and silently points to a cave entrance that is half hidden in the thick underbrush. Alkur stares at the forbidding hole in the rock. He knows he's going to have to go in there and he can already feel the anxiety in him. A cold stone forms in his stomach; he has a visceral fear of dark confined spaces. Is this really necessary? He asks himself, then turning to Ilax "Haven't we spent enough time looking into the darkness without this?" Ilax raises her eyes to his, saying reassuringly "I think you're ready. You can do this." He grunts and wonders.

Ilax's expression grows stern, and in a firm voice, she says "This is the cave of the shadow. It reveals your dark side on your journey through it. To succeed here, you'll have to conquer your fears and embrace your higher self." With scarcely a pause, she continues in a conversational tone, "Fear is the primordial force that stops us from growing into the light. It's odd but our greatest fear is facing ourselves. Living with that fear destroys us. Mastering our fears, that is, seeing them for what they are is the first step to discovering our divine destiny. In the cave whatever you think and feel happens. Any fears will become real. But you know how to tackle that. It's all up to you now. I must also warn you. You may also die in there as your fears grow real. Be vigilant!"

Alkur sighs with resignation. He'll have to do this. He composes himself and reflects for a moment on the task ahead. Settling on a nearby rock, he begins what he has begun to call his higher self meditation. He realizes he is afraid of facing himself.

He closes his eyes and calls on his guides and aligns his spirit with love and healing. With his hands on his heart he breathes deeply, chanting saying RA-MA-TI-MA on each exhalation. He pauses momentarily and feels the energies swirl within him. He bends over and picks up some of the damp earth, rubs it in his hands and then wipes his hands on his clothes. He feels strong. He is ready.

Alkur enters the cave and is instantly engulfed in darkness. With his left hand he feels for the wall and with his right hand above for the ceiling. Just two steps in, the passageway abruptly turns and narrows. He can barely fit through. The earth cool cave is suddenly oppressively hot. His heart is thumping and he has no idea what to do. He stops, his survival sense screaming to turn back. Stubbornly, he moves forward, slowly. He hits his head on the ceiling and drops to crawl on his knees. He is frightened now. Something scuttles lightly over him and he freezes. The only sound is his labored breath as he inches forward. The ceiling continues to drop. Now he is forced onto his stomach, wiggling through the sand in the black. He stops; wants to scream, to back away and get out.

The cave narrows even more, the ceiling now so low that he can barely move, wedged between the walls. He thinks, I am going to get stuck and die! It feels like a furnace and he can hardly breathe in the deathly quiet. He is afraid. It's too much. He wants to scream but he can't. He coughs and chokes on the dust. He gasps for breath.

He manages to roll over on his back and unexpectedly sees a projection of himself on the rock above. It shows a distorted, fearful face filled with contempt. Alkur can't close his eyes to block out the image. He watches scenes from his life and past lives flashing around him. I can't believe this selfishness, this ugliness is me, he thinks. He tries to back away but can't. He opens and closes his eyes as if not believing what he is seeing.

Then he remembers his training to tune into his higher self and allow the energy of love to neutralize the fear. He closes his eyes and begins chanting the healing sounds. The images slowly fade. Relieved, Alkur hesitates momentarily and then continues crawling. He thinks, it worked, the love worked.

The ceiling gradually lifts. Alkur rises to his knees and then slowly to his feet. The temperature cools comfortably. It is still pitch black as he feels out the cave's contours. He has no sense of direction whatsoever in the darkness and no sounds other than his labored breath. He has no choice but to face whatever lies ahead.

The cave tightens, the ceiling drops, and Alkur is on his knees again, crawling. He looks up and another image flashes on the wall ahead. It a cruel, demonic face that lashes out at others inflicting pain. The face seems to feed on others suffering and enjoying its lust for power and control.

Alkur closes his eyes in shame and regret. He feels the pain he's inflicted on others and himself. Remembering now what to do, he tunes into his higher self, tones the healing sounds and sends out love for himself and those he hurt in the past. He asks for their forgiveness and love. The image evaporates. He notices that the tunnel narrows abruptly. The only way forward is to lie on his side and slide forward using his hands to push his body along.

The ceiling is just an inch from his face. He opens and closes his eyes and it's all the same, just darkness. Then he screams, the noise echoing through the cave but disappearing as though absorbed in nothingness. He feels the hot cold onset of panic and a certainty that he will be buried alive. Ilax's words, "fear will become real" hit his chest like a punch. He thinks he's a dead man. Desperately, loudly, he calls out the healing sounds. The space brightens from an unknown light source. Alkur's fears quiet a little as he continues to wriggle forward, on his back now.

Another flash of dim light paints the ceiling. Great, he thinks, just what I need, another gruesome image. And he's momentarily aware that he had separated himself from his fears. This time the face he sees is a vindictive, vengeful self with a palpable blood thirst and glaring red eyes.

He momentarily hesitates and closes his eyes trying to turn away. He knows this energy, he lived this image for years; it drove him. He begins to weep then screams at the top of his lungs for forgiveness. He wails uncontrollably. The following silence is complete, wider and deeper than any silence he has known. But he feels a huge release. He tones the sacred words and love enters his heart. The face is gone.

Alkur is greatly relieved. He slowly rises to his feet and notices that the cave has opened. He brushes the dust and sand from his body and face and sees a glimmer of light ahead. Thank God, he thinks, this trial is over. He sighs then lifts his head to stand fully erect.

Alkur stops. As he adjusts to the brightness he can see in front of him a dark-like apparition blocking his path. It moves rapidly closer; its ghost-like appearance shifting into different forms. A dreadful hiss carries rancid breath to Alkur, who stares into the beast's eyes.

Alkur knows, instinctively, that this is the guardian of the cave and the keeper of his greatest weakness. He hesitates, closes his eyes seeking his higher self and guidance. In his heart, Alkur hears he must face the energy with love because the dark apparition is really an aspect of himself that he must embrace. It is the reason he is in the cave. He fills his heart with gratitude and love and slowly walks towards the apparition. As he gets closer he notices that the apparition starts to disappear.

Alkur walks towards the sunlight, changed and grateful. He thinks, now he's done.

He steps out into an open field. His footing feels dry; the sun must have erased the morning rain. He blinks in the sunlight and senses something alive nearby. His head swings to the right and he sees a new menacing like shape materializing before his eyes.

This is different, more aggressive than the one in the cave. The shape suddenly jumps in the air and kicks him in the chest knocking him backwards. Alkur lands squarely on his back, his head slamming into the hard ground. Before he can recover his breath the shape moves in for another attack. Alkur instinctively rolls to his right out of the line of attack and springs up. He still has trouble seeing in the brightness. The dark shape is relentless and reaches Alkur's neck. Alkur deflects, sidesteps and blends with the attack by facing the same direction. With the hands grasping the shape, Alkur launches it forward and away from him. The figure then turns and quickly grabs both of Alkur's wrists pinning them together in vice-like lock. Alkur steps forward and pivots facing the same direction. He then lowers his center while raising his arms in a sword-like fashion as he turns and slams the shape backwards. It rolls forward with a screaming sound and tries the frontal attack again. Alkur, seeing the creature's shadow gets his rhythm, sidesteps. With a cutting motion, he catches the shape under its head dropping it to the ground. Then as fast as it began, its over. Alkur looks around preparing for the next attack but the shape is gone.

Alkur is hyper-vigilant now, shaken but alert and ready for the next assault. He wonders what's going on. Nothing appears around him. Then, with sudden relief, he drops to his knees, exhausted, but alive. Thoughts aren't quite forming yet as he sees Ilax appears out of the trees with a thankful smile on her face.

"Alkur, congratulations." She extends her hand down to him, to help his rise. "You made it out alive." Alkur looks at her quizzically and surprised, saying "You mean there was a serious chance I wouldn't?" He rises with a more truculent note in his voice, "What was that last attack all about? I thought the cave was the challenge, and then out of nowhere, some 'thing' jumps me." He looks at her, demanding an answer.

Ilax half-laughs and replies "I guess the truth is that you must always be on the alert. You handled it well. Clearly, your warrior skills are still intact. But more important is to make the choice for love; the outcome is better." Alkur just shakes his head, "Ilax, for a sweet soul, you have an awful sense of humor."

She looks a little sheepish as Alkur's stern face crinkles into a grin. His shoulders drop as he relaxes, finally. From the sun, he guesses that he was in the cave for a couple of hours. But, it could have days or minutes. As he sighs, the fatigue catches up to him.

Over a snack of fruit and roasted vegetables, Ilax returns to business. Alkur finds that his respect for her has grown; she knows what she's doing. He's ready to listen again. Ilax says, "Your next mission is important and requires careful planning and diligence. You are to contact Am-ee-lee, a high ranking librarian in the Hall of Records. Do you know him?" She lifts her eyes questioning.

Alkur shakes his head and Ilax continues, "He's an interesting man, a long-time member of the Law of One. He knew about your father and the threat that the Temple of the Sun posed. He secretly organized and dispatched several missions to transfer vital religious, scientific and historical records for safekeeping around the globe. This was all part of the divine plan at the time and approved by the Intergalactic Council, fearful that sacred knowledge would fall into the wrong hands."

Alkur wonders who directs Ilax, and who is behind this mission. For probably the first time, he wonders about her private life. But he only says, "Does Am-ee-lee know about me and my mission?"

"He will soon enough. He is a peacemaker at heart. And he knows it is his destiny to safeguard our tribe's records." Alkur wonders if she knows everyone's destiny. He feels surprisingly humble with that thought.

Ilax goes on saying "Your role is to retrieve the skull from the inner chamber of the Temple of Thoth, without being caught mind you. You will then go to a safe house where you will stay while we prepare for a voyage away from Atlantis. I am afraid we have little time."

Alkur perplexed asks, "Who is preparing for the voyage and when and where are we going?"

Ilax ignores these questions. "Am-ee-lee will have the directions to the safe house."

Alkur always wants to know the full story, whatever it may be. Getting bits and pieces was hard. But Alkur nods, realizing that he trusts Ilax and the mission. And that's enough.

PART 2: A NEW LAND

*In this world, we are exiled from our
homeland in the world above.*

INCA SAYING

Chapter 25

MARCH 18, 2012
AVENIDA MERCEDES, APT # 61,
LA PAZ, BOLIVIA

I found myself retracing how I had found my career – how I was so lucky to find a perfect spot. Such introspection is uncommon, but today, it caught up with me.

As a child I loved exploring the hills near my home. I'd spend hours searching for rocks, stones, fossils, anything I could find. My rock and "sacred" object collections were mostly quartz and other crystals; they were my favorites because I could see through them. I'd peer at them looking for the hidden treasures within. Sometimes I saw rainbows, or heard sounds and even imagined I got messages. Each one had a unique personality to me. I even gave them names. I have no idea where the names came from, but like most childhood imaginary friends, the names stuck.

Papa and I loved to explore ancient ruins together. I'd pretend to be a famous archeologist; he'd be my trusty native carrier. I'd be world-famous; finding a lost civilization just like Hiram Bingham found Machu Pichu. Hiking through the old relics, we'd be lost in time.

Once I got to University, archeology became my way to rediscover my early creativity and passion. It was also an escape from the crazy turmoil following Papa's disappearance. It made me feel whole, purposeful, and complete.

University was great. All the students imagined being at the cutting edge of discovery and chased all sorts of theoretical constructs. I remember an American archeologist who specialized in pre-Colombian studies once presented his nutty idea that the survivors of ancient Atlantis migrated to South America and then, in the impenetrable jungles and the high Andes, built incredible cities and founded the Incan culture.

We, the students, laughed at the idea. I remember that my professor told me a legend talked about crystal skulls, not unlike the one that I found and a 13th skull.

I tried to recall what he had said about skulls, but it was gone. I'll track the American down on the internet.

Chapter 26

MARCH 19, 2012
DEPARTMENT OF ARCHEOLOGY
AND ANTHROPOLOGY OF BOLIVIA

The day started routinely enough. Eager to get started, I got to work about an hour early. I was surprised to find Oscar had beaten me in. We both usually strolled in just on time.

"Buenos dias, Oscar. How're you doing this morning? What's got you going so early?" I asked him as I walked into the lab. He was at my desk, peering at the skull. I noticed his black journal open with symbols etched across its pages by his right hand. I turned to toss my jacket on the coat hook.

At the time, I thought how diligent he was. But now I remember his surprised look when he saw me enter and how he shifted uncomfortably in the chair.

His answer was slow in coming, "I am... was trying to copy these etchings to compare with some of the drawings from the ancient Chavin culture, patron. You're in early. Ready for coffee?" We usually dropped by the snack bar for the first espresso in the morning, and then made a pot for our office. Oscar rose while he spoke; his eyebrows raised waiting for an answer.

I stopped; suddenly bothered that Oscar had taken the skull from our secure locker. Dr. Epis and Dr. Glasser had agreed that only Epis and I would retrieve and secure the skull each day. "Oscar, I thought it was clear. Our instructions were…"

"Yes, patron, I know." Oscar stopped without further explanation.

I looked at him with mild surprise. It was very unlike Oscar to break a rule or to interrupt me. I'd known him for over 12 years. We'd worked on many important projects together. He was very capable and completely trustworthy; this was completely out of character.

Nonetheless, I felt unreasonably irritated that he had handled the skull in my absence. Truth be known, I didn't want anyone messing with the skull. I felt responsible for it—its guardian. Oh well, no point in berating Oscar. He was probably just curious.

We strolled off for our morning libation, and to smooth things over, I casually chatted about the plan for the day. Oscar was nervous and acting strangely though, almost scared. I should have asked him about it at the time. Before leaving for lunch, I carefully locked the skull back in the cabinet by my office. I kept the key.

After a good lunch with a couple of colleagues, I hurried to run some errands. Checking my wallet for the dry cleaning ticket, the card the old man on the bus gave me fell out onto the pavement. Don Julio. I picked it up and flipped it over. There were the same strange words written in Spanish.

"The dark energies surround us but we can see their shadow."

What the hell does that mean? I wondered.

The meeting on the bus sure was curious. It popped into my mind that it's the kind of thing that is either forgotten quickly – or changes your life forever. I put the card back in my wallet.

Returning to work about two-thirty, I reclaimed the skull and set it on my desk. I just stared at it and smiled. Just like a child, I decided to call it "Che" after the Cuban revolutionary. He'd been killed in the early 1960's by the Bolivian military, not far from here.

I found myself relaxing, deeply and almost in a meditative state while I pondered the skull. Post-lunch sleepiness, I thought.

But it was more than that. My heart opened and I felt inner joy and sublime peace. The best way to describe it is that I felt connected in an odd way to "Che" as though the boundaries between us fell away and we merged. This is impossible to explain. I felt things that had eluded me for a long time.

Here I am a scientist, using emotional language. I don't do it often. I've always stuck to the scientific method of analysis, hypotheses and findings. It's impersonal, sometimes boring, but it's tangible and fact-based.

However, this inquiry was straining my rational, scientific approach. I knew somehow that I'd only learn the lessons of the skull through a heart connection. I'm either losing it completely or am on to something totally new, I thought.

Minutes later, I felt an incredible sadness. Tears welled up, and for no reason, I began to quietly weep. I got up and closed my office door. A doorway had been opened in my heart; maybe that skull was freeing me. I felt as if all the emotions I had rejected or suppressed, from childhood, were loosened. Thoughts of my father and mother came up and with it anger and resentment of not being loved as a child, of being rejected by them.

As a young adolescent, I always felt different and out of sync with everything and everybody. I did well in school, yet I had a hard time making and keeping friends. So I began to be quiet, to be distant. I withdrew. In school, teachers and friends brought this tendency to my attention. I'd even sought counseling years ago at the request of a girlfriend. Nothing really helped me cope. But, now the skull was reflecting these feelings back into my conscious awareness from my subconscious, maybe to be healed.

The message for me was clear. If you expect to find a higher consciousness, then you must heal and accept all the different parts of your personality. Accept and bring the hidden negativity and destructiveness into the open. I was not sure I was prepared for this. I was trying to understand and remain open to the possibilities.

Chapter 27

MARCH 24, 2012
AVENIDA MERCEDES, APT # 61, LA
PAZ, BOLIVIA

Since last week, the Institute's been in the throes of preparing for the annual trustee's meeting in April and all meaningful work on our discoveries was in hiatus. The offices were being repainted and carpet replaced. To meet insurance requirements, Dr. Epis had secured the skull and other artifacts in the Banco Central de Bolivia during renovations. So after, Oscar and I had drafted a benign, say-nothing paragraph on the skull for the trustees' brochure, we were done.

Somehow I kept thinking about my father and wondering what happened to him. I was suddenly eager to fly back to Argentina. I had no agenda except to clear my head and maybe, just maybe learn something about what happened to him.

My mother, who had died a few years back, had never really said anything about it. But I grew up with suspicions of deception and betrayal. How else could we account for his sudden disappearance? It must have been someone he knew. I knew that he had once been an aide to

Admiral Montes, the deputy naval chief. Did he know too much? Did they make officers like my father "disappear?"

Like my mother, many Argentines decided that their only hope to avoid the death squads and the increasingly savage repression was to leave altogether, if they could. Around two million did just that during the Dirty War. Peronists, trade unionists, artists, teachers and actors left; just about anyone falling into the category of "subversive" or "leftist." Many went to Mexico City, Paris and Rome; countries that had the reputation of being tolerant or even friendly to exiles from Latin America.

We went to Bolivia to be nearer to my mother's family. There was relative safety in Bolivia since my mother was a former Montenero, a guerilla. I had suspected this but never had the complete story till before she died. She also told me that Argentine intelligence agents were sent to find her and she had survived two kidnapping attempts. She changed her identity and we moved around a lot. At the time she never told me why.

Others were less fortunate. At least 12 Monteneros disappeared or were assassinated outside Argentina: four in Peru, two Uruguay, and others in Rio de Janeiro and Madrid. The junta was relentless. We were lucky.

After the Junta was gone, mother had made repeated inquiries through the Bolivian embassy for information about my father. A friend, a well-connected embassy employee, helped her contact the Argentine Ministry of Defense. They had no record of him. Probably lies. She even contacted the Commission that investigated the Junta, to see if he was mentioned in their report. His name was cited by a former prisoner as being at ESMA, the clandestine prison. However, no mention was made of his status. She was told the Commission did not investigate military officer disappearances. She filed the usual Habeas Corpus decree with the Argentine court to force the military to provide information on his whereabouts, but never heard back. She was too afraid to go back to Argentina. I have to hand it to her, she followed every lead.

Mother had kept some articles and journals from that time. In clearing out her apartment after she died, I had shoved it all in a packing box and stowed it on a back shelf of my closet. Now, I pulled out the battered cardboard box and went through the stack, page after yellowed page. The papers surrounded me as I sat on the living room rug slowly reading. It had been over 33 years since the junta. The papers were brittle.

A photo slid out from the stacks. It was an old picture, of a good-looking young man with a light brown hair and bright brown eyes in his naval dress uniform. His pensive, almost cerebral look suggested thoughtfulness and purpose. He looked so young. It was my father, probably taken before I was born.

I found my mother's old address book, and with it the name of an old friend of my mother's, Elisa Alvarez. She had worked as a clerk in the Ministry of Justice years before. It was a stretch, but Elisa was my first contact. I tried the old phone number. She was surprised, but delighted, to hear from me and invited me for coffee at her apartment whenever I was in town.

Carlos had recently returned from Argentina and had raved about a new jazz club there. I sent him a text asking for the name. Then I quickly made plans.

Chapter 28

MARCH 26, 2012
BUENOS AIRES

After a day of travel, I knocked at the faded door of the Alvarez flat in downtown Belgrano. Moments later, Elisa swung the door open; she paused then threw her arms wide with a welcoming hug. Elisa was a still attractive older woman, well-dressed with a dignified demeanor. I vaguely remembered that she was divorced; her two sons must be middle-aged now.

Waving to a slightly worn club chair, she said, "So good to see you Andres. I just baked some alfajor for our coffee." She smiled while setting a small tray with coffee and pastries on the table and told me to help myself.

"I was reluctant to intrude on you," I started, but she cut me off.

"Your mother was like a sister to me. I was so sorry when she died; I lost a very dear if distant friend." She went on to relay a couple of short anecdotes about their growing up together. The woman she described – lighthearted and full of fun yet serious about political matters – was worlds away from my quiet, sad mother that I knew.

Elisa pulled out an old leather album of photographs. She pointed out the pictures of my mother smiling with groups of girls, playing on the beach, and laughing. Then Elisa paused, and showed me a blurry photo of my mother and a light haired man along with another couple.

"Your father, he was good man. It was a difficult time. He and your mother were happy together."

"How did they meet? Do you remember? She never talked about it."

Elisa grew very quiet and looked out the window. It was a pensive look; maybe she wanted to guard a small private place. I remembered hearing that Elisa's sister and brother were murdered by the junta and that afterwards Elisa suffered a deep depression.

I instantly regretted opening up those bad times for her again. She had been so kind. "I'm sorry. I don't want to raise any sad memories for you. Thank you so much for sharing stories about you and my mother. It means a lot to me." We talked for a while, and later I thanked her again for her time and rose to go.

Elisa paused, and then stood up to show me out. Out of the blue she said, "Your mother loved you very much. She could not conceive due to a birth defect so when your father brought you home, she was ecstatic. A gift from God she called you." She smiled again and said "Please don't wait so long next time, Andres. Come again next time you're in Buenos Aires."

At her words, my breath caught and my heart started thumping. My legs and arms were suddenly numb. Somehow, I managed to thank her in a normal voice and, with a goodbye hug and smile, turned to leave.

I heard the door close behind me. I didn't move. It felt like a sledge hammer had nailed me, right between the eyes. I just stood at the top of the stairs, holding the handrail.

When your father brought you home... I was adopted. This was news to me, totally unexpected. How could my mother never say anything about it? I was dazed and beginning to get angry finding out something so basic in such a haphazard, oh-by-the-way comment.

Then my mind clicked. There was nothing in any of mother's papers about an adoption. Nor was there a birth certificate for me. She'd always said that it had been left behind when we fled Argentina.

But then I remember there was an article in the stack--testimony from a guard who was later accused of torturing prisoners. He had admitted to stealing hundreds of newborn babies from imprisoned mothers who later "disappeared." The babies were given to junta, military members and sympathizers.

I was glad to be alone to digest this news. I didn't know how to go from here. I almost laughed – the irony was inescapable. I had come to Argentina to solve one mystery and only found a deeper one. I was buried in secrets.

The next afternoon, I took a cab out to the old address. I would never have recognized it. The cabbie must have misunderstood me, I thought, looking around. I ended up asking an old man for directions. He just looked at me curiously for a moment, then smiled and said that he would take me. Although, I tried to decline, he insisted, and was already walking with me pointing at buildings a couple of blocks away. I finally said, "Gracias ... I've got it." He stopped then waved goodbye and headed off down a side street.

Finally, I saw some familiar landmarks, the cafes and stores. Then, there was the old apartment building. The façade was slightly changed, probably from updates over the years. I took a couple of pictures for the heck of it; I never planned to return. I had an itch to knock on our old door, to see who was living there, but decided against it. I had nothing to say.

I thought I'd feel something seeing the old place. But no warm memories came. I just had the creepy feeling that I was being watched. I chalked that up to our long ago escape and was suddenly ready to leave.

I'd recovered, somewhat, from the shock of the day before and decided to resume the search for the man I knew as Papa. The Biblioteca National de Bueno Aires was my first stop. There, I found the old Commission report but it didn't include a list of junta officers. The library staff assured me that no such list existed. One librarian looked severe saying "any such lists were destroyed years ago." She must have pegged me as a trouble-maker.

However, their collection was a gold mine of articles and reports about the junta's activities between 1976 and 1983. One piece in particular hit home. The newspaper described the trial of an officer accused of torture and murders committed in the ESMA. It said another officer, scheduled to testify for the prosecution, had been found dead in his cell probably a suicide from cyanide poisoning.

The article was relatively recent, a vivid reminder that elements linked to the past repression were still alive and well in Argentina. There was a picture of ESMA: beautiful colonnaded white buildings with red-tiled roofs sitting among graceful trees in a park-like complex. I knew it was a large detention and torture center; I hadn't realized that almost 5,000 people died there in the junta years.

Another blurb reported that human rights associations blame the junta for the arrest, torture and death of 30,000 people, mostly trade-union and student activists, accused of being communist sympathizers. Only a handful of cases against the perpetrators ever reached the courts, despite the 2003 decision by then-president Kirchner to annul amnesty laws passed in the 1980s. Many of the junta's henchmen are believed to still be free and living in Argentina and abroad to this day.

I couldn't get that out of my mind. Many are still free and... living abroad! Enough. Some music and a thick steak were in order.

The next day, I went over to the ESMA complex, where Papa had worked. It was peaceful and, frankly, elegant. It's now Latin America's largest human-rights museum, erected in defiance of the oppressors and in memory of the victims. The "Mothers of the Plaza de Mayo" group had converted one building into a cultural center; another would soon house the National Memory Archives. It was hard to believe that this beautiful site was, in fact, the "Auschwitz" of Argentina.

Strolling around, I came across a building with thousands of pictures of people on its walls. I first assumed that these were the people who had been prisoners here. But, on an adjacent wall were pictures of men in military and police uniforms with name, rank and service numbers. I looked around for the curator's information page but there was no explanation for this exhibit. These men could be victims or perpetrators. How odd, but perhaps how just, to display them together.

I studied the photos closely looking for Papa's face that I dimly remembered. One face stood out from the rest and I found myself starring at it. It was not Papa, my adopted father, but an unidentified stranger who looked just like a younger me. It could have been a mirror; the resemblance was uncanny.

I came looking for my father. Had I found him?

I took a photo of the picture with my phone.

Chapter 29

MARCH 27, 2012
AVENIDA MERCEDES, APT # 61,
LA PAZ, BOLIVIA

The trip back from Argentina was uneventful.
I shoved the news about being adopted to the back of my mind. The shock was gone, replaced by regret that mother never told me the truth. But, I couldn't regret everything. After all, I was confident in my-self, satisfied with my career, and enjoyed good friends. That I had no real clue as to who my parents were didn't change anything important.

The phone light was flashing with a new message when I walked in from work. I punched the red button and heard a heavily accented deep voice, "Buenos dias, excuse me … We met, briefly, on the bus. I think we should talk … it's about your work … and your family… Excuse me for intruding. My name is Don Julio and… Beep beep beep." The message was cut short. I replayed it a couple of times. And how did he get my number—it's unlisted?

Thinking about what to do, I opened the refrigerator searching for a quick bite. With a cold beer and a small plate of ham and cheeses,

I went back to the living room and sat in my usual TV watching chair. But I didn't turn it on.

I pulled Don Julio's card from my wallet and tapped it on the table. Don Julio. I thought our meeting was an odd random encounter. The sort of nothing things that occurs from time to time. But he knew me, where I lived and what I do. He must have followed me to know which bus I took. He must have planned it.

Slumping back in my chair, I decided to pay him a visit. After all, I had nothing to lose. He's just an old man. But if he knew something about my parents, about Papa, then I had to follow up.

A quick phone call and then I set the empty bottle and plate on the kitchen counter, slung my jacket over my shoulder and headed out to find Don Julio.

I drove through the outskirts of La Paz along a long narrow road lined with large eucalyptus trees. He had said that he lived about 20 kilometers outside the city in a small house about 100 meters from the main road. The directions were clear. There weren't many neighbors. I'd know the house by the chickens and pigs in a fenced lot next door and the black Honda motorcycle parked by the front gate.

I parked the car on the gravel drive then walked through the open gate to the small courtyard. I knocked a few times on the door but got no answer. Odd, he should be expecting me.

Then, I heard footsteps behind me and turned to see a small hunched over old man with a multicolored Andean cap on his head with the flaps hanging over his ears. Yes, it was my acquaintance from the bus. He greeted me with a smile and unexpectedly firm handshake. He said something in Quechua, his native Andean tongue which I assumed to be a welcome. Then he motioned me inside and pointing to a cushion on the cement floor invited me to sit down.

It was a very simple room with white walls and a single picture on the wall. Next to the cushion stood a low table with a jug of water and a framed picture of Jesus with rosary over it. It was graceful if austere; the home of a man who didn't care about, or couldn't afford, possessions.

Don Julio walked into another room and came back with a pitcher of hot liquid which he poured into a cup. He handed me the cup. I looked at him as he picked up a large bowl from behind me and then settled on another large pillow on the floor. He smoothed a cloth on the floor between us then took the bowl, which I could now see was filled with coca leaves and began to chant in Quechua. Always interested in cultural rituals, I watched quietly but thinking I hope I'm not being baptized or anything.

He raised the bowl above his head; I assume asking for the blessing of the spirits. I often found rituals stilted and false but this was comfortable filling the room with an easy peace. Don Julio lowered the bowl and spread the leaves on the cloth. In broken Spanish, he asked me to choose three leaves, which I did. With those leaves in his hand, he resumed chanting.

Okay, time to move this forward. I interrupted his cadence, saying "Thank you for inviting me Don Julio. But who are you?"

He didn't miss a beat.

"Let's just say that we were destined to meet, Andres."

I found out later that he had lived through the Argentine junta's darkest years. He was a distant cousin of the Army Chief of Staff, then the President of the Republic. Don Julio had turned against them when he found out about their excesses. He'd been arrested then tortured in a Buenos Aires jail. His escape, dressed as a cleaning woman, was a good story and one of the few successful escapes. He went underground, fled to nearby Uruguay and eventually Bolivia.

He was back chanting. After a few minutes, he stopped and asked me in perfect Spanish, "Why have you come? The spirits need to hear your words to attune to your energies and set the intention for your needs."

I was a little surprised by the question since he had invited me. And his now cultured accent.

But the ritual had put me in a calm and accepting frame of mind, so I repeated, "Yes, thank you, Don Julio, for seeing me. Your phone call was timely. I've just come back from Argentina, a trip prompted by curiosity about my family. I have come tonight because you said you know something about my father."

"I see," he nodded looking at the floor.

He gave me back the leaves. "For each leaf, ask a question of me. The spirits through me will answer you honestly."

Then, he began muttering in Quechua while I watched, lightly rubbing the leaves between his fingers. I sat still, my mind caught between old fables of genies in bottles and carefully considering what questions to ask. After a few minutes he said,

"The man you call your father is here now, with many other angelic beings. He is protected and loved by them." I can only surmise that he meant that he is well. I wanted to know more.

"Can you tell me what happened to him?" I handed him one leaf, which he took and laid on the cloth.

He paused, then said, "The person you call your father was a man of principle. He was a naval officer, a patriot really. He loved the Navy. But, he was an independent thinker and had the wisdom to know that he had to follow his heart."

He paused, looking at the leaves. "When the Argentine junta came to power, it broke him. He lost the love of his career. He felt personally betrayed by their corruption. But his sense of duty pushed him to go along with the junta for a while. The sight of his fellow officers becoming willing accomplices in illegal pursuit of enemies sickened him. He had not signed up for this perversion of his profession."

A sadness filled Don Julio's face as he continued, "He considered resigning, but the junta declared a national emergency which halted all government resignations. Other options, like desertion or protest, carried heavy penalties for himself and his family. He knew he was stuck with no way out. Early on, before he saw the regime's evil, he was trained in anti-subversive techniques. He was highly respected, a rising star being groomed for higher rank. His father had been a high ranking naval officer.

He was secretly assigned to infiltrate subversive organizations and identify traitors. He led commando teams which captured dissidents. He knew those he captured were later tortured and sometimes executed at EMSA and the 50 other detention centers in Argentina."

I was silent, wondering what the tipping point was for my father and, in the back of my mind, how did Don Julio know this?

Don Julio went on, "One day he brought in a two women accused of being Montonero rebels. He was assigned to interrogate them. One woman was very resistant to the questions and your father found he couldn't subject her to the usual protocol: electric shocks, beatings or water-boarding. Instead, he admired her strength and loyalty." Don Julio poured some water and took a few sips. Before, his eyes were mostly focused on the leaves between his fingers. He was watching me now.

"He certainly did not anticipate having strong feelings for a prisoner – or to find that the attraction was mutual. Her name was Elizabeth. She was striking, exotic really, with hazel eyes and delicate slender features."

"My mother?" I asked confused. I didn't hand him a leaf this time.

"Yes."

Don Julio pauses, "Eventually, he got her released and after a time, they married. That event only served to alert the Naval Intelligence Service that he was a possible traitor. Your mother was a leader with the Montonero guerillas; the government held her responsible for planning attacks against the military. None of this was ever proven, of course. Even the man you called Papa was not certain of her role although he suspected it."

"What happened to him the night he did not come home?" I asked.

"He was hiding nearby at the house of a friend. But the friend turned him in and he was arrested.

I nodded my head, "I knew it!" Don Julio's story only provided details for the history I already knew in my bones.

"Despite torture, your father refused to implicate others. He was labeled a traitor and imprisoned to await sentencing by the military magistrate. His father tried to intervene, but was not successful. His father died a short time later of a broken heart, his son never knowing his fate."

"What happened to him Don Julio? Can I talk to him now?"

The old man hesitated for what seemed an eternity and nodded, "In spirit, of course. You'll sense his presence around you in daily life. He will send you signs that he's there. He wants you to know that the past is past, don't dwell there and pick over old events; you must move forward to live your life fully now. The angelic beings around him are all nodding." Don Julio smiled.

I just sat there absorbing all of this and wishing that my mother was still alive. Had she known all of this?

Don Julio looking at me asked, "You've had your questions. Has this helped?"

I still held two leaves in my hand but knew I had been used up my time. "Yes, thank you."

I still didn't know how Don Julio knew me or anything about my family or why he contacted me now. Frustration shot through me. Why was everything one step forward just to find another mystery.

That annoyance dissipated almost immediately. I rose and thanked Don Julio again. As I reached in my pocket for the car keys, Don Julio handed me a small wooden box. Inside was a tiny crystal skull. I rolled it between my fingers as we walked to the car. We'd circled back to something but I didn't know what.

Don Julio stood quietly. His words, as I opened the car door were, "Take care, my friend. The dark energies surround us but we can see their shadow."

He smiled. "Vaya con Dios." "Be with God!"

Chapter 30

APRIL 1, 2012
DEPARTMENT OF ARCHEOLOGY
AND ANTHROPOLOGY OF BOLIVIA

I got up an hour earlier this morning eager to get back to the lab, back to normal. The renovations were done and work could begin again. The Buenos Aires trip and Don Julio were already receding into the past. I tucked the tiny skull that Don Julio gave me in my pocket. I wondered if there was a message in it for me. I thought about getting a hole drilled in it and adding it to my key chain.

The symbols on the skull had been hovering in the back of my mind. We hadn't found any pre-Colombian work with similar designs and carvings. But, while showering I had remembered some early African carvings that may be similar. So, I asked Oscar to check out some of their civilizations in hopes that we would find something.

After grabbing a sausage and hard roll, I almost ran out of my apartment. When I got to the lab, espresso in hand, it was clear that someone had not locked up properly. My office door was ajar. Pushing the door open, my breath stopped. Papers and artifacts were strewn on the floor, the file cabinet drawers hung open; it had been ransacked. My desk drawers were partially open and documents I had left neatly stacked on top were fanned out and scattered.

I ran over to the hallway cabinet where the skull was secured after its return from the bank. A chill ran through me – the door had been pried open and the shelf where the skull was supposed to be was empty. Some of the other pieces, mostly ceramics, had fallen and lay broken on the floor. But the skull – it was gone. Shit! Oscar surely would know.

I immediately called security to report the theft and vandalism. Two officers arrived about five minutes later. One was a lean elderly man of about seventy and the other, well, he couldn't have been old enough to drive. Both walked around shaking their heads wondering aloud what could have happened.

I called Dr. Epis to let him know of the break-in and the missing skull. He told me to call the police immediately; he would call the public relations office to work up a short statement. I guess it is good I wasn't in top management. Public relations were the last thing on my mind.

I dialed Oscar's number; he would be upset, too. With all the work he'd devoted to this project, he deserved to know the situation right away. There was no answer. Must be in the shower, I thought. I called repeatedly while waiting for the police to show up. The Institute's security people were useless; they clearly wanted to turn this over to the police as soon they could.

After awhile I called again. Still, no answer at Oscar's. Checking the clock, I realized I must have missed him and he was probably on the bus now headed to work. He could be running late, which would be a first. Unless… unbidden the wild hair idea that Oscar might be involved in the skull's disappearance landed in my head.

It landed firmly, I couldn't dislodge it. He had been acting strangely since the day I had caught him with the skull.

It seemed like my predictable world was rolling sideways. Things were coming apart all over Bolivia. A cholera epidemic in the countryside was spreading to La Paz. An Andean terrorist group, affiliated with Al Qaeda, was blowing up banks and ATMs in and around the city.

Kidnapping had become a regular industry in Bolivia. Unemployment was skyrocketing. Crime was up. Even the economy was haywire. The papers warned of spiking inflation and currency manipulations; for some, life was unaffordable. There had even been an assassination attempt on President Bedoya while he was visiting Venezuela. The whole country was on edge. Maybe I was becoming paranoid, or just becoming more attuned to the effects of the real world energies on my consciousness.

The police finally arrived with a photographer and detective. The next few hours were spent making statements, explaining the significance of the loss and recounting our security procedures. As we went over the scene again, it was clear that the skull was the only thing stolen.

Enough pieces of the other missing artifacts were found to identify them. Some valuable antiques had been tossed in the corners of the office, which I would have thought would be taken and fetch a nice amount on the black market. Some could be repaired, but most were destroyed. It was obvious that the thieves weren't working for a pre-Colombian art collector.

Oscar never showed up at work, nor had he called in, and it was already late afternoon. As soon as I finished with the authorities, I tried his phone again. Getting no answer, I just sat down pondering what to do. I then pulled on my jacket and headed off to get my car so I could find Oscar, leaving Dr. Epis amid the wreckage. I'd clean things up tomorrow after the police left.

Chapter 31

APRIL 2, 2012
OSCAR'S HOME

I drove directly to Oscar's home on the outskirts of the city. While skirting the evening traffic, I had at least a couple of conversations going on in my head. My kinder self said things like I hope he's not ill or anything. My skeptical self knew he had been evasive lately and suspected that he knew about the missing skull. Finding him would answer these doubts.

His beat-up old Toyota was parked in the garage next to the house. He couldn't get very far without it since the city bus didn't come out this far. Although the vehicle bore evidence of hard roads, the house itself, at the end of a cul-de-sac, was tidy and cared for. The lawn was recently mowed and the fall flowers were just beginning to fade. The house was dark.

I parked and walked up the flagstone path to the entrance and knocked. There was no answer; nor did any lights go on in the house. I didn't hear anything from inside. After a few minutes, I went around the fenced yard, trying to see inside the house. I peeked in the first floor windows, at least those without shrubs, but couldn't see a thing.

I dialed his home number on my cellphone and could hear the ringing inside. No answer. I tried his cellphone; again there was no answer. Perhaps he really was ill and was asleep. Or maybe, he was visiting his mother who lived nearby. She's getting on in years, maybe she needed help.

I called her. Over the years, we had met a few times. The last was at a reception for Institute personnel where Oscar had received an award for his research into the Chimu culture. The phone rang; she answered after the third ring, "Bueno."

"Senora Mendoza, this is Andres Parades from the Institute. How are you today?"

"Oh, Dr. Paredes, how nice. I'm well. My arthritis is a little noisy this morning, but at my age ... How are you?"

"Fine, fine, thank you. I was trying to reach Oscar, but haven't been able to find him. We've had a situation at work that Oscar needs to know about. Do you have any idea where he might be?"

"Oh, Dr. Paredes, I wish I knew." Her high pitched voice sounded worried. "Oscar usually calls by this time, but I haven't heard from him all day. I just assumed he had gotten busy at work; he's been so preoccupied lately. If he's not there, I don't know where he'd be. Perhaps he stopped by the market on his way home. Is there anything I can pass along to him when he calls?"

"No, nothing to pass along, but thank you Senora." I didn't want to worry her so I didn't say that he had never shown up at the lab today. Then I changed my mind. "Yes, senora, please have him call me a soon as possible. Something important. Thank you senora."

I thought the conversation strange. Oscar typically checked in with her three or four times daily. She was a widow and didn't leave her home very often except for the market. She didn't suggest any other friends or places he'd hang out and I didn't want to press her.

Amazing, I'd worked with him for years and now realized I knew nothing about his personal life, except that he was very quiet on his private life. Where would he go if he were in trouble? Should I file a missing person's report because he didn't show up at work? I didn't think so. It's too soon and I had no reason to think he didn't just go to a matinee or something. Other than that he never missed work.

Something was wrong. I could feel it. I was tempted to call his mother again but didn't want to add to her concern. I rang his cell phone again; same story, no answer. I was just about to head home when I remembered that Oscar always kept an extra key under the doormat by the back door, just in case. Always meticulous, that was Oscar. I walked around the back and, sure enough, found the key. I unlocked the door, and stepped in.

That's when it hit me. A horrible stale odor of filth, rot and garbage slammed me like a wave. The oppressively sweet smell crawled in my nose. I choked trying not to breathe. It was dark in the house. Covering my mouth and nose I felt along the wall for a light switch. Finally finding one, the kitchen was flooded with a yellow haze.

The table and garbage pail had been overturned. Righting the latter, I saw the trail of blood leading to the living room. Crossing the threshold, I saw Oscar; he's lying on his stomach clutching the carpeted floor in his right hand. There was blood everywhere. I knelt over him, feeling for his pulse. Nothing discernable, no, maybe a faint echo. I whispered his name, "Oscar, Oscar. What happened?"

There was a large pool of blood under his head. Gently, I turned him over. His ashen face and eyes stared blankly at me. He looked dead, his throat slit from one end to the other. His clothes and body bore the marks of a desperate struggle. I turned away and fumbling for my cell phone, trying not to throw up.

"Oscar, I'm getting help. Stay with me." I dialed the emergency number, then reached to hold his shoulder. I looked around the room. It was a mess. My friend had not gone down easy. Suddenly, I heard a gurgle, a slight gasp.

I looked at him and he looked at me, his eyes blinking and staring at me. He tried to smile, through his bloody teeth, the blood seeping from his mouth. He tried to move his lips, but couldn't. Then he raised his arm slightly pointing behind me. I looked over my shoulder to where he was pointing.

I knelt down and placed my ear near his mouth. "What is it Oscar? Perhaps you should be quiet. I'm calling for an ambulance. Hang with me amigo."

"Patron...I am sorry...know..." he whispered.

"Know what?" I asked. He shouldn't be talking.

"The ..." he whispered.

"The skull?" I had to say it.

He tried to answer. His lips moved slowly and his eyes blinked repeatedly as if relaying a message. He waved his arm slowly, and then abruptly grabbed my hand, let out a long gasp, and died.

That's when the dispatcher answered the call. I called out Oscar's address and yelled there had been a dreadful thing, my friend was dying. I repeated the address and hung up. I felt for his pulse. Nothing at all now. I tried pumping his chest, but blood just squeezed out from his neck wound in small spurts. He kept staring at me, eyes glazed over, blood seeping from his mouth. I lifted his head and gently closed his eyes.

Suddenly, lights from a passing car illuminated the front windows. We were at the end of the street – no one ever drove down here. I placed Oscar's head gently on the floor and rose to stand to the side of the window. A moment later, the car passed by slowly; the two men in it were intently focused on Oscar's house. Their faces were lit up by the streetlight that was now flickering on. Two minutes later the same car drove by, but with no lights on. The car looked like an old Ford Falcon.

My precarious situation dawned on me. Someone had murdered Oscar; he had tried to tell me something. The murderer could still be here or in the car cruising the neighborhood.

I crossed the room to Oscar's home phone and dialed the emergency number again. This time, I asked a different dispatcher for the police. Ambulance sirens screamed from out on the highway; they'd be here in a minute. I hurriedly looked around the house for anything unusual. Oscar was saying something – what was it. If he had the skull, where would he keep it safe?

Oscar was a cautious man, not one to take chances with things. Then an old memory emerged. He had a surprise gift for his mother and he had kept in his car so she wouldn't find it when she lived with him. The car! Of course. I opened the front door and trotted out to the garage. The car appeared untouched as I peered in the front seat. I tried opening the door. It was locked. I looked around the garage for something, anything.

With a short piece of pipe I smashed the driver's side window. I hurriedly checked under the seats and trunk. Nothing. I slid partway under it and using penlight on my keys scanned the underside. There, under the engine manifold was a bump. I crawled out and popped the hood peering into the engine compartment. Lodged behind the battery was a black bag. I reached inside and pulled out an object wrapped in a white cloth.

It was the skull.

The ambulance was pulling up in the driveway and I hurried out to meet the paramedics. I slipped the bag with skull inside of my light jacket and then waved my hands and called out "Senores, inside. My friend is inside." I motioned to the front door which I'd left hanging open.

Before the police arrived, I shoved the skull under my camping equipment in my car's trunk. I didn't think the paramedics saw me.

Chapter 32

APRIL 2, 2012
THE AVENIDA BOLIVAR POLICE STATION

Police Captain Enrico Bedoya slouched forward, his elbows on his desk as he scanned the first few pages of a folder just handed to him. The Captain nodded to the young patrolman, dismissing him. He then adjusted his tie and unbuttoned his collar as he reached for his lit cigarillo. He was a short, dark, overweight man, middle-aged with more stomach than hair.

The room was still; even the fly on the window was quiet. After glancing at the papers, he looked up slowly with a searching expression look on his face,

"Doctor Paredes, our forensics evidence places you at the scene of the Senor Mendoza's murder. Your prints, and only your prints, were found along with Mr. Mendoza's. Do you understand what this means?"

I said nothing.

"You are our primary suspect. Comprende?" He paused, and then said "Tell me again what happened."

I nodded. "As I said before, when Oscar didn't show up at work at the Institute, I called him. Several times. You have to understand that Oscar was never late, never absent without letting us know; always punctual. When I couldn't reach him, I called his mother to see if she knew where he was. Oscar stayed in touch with her, she's an elderly widow and he's an attentive son. However, Senora Mendoza had neither seen nor heard from him all day. That, in itself was usual. I was worried so I drove out to his house. I … "

Captain Bedoya cut in, "That is very noble of you, Doctor Paredes, to run out the door to check on a colleague. Do you do this often?"

"No, it's just that…" I began to explain about the robbery but the Captain interrupted, "What was your relationship like with Senor Mendoza?"

"We were friends, well, not social friends but long-time co-workers. He was my assistant at the Institute. We have worked together for over 12 years." It was just as well that he stopped me. I hadn't figured out what to say about the robbery.

"Were there any complications, arguments between you?"

"No."

"Professional jealousies? I understand that the Institute has announced some important finds recently."

"No, we each have, had, our own special interests and our work was collaborative, not competitive." His look stopped me short.

"Are you looking for a motive for murder?" I felt incredulous. I leaned over the desk as it finally dawned on me that the Captain was serious considering me as the possible murderer.

"Perhaps." The Captain's eyes never left my face. Without looking down, he gathered the papers in a stack and tapped them on the desk top. I pulled my hands off the desk top, back to my lap.

"No, there were no personal conflicts. We had our occasional disagreements, but they were professional, nothing personal or long-lasting."

"So the last time you saw him was yesterday." His statement was really a question.

"Right."

"Please continue. What did you see when you got Senor Mendoza's house?" His bland expression revealed nothing but mild interest.

"When I got there, I knocked on the door. His car was in the garage so I expected him to be there. When he didn't come to the door, I called his cell. I heard it ring, but Oscar didn't pick up. Then I remembered that he kept an extra key under the back door mat." I saw the Captain shake his head but went on "That's how I got in the house – and found him lying there. I thought I picked up a slight pulse but when I turned him over, I saw the gash..." I paused, slightly sick at the thought, "and he was dead. I was already calling the ambulance. Then I called you all."

"Did you see a weapon or knife by Senor Mendoza?"

I tried to remember. "No, no. But I didn't think to look for one."

Captain Bedoya listened attentively and then put out his cigarillo in the ash tray. "Doctor Paredes, can anyone confirm your story?"

"No, I was alone. I didn't see anyone. I had called Sra. Mendoza before going to the house – she can confirm the time and that I was looking for Oscar." I paused, this sounded far-fetched perhaps, "But I did notice something."

"Si, please continue."

"There was a green car; it looked like an old 1963 or 64 Ford Falcon that drove by the house a few times. The second time, it went by with the headlights out. It looked like some men were looking at Oscar's house, and then it drove off. That's all I could see. It was dark."

"Had you ever seen this car before?"

"No." Stories of the cars that the Argentine junta used popped in my mind, but I didn't mention it. That really was too far a stretch.

"We'll check it out. Perhaps someone else in the neighborhood noticed it."

He glanced at a document again, then continued, "Oh, my team noticed that the car in the garage had a smashed in window. From the glass on the seats, it must have been recent. Perhaps the murderers were looking for something. Do you have any idea what?" The Captain was watching me closely now.

"I…don't know, maybe." I've never been a good liar – and felt like my face gave away my effort to evade the question. Did he already have my fingerprints from the car?

Captain Bedoya slowly leaned forward placing his hands over the papers and looked attentively at me. "Is there something that you are not telling us, Doctor Parades? It is always best to be completely clear."

"No, Captain, that's it." I nearly choked trying to appear calm.

"Well then, Doctor Paredes, I have been in this business for over 30 years." He continued in a conversational tone, as though we were just chatting over coffee. "I plan to retire to Santa Cruz next year to return to my farm and take care of my parents. A lot of strange things happen in this line of work. And I don't mind saying that this case strikes me as being one of the strangest. You see I have a theory."

His voice went on as if reciting a lesson, "The murder of your friend was a professional job. Narcos maybe. Can't rule them out. That means probably two or more people were involved. They knew what they were doing. They did not break into the house; they waited for your friend to come home."

"What I am puzzled about, Doctor Paredes is what were they were looking for." He stopped talking for a minute, maybe longer.

I didn't break the silence.

He started again. "When they did not find it, it appears they killed your friend. Perhaps he was of no further use to them. He put up a good fight. I believe that your friend was drugged and then killed to make it look like a robbery. I'm also thinking that maybe, just maybe, these men are after you next, Doctor Paredes. Who knows? I hope we find them before they find you." I listened without a comment as he wrapped up his sentence with an almost philosophical shrug.

His voice grew harder, "Do you think Oscar stole… the skull?"

I froze for just an instant. "No, I can't believe … He was scholarly, not like that …" I don't know what the Captain saw in my face.

"Or, did you?"

"No, never, it was our most important archeological find to date."

Captain Bedoya rose from his desk, putting out his cigarillo. "We'll be in touch doctor. Please let us know of your whereabouts daily. Don't hesitate to contact us if you discover there is something more to share or if you notice something unusual. That is all for now. Also, you have my personal number in case you need it." He rose indicating the interview was over.

"Yes, of course." I rose too, and turned to the door. Then he called me back.

"Oh, Doctor Paredes, one of my very observant officers found this." Captain Bedoya reached down to a drawer in his desk and pulled out a black bag. "I thought it probably belonged to the Institute and you may want it. But was it worth his life, Doctor Parades?" He smiled as he lit another cigarillo.

I took the bag, thanked him and walked out. Just outside the building, I looked in the bag and found Oscar's work journal.

Chapter 33

APRIL 3, 2012
AVENIDA MERCEDES, APT # 61,
LA PAZ, BOLIVIA

The events of the previous day clouded my mind as I stepped in the bathroom to shower. I had slept only fitfully.

I could not believe Oscar was gone and that I was a suspect in his murder, and possibly the next victim. The Captain hadn't said anything about police protection; I wondered if I should have asked. But with the police following me I'd have no room to try and clear myself of the murder.

I felt sorry for Senora Mendoza and tried to comprehend her grief and what she must be going through.

It was obvious that I needed to do something about the skull. I let Dr. Epis know that I had it. He'd want it returned immediately, of course. I felt strongly that it was no longer safe at the Institute. The skull was the key to everything. I had to assume that the killers must know by now that I had it.

Carlos would have some ideas. He was a wild card, always up for adventure. Was it fair to bring a friend into potential danger? No. Just as quickly, my inner voice said that a good offense will beat the defense. I needed to go on offense.

After dressing and downing a quick espresso from my rickety old coffee maker, I pulled out the bag with the skull. The night before, I'd hidden it in the vacuum cleaner bag hoping no one would search that if they broke into my apartment. I unwrapped it and shook the dust off it. It was unharmed by its escapades.

Then I saw a picture fall to the floor. It looked like a photo of an oil painting. A strikingly beautiful woman looked back at me; she had a foreign look, high cheek bones and lovely green eyes. She was dressed in an elegant silk robe, but the garments looked old, from an ancient civilization perhaps. This photo was not there before, I was certain. Oscar must have added it.

I wondered if I should call the Captain and let him know but then I'd have to say I had taken the skull from the crime scene. I was not ready to do that. I examined the picture carefully, looking for a photo shop's name or something. There was nothing, of course.

It briefly crossed my mind that this woman was like the one from the Alkur story that continued to fly out of me from time to time. I sat back on the sofa, tossing these thoughts around without conclusion. I must have dozed off. When I groggily woke up later, I reached for the picture again. She sure looked familiar.

Damn, I'm late to work. Once I get this all figured out, I'm taking a long vacation.

Chapter 34

ATLANTIS

Earthquakes are more common now, as a tense watchfulness descends filling the air with a sense of impending danger. For days, a humid, sultry sulfurous cloud hung over the city. Many are fleeing the city and the erupting Mount Atlas.

There is a sense of imminent catastrophe, yet, life continues, perhaps in a new normal. Boats ferrying people to safe havens jostle in the city's canals, some are headed to the leeward side of the island, others on longer voyages to foreign shores. Boat captains were making more money than ever before.

King Amillius, concerned by the unrest, asked Salkuzzar and The Temple of the Sun to help calm the populace. A high priest was sent to observe the mountain's behavior from a nearby shrine. The signs were not good. It didn't help that the chief astrologer foretold the destruction of Atlantis and blamed the Temple of the Sun for angering the gods. The announcement fueled more unease within the already anxious population.

Many in Atlantis remained skeptical of Amillius' calming proclamations; they could see that the rulers and priests were making their own hasty preparations to leave the island. Some had already gone. Salkuzzar had ordered that his valuables—the gold and crystals, his robes and jewels be loaded onto his personal boat by the temple for a swift departure, should circumstances warrant.

This morning, an eerie calm greets the sunrise, obscured by ashy haze. Loud claps of thunder from the mountain are heard; the sound, much like large artillery shells, screams like a shriek and echo through the city, rattling homes and terrifying the people and animals.

The summit, hidden by clouds, gives off a deep rumbling every now and then. The mountain casts a yellow and red glow up in the sky. In the distance an enormous bulge is seen on its southeastern side, a fearful omen of its imminent eruption.

Alkur's has been awake for hours, hastily readying supplies for the voyage. Food and casked water are in short supply. Alkur's need to stay hidden, away from Salkuzzar and his cronies makes preparation that more difficult. From the mountain's signs, he knows he does not have much time. His only hope is that the general disarray will hamper the Temple's efforts to find his hiding place. Surely, by now, Salkuzzar's men have discovered that the skull is missing from the temple. They would search for it. They would be ruthless and desperate.

As evening falls, Elchi, the boat captain, and his handpicked crew are awaiting Alkur's arrival. Elchi is one of the finest seamen in the region; he once served as the King's personal navigator. He had also been a close friend of Alkur's father and follower of the Law of One.

The plan called for Alkur to sneak under cover of darkness and rendezvous at the main pier at Elchi's ship, Poseidon. There was a strict meeting time. Alkur could be early but not late. Alkur had never met the boat captain but had a description from Ilax. Elchi would recognize Alkur by the sack he carried, a pre-arranged signal.

Alkur pauses during the day to think of Ampero. He misses her and feels that the new direction of his life is somehow taking him even further away from her than death. He wishes to see her cheerful countenance once more. The day drags by.

Long after darkness falls, Alkur slips away from the house and walks silently towards the pier. The dark brown bag on his shoulder holds the skull and some personal belongings. He almost laughs; after the fire, he doesn't have much left.

Ilax's admonition to travel light was unnecessary. Alkur chooses to walk through dark alleys to avoid being seen, although taking the bridge to the center island would be faster. But the king, chief priests and military leaders resided there and it was always heavily guarded. Instead, Alkur will cross the bridge furthest from the palace where the gates were not as heavily manned.

Alkur quickly strides along the road's edge, glancing back to see if he is being followed. Sometimes he stops and listens, other times he just crosses to the other side. No one follows.

Then he notices a silhouette against the gate lantern; it's a soldier in full battle gear guarding the roadway. Alkur stops. The soldier has seen him and is walking towards him, his face hidden in the dark. Alkur fumbles for a moment; he thinks about turning for the next alley but hesitates. Changing course now will look suspicious.

The soldier calls out, "Stop there. What's your name and business at this late hour?" His sword points at Alkur's feet.

"Alkur, my name is Alkur." He stops and turns slightly to keep his face in shadow.

"What brings you here Alkur, at this late hour? There is a curfew tonight." The soldier doesn't sound alarmed as he waits for Alkur to speak.

"I am sorry. I am... was unaware." Alkur speaks trying for sincerity in his voice,

"Where are you heading?" The soldier glances back at the gate. As he does, Alkur gets a glimpse of his features. It's a stranger to him.

Alkur clears this throat, "A friend's home. I must have gone the wrong way in the dark..."

The guard looks hard at him, a tinge of suspicion in his tone, "What's in the bag?"

Alkur hesitates and with a small smile says, "My friend is in need of clothes and some food. His home was damaged by tremors two days ago."

The soldier nods, and says "I will need to check the bag."

Alkur straightens assuming a military bearing. He impatiently asks in an annoyed tone, "What's your name soldier?"

"Brachieos." The soldier is cautious; he doesn't like this sudden challenge.

"Well, Brachieos, I am Alkur, a former chief of Arms in the King's Palace Guards. I object to this intrusion. Do I need to advise your Commander?"

The soldier pulls himself to attention, "I apologize sir...; but I have my orders...however if what you say is true the search will not be necessary." He frowns slightly but says, "Be careful, there is much unease now."

"Yes, I will." Alkur stands without moving.

"It is dangerous out. I suggest you find your way back home and see your friend another time."

Alkur pauses. He doesn't want to draw more attention to himself. "Yes, of course, you are right. Good night."

The soldier watches as Alkur turns and begins to walk back toward the alley. Alkur hurriedly turns and slides into the alleyway he saw earlier. At a brisk pace now, he trots to the next bridge. He's lost precious moments.

About half an hour later, Alkur sees the pier. As he rounds the corner, he's met with complete chaos. The smoking lamps along the wharf reveal men, women and children struggling with boxes and bags as they hurry to waiting ships. Others wait in groups alongside where loud voices negotiate passage, haggling over fares and the chance for escape.

Alkur is stunned with the noise and crush of fearful people. Atlantis, how sad you've become, he thinks. In his mind, he knows that the beautiful city, its magnificent temples and gardens, will soon be gone, covered in ash and liquid stone. But his heart breaks at the sight of the doomed people. Events are unraveling and fast. Ships are cluttered with cargo, the crews so eager to get underway that crates and passengers are tossed chaotically on the deck. Suddenly, the ground begins shaking and large waves lash the ships that lie docked.

Elchi, a tall middle-aged man, sees Alkur approach and waves him to hurry up. As Alkur joins him, Elchi grabs his arm and pushes him towards the docked ship. At the same time, he shouts to the crew to prepare for an immediate departure.

The eastern sky is just turning gray with the dawn. Alkur runs up the gangway as ropes are pulled from the pier; Elchi is right behind him, moving surely to the wheel. The oarsmen below begin to pull the ship away to the muffled beat of a drum. It's taken only moments. Alkur looks back at the frightened crowds on the wharf, knowing their fate. As the ship moves, their cries grow quieter and the faces become indistinct. Alkur takes a moment to say goodbye. The panic of the shore gives way to the rhythmic sway of the sea.

Finally, Alkur looks around the crowded ship. It's a mid-sized cargo ship, with several cabins for passengers. In the gathering light, he sees Ilax standing close to Akaus, a princess and friend of Ampero's. Akaus is famous for using music to disperse negative energies. Alkur has known her all his life; he loves her like a sister. They are both mesmerized at the last sights of Atlantis.

Am-ee-lee, the librarian who found the safe house and Asa-masa-me, a priestess and master linguist stand by the bow. They are looking forward, watching the mountain as the Poseidon winds her way through the crowded harbor and out to sea. Asa-masa-me glances to the side and seeing Alkur nods slowly. Alkur returns the salute, glad that her expertise in ancient cultures and languages are in the party.

On the port side, Ax-Tos, a physician and priest in the Law of One, is shouting warnings to a small vessel that is tossing against the Poseidon in the waves. Alkur recognizes that the physician, known for his genius in medicine, is now turning his problem solving skills to navigation. There's nothing like an urgent, immediate problem to keep the sorrow of leave-taking at bay. Caphala, a young soldier who trained under Alkur, and then became a historian within the Temple of One stands by Elchi at the helm. Alkur walks up to and embraces Caphala. He is pleased with the group sharing this adventure. Leaving his spot along the rail, Alkur stumbles towards the others to greet them. He staggers in the unfamiliar sway of the ship. Alkur looks up to see Elchi laughing at him between shouting directions to the crew.

The palaces and the temple of Poseidon are now barely visible through the smoke and haze as the ship gains momentum out of the harbor. At the sound of another thunder clap, all eyes are on the city. They can all see the shaking intensify and, one by one, the splendid homes and temples begin to disintegrate and disappear in clouds of dust. In horror, they watch as the mountain belches large dark clouds casting a blanket of darkness over them.

Suddenly, a terrible explosion and roar shakes the vessel, lifting it off the sea's surface. The Poseidon slams back down in the waves. From the bulge on the mountain, an enormous orange cloud of hot ash descends and engulfs the city, incinerating everything. Within its superheated core, continuous lightning flashes are heard followed by thunderclaps that sound like cannon fire. The roar feels like a thousand elephants charging. In just moments, thousands of people, animals, homes and fields are vaporized by the superheated cloud. The cloud continues on its destructive path and soon reaches the harbor catching ships and people in its hot embrace. Ships are afire; the anguished cries of passengers and crew are muffled by the enormous roar.

A surge of superheated air sweeps over the Poseidon hurling it across the water. Alkur, holding fast to the gunwale, feels a blow to his body and gasps as the hot ash covers him. Screams are heard all over the ship as people are knocked down by the blast or fall under the clouds of hot ash. Fires break out. Alkur, recovering, pulls his tunic over this mouth and runs to help Elchi and the crew put out the fires on the ship's deck. The vessel's outer hull is completely covered in a dark brown ash as are the interior surfaces and compartments. The visibility is only a few feet, but the ship remains upright. Elchi is everywhere, directing the effort as the fires succumb. Seeing their distress, Alkur runs to help Ilax and the others covered in ash.

Someone yells "Look!" The cry carries above the chaos.

The peak of Mt. Atlas is exploding. Suddenly, a shower of fiery boulders is flung into the atmosphere and with a piercing whistling sound it rains on the city and the ships. Another thunderous clap reverberates across the ocean rattling the ship's timbers and sending terror into its crew and passengers.

By nightfall, Alkur sees the island in the distance burning, illuminating the oil-black sea for miles. A strange calmness settles over the Poseidon. Alkur catches glimpses of the tired and terror filled faces of the crew as they steadily keep the beat bringing more distance between them and the island. They've been working for hours; they must be exhausted. Alkur feels new respect for the crew and Elchi; he takes a pitcher of water below just in case the oarsmen need it. He should have known, Elchi has already provided for his crew. Alkur is numb; feels gratitude for surviving, yet is emptied by the sorrow of all that perished. He thinks of all the friends and their families who had no way out. He never imagined something as terrible as this.

Elchi slowly walks up to him and puts his hand on his shoulder. Silent, they are together but lost in their own thoughts. Elchi says quietly, "We should be further away by now. Some odd currents, whirlpools almost, keep pushing us back to Atlantis. I can't push the men any harder, by god, they've given their all."

Alkur nods in understanding, then catching Elchi's eye, says, "We are so fortunate to have escaped. I can't say how grateful I am." Elchi looks back at the island, barely visible on the horizon. Ash clouds completely obscure the night sky now, yet even as they gained distance the smell of sulfur is persistent. Thousands of fish float lifeless on the surface.

Most passengers are dozing on deck when the calm is shattered by a loud explosion and rumbling. Some, those passengers that could, rise to face the island. The entire sky lights up like a candle as bright as the sun. Then, the light disappears and a large rumble throbs through the ship. They are transfixed by the sound. The wind picks up. All are silent and anxious as they peer into the dawn sky.

Elchi shouts to the crew and points towards the horizon. A white line on the horizon is rapidly approaching. Elchi immediately shouts, "Hard starboard, now! Everyone, get below ...now... and hold on!"

Immediately the ship turns. Elchi knows their only chance is pointing the bow into the rising wave hoping they will survive the impact. As the passengers scramble below, they catch sight of the immense wall of water approaching from the east.

They brace and wait.

Chapter 35

The midmorning heat is oppressive. Alkur must have been knocked down and out by the massive wave; looking around, he sees others in the cabin looking dazed. Someone had thrown a light robe over him. Slowly he rises to his feet and climbs back on deck; it's a scene of utter devastation and horror.

The surface still froths with seismic agitation and waves pound the ship. All around him, the gray sea is littered with miles of floating debris, boards, sails, ropes, oars, and the remnants of ships and vessels caught by the giant wave. He thinks to himself it's the debris field of a vanished civilization.

Corpses both human and animal rise and fall in the water. Some bodies appear to be asleep, others are being torn apart by packs of roaming sharks. There, the whitecaps are a frothy red color. The whole sight is surreal. It's a glimpse of hell, he thought.

Elchi is at Poseidon's bow carefully guiding the helmsman through the debris field; Alkur is again struck by his expert seamanship as he shouts commands and motions with his hands to warn of what lay ahead. Elchi is an impressive man, thought Alkur, and the reason he and the others on board were still alive.

Alkur sees a few people huddled on deck, holding firm to the boat as it rocks. Akaus looks out to sea, softly singing a quiet melody to herself. It's a serene moment in the midst of the chaos. Ax-Tos, the doctor, is comforting two of the crew who suffered broken bones when the ship was shaken.

Elchi orders a slight change of course and the helmsman leans on the tiller as the oarsmen adjust their rhythm. It's a synchronized dance. Alkur approaches Elchi to offer his assistance, but Elchi just gives a tight smile, saying "We are making good progress now, the wind is with us and some of the sails are still functional. We were very lucky. The gods must have held us closely."

Alkur asks, "Did everyone make it through that last explosion?" Elchi shakes his head, "As far as we can tell. That was a wild, enormous wave. I've only seen one like that before. It damaged the bow, but we'll be all right as long as the seas stay light. When we get to a calm period, we'll slow to repair it."

Alkur notes that repairs will be made at sea. There must be no safe harbor in sight. He agrees with Elchi's assessment, "Yes, we have the gods to thank for this. What can I do?"

"My crew has most things in hand. But, if you and Caphala could check the holds for timber and tar to make repairs that would be helpful. Also, we need to check provisions. Also set some barrels to catch rainwater just in case. It's a long and difficult voyage ahead." Turning to scan the clear sky, Elchi sighs, "Let's hope that the weather holds."

Alkur smiling answers, "Your leadership and skill, by the grace of Poseidon, has brought us through. I'll go round up Caphala."

Elchi responds, "No damage to the hold, but we lost some of our stores. We have enough water and food for maybe 20 days. That's if we ration. After that we better enjoy fish!" smiling.

Suddenly, a lookout calls out, "Ships ahead!"

All eyes search the western horizon. Before long, they spot a small armada of warships silhouetted against the morning sun headed directly at them. Soon the towering sails with the Poseidon trident and the red and white flag of Atlantis are seen straining in the breeze. It looks like a flotilla of warships returning to Atlantis. The ships approach in lengthy swaggering strides. Two of them have bows carved with the distinctive curves of a large bird of prey leaning in to strike. Others display the shapes of menacing serpents.

Before Elchi can order a change of course to avoid the rushing flotilla, the warships themselves simultaneously disperse on either side of them in a precise maneuver coordinated with flags and hand signals. Some shouts are heard between sailors on the vessels. Moments later, the warships pass on both sides of the cargo ship, hissing through the water. Troops of bronze warriors and seamen crowd the high gunwales looking down at the cargo ship. Alkur and the rest of the crew look at them. There is an eerie silence and no exchange between them as the ships pass.

Atlantis was an empire and her reach knew no bounds. These ships were returning to their home base with bounty from some far off land. Alkur felt sorry for them for their beloved land now lay beneath the sea; their families and loved ones had certainly perished. Surely they must know that something devastating happened. The spotty debris still carried on the surface was a clear signal of disaster. Some of Elchi's crew waved, others stood with their hands on their hearts making a subtle gesture of respect, a connection beyond words. There is no response from the ships. The small fleet vanishes into the vast horizon.

A short time later, freshwater flasks and rations are passed around as the seamen and officers resumed their duties. Elchi has assigned small tasks to everyone in the party. The wisdom of keeping everyone occupied and contributing is comforting. Everyone is important here.

Alkur climbs below decks and encounters Am-ee-lee, the librarian sitting on a box holding the skull in his hands. He looks at Alkur gravely, clears his throat, and then says, "Alkur, our most critical task is to safeguard the skull for the future. Shouldn't we be honest with everyone and tell them that we have the sacred skull with us?" Am-ee-lee expects Alkur to agree; his tone indicates that sharing the information is the only correct action.

But Alkur hesitates. After a moment, he says in a thoughtful way, "Yes, in due time. But for now, let's not broadcast that fact. It could distract the crew or worry the passengers. We owe Elchi our full attention right now."

Am-ee-lee ponders this statement, then nods in agreement and places the skull back in the canvas bag and ties it. They look at each other for a minute or two, and then smile acknowledging their partnership in a sacred trust.

Walking back topside, Alkur sees Akaus leaning against the side of the ship. She is wrapped in a blanket despite the heat of the day; her blonde hair blows freely around her face. Alkur knows that she is a gentle, loving soul. The turmoil and desperation of the past few days must have taken a toll. She's caught up in her own thoughts, staring at the blue sky. Alkur approaches and places his hand on her shoulder as he kneels beside her.

"Akaus, I am glad you're here with us. Thank you for the beautiful music the other day. It was a moment of harmony in the chaos." As she turns a sad face to him, Alkur asks, "How are you doing?"

"I'm fine, well, as fine as can be today. I really believe the angels of Atlantis are with us. You know, it's a miracle I'm here. That dreadful night before the volcano blew up, I woke up in the dark and, without knowing why, walked to the harbor. I didn't bring a thing. Elchi happened to see me at the edge of the crowd and told me to board. I didn't plan on this." She stared out at the sea, a bewildered look flitting across her face.

Alkur nods at her smiling and says, "Some days, we're surrounded by miracles."

That night Elchi gathers the group, passengers and crew, together on deck. The moon rose low in the sky, sending white ribbons of light across the sea. A calm breeze lifts the sails. Elchi looks around, the faces watching him showed a mix of mix of fatigue, anxiety, interest and anticipation.

"I am grateful to all of you and the gods. We've been lucky to have escaped the destruction of Atlantis and survived the wild sea. I know we share the grief of our loss and some apprehension about the future. If I could I'd restore what we had before. I can't – none of us can." Elchi stops, searching for the words that will pull the group together. "I won't mislead you; our voyage to a new home may be difficult and may be long. To survive, we'll need to work together as a team. Everyone will have jobs to do. It may sound odd but kindness and generosity of spirit towards one another as we do our tasks will be essential. It's a small ship and I have no illusion of what is in store for us."

Elchi pauses to let his words sink in. "Alkur, could you talk about the provisions now."

Alkur, leaning against the gunwale straightens to address the group. "We have a limited amount of rations. Caphala and I are working on a distribution plan, which will be strictly enforced. Of course, suggestions are welcomed."

He pauses and continues in a matter-of-fact voice, "Also, I want you to know that we have brought sacred skull of our tribe Thoth with us."

There are surprised looks on many faces. Alkur still did not know who Ilax had confided in besides Am-ee-lee. Looking around, it couldn't have been many. Some look at each other perplexed; a couple of people look relieved. Alkur sees Ilax nodding with approval at this announcement.

Alkur went on, "We have been entrusted with a sacred duty—to safeguard the skull until the community of One is restored. We must pray for guidance and good fortune as we move forward."

Elchi proceeds to give out assignments for the next few days. The next morning Alkur and Ilax conduct a brief ceremony of love and celebration for the passengers. They set up an impromptu altar on the deck, with the skull and some crystals on a colorful woven cloth. In the silence, they give thanks and ask for guidance and wisdom for what lies ahead.

Chapter 36

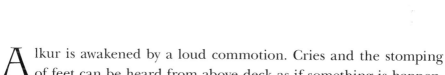

Alkur is awakened by a loud commotion. Cries and the stomping of feet can be heard from above deck as if something is happening. Elchi's face appears in the doorway, a determined and worried look shadows his eyes. He shouts at Alkur, "Warship, coming fast, probably a renegade vessel. I need all able men topside now. Weapons ready."

Alkur jumps out of his hammock, shakes Caphala and Am-ee-lee awake, saying that they we're needed topside to fight, now. Caphala swings out of bed grabbing his scabbard; Am-ee-lee, a trace slower, reaches for his sword and dagger.

Alkur's heart is pounding as he clambers up the ladder and sees the crew assembling weapons, chains and ropes and finding their spots in the rigging or along the gunwales. Elchi is giving orders while he, and his look-out posted above, peer into the darkness to keep track of the on-coming ship. Lights on deck are doused. Suddenly, it's quiet.

Everyone is tensely watching the large silhouette on the horizon. In the faint light of dawn, the warship's sail appears to be barreling towards them.

Elchi yells to his helmsman, "Trio, starboard, NOW!"

As the ship turns to avoid the seemingly inevitable collision, the warship also changes course sailing directly at them at flank speed. A hail of fireballs from the renegade ship light up the sky. Some burst explosively overhead, most land on the ship, sending hot fragments slicing along the deck.

Like a scythe running through wheat, men are cut down and Alkur is flung backwards as a large fragment hits his sword and ricochets off his chest. He quickly rises to his knees and is thrown back again as both vessels collide with an enormous screeching roar.

Alkur scrambles to his feet and rushes forward to join Elchi as the men try to prevent the warriors from boarding and taking the ship. Men clad in black are jumping from the tall warship and swinging over on ropes screaming and swinging wildly with swords, spears, lances and knives. The fighting is brutal and hand to hand. In the pandemonium Alkur struggles to identify friend from foe.

The warriors have armored vests and masked faces making them look like pirates not soldiers. One charges across the short deck towards Alkur with a spear. Alkur quickly sidesteps and cuts him down with a sword strike to the temple splitting his skull. Another appears on Alkur's right side; he is downed with strike to his midsection.

Elchi shouts to the helmsman "Hard port, hard port" trying to disengage the vessels. Nothing happens for a small eternity but then, with a jolt, the vessel begins to move away. Some of the warriors, seeing that their ship is loose, jump back, while others fall into the ocean between the vessels. Clinging to the side of the warship, some are crushed when the ships rub against one another in the churn.

The deck is slippery with blood. Alkur sees Caphala thrusting his spear into the chest of another warrior. Alkur runs a few steps forward to strike down another warrior coming up behind Elchi. Suddenly, he is hit in the back and falls headfirst to his knees. He turns to see a black clad warrior raise his sword to strike. Alkur shifts his left knee and just as the warrior slices downward with his sword, Alkur sweeps the warriors right leg from under him, severing it at the knee. He buries his sword in the warrior's chest as he falls. He stops, panting, heart pounding and looks quickly from side to side.

It's over. The warship slides away, fires burning on its deck. Elchi and his men let out a loud victory cry. Then there is the carnage. Dead bodies and pieces of bodies litter the deck. Some of the crew are dead and injured, but most are relatively intact, tired and relieved. The bodies of the dead attackers are stripped of armor and weapons and unceremoniously tossed overboard.

Alkur doesn't see a reason for the attack. The cargo ship is riding high indicating a relatively empty hold. Maybe pirates, he thinks, but... maybe not. The attack was well planned and deliberate. Alkur senses Salkuzzar is behind it.

Elchi comes up along Alkur's side. They are both bloody, clothes torn, still on edge from the fighting. Elchi's hands are shaking as he says, "Alkur, we have one captive. In concert with the law of the sea, he'll be executed for piracy and murder. After that, we'll convene to discuss the attack and preparing for the next one ... if there is a next one." Elchi starts walking away but Alkur calls after him.

"Wait. Let me talk to him. He may know why we were attacked." Alkur needs to understand the why – it doesn't make sense.

Elchi is not used to people suggesting a different course than the one he plotted. "He is better off dead; I'll not keep him alive. Our provisions are low enough as it is. And he's a pirate." He looks at Alkur then continues, "You have a few moments, my friend." Elchi walks back to where his wounded are resting alongside the gunwales.

Alkur steps over some sprawling ropes and remnants of broken crates to reach the corner where the wounded warrior waits for his death. Caphala stands near him, waiting for orders to dispatch the boy. Alkur thinks, my god he can't be older than twelve or thirteen. But his eyes look very old.

"Water!" Alkur snaps to a young crew member. Moments later, he holds a flask to the captive's mouth, allowing him to take a swallow. "Who are you and who sent you?"

The boy looks at him with empty eyes and slowly lowers his head. "I'm Mitfor. We left from Salaet two days before Atlantis erupted." He coughs and a little blood sprays into his lap.

Alkur knew of Salaet. It's a small island on the leeward side of Atlantis. It had a reputation as a place of corruption, piracy and lawlessness. The original people from Salaet and their sinful ways were blamed for the first Atlantean cataclysm. The stigma carried through generations; their descendants were never integrated into Atlantean society. Legend held that there was one motto, "We are from Salaet, we do not forgive; we kill." The Sons of Belial had for generations recruited them because they were ruthless and fanatic fighters. Assassins.

"What was your mission Mitfor?"

Silence, then a shrug and he muttered "To intercept and destroy you."

"Was Salkuzzar behind this plan?" Alkur watches carefully.

"Who?" The boy's head droops again.

"Salkuzzar!"

The boy stares straight ahead and says nothing.

Alkur growing impatient, snaps again, "Tell me, did Salkuzzar send you to attack us?"

Alkur could tell that the boy is slowly slipping away. He coughs and gasps, looking to the flask for another drink of water.

"Salkuzzar? Did he send you?" Alkur holds the flask in front of Mitfor's face. Mitfor nods slowly. Then a glimmer of life shows in Mitfor's eyes. He looks at Alkur with contempt, smiles showing his blood covered teeth, and reaches for Alkur's tunic.

"It is dark…" He breathes his last.

The skull! Alkur has a sense that Salkuzzar was after it. There was no other explanation. Alkur bolts from his spot by the dead boy and rushes to Am-ee-lee to make sure the skull is still on-board.

Chapter 37

The days are long and hot as the Poseidon alternatively sails and drifts to an uncertain future. Supplies are low, maybe four or five days of provisions are left at best. Water is the most pressing concern. Some had been collected the previous evening when the crew used the sails to funnel rain into water barrels during a squall. But not much was gained. They would need to conserve.

For the most part, the passengers and crew are quiet. Elchi had firmly indicated that no squabbles or incivility would be tolerated. The ship was too small to hold discontent. Ilax and Akaus consciously maintained positive energies to help lift the spirits of everyone. Quiet Am-ee-lee surprised everyone by telling marvelous stories filled with heroes and happy endings every evening. And Akaus, always serious and with a far-away look in her eyes, had become a gentle prankster. Her laughter, a balm to stressed souls.

As always, diligent Elchi mans the helm. This afternoon, Alkur leans over the gunwale with the breeze blowing his hair back and the cool ocean spray sprinkling his face. They are both brown from hours in the sun. A comfortable friendship has grown from mutual respect. Elchi calls to Alkur, "I can see you have the sea in your blood. By the time this is over, you'll be an old salt. I'll have to find a ship for you to captain."

Alkur laughs knowing that he could never commit to a sailor's life. "I can see why you went to the sea, Elchi. There is freedom out here, the sense of oneness with everything, all in perfect harmony and flow."

Elchi nods, saying, "Yes, one can easily lose himself at sea. But you also own it – own the responsibility, own the hard work, own the stars at night." Elchi pauses watching the horizon. "We've entered into a new current my friend and there's more moisture in the air. We're moving steadily now with winds increasing the pace. I suspect we are getting closer to land. It's been 12 days since the destruction of Atlantis."

The calm is interrupted an hour later when the lookout begins shouting and pointing to the horizon. All at once, passengers and crew alike run to the gunwales, some climbing the masts to get a better look, others shouting and laughing. In the distance looms the outline of a large landmass. A few are embracing with relief and excitement. Just moments before, the group was living in a state of subdued resignation. Now, the mood is exhilaration. They had done it. They had survived. It's time to dance and celebrate. Alkur grins with pleasure at everyone's happiness.

Elchi is more tempered in his zeal. He scans the horizon through his long distance crystal glasses. The landmass appears very large. Its deep green hue suggests dense vegetation, probably a jungle surrounded by high mountains.

Elchi looks for a place to bring the ship in safely. The best approach, he decides, is to use the current to bring them parallel to the coast. They can run along the coast until he sees a place to dock or beach the vessel. To the port side, Elchi sees large sea birds searching and diving in the surf.

As they approached the land, an unusual panorama unfolds in the sky. On his right, Alkur sees a dark foreboding storm cloud swelling and rising. In it dark shafts of rain fall in a curtain to the ground. On his left, there is a pink-magenta-purple sky with all the colors swirling over the blue grey background. A shot of clear light illuminates the sea. Light and dark, Alkur muses. It's always light and dark.

Ilax strolls over, and wraps her arm around Alkur's waist. She looks tired, yet happy. Alkur says, "I have to admit, I'm glad this part of our journey is almost over. I'm hungry to walk in straight lines on land, not just circling around the ship. Can you tell me what lies ahead for us, Ilax?"

Ilax half smiles at his question. "You always want to know, Alkur. Patience is not one of your inherent strengths. Of course, one must be prepared, especially for new situations."

"It's always the same challenge, Alkur. To use your power as you have already; to face your fears and to accept the duality of the world. Don't worry. Trust!"

Alkur smiles with resignation. "And you Ilax are always the same. I never get the practical answer; it's always the spiritual perspective. But I'm used to it – and can always use the reminder."

That afternoon, the Poseidon drifted in the current. The crew was on alert, ready to row or sail should danger appear. Elchi watched the rocks on the shore with concern; it could be a rough time ahead. But for most, the excitement grew as the beauty of the land was visible.

In the dense vegetation adjacent to the white sandy beach, a dark-skinned man crouches low. He peers intently at the strange object on the horizon. He leaps to a nearby tree and begins climbing. Once at the top he grabs a large conch from his waistband and, blowing into it, sends out a low-toned but loud whistle. He drops down and trots off into the jungle.

Chapter 38

Elchi struggles to maneuver the ship safely towards the shoreline. As it neared, the waves grew larger and thundered as they crashed on the reefs and rocks. A small sandy bay lies ahead, but the current is working against them, drawing them dangerously close to the rocks. All hands are rowing vigorously. Elchi shouts at the helmsman as the ship's bow rises and falls abruptly in the rough surf.

Elchi calls to Alkur and Am-ee-lee who are both bracing against the gunwales to avoid being thrown overboard. The others had already gone below. "We may have to beach here before she is torn apart. The current is too strong." A moment later, he shouts, "Hang on!"

The ship dips abruptly into an enormous swell then pitches up on a starboard roll. Before she can right herself, another enormous wave slams into its side tilting it perilously close to capsizing. For a split second, the ship rests on her side, the masts dipping into the water. Another swell hits it turning it completely around still parallel to the waves.

Elchi desperately shouts commands but cannot control the ship. Screams are heard as oars break like matchsticks; the ship shudders and cracks as timbers give way. Some of the crew are knocked over by the force, some tossed into the churning waves. Suddenly, the ship is upright again, but the main mast is broken. Ropes and sails drape over the deck.

Elchi screams over the chaos, "We must abandon ship now. It can't be saved. Get everyone on deck; we'll launch the small craft if we can." Two small dinghies hung over the back. They would never hold everyone.

Alkur nods as the ship shudders again. The masts shatter and come down smashing the deck with a loud noise. Two crewmen are crushed, their limp bodies protruding from under the mangled heap of wood and rope.

Alkur barely holding on makes an attempt to help them but stops, realizing it's no use. He shouts to Caphala, who is nearby, "Caphala, gather everyone together now..."

Before he can finish the sentence, he is thrown backwards onto the side of the ship and over the gunwale. Tumbling under the water, out of breath, confused, and entangled by ropes and loose gear, he desperately reaches for his knife and cannot find it. Something hits him on the head plunging him further into the depths. He is now directly under the sinking ship. Desperate for air he finds the knife and with his last bit of his strength he cuts himself free. He swims away and then pops upward. His lungs are near bursting point as he breaks the surface wasted and out of breath, but alive.

Alkur sees the remains of the ship tossed in the surf but cannot see the others. Struggling through the debris, he loses sight of the ship then the dreadful realization hits that the ship is gone. Only a few pieces remain above the waves.

He barely keeps his head above the water as waves shove him towards jagged rock outcroppings ahead. Even at full effort, he can't make any headway against the current. Just as he is about to be smashed on the rocks a tarry wood board bobs up by his right hand. He grabs it to ward off the rocks. A dead body floats nearby.

Holding the board with both hands, Alkur eventually gets some tenuous footing in the sands and is cast onto a white sandy beach, bruised but alive. He crawls up as the waves alternatively push and pull against him. He sees Ilax further down the beach and then some of the others huddled by some logs. He makes out Caphala and then sees Asa-masa-me struggling in the swells. Alkur pushes out to her and pulls her up on the beach. Elchi paces back and forth on the beach hoping to see that some of the crew has survived.

Miraculously, the passengers all arrive on shore wet, dirty, scared and spent. Few talk as they collect themselves. A lot of the crew is missing; Alkur sees none of the oarsmen alive. Elchi still watches the waves. Alkur sees a clump of debris tucked by the rocks. Tangled in a pile of ropes, lies the bag he brought on board. Alkur shoves the hemp and seaweed aside as he quickly checks and sees the skull is still intact. His relief is palpable; at least he'll have some good news for Am-ee-lee, Ilax and the others.

Alkur stops for a moment to examine the island where they've been deposited. It's hot and humid; the uncomfortable temperature is barely relieved by the on-shore breeze. A few large bugs hover nearby. Dense vegetation lies between the beach and the nearby mountains. An occasional earthy scent wafts by as the breeze shifts. The hills cut off any view of what may lie further inland. The beach is strewn with hundreds of coconuts. Large shore birds watch as they circle in the clear sky.

Alkur steps through the thick sand to the other survivors. He's missing one sandal and the sand is hot. Ax Tos is wrapping Caphala's lacerated arm with some torn clothing, It's not serious, but infection would be devastating. The others have scratches but no serious injuries. So far most of the crew is still missing, presumed drowned. They must have gone down with the ship, he thought. A few bodies are beginning to wash ashore. Caphala, Alkur and Elchi enter the surf and retrieve as many as they can. One of the first they catch is the young cabin boy. Later, they will bury them, that is, if they find something to use as a shovel.

Alkur and Elchi wander the beach to see if they can find anyone else. All they can see is debris and a field of destruction. They walk along the beach picking up items that can be salvaged. Elchi is silent. For the first time, Alkur sees his confidence and swagger diminished; the loss of his crew has hit him hard.

Caphala had ventured into the forest and returns with a bag of fruits--papaya, mangos and a funny green looking thing. He hands out the fruits, saying "I don't think we're alone here."

He hands an odd shaped melon to Ilax, "Here, try this one." As she sinks her teeth into the juicy pulp a sigh of relief comes. "Delicious... it's tart. Thank you; I just couldn't face another hard biscuit and jerky." The others gather around surveying the bounty for their own choices.

Caphala returns from a quick look of the area. He addresses the group, "There seems to be a narrow trail that goes up to a waterfall and lake."

"Oh, a lake!" Akaus grins with pleasure and says, "I can't wait to wash this salt water away." Ilax nods in agreement; the juice has already made her hands sticky and attracted a couple of flies. She waves them away, "Let's head up to the lake this afternoon. Caphala, could you point the way?"

He replies deliberately. "We'll need to check with Alkur. Until we know what or who is on the island, it's probably best to stay together."

Alkur arrives in time to hear the last statement and quickly weighs in, "We need to salvage what we can from the wreck before the sea swallows it all and set up a small, covered camp for the evening. Am-ee-lee and Ax-Tos, find a level spot by the rocks and out of the surf zone. Set up lean-to structures with timber and rope. Cut branches to give us some respite from the sun. See if you can find firewood. Elchi and Caphala, come with me to pull debris in. Ilax and Akaus, go through the stuff that has washed up. I've already seen a barrel, bits of sail and some clothing. Get it all together over there." Alkur waves towards one of the rock piles. Pointing in a different direction, he continues "We'll bury our dead back at the forest edge; its sandy but we can cover the grave with small rocks. Elchi, have we missed anything?" Elchi shakes his head, glad that Alkur is organizing the group.

After a restless night, Alkur and Caphala set out in the early morning to explore the area with the intent to find fresh water, more fruit and any trails. As they hike through the dense brush they see some small paths suggesting animal, maybe even human life. But often as not, the trails disappear a few yards ahead.

After about an hour, Caphala senses something ahead and silently motions for Alkur's attention. A small clearing appears beyond the trees; it's grassy and must have been tended. Soon, they're looking at what must be an ancient temple right in middle of the jungle. Alkur and Caphala trade a startled look. "Amazing," Alkur whispers. "Look at the proportions and the engineering. This is not a primitive effort." Caphala points to a number of smaller buildings lying just behind the temple. Some are circular, others are rectangles. They appear to be precisely arranged around the temple steps.

"Remarkable, look at the stones! It takes advanced technology to get such a uniformly smooth cut not to mention the accurate placement," Caphala is clearly intrigued with the artistry of it all. Alkur remembers that Caphala's father was an architect of some distinction in Atlantis. Atlantis, he sighs, remembering.

Caphala is still studying the workmanship "There must be a quarry nearby for such large blocks. And workrooms for the carvings." He walks slowly circling one of the smallest buildings.

Alkur's thoughts wander to the compound's purpose. "Do you suppose these are for worship or conducting funerals? They look too fine for shops, schools or homes." He strongly senses that this is in a power place, perhaps an ancient portal. It was common practice at home to set temples near energy vortices. "But where are all the people?"

"I don't know; it just seems spooky that no one is here." Caphala replies. He's suddenly eager to move on. Without discussion, the men continue down the center corridor of the grounds. At the far end, just past some tall trees, is a larger and more elaborate structure with extravagant carvings around the base and up the semicircular steps.

Alkur starts up the stairs as Caphala stoops to examine the carving of a bird. He looks up and calls to Alkur, "Hey, this looks like one of the eagle carvings at the Temple of Pfuerto. In fact, the stone base is just like that Temple."

Alkur reaches the top. A deep hole had been drilled through the rock. Next to it, a small carved pipe poured water down through a series of carved channels. Both men dip their hands into the water; it's cool and clean. They taste it. It is refreshing and with just a slight hint of limestone. "It's a successful, surprising morning so far" chuckles Caphala as he starts to fill one of the jugs they carried.

As he pulls out another jug, Alkur answers, "We just need to find the people. The quiet is strange." He notices that the birds had stopped their incessant calls. It was strangely still. He looks around again, looking for any sign of life.

Caphala's comment about the similarities with the Pfuerto temple starts Alkur's thoughts down a different path. Could this compound have been erected by survivors from the earlier Atlantean cataclysms? Are they on a journey traveled before? A deep sadness catches him unaware; something has triggered vivid memories of his father. It's as if he can feel his father's presence near him. He stops and looks around. It felt so close, so intimate as if he was walking with him once again.

Caphala is already heading back to the beach. "Alkur, let's get this back there. We still have to pick more fruit and gather wood."

Alkur hesitates momentarily still caught up with the feeling. He slowly walks away.

Chapter 39

The warriors move silently through the jungle. Barely indistinguishable from the shadows, their faces and bodies are covered in black and white paints. Their eyes gleam with purpose, like revolting zombies ready to pounce on their human prey. The only hint of their presence is the occasional warning shriek from a bird or tree monkey. Then, as in a precise maneuver, they lie motionless in the darkness, under the dark jungle canopy, waiting. For days they had closely watched Alkur and the group, tracking them since their arrival to their land.

Caphala is in the lead as they slug through the dense brush, hacking their way with swords, sticks and their bare hands. It's exhausting work. The heat surrounds them like a blanket they can't shake off. A few hungry insects feast on this new prey. The land is full of opposites, Alkur muses, as he brings up the rear of the party. The virgin trees, foliage and sounds appear like a land beyond time, with no trace of civilized life. Yet, the temple site indicated a sophisticated society of some kind, he thinks.

Suddenly, Caphala signals for them to stop. He motions Alkur to come forward and points to an abandoned village in the distance along a river. There, thatched huts made of a brick and stone are clustered, but no apparent sign of the inhabitants. No people, no domesticated birds or animals, nothing moved or made a sound.

Caphala sensing danger says, "I don't know about this one Alkur. It looks abandoned, but it doesn't feel and look right to me."

Alkur senses Caphala's apprehension and knows to trust him. Caphala is one of the best, a skilled warrior and tracker. Alkur readjusts his position and replies, "Yes, something must have driven the natives away; I hope it wasn't us that frightened them. You stay here with the group and I'll go investigate. If I'm not back in an hour, reassess the situation and, if possible, come for me."

Alkur breaks away from the group, and as quietly as he can, treads through the brush towards the village. Like Caphala, he senses danger and is alert for anything unusual. There has been uneasiness in their travels for the past couple of days. They could be walking into an ambush. Alkur skirts the huts avoiding the center of the village. At one, he peers in and sees a small wood fire still burning, plates of food with eating utensils, blankets and other household goods. Whoever was here left in a hurry, without carrying their possessions. Are they hiding in the jungle watching? Are they friendly?

Alkur makes his way back where the group anxiously awaits his report.

"The place is empty. They must have left in a hurry. Let's move on and get away from here and keep on the alert. If they are watching, we don't want to provoke any trouble by stealing their food."

Caphala and Elchi nod in agreement. The others pick up what little they've been carrying and wait for Caphala to lead them off, back through the scrubby undergrowth.

They stop to rest along the river perhaps a mile from the village. It's a little cooler here, shreds of a breeze travel along the water. Ilax starts re-winding the light cloth she's wrapped around her legs to protect them from the tough brush. Ax-Tos lies back against a tree and watches the river flow by. He's thinks, "If only I had some string and a hook, perhaps we'd have a fine dinner tonight. Wonder what's out there."

Alkur finds a space beneath a tree a little apart from the others. He feels very responsible for the group and in need of some guidance. He carefully unfolds the bag and places the skull on a cloth he's laid out. Alkur closes his eyes but finds it difficult to connect with the skull. His mind is too full of their troubles. He takes a few deep breaths to center and ground and brings the energy of love and gratitude to his heart. This works and he asks, "What will we face on this journey?" He feels himself sink into a deep state of inner peace. Next, he sees himself suspended over a large turquoise-blue lake. In the lake's center is an island. He descends onto the island and is engulfed in a white—yellow prism of light. He is surrounded by what appear to be dark skinned beings dancing ecstatically around a large bonfire. It feels like he is witnessing a celebration ceremony. Alkur feels compassion for all life and Oneness. Suddenly, he is jolted back in his body and looks up to see Caphala standing over him.

"Alkur, we're ready. It will be getting dark soon. We must find a campsite. Do you need some water? I've some left in my flask."

Alkur shakes his head admiring, not for the first time, Caphala's perception. He's a natural leader, always aware of the needs of others. I can trust him, Alkur thinks. As before, Alkur takes the rear spot in the line as they walk further into the jungle.

A short while later they notice a well-trodden path. Caphala stops and waits for Alkur's advice. Alkur knows something is not right, but does not know what. The tall grass and trees darken the trail further on, a perfect setup for an attack. Alkur turns to Caphala, "I'll take lead for a while. Pass the word for everyone to keep their eyes open. This could be dangerous." Caphala nods.

Then, Alkur sees a slight movement ahead and a rustling on his right flank. Turning quickly, he hears a crunching sound to the rear. He yells, "Everyone freeze. Don't move. Stay where you are!"

As they stand there, the ground around them starts to move in a surreal dance, mounds of branches and bushes slowly coming at them from all directions. In unison the motion stops. Dozens of black-faced warriors emerge like a strange mist. Their bodies are covered with leaves and branches; they hold spears at the ready. Some, armed with bows and rope like sling shots, appear posed to attack. Alkur slowly raises his arms as a gesture of peace. His sword remains sheathed.

A small elderly warrior armed only with a short spear approaches cautiously. In addition to his camouflage of foliage, he wears a large headdress and face paint. Alkur assumes he is the leader as the warrior walks around the group as if trying to decipher their intention. At his signal, the warriors close ranks around him and the group.

Alkur thinks to call Asa-masa-me just in case she can help with communicating, but before he can, he hears a commotion from the rear. Two warriors have already grabbed her; the threesome shuffle forward to the presumed leader. The two warriors let go of her but stand close by. Asa-masa-me has a flicker of fear in her eyes as she says to Alkur, "I was trying to speak with them. We didn't connect."

Alkur looks at her, still trusting her skills, says "Ask them what they want."

Looking at the leader, she uses hand signals to relay the question. He doesn't understand. She tries some early Atlantean dialect, but the leader just looks at her. Asa-masa-me tells Alkur with a note of chagrin, "I'll try something different next time."

Then the old warrior smiles and signals with his spear for the warriors to move them all along the trail. Alkur nods at Caphala and Elchi to comply; they have no choice at this point.

Chapter 40

The natives lead Alkur and the Atlanteans on a grueling hike through dense jungle and finally reach a small village perched next to a large and stunningly beautiful lake. Alkur sees small islands dotting the surface out to the horizon. It reminds him of the Atlantean coast, complete with sparkling blue waters and bright green foliage. The village huts are made of wood and mud with thatched roofs. As they pass through the village center, men and women gather to watch. Small children stare as they walk by.

They are taken to a nearby open field rimmed with large trees. A large fire pit sits in the center of the field, with some rock seating along two edges. For Alkur, the scene is eerily reminiscent of his dream meditation the day before.

Despite some apprehension, he's fascinated with these natives, the village and their way of life. They have a mix of technology and primitivism that's intriguing. He thinks, it's just a matter of assuring the warriors that we are peaceful and have no evil intent.

Ahead of him, a heated conversation erupts between a warrior and the leader. After silencing the agitated young man, the leader approaches Alkur as though he's the next problem on the day's list. The leader stops a step away and just looks at him intently. Alkur senses a connection with this man; they were destined to meet. Another angry looking warrior arrives, and emphatically relays warnings or threats while pointing menacingly at Alkur. Undeterred, the leader still looking at Alkur raises his left arm signaling the warrior to stop. Frustrated, the warrior pauses then speaks again. The leader ignores him. The warrior, fed up, turns and strides towards the village. The rest of the tribe stands around watching with interest.

Asa-masa-ee slides through the group to stand next to Alkur. "I may be able to help. They're dialect sounds similar to old traditional Atlantean."

The leader looks at Asa masa-ee and nods as if realizing her skill in languages. As he begins to talk, loudly and with a touch of ire, she begins to translate.

"He is angry at us for dishonoring their sacred grounds when we first arrived... I think he is saying they observed us on the beach and were afraid."

Alkur nods, "the abandoned village."

The leader continues to speak.

"I believe he is talking about the temple. The site is one of their most holy grounds, where they bury their ancestors. He says we have dishonored it."

She hesitates and Alkur looks at her, his mind scampering back to when they climbed the height and filled their flasks. He glances at the leader. She continues, "He says many who arrived before us desecrated their land and the monuments built to honor their gods. We are not welcome here."

Alkur looks back to Asa-masa-ee and steadily replies, "Can you tell him we mean no harm; we were shipwrecked and lost." Caphala and Elchi, who had moved near Alkur, both nod their heads indicating agreement with Alkur's statement.

Asa-masa-ee begins to talk and uses her hands to emphasize Alkur's message. The leader is fascinated that she can speak their language. The warriors look around at each other, surprised and a little confused.

Before long, drumming is heard and the group is escorted to the village center, and through hand signals, directed to sit down. A large crowd gathers. Something important is about to happen. All the heads turn toward the entrance of a large hut. A tall man walks out followed by the leader. The man has a headdress made of leaves, animal feet, chicken skulls and animal horns. Alkur's party is transfixed at his imposing figure. In his right hand he holds a wooden staff intricately carved to display a serpent head and the bust of a large bird. His face is black with white stripes. With a serious look, he surveys the scene, raises and points his staff at them and begins to speak angrily.

Asa-masa-ee grabs Alkur's hand and whispers, "He must be the medicine man or spiritual leader. He is very upset at the sacrilege we've committed. He says we are an evil omen, cursed and must die."

The man faces the leader, his fury is unmistakable. The chief nods.

Asa-masa-ee looks at Alkur and the others with concern. Alkur tries to stand, but is stopped when two warriors shove spears against his chest. The chief didn't notice.

At first, Alkur does not notice as the young woman emerges from the large hut behind him. She's draped in blankets and has a dark complexion, hazel eyes and long brown hair arranged down her shoulders. Two elderly women walk beside her, helping her. She walks with slow measured steps toward the crowd occasionally helped by the women. The crowd bows respectfully and creates a path for her.

Reaching the center, she stops and bows to the leader. After a quick contemptuous glance at the medicine man, she begins speaking quietly. From where Alkur stands, it appears whatever she is saying is provoking an angry reaction from the medicine man. She looks squarely at him and angrily admonishes him. The medicine man, startled and angry, abruptly walks away. Her energy expended, the elderly women grab her arms and help her back to the hut. As she is whisked past the group, she glances at Alkur. There is a hint of a smile in her countenance and soft eyes. Alkur feels a jolt as his eyes meet with hers. He feels a connection. Then she's gone.

After conferring with the head warrior, the leader directs that the group be given beds and provisions. As they are led away, Alkur and Asa-masa-ee breathe a sigh of relief. Alkur realizes he is very tired.

That night Alkur is awoken by Asa-masa-ee. "Alkur, I just overheard an argument I think, between the leader and that young woman. The leader blames her for our arrival; he says we must go. She accuses him of being superstitious and listening to the medicine man's message, which is always fear and death. She tells him we are harmless and that she psychically traced our journey from arrival on their land. She said that we and their tribe were destined to meet, that the hands of the Gods are in this. The leader disagrees. He says foreigners have always brought ruin, exploitation and slavery."

Alkur interrupts, "What is meant by ruin, exploitation and slavery?"

She shakes her head and continues, "I don't know." But then she says, "The woman felt we can help them deal with some labor camps. The leader will bring it before their council for a decision."

Alkur pauses to take it all in and ponders what to do. "Thank you for letting me know. Let's get some rest." After she leaves, Alkur can't sleep. Restless and knowing that he is somehow responsible he begins to think through their options. He needs to talk to Elchi and the others; perhaps Ilax would have some guidance. But he doesn't want to rouse the camp by looking for them all. It will have to wait.

At dawn a couple of women bring water for washing and then the warriors come back and escort them to a large hut. On the way, Alkur tries to assure everyone that they are safe for the moment.

Inside the hut are the chief, the medicine man, and a host of tribesmen and women sitting cross-legged. Alkur guesses that the men in front must be the council members. Alkur and the group are placed on the other side of the hut. A small fire in the center warms the morning air; a small table, perhaps an altar, is covered with precious stones and statues. Outside, the entire village gathers to await the council's decision.

Alkur and Asa-masa-ee are pulled from the group to stand before the council. The other survivors from Atlantis look tired and nervous.

After all their travels, does it end here? Their eyes show a mix of resignation, hope and uncertainty. Alkur sees the young woman being helped to a place near the center of the floor next to the other women. The leader, holding a large crystal, rises gathering everyone's attention. He begins to speak.

Asa-masa-ee translates for Alkur, "He, Rariru, the chief is telling them the council session is now in order. He is reminding them that those who wish to speak must first pick up the sacred crystal." The leader points to Alkur. Asa-masa-ee continues, "He says we bring evil omens and threaten their way of life. It's an evil they know all too well from previous strangers. He says we must be destroyed. We desecrated their burial grounds and that shows who we really are. He asks for advice from the council before making his final decision."

Alkur looks at the chief as she continues, "He's pleading for the council to vote that we should be executed." Asa-masa-ee's face is tight with fear. They both watch as some of the tribe nod in agreement, others remain silent and expressionless.

The young woman, who Alkur has named "hazel-eyes," glares angrily at the leader and then looks at Alkur. Then, an elderly, very distinguished looking man walks up to the leader, says a few words privately and takes the crystal. He walks towards Alkur's group and carefully appraises everyone then motions for Alkur to come forward. Alkur rises and walks to the center of the room. The older man inclines his head slightly and places the crystal into Alkur's hands. He slowly walks back to his seat on the council and sits down, waiting expectantly. All eyes are on Alkur and the room falls silent.

Asa-masa-ee moves forward to stand by Alkur and, at his direction; they kneel in front of the council. Alkur starts talking as Asa-masa-ee translates.

"I am Alkur. We are from Atlantis, a land far from here. Our island home was destroyed by a volcano. We escaped on a ship. We sailed for many days until our ship was wrecked off your shore. We are alone and in search of a new home."

Alkur pauses, his expression is earnest and serious. "We are sorry that we did not understand about your temple. We apologize for any disrespect. We are peaceful people. We intend no harm; we only want to start a new life here. We believe in the Law of One, equality, love and freedom." Alkur looks around the room to see the reaction to his speech.

Some look skeptical while others are simply amazed to hear something very like their language being spoken. The elders were listening and occasionally leaning toward one another with comments. Alkur feels he hasn't convinced them. Alkur turns and asks Asa-masa-ee to have Am-ee-lee bring the skull. She turns, whispers to Caphala and turns back ready to translate as Alkur continues.

"When we left Atlantis, we brought our sacred teachings with us. Our beliefs and the wisdom of our elders are with our crystal skull." Am-ee-lee hands the bag to Alkur. In a dramatic flourish, Alkur pulls out the skull and raises it with both hands. Suddenly, a collective gasp is heard; some council members stare and cry out in disbelief at what they are seeing. The leader stands and points at the skull angrily shouting. The shaman abruptly stands and backs away in horror.

Asa-masa-ee translates, "He says, I told you these people are evil— they come from the same place as the evil One." Asa-masa-ee is scared now. Alkur, reacting to the heightened energy in the room, snaps at her, "Ask them what it is they fear. Tell them we come in peace!"

She starts to talk but Rariru interrupts. She translates, "he says, they've been persecuted, brainwashed and enslaved by a powerful entity that came with a crystal skull like that one. Those evil people arrived not so long ago. When they came, they said they came in peace. And their crystal skull carried magic. But they were evil; their leader made war and made us work mining for copper. Too late, we realized that the foreigners were ruining our land and our lives. People who refused their rule were enslaved and their families massacred. The evil one used a noise generator that alters emotions to control and enslave huge numbers of people. Sickness, depression and other previously unknown maladies afflict us. And now you are here with a skull. The same. No more!" The leader shakes with fury and frustration. Asa-masa-ee catches her breath, stunned by his words.

Alkur stands silently. He listened carefully and now the two big questions that trouble him are who is the dark Leader, and how can he, Alkur, convince the council that they are not the same.

A moment later, Alkur looks at Asa-masa-ee and tells her, "Thank him for telling us what happened here. We are very sorry for these evil doings. But we are not of the same energy as those who preceded us. In our land we also faced similar trials and evil. That is the major reason that we left and are here now. We may be able to help." Alkur watches the council as she speaks.

As she finishes, there is a long period of silence. For a moment, Alkur stood, still, before them, the small fire dancing in his eyes. For a timeless moment the world seemed quiet. They all remained impassive.

One of the Elders whispers to the leader and then for a few moments the council quietly, calmly discusses something. Imperceptibly, they reach a decision. The leader speaks and Asa-masa-ee translates, "How can we trust you?"

Alkur almost smiles, "You have my word."

The young woman in the circle slowly stands and reaches for the crystal. Alkur hands it to her. With confidence and serenity she addresses the council. Again, Asa-masa-ee translates, "She is asking the council to welcome us and consider our offer of help. She says that she had foreseen our arrival – that we are not like the evil men who came and destroyed our peace. She says if for no other reason they must accept us because they have no other option and must think of their children now and their future. The stakes are high. She is imploring them to step up to the challenge and regain their freedom and dignity once again. That's all she said to them."

The young woman puts the crystal by the fire and slowly returns to her seat. Looking around, Alkur can see that her words hit home. The elders are moved. They glance around at one another and then nod in agreement. Rariru stands, listens and then makes a brief statement. All at once drums began beating throughout the village.

Alkur faces the group and says, "Are we part of the tribe?" Asa-masa-ee repeats the question, relief coming through her words. Rariru nods in assent. Then he turns to talk in low tones to the council. Asa-masa-ee can't quite hear everything he says but she says, "He's holding a closed session with the elders. I'm not sure, something about consulting an oracle."

Chapter 41

Dark human shapes glisten with sweat in the stifling midafternoon sun. Slouched over underneath their heavy loads, they trudge slowly up the hill. Others nearby crouch low to the earth leaning against the trees for whatever shade they can get. The dim light reveals their terrible pain; despair and abandonment is etched on their wet faces. The eyes say it all—sunken, enormous, vacant, the depths of which what their life force is fading away. Some have given up all hope and withdrawn to die. The others don't even bother to look at the motionless, distorted shapes. They know they were all dying anyway, captives in a nightmarish world, shadows of themselves, skeletons of disease and starvation.

Imprisoned against their will, they came from the deep recesses of the land, away from their tribes. They are lost in unfamiliar surroundings and fed only small portions of questionable food. They work under the watchful eyes of their despotic masters as slaves. This is the impenetrable darkness that they face.

A familiar loud noise is heard as the soil shudders. The rumble brings no reaction from the men; the dangers of frequent cave-ins are well known. They happen more and more all the time as if the earth is fighting this invasion to its body. Once down in the recesses of the mines, there are frightening noises, dust, unbearable heat and darkness. This must be hell itself. But, the work goes on.

The men cannot see it, but know that it exists. They call it "the machine" -- a device that emits a subtle barely audible noise, but it is very effective. It is like a disease that takes hold and spreads. The only cure is to run away. It frightens the animals; some flee and some just die. For the most part, this green hell is devoid of life. The tribal elders say that in their shamanic journeys they have witnessed the machine's dreadful power: the sudden loss of the life force, the overwhelming sense of dread and fear, depression and resignation to one's fate. The shamans have tried to neutralize its effects but are powerless to stop it. One tribal elder described the situation as having "two types of people now – those who are dying and those who waiting to die."

Suddenly, piercing screams are heard echoed with cries of desperation. A man is being dragged away by two husky guards. His voice is incoherent, his eyes bulge as he pleads one last time. There is no mercy. Some workers stop to stare while others turn their heads away. The guards know this small drama is a way to enforce obedience. There is no tolerance for rebellion, no quarter given to insubordination or lesser infractions. In this place there is no trial and only one path -- death.

The man is dragged to a small plot of dirt in the niche of a wooden fence, then up the steps to a makeshift platform. A hooded man awaits standing with an enormous ax. The victim writhes frantically in a last ditch effort to live. It has no effect on the captors. The men toss his body on the platform then tie straps around his arms. His victim's body shakes; he is past screaming now.

The executioner's blade swooshes downward landing with a loud thud. Then there is silence and the headless body twitches spastically, then lies still. His body withers with a last kick of the feet. The guards wait a moment then calmly remove the corpse as two prisoners are summoned to clean the platform. The executioner steps down, trading an unconcerned comment with another guard.

Work slowly resumes.

Chapter 42

Half hidden by the trees, dark shadows slide by. Streams of half-naked, dark-faced bodies move silently with spears in their hands, bows, arrows and shields. The bushes move, the soft grass sways, and then it becomes still. In the distance a lingering haze obscures the village. The men lay waiting for the right time, the right time to kill and capture this tribe that hasn't submitted. They must be punished, examples to all that no mercy is shown to the defiant.

Night falls and village life begins to ebb slowly as if on cue. Another day is gone. But a subtle sound, barely distinguishable to the naked ear, penetrates the darkness like a heavy blanket. It hums a perceptible and numbing sound disturbing the energy field.

Alkur is unable to sleep and tries to tune out the sound, to neutralize its effect with his breath and mind-focus. He feels the slight tingling between his eyes and the fogginess of his senses. His mind begins to wander, thinking of all they have endured thus far and still facing an uncertain future. He has a flash of pride in the Atlanteans – they have shown strength and resilience. He takes a moment to pray that the elders get an omen of good fortune from the oracle. He prays that they accept them all. He can't fathom the alternative.

As Alkur finally drifts off to sleep, he sees himself in a large open field of yellow orchids and green grass. Ampero is with him; they hold hands and play like children. How happy, how free they were; destined to be together in this lifetime. Ampero breaks away from him and as she runs she looks back at him, smiling and laughing. She runs until he can't see her anymore. Alkur feels the terrible sadness as he calls her name to no avail. She is gone. He awakens feeling lost and alone. Alkur closes his eyes again, hoping for a different dream.

Suddenly, loud noises startle him awake. Instantly vigilant, he crawls to the hut's entrance. Peering into the darkness, he hears loud screaming and sees people running wildly in all directions.

A fire has engulfed a hut on the village edge lighting up the chaos in silhouettes. Alkur runs out to see that the fire is devouring Rariru's hut. Dark shapes with spears are roving through the village indiscriminately maiming and slaughtering the screaming villagers and torching the huts.

Alkur shouts to Caphala and Elchi while running to the huts where the others are staying. He sees Ilax and the others huddled inside; Alkur yells at them to stay put.

"Caphala, Elchi, stay here and guard the others; let no one enter."

Alkur runs towards the burning hut. He grabs a spear from a dead villager and peers in. The intense smoke and flames obscure his sight but as he enters he sees Rariru lying on his back; he'd probably been caught in his sleep. Dead guards with arrows littering their bodies lay nearby caught unawares in the initial attack.

Alkur surprises one attacker by grabbing him from behind and throwing him on his head breaking his neck. Another attacker lunges at him with a spear which Alkur deflects with a parry from his own spear as he thrusts it into the attacker's stomach. He quickly swings around in time to notice Rariru has rolled to his stomach in a desperate attempt to reach for his weapon as he is about to be stabbed by an attacker, Alkur turns and impales the attacker with his spear. Rariru looks up surprised as Alkur reaches down with his arm and lifts him to his feet.

Rariru runs past Alkur shouting orders to his men who begin to rally around him. Warriors appear and join him in the fight. As he gives commands and presses an attack, the villagers regain the initiative. They advance on the attackers, cutting them down like cane as they flee back into the forest. As suddenly as it began, the fight is soon over. The villagers gather weapons and post guards, preparing for another attack.

With the fighting done, Alkur trots back to the Atlantean huts and sees Caphala and Elchi swords in hand poised for action. There are almost a half dozen dead strangers strewn about the hut. Alkur calls out, "Are you alright? What happened?"

Caphala, still tense, gives a half-smile and says, "Well, they got more than they bargained for."

Elchi nods and adds, "Everyone is alright." Alkur smiles, grateful that everyone has survived. Ilax, who has been standing in the hut door, now reaches for Alkur's hand. Ax-Tos grabs his satchel with medical supplies and runs to help the wounded.

Moments later, the warriors let out a fierce victory cry that echoes through the village. They have faced a hardened enemy and won.

That evening the villagers celebrate their victory with a fire and water ceremony. A young warrior was sent to invite Alkur and the group to attend as the guests of honor. As Asa-masa-ee translates, Rariru recognizes Alkur, Caphala and Elchi for their bravery and saving his life and the villagers. The elders stand and lower their heads as a sign of respect to the Atlanteans. Alkur sighs slightly, glad that some measure of trust has been won.

At the far end of the village, the medicine man moves quietly in his hut. He assembles a circle of bones and sacred carvings and sprinkles it with a white powder and dark liquid. As he chants, darkness envelopes the hut; a foreboding sign of dark energies being manifested.

PART 3: CONFRONTATION

I believe that what we become depends on what our fathers teach us at odd moments, when they aren't trying to teach us. We are formed by little scraps of wisdom

UMBERTO ECO

Chapter 43

The next morning the village begins to return to normal, people going about the mundane tasks of cooking, washing, gossiping and daily chores. The sun was already up when a young boy appears at Alkur's hut, calling out something and waving frantically. The boy turns and trots around the sides of the small dwellings, headed to the other side of the village. Alkur grabs his weapons and almost stumbles as he follows.

The boy stops at the hut of the chief's daughter. Inside, Alkur finds a grave scene. The young woman, Hulos, lies on a mattress of smooth cloth stuffed with leaves. She is covered with soft blankets but still trembling with fever. The chief and several older tribesmen surround her, chanting in loud voices and placing what appears to be sacred objects around her. The medicine man is nowhere to be seen. Her eyes are shut and, except for her jaw, which tightens to try and quell the shaking, her face is serene and calm. Her skin, damp with fever, has the grayish hue of someone close to death. Grief and confusion are mixed on the faces of all those gathered around her. Some women are visibly distraught and softly crying.

Alkur turns to Asa-masa-ee, who had followed him through the village, and says, "Ask the chief what is happening. What can we do?"

After a brief conversation she returns to Alkur. Rariru watches them from across the room.

"He is afraid that his daughter is dying. Despite all their chants and potions, she seems to be slipping away. He asks, "Can we help?""

Alkur looks at the woman, concern in his eyes. He says only, "Ask Am-ee-lee to bring the skull. I need you, Ax-Tos and Ilax with me now." Alkur nods in Rariru's direction to let him know that they will try.

Asa-masa-ee scurries past the elders and out of the hut to quickly find everyone. Rather than approach the sick woman, Alkur studies the space around the low bed. He reaches over to slightly shift a few of the objects and is met with some questioning looks. But he keeps on, makes a few minor changes in the room and stops. This will do for the healing, he thinks.

Asa-masa-ee walks in with Ilax, Am-ee-lee and the others. The skull is hidden in the old satchel. Alkur says quietly, "I need all of you to hold the energy as we do a healing for Hulos. She is very sick and may die. Akaus, I need you to bring in a sacred Atlantean chant—a beautiful song to raise the vibration. Ilax you will be my anchor to ground her energies and fill her with the earth energies. Ax Tos, I need you to observe her vital signs and anything that needs to be done as we proceed. The rest of you hold the energy." They are silent, waiting for the healing to begin. Ilax and Akaus focus on quiet prayer, both glad to once again remember and relive their familiar Atlantean practices.

Alkur turns to Asa-masa-ee, "Please ask the chief to have his people form an outer circle in this space. I need them to invoke the healing spirits of their tribe and to raise the vibration, to chant, burn sage; whatever. We must make this space buzz with the healing energy of unconditional love." As he speaks, he motions the others to form a circle around the woman.

After a moment the hushed room begins to stir with low tones of rhythmic chanting. Alkur steps to the blankets where Hulos is lying and opens his bag. He places crystal stones around her, and the skull near the top of her head facing her. He slowly raises his hands and sets his intention to expand his energy field into a ball of white light. He invokes the energies of love, light and healing in the name of the Spirits of Atlantis, and asks the ancestors, angels, and spirits of this new land to join the healing ceremony. Akaus' voice joins the chanting, her soprano lightly blending with the tribesmen's lower tones.

Alkur kneels and placing his hands over the skull begins to chant the sacred sounds: AKMA-LA, AKMA-RA-LA, AK-RA-NA, and AK-El-KIBA. He circles his hands over the woman's body, not touching her, but as though spreading a healing breeze. Ilax moves forward and, with her eyes closed, holds the woman's feet; Ax-Tos gently takes her hands, chanting aloud.

Alkur, picking up on a hostile energy, suspects that she may be possessed by an entity. With his intuition and using his fingers as a long etheric crystal sword he begins to cut the energetic cords around Hulos' body that hold her to the darkness. Then, placing his hands on her right arm, he begins to channel healing energy and the vibration of love into her blood. After a few minutes he slowly places his left hand on her solar plexus and the right on her navel sending loving healing energy to her. The tribesmen watch warily; this is a new healing practice and they don't know what to expect.

Suddenly, she begins to move from side to side. Alkur suspects that the entity in Hulos may be an ancient tribal demon, tied to their ceremonies and the negative energies in their environment. The entity has become part of the tribe preventing them from a healthy connection to the earth.

A couple of women gasp as Hulos begins thrashing about uncontrollably. Everyone is watching her now and the chanting seems to increase in tempo as though to combat something. The entity knows it has been found out. Alkur knows there is no stopping now. He must continue.

"I ask the ancestors and angels of Atlantis, Melkizadeck, Thoth and the inter-dimensional beings of light to be present and to stand against the darkness that would interfere" Ax-Tos begins humming a new strain of music while nodding to Alkur.

Still chanting, Alkur creates a golden pyramid of light around Hulos. In the pyramid he draws an inter-dimensional window to capture and release the entity. This was an effective Atlantean technique for releasing earthbound entities to the light.

"I command you to leave in the name of ...."

Suddenly, a raspy voice is heard as Hulos screams in her native tongue, "You will not, cannot make me leave... I will destroy you!" Her entire body distorts and writhes. Her loud cries are frightening. With her eyes bulging, she claws at the air, at her face, at Alkur, like a wild animal. Alkur continues to command the entity to leave,

"You will leave now!"

The villagers are looking one to the other, very uncertain and scared. The chief stares in horror at his daughter. As their chanting subsides, Akaus' clear tones take over the hut.

Still the entity resists. It becomes even stronger as Hulos' upper body comes off the bed. She screams wildly, in indistinguishable words and sits up clawing at Alkur and then falling back. She does this again and again. Some in the inner circle start to back away.

"Keep chanting...don't stop!" Alkur says sharply.

A sudden movement from her navel to her left shoulder captures his attention. Alkur follows the energy and places his hand on her shoulder. It moves again not wanting to be found. Hulos shakes uncontrollably. The entity is still resisting. Alkur uses all his power and strength to hold the energy.

"I ask that the Spirits and angels move deep inside Hulos and find the dark one. In the name of the light, bind it in the pyramid of light. The pyramid of light surrounds the dark one now!"

Alkur sees the entity emerge from the woman's stomach and enter the pyramid's window. The energy in the room shifts; a sudden cold wisp and a shadow-like presence flits by. The skull is lit up. A second later, there is a piercing clapping sound and a sudden rush of air. Many cover their ears as the hut and ground shake as though buffeted by a strong wind. Alkur senses that other entities living in villagers and connected with the Hulos entity have also left. It feels like a huge storm has abruptly cleared; it's finally over. Hulos' face looks normal as she slowly opens her eyes. One of the women, smiling broadly, steps forward to wipe her brow.

The chief looks to Alkur with relief and a touch of wonder as the tribesmen carefully step to the rear, giving plenty of room to Alkur and the other Atlanteans.

The people now see Alkur as fulfilling an ancient prophecy. It fore-told generations before they had been visited by a fair skinned, red-haired wise man and healer who became a leader-priest. They called him At-ach-u-chu, the teacher of all things: arts, agriculture, religion, astronomy, weights and measures and government. He was a very power-ful, yet gentle man who led the tribe in rebellion against an evil ruler, but was imprisoned and executed. The people revered him. The old legends said he had come from a distant land in the East and settled in a lake after surviving a cataclysmic deluge, the Unu-Pachacuti.

Many now see Alkur as their new leader and only hope against the evil ruler.

Chapter 44

Later that day, while many natives are gathered in the village center working, Alkur joins them feeling ready to take up the next challenge. He notices more friendly faces in the village, and an air of lightness in the community. He sees Caphala smiling and gesturing with a group of young men; Elchi is drawing something on a rough bark leaf that has captured the attention of some of the older tribesmen. He finds Asa-masa-ee learning from a shy woman how to weave the amazing patterns. Smiling, he interrupts and says, "Let's ask the chief what he knows about this sound generator."

The three of them stand in the shade of an ancient tree as Asa-masa-ee translates, "The natives call it the darkness. He says that his tribe has been under attack by a very powerful energy for a long time. The evil one uses the darkness to bleach out the thoughts of his subjects ensuring total submission. Resistance means certain death. The darkness emits a subtle frequency that alters a person's perception and renders them powerless, numb and confused."

"We've felt this oppressive force since our arrival." Alkur says. Asa-masa-ee continues, "They have resisted the evil one with some success. They are the only tribe that has not submitted." The chief has a small look of pride although his face is creased with worry.

Ask him, "Who is the evil one?"

"He says he is a fair skinned, tall bearded man who, like you, said he came in peace from faraway in the East. But he quickly began to exploit them for material wealth, robbing the earth mother of her gold and copper. They took much more than they need for their buildings and ceremonies."

She pauses to listen, then continues,

"At first, he demonstrated magical healings and showed us new and better ways to mine the earth. It was only later we could see in his heart his intention to enslave us and destroy our families and our traditions. He said he wanted a better life for us but he was really just after the metals. Our ancestors called it the dark spirits and they've come back to punish them."

Alkur asks, "How has the tribe resisted for so long?"

"We identified the frequency and, through collective will and the protection of ancestral energy shields, have neutralized some of its effects. It doesn't always work."

Alkur asks, "Ask him, what is this ancestral energy shield?"

"It may be our greatest possession. It's a blanket of white light energy invoked through rituals. It protects the entire village and its occupants; a gift from the ancestors who foresaw that this evil would happen and wanted to give us a way to survive."

"He says the shield has weakened over time; its vibrations cause confusion and allow the bad energy to infect the village. He believes the entity you removed from his daughter was part of the assault, and that the entity had beckoned the evil one's warriors when they attacked."

"Tell him I suspect he is not being truthful about what is going on in his tribe."

Rariru looks intently at Alkur; his immediate reaction toward being challenged is quickly overcome by his need to find out what Alkur might know. He whispers slowly to Asa-masa-ee. "He feels there is a traitor within the tribe who is working for the evil one." The chief looks warily around them; no one is near.

"Does he have any idea who it may be?"

"He has his suspicions but is not certain."

"Do they know where this generator is?"

"He isn't sure, but it may be in a cave on a mountain very close to the evil one's camp."

"Ask him where the main camp is."

"He says it is two-day journey up river, north of here."

"Tell him we need to find a way to destroy the generator to help release those who are in bondage and ease the attack on the tribe. It's only a matter of time before the evil one disables his defenses and takes over. There will be more attacks. From what I have seen thus far, it may be sooner than later." Alkur and Rariru stare at each other for a long moment before Rariru murmurs something.

"He agrees and is willing to develop a plan."

"Good, let's get started."

Alkur summons Caphala, Elchi and Ilax to Rariru's hut. The shaman and the warrior leader, along with some of his best fighters, are already there. Rariru draws a map on the ground and throughout the day they develop an ambitious plan.

It calls for an assault group, under the cover of darkness, to move up along the river for about a day's journey. From there, it will take about two days to trek over difficult and dangerous terrain to get to the mountain cave where they hope to find the generator. They will have to travel quickly and quietly. Rariru asks his warriors to comment. There is a lively exchange and the head warrior points to Alkur, shaking his head. Several other warriors sit back to listen.

Asa-masa-ee leans over to Alkur and the others and says "The chief wants to know what you think about their plan." She points to the lead warrior, "Chulki is not happy with it. He says it's too risky. The river is unpredictable with very strong currents this time of the year, and the route puts them through an ancestral burial and ceremonial area. It is very sacred and prohibited to pass without special permission."

"Assuming they gain permission, the warriors would then have to cross land in the daytime exposed to enemies who know the terrain well. Most enemy warriors were captured from villages that border the river. The men don't want to enter the lands of other tribes without permission. There have been too many deadly clashes in the past and there is no trust. Also, he wants to use a small number of his men and does not want to include any of us." She looks around at Alkur and the Atlantean men.

Alkur is perplexed, "It's a good plan as long as we have the element of surprise." Elchi and Caphala nod in agreement.

"Tell the chief we have experience with crystals, and this generator sounds similar to a device we had but was stolen from our land. Caphala and I are former soldiers and well trained; Ilax is a powerful shaman who can use and read the energies of the land. We can help his warriors." As an aside, Alkur turns to Elchi and says "I will need you to remain in the village and guard the skull." Elchi nods in understanding.

Asa-masa-ee shares Alkur's comments with Rariru. Chulki leans in to listen to her words. A brief discussion follows then Chulki looks at Alkur and nods.

Asa-masa-ee says, "It looks like you're in. Does this mean I can go as well? You will need me to translate."

Alkur hesitates but knows she is right. She will be needed.

Alkur suggests creating a small force to disable the generator. He draws a replica of the old Atlantean machine and, with a lot of animated discussion between Ilax and the warriors, they decide how best to disable it. It will take two people at a minimum. After a few days of careful planning, they're ready.

Chapter 45

The canoes ease down the ink black river, drifting into the heart of darkness on the moonless night. The silence is impenetrable, interrupted only the hissing sound of the quiet oars as they glide on the still water. Occasionally, there is a splash, maybe a fish or land creature or worse an enemy sentry alerted to their passage. The shapes and shadows of the trees on the banks wave ominously in the dim starlight. They look like giant creatures or savage warriors ready to pounce at a moment's notice.

They had been traveling for hours; daylight was creeping into the sky. A few birds call to each other in the forest. Alkur sits low in the second canoe; next to him are Ilax and Asa-masa-ee. In front, as a dark shadow, Caphala sits with Chulki and some other warriors. Two more canoes ride astride the pair.

Alkur sees that the river is narrowing and they are approaching a large cluster of trees on the left bank which signals another waterway. As they slip into the entry, the warriors slow their speed and on cue place their right hands to their chests while holding the oar in the left in a traditional salute. One of the warriors in Alkur's canoe, Patob, quietly explains to Asa-masa-ee, "This is our sacred ancestral land, the burial grounds for our people. We must show honor and respect. They are requesting a safe passage for us."

They slowly drift forward as if propelled by a mysterious energy. The air is still. The dark water mirrors the trees and sky above it, giving it a beautifully ethereal appearance. Alkur is mesmerized by the stillness, despite the occasional cry of a bird or monkey. It's otherworldly.

On each bank are dark silhouettes of mounds topped by small structures. As the light grows, it's clear these are carefully tended, sacred burial chambers, Alkur guesses. The birds are quiet now; the only noise is the water ruffling against the canoe. Alkur looks around. He feels a strong spiritual presence reminiscent of how he felt in the temple with Thoth, a sense of peace, reverence and ancestral protection. Glancing at Ilax, he can see that she also feels its mystical charm. The hours pass slowly.

The canoes stop at a low clearing where the Chief disembarks and walks ashore. Patob again explains, "Rariru, is asking the guardians of the river to bless us and our mission."

Moments later, they are again drifting down the river. Maneuvering around a small bend, Alkur senses a movement on the river bank to the right. Some of the warriors also catch the change, but it is impossible to distinguish any shapes. Several heads turn; all scanning the underbrush. Alkur is certain he saw something, a subtle movement, like smoke in the dark. He feels uneasiness in his gut, a sensation felt before a skirmish years ago when he was with the Guards. Something is not right. He looks over his left shoulder at the other bank and again senses more then, sees a slight motion with his peripheral vision. We are being watched, he thinks. Instinctively, Alkur presses his hands on Ilax pushing her further down in the boat. Asa-masa-ee crouches lower. They were in danger and about to be attacked – worse, ambushed, he thought. His body tenses up.

Suddenly, a barrage of flaming projectiles lit up the sky. They shriek past their heads and some land on the canoes amongst them. A loud thud hits the warrior adjacent to Alkur as a flaming arrow through the chest knocks him overboard. The arrows' swoosh sounds like a thousand birds flying overhead.

In the dim light Alkur sees a canoe drifting aimlessly towards the right bank afire. Loud shouts are heard as the warriors row furiously to escape the trap. Ilax screams. Alkur turns abruptly to see her holding up a dead warrior with an arrow protruding from his neck. He shoves the body to the side and pushes her back down to the bottom of the canoe. Their only hope is to get quickly further down river.

Suddenly, the canoe hits a huge rock that stops it in its tracks. He screams to the others, "Get down! Get down!"

No one hears him in the confusion except Asa-masa-ee who screams the message out again and again. The water around them erupts in loud splashes mixed with loud thuds as stones crash into the sides of the canoes. Alkur grabs a paddle and desperately rows past the rock and then the boat snags on another underwater object. Most of the warriors in his canoe are dead or gravely wounded. They are sitting ducks. Without forward movement, they will be slaughtered. He pushes with his oar against the object but is unable to free it. In a last ditch effort he jumps into the water and tries to push the canoe but it's firmly caught.

Alkur reaches for Ilax, and grabbing her arms pulls her into the water headfirst. He points towards a low rise on the river bank and reaches back into the canoe to hoist one of the wounded warriors. The water is up to his shoulders and they move towards the bank struggling with the current trying to stay upright.

"Stay together" he calls, then "Where is Asa-masa-ee?" As the water tries to peel the warrior away, Alkur tightens his grip on the man and keeps calling, "Asa-masa-ee! Asa-masa-ee!"

Ilax and Alkur, still carrying the native, struggle to climb onto the bank. They are exhausted and running on adrenaline. Setting the wounded man under a low plant, Alkur tersely shouts, "I will be back", and slides down the bank. He swims to the canoe, still stuck in the river, to find Asa-masa-ee. But it's empty. She's gone as are the warriors. The projectiles continue to fall around him. Alkur looks wildly around to see any sign of them.

He hears Ilax scream. "Alkur"

Alkur swims back, climbs on the bank and sees Ilax lying on her back trying to fend off a black clad enemy. As Alkur rushes in their direction, the warrior standing behind her raises his arm to throw a spear at Alkur. In an instant, Ilax cries "no" and jumps up, lunging at the warrior and placing herself between him and Alkur.

The spear penetrates her right shoulder and she screams, falling to the ground gasping and holding it with her hands. Alkur instinctively rolls on the ground away from the line of attack, and leaps headfirst into the brush, pursued by what seems like a dozen dark shapes. He cannot see clearly but turns and feels a sharp piercing blow to his back and thigh. He lets out a loud scream and hits the ground. He tries to get up and falls again. He looks up to see the shapes of camouflaged warriors standing over him bow and arrows and spears pointing at him and muttering strange sounds. He is breathing hard now and in shock from the pain. He knows he is gravely wounded. He tries to get up and is stabbed in the stomach. He blacks out.

Chapter 46

Alkur is motionless, lying on his back on the wet, matted floor. He can hardly see or move. The walls enclosing him are craggy boulders with strange colors as if they were painted with metal. It is lit only by a small open crevice. The heat is oppressive laced with the smell of decayed flesh and fear. His feet are shackled to a large cage like door with an enormous lock. As he groggily regains consciousness, he tries to clear his mind, to ground himself. Tears well up in his eyes when he thinks of Ilax. He would be dead if not for her sacrifice. He starts to feel the shock, grief, anger and hopelessness of the situation. His friends are lost, the tribe that trusted him was murdered, and he is helpless, tied up like a dog. Another deep breath. He thinks, could I have prevented this? What has happened to Caphala and Asa-masa-ee? Is this where the adventure ends? He can't bear to speculate their fate and drifts off to blackness.

Time passes. Alkur catches himself straining to move and stops to take stock of his injuries. He must have lost a lot of blood; he feels weak and foggy. He closes his eyes and concentrates. The air is musty. Alkur begins to intone the Atlantean healing sounds and moves his left arm until it rests on the wound to his stomach. It's superficial, sparing vital organs and the blood has already coagulated and hardened around it.

However, the back wound is another story. He cannot move his right arm and when he does finally manage some shift, the pain is raw, piercing and unbearable. He tries to roll over on his left side elevating the area. He concentrates, visualizes a steady stream of violet-white light entering the wound's cellular structure healing it. He does this for quite some time and then tries to sleep.

Alkur wakes up when the cell door is opened. In the entrance, a large man with a sword in his hand looks down at him with contempt. Two large guards pass him in the doorway, then grab Alkur under the arms and drag him to his feet. Alkur can't help but groan with the pain.

He is taken through a dark corridor and a series of passageways then up a flight of stone steps and into a large, open courtyard surrounded by enormous trees. The guards pull him along; he misses steps and can barely keep up. The pain in his back is excruciating. But he forces himself to carefully observe everything and count his steps to memorize the route. He is taken up a very steep staircase emerging at the top to see an enormous wooden structure.

Inside, large burning lanterns are mounted on a series of tall wooden poles. They illuminate a most gruesome scene. Corpses, some hanging by their necks, other visibly mauled, eviscerated, burned and broken, are tied with ropes and vines decorate the poles. Mouths hang grotesquely open showing their last agonizing moments. The guards walk by without a sideways glance. The stench fills Alkur's nose and throat. At the end of the corridor, he sees hundreds of people, some are half-naked with spears or bows and shields. Some have blackened faces, others covered with a greenish-yellow substance, bronze and glittery, and on their bodies around their neck or waist hang artifacts of heads, necklaces, bones, and knives.

The natives move aside creating an eerie passage for the guards and Alkur. Their wild expressions give them a menacing and supernatural look. Alkur cannot believe what he is seeing; they look inhuman. Then, he sees ahead of them a man, sitting on an elevated throne-like platform. Shadows from the simmering rays of daylight in the passage-way give him a mystical other-worldly appearance.

As they approach the platform, the guards stop and release him. Unable to stand, Alkur falls to the ground landing on his left arm. The man steps off the throne and approaches him.

Alkur looks up to see a short, thin, cadaver-like man, shriveled with age. His bony head is covered with a black headdress; his shoulders carry a cloak made of an unknown material. His piercing eyes are dark; his shrouded face is white and thin with a narrow nose and purplish lips. Alkur realizes that the cloak hides his true appearance and makes him look bigger and ominous than he really is. The man supports himself on a gnarled, but intricately carved cane. Large gold and copper necklaces adorned with precious stones burden his neck. After a minute of silence, Alkur has to look away. So this is what evil looks like.

In a scratchy voice the man speaks "My warriors tell me you fought them bravely. You were taught well."

Alkur recognizes the voice: the accent, the pitch and tone. He knows it well. It is Atlantean.

"Who are you?" he asks hoarsely.

The man ignores Alkur's question and goes on, "My scouts reported your arrival before you reached our shore. We were destined to meet, so here we are. We've been expecting you."

"Where are the others?"

"You must be referring to the other members of your group. They resisted and were needlessly slain. If you are concerned for the woman with the dark hair...she is alive."

Alkur figures it must be Asa-masa-ee or Ilax. "You must not hurt her."

The man looks at him with renewed interest and smiles, "I admire your concern."

Glancing to his right, Alkur sees a familiar figure, the shaman from the village. It's instantly clear that he betrayed his own people and Alkur knows his betrayal is the reason they got ambushed. The bastard, Alkur thinks! Alkur glares at him and, in a moment of anger, tries to rise to confront him. He cannot. He falls heavily back to his knees. The guards start to move towards him, but the man motions them to back away.

"You must learn more self-control." The man chuckles to himself. "Tonight you will be my guest of honor." He turns and walks away disappearing into the shadows.

That evening Alkur is brought to a courtyard where there is a large gathering of people. He is still dirty, unshaven and matted with blood. The people pay no attention to him; they are waiting with cheerful anticipation. Soon, loud drumming announces the arrival of a large entourage with warriors clad in green and bronze leading a procession of men in various types of exotic costumes. Alkur wonders if these are the conquered tribal leaders and their shamans, or some local aristocracy. The cloaked man from earlier comes in seated on a large platform, carried on the shoulders of warriors. The people bow and prostate themselves as he passes, some of the warriors cheer raising their spears into the air in adulation.

As the men pass, Alkur sees another captive walking slowly behind. He cannot believe his eyes. It looks like Hulos, the daughter of the chief. She stumbles along, shackled at the ankles, and with her hands bound in front of her. A long robe covers her head and body. Alkur's mind races trying to comprehend what he is seeing. The village! They must have taken the village! What about Elchi? The skull?

The cloaked man's palanquin stops and he is slowly lowered. He stands absorbing the crowd's admiration, and nods as they fall to their knees and bow in reverence. He speaks to them in their own language. Murmurs are heard through the crowd as they listen, some begin to sob while others stand and sway. Suddenly, with the swift move of his hand, the guards walk into the crowds and bring two men out towards him. Their hands are roughly bound behind their backs and they are shoved to the ground. The men look at each other and around them, frightened and surprised. The cloaked man starts talking again, his tone taking on the serious and even cadence of pronouncing a sentence. One of the bound men shouts back defiantly while the other moves his head glancing wildly at the crowd. They are taken away by the guards. Alkur wonders whether he will find them on one of poles he had seen earlier.

Then the cloaked man waves and a large black bull is led into the arena. Its legs are then tied together and a harness placed around its neck. Two men from the crowd appear with large axes and on signal they begin hack into the buffalo while other men hold the ropes. Flesh is sliced off the animal as it falls to the ground roaring agonizing sounds. Its eyes are huge but empty. The crowd watches, transfixed. In a few minutes it is over and the beast lies still. People rush up to the remains, pulling pieces of flesh off the carcass then placing them on a large fire. A few of the more excited younger men are spreading warm blood on themselves as if performing a ceremonial ritual.

Alkur is brought forward and pushed down by the cloaked man. He ignores Alkur, and signals to his servants to begin passing the food and drink. There's a flurry of activity as people gather near the fire and settle in groups to eat. Drumming continues in the background.

"The natives believe their gods are angry with them, so we sacrifice the animal to please them." The man doesn't look at Alkur, he's watching the people with a hint of contempt.

Alkur finds his voice, "What about the two men; were they part of the sacrifice?"

"We deal with crimes justly here. The two men are petty thieves caught by their own kind stealing. The natives have their methods of dealing with this and I have mine. I believe mine to be more effective if a bit more harsh."

"I see." Alkur's voice is now clear and calm. He treads cautiously as he inquires further.

"What happens to those who wish to live unmolested?"

"We deal with problems swiftly. I offer everyone the opportunity to join us. If they refuse, I make another offer, perhaps even a counteroffer. I don't take refusals lightly. Further resistance is not allowed. They soon get the message."

"Those on the poles." Alkur's leaves the question hanging.

The man looks at Alkur for the first time. "One tribe has resisted my authority for some time. It's a bad example. I haven't destroyed them, yet, and am ransoming some of their people."

"The chief's daughter"?

"That's right." He pauses and then says, "I know all about you, Alkur." His eyes return to the crowd who remain contentedly eating before them.

"How do you know my name?" Alkur guesses that the shaman described him in earlier communications.

"Suffice it to say, your arrival was foretold by my people years ago. I am Saail."

Alkur's thinking suddenly clears, Saail... I know that name. It was tied up with my father and Salkuzzar. Alkur is surprised to find his memories have clouded. Atlantis seems so far away and so long ago – a past life he may have read about.

"I arrived here like you, a refugee in an unknown land, far from Atlantis." He sighs and looks at Alkur for a moment, possibly remembering. "We had a very advanced civilization. I was a high Alta priest of the Law of One, helping to rebel against the Sons of Belial."

His face clears and his eyes grew cold. "I was selected to infiltrate the Sons of Belial and steal their plans. However..." Saail laughs, "I was in fact secretly planted into the Law of One by Belial himself tasked with exposing and destroying it."

Again, he glances at Alkur. "I knew your father, a wise but stupidly stubborn man. He discovered my treachery and exposed me first." He pauses, and looking at Alkur without expression says, "You look a lot like your father. Even without my intelligence sources, I would have known you as Ellm's son."

"I won't bore you with the whole history. My failure angered Belial and I was banished from the order and Atlantis. The rebellion by the Law of One failed and many were executed. Your father became the hunted with a price on his head. Yet he, like you, escaped. He had to save his life. It was only later that your father arrived to this land. This was no coincidence. The Gods planned it this way. We were destined to finish where we left off." He smiles.

Alkur is confused. His father was died in the fire…or was he? He remembers: This is Salkuzzar's father. He keeps his face void of expression, which isn't too difficult since it is coated with dirt and blood.

"What… happened?"

"Your father taught the natives well. His growing stature and power directly challenged my reign. I had no choice but to confront and destroy him."

Alkur repeats slowly, "What happened to him?"

With his eyes on the crowds, Saail says in a matter-of-fact tone, "After many years of fighting, he was destroyed of course. He was very brave. Anything more, you'll have to find out from the natives. It's not worth discussing."

Only his fatigue keeps Alkur from reacting. Did this mean his father didn't die in the fire and that he is now sitting next to his murderer? They fall silent, perhaps nothing more needs to be said.

Throughout the evening, dancers and musicians play before Alkur and Saail. Food is plentiful but Alkur's mind is scattered. What happened to his father? What would happen to Asa-masa-ee and the chief's daughter? Where is Caphala and Elchi, and Rariru? His head nods. He is too tired and drifting.

He begins plotting his escape.

Chapter 47

Alkur is back in prison. The pain from his wound has lessened, but he finds his muscles still fight him when he tries to move. Drumming and loud voices filter through the camp. He is not sure how much time has passed. Alkur slowly moves to the door and peers through its small window. Outside, Saail is surrounded by loyal native tribesmen while it looks like tribal chiefs in their ceremonial regalia are presenting some sort of tribute. Saill, atop his throne, receives the gifts like a god. Alkur almost laughs, thinking how godforsaken this place is.

He crawls back to a corner of his cell and rests his head in his hands. His eyes close. He's ready for the lessons of the past. Alkur quiets his mind and fills himself with energy. He grounds and aligns his energy centers. He concentrates on his third eye and attunes himself to his line of intentionality, expanding his energy field till it fills the room, then the camp, then into the land, the sky and across the universe. He is lighter and freer as he ascends into the sacred space of his multidimensionality.

Alkur finds himself following on a dark path through an ancient forest with enormous trees. The trees allow the sky to send only wisps of light to the path. Ahead, the path forks. The main trail leads to a clearing; it's well-trodden and the way is clear. The other branch is less so, with high grass and bushes obscuring the way. He stops, looks in both directions to decide which one to take.

A noise startles him awake just as he was about to choose. The dream is lost as guards enter and pull him to his feet. Roughly, he is jostled along a track by a river. It looks eerily like the area where they were ambushed. He wonders again where the others are, and where Hulos is being held.

After a while, they arrive at a small clearing with an elevated hut in the center. Alkur is shoved up the steps and nearly stumbles into a spacious, beautifully decorated loft. The floor is polished mahogany and the room is open to the forest canopy. A stone hearth with a small fire stands in one corner.

Sitting on an improvised stretcher is the frail figure of Saail. He motions Alkur to come forward and sit; at a second signal the guards bow and back away.

Alkur looks around, then says drily "We have to stop meeting like this." His even tone belies the sarcasm of his words.

Saail looks at him and without any greeting asks, "What is your mission?"

Alkur looks at the floor ignoring the question. Then he again looks out at the treetops watching the nearby birds. Their colorful feathers are unusual and new to Alkur.

"Make no mistake, we knew what you were up to before you began."

"Then, why ask me? You have your sources among the locals. And who is 'we'?"

Saail pauses. "You surely have grasped the consequences for those who rebel. They hang from the stakes at the camp's entry as a warning to everyone."

In a moment of cool clarity, Alkur realizes that he won't be killed today. Saail needs him for something. In a conversational tone, Alkur asks, "What do you want from these people?"

"These so-called people have given their complete allegiance to me in return for their freedom and security and an interest in the spoils."

"What do you give them that they do not already possess?"

Saail almost laughs, "A greater vision of themselves, being part of something greater than themselves. They can …."

Alkur cuts him off. He doesn't try to disguise his contempt, "You've enslaved these people to suit your own selfish desires. They've been forced, against their will, into submission. There is no freedom here— no hope for them and their culture. This is a sham, a lie and you know it. Don't bother to feed me your empty rhetoric."

Saail leans slightly forward and shouts, "Enough!" The guards are surprised at the sudden outburst. They quickly recover and look straight ahead. Alkur knows he has pushed a sensitive button. Interesting, he thinks, there must be a way to use this.

In a slightly lower voice, he continues, "You don't tell me about what is right or wrong. You very much forget yourself."

Saail, sits back and looking relaxed, says "You will tell me where the skull is."

"Skull?"

Alkur looks at him and realizes that Saail must have known about it from the shaman. This is what he meant by 'we knew what you were up to.' Perhaps negotiation and not denial is the best approach.

"Release my friends and the chief's daughter."

Saail abruptly laughs and then shakes his head. "Do you think for a moment that I will allow you to dictate terms to me?" He laughs again, and then says seriously, "You have until sunrise tomorrow to think this over. I want the skull. At that time I will decide your friend's fate."

Saail motions to the guards. "Put him with the others." Alkur is grabbed on both sides and escorted from the hut.

At the edge of the clearing, one of the guards ties a blindfold around Alkur's head. From the terrain, Alkur realizes they are on a different path. He hears the river, yet he knows he is going somewhere new. He still hears drumming, along with a humming sound and can feel the hot, sunlight on his back. They walk for some time before the guards stop and remove the blindfold. Ahead of him, Alkur sees two warriors with tall spears standing in the sunlight guarding a large hut. He is pushed into the hut and falls to the floor. His eyes take a moment to adjust to the dark but then he sees Asa-masa-ee leaning against the wall and Caphala lying on his back resting on his arm, the other covered in blood and in a sling. They share glances of welcome and relief. They are together once again.

Chapter 48

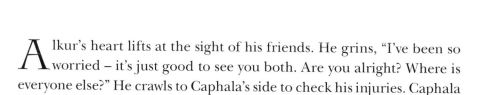

Alkur's heart lifts at the sight of his friends. He grins, "I've been so worried – it's just good to see you both. Are you alright? Where is everyone else?" He crawls to Caphala's side to check his injuries. Caphala raises his arm saying "It's nothing. Just a small tear." Alkur embraces both of them in turn then sits against the wall.

Asa-masa-ee, tired but relieved, says "We thought you and Ilax were dead, Alkur. We didn't know what happened." Like the men, she is dirty and her clothes are scuffed and torn.

"Ilax was with me. In the ambush, our canoe got stuck in the river and we had to leave it. The last time I saw her, she was trying to protect me from an attack. She was... I don't know what happened after that." His voice trails off a little; his own words ring hollowly in his ears. He thinks he should have taken better care of her.

Caphala interjects, "Our canoe overturned during the ambush and we were carried downstream. By sheer luck, we escaped the fighting. The others were not so lucky. We made our way out of the water into the jungle and evaded them as long as we could before their trackers caught up to us. We've been here ever since. They feed us and keep us alive – but we don't know what's going on."

Alkur nods, "I don't know much either. But ..."

He starts to tell them about Saail when Caphala interrupts, "We've heard rumbling sounds coming from up river. Most nights there is a lot of commotion. As if they are mobilizing, as if something big is imminent."

Alkur considers this. "They have captured Hulos, the chief's daughter, and say they are going to ransom her in exchange for the tribe's submission. Their leader, the one who has enslaved most of the natives, is from Atlantis. He came here years ago." He pauses, "Do you know where Hulos is being held?"

Asa-masa-ee and Caphala trade looks and both shake their heads. In the meantime, Asa-masa-ee has peeled back the rough cloth on Alkur's wounds. "Hold still and let me clean this." She reaches for a small bowl of water. Alkur's breath catches as she pulls the rags away from the open wound.

After a moment, he says, "We must find her. They won't expect us to help her; we may have the advantage of surprise."

"How do we find her, penned up here?" asks Caphala

"I don't know. But we must find a way. Together, we can figure this out."

Asa-masa-ee ponders a moment then says, "Let's go over everything we know about where we are and the men that captured us."

Caphala snorts, "Well, that's not much, but it's a beginning." They begin going over what little they've learned.

That night Alkur begins planning their escape. Just the idea of taking action raises his energy and optimism. They must first find the chief's daughter and then the low frequency generator. After all, that was the original mission. It must be destroyed to keep the low energy from sapping their will. Along the way, he and Caphala must find weapons. Surely, Saail and his forces had decimated the village to capture Hulos. He had to assume the village was completely destroyed. But then, how could he ransom her? And what about the others? Elchi must have hidden the skull or else Saail wouldn't ask for it. Or would he? Alkur feels his thinking twist – he's making it too complicated. Keep it simple. Find Hulos and the generator before they are all murdered. It's only a matter of time. Better act now.

That night he can't sleep. The pain is growing unbearable. He tries the Atlantean healing sounds again, but doesn't feel the same focus and effectiveness. By the time dawn slips between the slats of the hut, Alkur is sharing his plan with Asa-masa-ee and Caphala. In a hushed tone he tells them;

"We must check the guard's shift, their habits and routines."

Caphala had already considered this, "The guard's change every morning. They seem to ignore us most of the time."

"Good."

"Alkur, it will be very difficult to get past them through the main entrance and even if we did neutralize them, it would raise an alarm."

Alkur nods in agreement. He is right. There has to be another way.

"Let's dig a hole by the far wall of the hut large enough to crawl out. The soil seems soft enough and I haven't heard anything going on back there; it must back up to the forest."

Caphala and Asa-masa-ee look disapprovingly at Alkur as he continues, "I'll sneak out this evening, get some bearing on our situation and return later."

Caphala hesitates. "It's too risky. You don't know where she is, or if she's alive. There are people running all around here. Besides, the guards will notice your absence. They check every hour or so. It makes more sense to escape together, head for the river, find others to reconstitute our forces if we can and attack later."

Alkur considers this for a moment, then counters. "If we all go together, we may all be lost. But if I go alone, and something happens to me, at least you will be alive and ready to follow."

Alkur goes on, "Remember, we're here to destroy the generator and live another day. Besides, Hulos may know what's happened to everyone and whether her father will attempt a rescue or an attack on the generator. That is, if he is still alive. I think we need to find her first."

Caphala reluctantly concedes. As Alkur and Caphala begin digging with a couple of broken roof branches that had fallen into the enclosure, Asa-masa-ee scoops up the dirt and shapes it into the crude form of a sleeping Alkur. They each keep watch on the guards outside.

In the early morning darkness, Alkur eases his way through the short tunnel and quietly crawls away from the hut. So far so good, the guards are sleeping. He stops to cover the outside hole with a few large fronds lying nearby.

Creeping through the darkness, he hears screaming and loud laughter ahead. Alkur drops into the brush for a moment and then cautiously rises behind the trees to look ahead. The screams are a woman's and grow louder.

Outside a small hut, a group of men are drinking and appear to be grabbing at a young woman, pulling at her clothes and pushing her down. She fights back but can't get away from the men who are laughing and now beating her. Suddenly, she rises from a crouched stance and swings hard, hitting one of the men square in the face. The laughter trails off. The man slaps her and throws her to the ground then grabs her arm to drag her toward the trees a short distance from where Alkur is hiding.

Alkur drops to the ground to avoid being seen. The man is small but powerfully built. As the woman tries to crawl away, he just tightens his grip on her arm. She screams and kicks. The man smiles meanly, revealing black and yellow teeth and almost casually sits on top of her. He holds both her arms down and leans in to nuzzle her neck and body. The woman screams and writhes desperately trying to free herself. He slaps her, and is about to punch her when Alkur steps behind him and with his right arm encircles his neck, abruptly pulling him backwards. Alkur throws him headfirst over his hip onto his head, breaking his neck. He throws the limp body to the ground.

The woman looks up alarmed as if she can't believe what's happened. She tries to scoot back, away from the new stranger. Her fear fades a little as Alkur motions for her to be quiet and she recognizes his face in the starlight. He extends an arm to her and in the darkness, whispers, "Hulos!"

Chapter 49

Hulos lets out a deep breath; she has a relieved smile but points, jabbing her finger, towards the group of drunken men who are staggering about and talking in slurred voices close by. Alkur thinks, better get out of here before they begin missing this guy. He gently wipes the blood from her forehead then turns and motions her to follow him. Still crouching, they try to quietly scurry into the forest. A short time later, they stop to listen. They hear nothing but the rustle of a breeze in the foliage.

Off to the right, an elaborate house stands alone in a small clearing. Hulos grabs his hand as she points it out. The grandness and permanence of this hut indicates a resident of some importance. Alkur guesses it must be Saail's but there are no guards in sight. He barely makes the presence of the palanquin next to the house.

Alkur motions for Hulos to hide and wait. She kneels in the brush, her head bowed below the thick leaves. Alkur slowly scans the clearing and not seeing anyone, trots low across the open ground to the house. He silently climbs the steps and slowly moves through the entryway. His eyes used to the darkness, Alkur makes out the figure of Saail asleep on a bed pushed into the corner. Alkur runs through his options – the thought of killing him now seems like a good idea. He starts across the floor but realizes he can't do it. He stops; why does this keep happening to me he wonders.

A commotion comes from behind. He turns to leave but is immediately surrounded by a menacing mass of bodies with spears, bows pointed at him.

Two guards grab him and push him forward, back into the room. Saail walks from behind a dark passageway adjacent to the bed. From under the bed blanket, a small boy emerges. With a smirk on his face, Saill says to Alkur, "I've been expecting you. Predictable."

A guard knocks Alkur to the ground. Alkur regains his footing but stays low. He stares defiantly at the small dark figure of Saail.

"It seems you have company with you." Saail watches as the guards bring in Hulos.

Saail, in a voice that signals his patience is running thin, says "What were you intending to do? Kill me once and for all?"

"It crossed my mind."

"Of course, you could not go through with it. Were you afraid of acting on the darkness within, or perhaps you only had pity for the fate that would befall your comrades if you went through with it?" Saail seems vaguely curious.

Alkur looks at him then turns to see the others. Yes, it was true. He could have attacked -- but he would only have killed a child. Saail would have survived and his friends and he would have died. If he had managed to find and kill Saail, perhaps then his empire would crumble. He looked at his hands and knew he could dispatch him even now, break his neck before the guards could stop him. He would die of course. But it would be succumbing to the darkness. He'd be just like Saail. He has total freedom to choose, yet can't. The thought just hangs in his mind. He hesitates. The moment passes and he does nothing. He says nothing. He thinks how odd it is that he's not afraid. He feels nothing.

"Tell me, why are you really here? To finish what your father could not do?"

You're greedy Saail just like your son, Salkuzzar. But worse, Alkur thought. He's silent as the lessons of the past swarm into his consciousness. He's calm and grounded.

Saail watches; he must see the determination etched on Alkur's face. "So, it's true, you're here to avenge your father's death." His sarcasm is unmistakable. "You may even have a cock-eyed notion to bring justice here. Am I right? Your father tried and failed. He was, at the end, a worthless man."

Alkur tenses at the defamation of his father. It's obvious that Saail is trying to provoke him with contempt. Alkur struggles to maintain his composure. He takes a deep breath and starts to raise his energy.

"You are a fool to think you can destroy me with your power. I am stronger. And even if you did get rid of me, my spirit will live on."

Unexpectedly, Alkur feels a sudden peace course through his body as he looks directly into Saail's eyes. Beneath the decayed flesh and sunken eyes, he sees a spark. There's a glimmer of light; it must be Saail's higher-self energies. In those dark eyes, Alkur sees the mask of darkness, fear, and corruption surrounding and choking Saail's soul. He could feel it before but now he sees the mask that hides his weakness and the frantic ego lashing out to project its energy. Evil cannot love, it can only control others.

Like Saail, Alkur realizes that he too has been living his whole life in a fear that he's been unable to face and transform. In many ways, he's like Saail; he's afraid of his own power, of losing everything, of not being in control, or being insignificant, a fate worse than death itself. This is what he's been fighting all along -- a perpetual darkness masking his true essence and the core of his being. And that's manifested. But he sees that he has a choice now.

Alkur says, "You're gravely mistaken. You won't destroy me as you did my father."

Saail laughs quietly but there is steel in his voice, "No, you'll see that it's you who are mistaken ... about many things. I can feel your anger and hatred. Yes, my friend, you've been betrayed too. Only, I chose to face it and seek my own justice through strength and power. I haven't done so badly, wouldn't you say?"

He tilts his bony head back lightly as he smiles. "Go ahead; you want to kill me. Try. Be like me. We will become one with our mutual hatred." His laughter trails off in a sigh.

Alkur is confused again. What to do? He feels alone, lost. Follow your heart.

For a brief instant, Alkur sees a murky image of himself standing over Saail's body. He'll be known as the one who saved them.

Follow your heart.

Looking at Saail he finally speaks, "You and I are more alike than you may think. I will not fight or kill you. No. I will not lower myself and yes, I hate the dark energies in you and can see what they are doing to me, but I can also see the divine spark of your soul essence. Saail, you just don't see it as I do. I chose to acknowledge this and to change."

Alkur thinks, if there was ever a time to receive your guidance it's now. Don't let me down, Thoth.

Then, Alkur rises and approaches Saail. The guards tense but do not move. Standing there, Alkur looks at the wrinkled white face, smells the corrupt breath, and takes in the death grin. He looks at Saail with deep love and compassion. Alkur places his hands on Saail's shoulders. The guards are speechless, waiting. Saail starts to back away, but can't.

Alkur begins chanting, invoking the powers of spirits and angels, as he channels healing energy through his hands and heart. Saail is frozen. His eyes close slightly as if in trance. If a dark heart is touched by pure compassion and forgiveness, it can experience love again. No one is beyond redemption. Alkur with his eyes closed then moves his hands to the sides of Saail's head.

Then, abruptly, Alkur sees Saail transform into a huge, hideous creature that lunges at him knocking him backwards. The rest of the room is in a fog. Alkur can't move. He remembers the trials of the cave and the creature that was defeated with love, not force. He tunes into his heart and continues to radiate love while calling in all his helpers.

He notices the creature that was Saail slowly shrinking and beginning to dematerialize.

Alkur then sees the spirit of his father Ellm in front of him in a white golden light, watched and protected by an entourage of enormous light beings that have moved between himself and the creature.

Saail's limp body lies on the floor. He appears lifeless. He watches as his father reaches for Saail as if inviting him into the light. Saail tries to hide by crawling away, as if feeling unworthy and shameful to be seen in the light. Ellm walks towards Saail and, after a short exchange, they both enter a column of light, hand in hand. Alkur knows that Saail's spirit has entered a different dimension of consciousness and that they are old souls, old friends, old enemies that have spent lifetimes together, helping each other's soul evolution.

Alkur stares at the lifeless body of Saail in the flickering light. He walks to it, kneels, touches his face and closes Saail's eyes.

Chapter 50

The camp is under attack. Loud cries and yells cut through the darkness. Alkur moves to stand next to Hulos; he quickly looks around to assess the danger. The guards, who had been standing dumbstruck, suddenly fall cut down by spears and swift swords. The young boy huddles under the bed. In the distance large jumping flames engulf the camp.

Alkur runs to the entrance, and amidst the chaos is surprised to see Rariru and a small contingent of warriors searching the huts before they are set afire. Their eyes meet across the fire light smoke. Alkur pulls Hulos out of the house, and they run towards the trees. Even at some distance, Alkur sees Rariru smile as he runs to them. His gentle embrace of Hulos says it all. Behind him, one of the warriors torches Saail's home.

Alkur looks around for Caphala and Asa-masa-ee in the confusion. He runs along a dark trail, past burning buildings to the hut he had escaped only an hour before. It was empty, and floating embers were blowing onto the roof. Where are they? He thinks they may have used the chaos to escape, they'd probably head to the river. But, as he moves away from the camp, Alkur hears a low throbbing hum. He follows the sound.

The cave hiding the crystal generator is concealed beneath thick underbrush half-way up a mountain, just a short distance from the camp.

Asa-masa-ee had said that the natives called it the mountain of fire for its powerful and strange energies.

The sun is beginning to rise as Alkur finds the trail. From his vantage point below, he sees guard posts along the winding path, and further up the mountain steps have been cut into the rock. Guide ropes are anchored to the rock and the trail is lighted with flaming poles that finish at the large carved out entrance.

Alkur is torn between confirming the generator's location and destroying it, or looking for his friends. I've got to go for it while everyone is at the camp fighting fire, he thinks. This could be the best opportunity. A few of the warriors have followed Alkur and stop with him at the bottom of the hill. After a moment, Alkur scrambles up the trail, stopping every minute or so to look ahead for trouble. He knows that the warriors have his back. It's a hard climb even with the guide ropes. At the top, he sees the valleys and rivers below. The generator must be able to stun across nearly a hundred miles.

As they approach Alkur can see the generator. The six-sided stone crystal generator is huge, cylindrical in length, and carved like a prism along the top and bottom. A moveable capstone sits on top, used to concentrate incoming rays of energy and distribute current out across the region. The great crystal is mounted just outside the cave entrance on a large wooden platform maybe twelve feet off the ground. Enormous wooden logs act as wheels under the platform and move it to and from the interior of the cave. Alkur recognizes the design. The one in Atlantis had collected solar, lunar, stellar, atmospheric, and earth energies, and by concentrating those could generate the power to illuminate Atlantis. This model had evidently been reprogrammed by Saail to emit frequencies of despair and defeat. Just being near it slowed Alkur down.

Looking down the other side of the mountain, Alkur sees hundreds of small human shapes, covered in dirt and sweat, trudging slowly up and down the hill. Even at dawn, they are working, slouched over under their heavy loads of yellow and red rocks. Here he sees the remnants of the Saail's forces. Native guards, armed with spears, keep close watch on the miners. Everyone avoids the cave. The dreadful hum is directed toward the mines and, the closer one gets, the worse the effects.

Alkur looks in horror at the mining scene below, as Rariru and his war party climb the mountain. Alkur stops behind a rock at the entrance and watches them rise along the trail. This is good news; it must mean that the opposition in Saail's camp has been vanquished. As they grope their way to the top, he sees that they've put something over their ears to muffle the low throbbing, and they are communicating by hand signals.

Without warning, a group of guards rush to the cave entry to stop the warriors. The fighting is brutal, and hand to hand. One by one, the guards are cut down by arrows and spears. In the commotion, Alkur can see some guards begin to pull the generator into the cave. Afraid they may hide it, Alkur rushes ahead, knocking one guard down and spearing the other.

He knows the only way to dismantle the generator is to remove the large capstone. He remembers Ilax telling him that in early years, Atlantis had been taken over by the Dark priesthood, and that they had used a low frequency to confuse and cripple their opponents. Alkur is pretty sure the generator is the same thing. She had also warned him that anger, fear, or any negative emotions could make one vulnerable to the dark energy forces.

Alkur feels the menacing energy coming from within the cave. He has to think fast. Then, he recalled Ilax telling him that he had all 12 of the universal life force strands within him – and that was the unique inner power of the Atlanteans. With focus and concentration, he could manifest anything he wanted and even change matter. Since Atlanteans believe all matter is alive, it was amenable to change if directed by universal life force energy.

Alkur feels the confidence surge through his body. He just needs to get to a state of complete harmony and love, which is the highest possible vibration. He could then reprogram the crystals with his energy. Ilax had told him the theory, but she never taught him exactly how to do it. Alkur thinks, focus on the crystal, transmit positive energy and the low frequency will stop. Great. How?

Turning his back on the men still fighting on the bluff, Alkur momentarily tunes into the energies of light, bringing them in for strength and protection. He begins to send the energies of light to the capstone. Nothing seems to happen. He tries again. Nothing. It feels blocked. He then invokes the powers of the highest realms, and requests that the crystal capstone be deprogrammed. Again, he feels the dark energies resisting.

Through the mayhem, Hulos appears by his side. She smiles tentatively and points at the generator. Surprised Alkur looks at her and nods. She knows, he thinks, she knows that together they can neutralize the dark energies. Without words, they both align their energies and hold hands. There's an immediate shift in the frequency.

Hulos pulls him up and walks toward the generator. Together they climb the platform, Hulos in the lead. At the top, they face the enormous quartz crystal. It is throwing off beams of dirty yellow and brown light coupled with a distinctive low vibration humming sound. They cover their ears and push the stone trying to dislodge it. It barely moves. Again they try, and finally feel it shift slightly. Another warrior climbs on top and with their combined strength; they push the crystal off the platform. It crashes to the ground below, seems to pause mid-air and then bounces down the mountain side.

Suddenly, the sounds stop.

Alkur and Hulos embrace with surprised looks on the faces. They have done it. He turns and sees that it is Patob, the young man from the canoe, who has helped demolish the machine. "Well done!" he slaps the man on the shoulder then turns to hug Hulos again.

Chapter 51

The celebrations last long into the night. Despite the damage done to a number of huts in the camp from Saail's attack, people are hopeful and cheerful. Families gather around a huge bonfire blazing in the central clearing.

Rariru, Alkur, and the others share the warm firelight on the cool evening, singing, dancing and telling stories. There's a huge sense of success, accomplishment, and new found freedom. Most of Saail's warriors readily surrendered and quickly left to return to their villages and rebuild their lives. Now freed from the caves, the men are once again reunited with their friends and loved ones. The mood is festive, flushed with relief that the terrible pain and suffering they have endured for so long in finally is over. It's tempered only by the sad memories of those who did not survive.

After a long, soothing bath and delicious meal, Alkur walks around the village quietly. He's glad for the celebration and grateful that the worst is now behind them. Everyone is accounted for except Ilax. He wonders what happened and whether he will ever see her again. He knows that without her, he would never have been able to reach out with love and compassion to evil. Alkur is still light-headed with that amazing revelation.

As he rounds a small cluster of huts, Alkur sees Hulos standing away from the fire looking up at the starlit sky. She was part of the miracle. As he approaches slowly, she turns to face him. Without thinking, he reaches for her hands and holds them tightly. Her eyes are happy; she's pleased to be near him. Alkur gently pulls her closer to him and kisses her firmly on the mouth. He holds her tightly, feeling her breathing. She closes her eyes, and she begins to kiss his neck and tears run down her face. He gently wipes the tears from her face and leads her to an abandoned hut. She whispers to him gesturing with her hands to her mouth and heart smiling to get the sounds right, "I... Hulos."

Alkur surprised to hear her speak his language says, "I know, Hulos. I am Alkur."

As he lies next to her, he smiles as he looks into her sparkling eyes, and gently traces his fingers around her face. He then kisses her mouth slowly moving his hands to her breasts. That evening they make love.

The next morning, Rariru and tribal elders lead Alkur and other Atlanteans to the village's ancient burial grounds. It was a different route, walking easy trails through cool forests, not along the river. After several hours, Alkur sees the familiar stone structures they found when they first left the beach. Rariru slowly climbs the steps to the large flat rock. It was here that Alkur and Caphala had filled their flasks with water.

Rariru ceremoniously turns to face the small crowd. After a brief moment of silence, he beings speaking. Asa-masa- ee translates,

"We gather here as one, members of different tribes and races, to celebrate our freedom. We honor our ancestors for their wisdom and guidance in leading us to this sacred moment together. We acknowledge with gratitude our forefather At-ach-u-chu, the fair skinned man of peace, who came to use and gave us hope, freedom, and above all, his love."

Rariru pauses momentarily looking at Alkur and continues, "His spirit lives with us again and, all our ancestors will guide us as we move forward."

Afterwards, Alkur cannot help but feel his father's presence. Only this time, love, not sadness fills his heart. It's always been there under the grief and anger. Now, his heart can feel love, once again.

Then Rariru signals to Alkur to come forward. Not sure what was going on, Alkur climbs the steps and stops in front of Rariru and bows his head. Reaching into a narrow channel adjacent to the rock platform, Rariru fills his hands with water and drizzles it over Alkur's head. He embraces Alkur and nods approvingly.

Asa-masa-ee steps up to Alkur as he descends the stairs. She says, "The chief said the water purifies and blesses us. It cleans the old energies so the new may come in." While she speaks, the others line up for Rariru's water blessing. To his surprise, Alkur is moved by the ceremony. The ritual is comforting and starts a new life for everyone there.

As everyone gathers afterwards, Asa-mas-lee tells Alkur that Rariru wants Alkur to accompany him. The three of them walk along a narrow path out of the forest, and into an open field of high grass and beautiful multicolored tropical flowers. A stone pyramid, built with a flat spot on top, sits in the middle of the field. It towers over them as they grow close. Each side of the pyramid is carved with inscriptions and pictures. On one facet is a picture of a man holding up a small child. On another, there is a scene of an earthquake or volcanic eruption and its chaotic aftermath. The third depicts a mountain emitting strange lines, scattering over the valleys. On the last rock surface is a group of people standing by a lake in the midst of brutal fighting. On top of the pyramid, there is a skull carved from stone. Alkur is struck by this. All his experiences, and maybe those of his father – are etched here.

Rariru addresses those gathered. As Alkur listens Asa-masa-lee tells him, "Under this pyramid is where your father is buried Alkur. We will never forget what he gave us and honor him as one of our own. His spirit lives in us."

Alkur struggles for a moment to find the right words, then with tears in his eyes says simply "Tell him I am very grateful."

Alkur slowly walks up to the pyramid. He kneels in front of it alone and grateful to be reunited with his father once again.

Rariru then invites Alkur to perform a healing ceremony. Alkur decides to use water and fire since both are elemental forces that cleanse, purify and transform. They help bridge the chasm one feels when the world changes so quickly, as they have experienced.

A little while later, everyone convenes by a circle of stones in a clearing. In the center there is a large hole filled with branches and timber. Rariru asks all to gather closer around the circle then nods to Alkur to begin. Alkur smudges himself, and then the entire group, with sage. Its fragrance drifts upward into the crisp air. In a gesture of respect, he lifts both hands skyward, offering the remaining sage to the gods.

The fire is lit. Alkur acknowledges the five directions, and calls in the spirits and powers of creation to pay attention and hear the prayers. Then he opens the doorways that lead to the spirit world and invites the spirits to observe and participate in the ceremony. He calls upon the Creator above and the ancient Earth Mother below. Lastly, he acknowledges the indwelling spirit, and declares the circle open and activated for ceremony. The fire is now ready to receive prayers. Alkur approaches the fire first for his own communion with spirit. Soon, Rariru and all those gathered approach the fire and kneel before it. They are all communing with spirit in a timeless exchange of humility, love and reverence.

In the ceremony Alkur sees images of his parents walking towards the fire holding hands. He knows that now he can hold their memories in his heart with love and finally forgive himself and their murderers. He has found peace.

Chapter 52

The orange-reddish glow of the sun as it disappears beyond the lake creates a surreal kaleidoscope of color on the barely rippling waters. The forest on its banks forms broad shadows resembling ancient deities. A cool breeze cleans the air.

Alkur stares over the lake, caught up in his own thoughts. He realizes how much he has changed, the journey has profoundly transformed him, and he's grateful. He's had to face himself and his dark side. He realizes how close he came to almost losing that fight. As he watches the sky darken, he commits to integrating and becoming the change he's tasted. Memories of his life in Atlantis, and Ampero, slip in. A part of him still longs for the land of his birth.

"Alkur."

He turns. She has come upon him through the dusk.

"Ilax!" Alkur smiles broadly, he's glad to know she's survived. They hug and hold each other just to be sure. Releasing, he steps back to look at her. She's radiant in a brightly colored native tunic which makes her luminous green eyes look as mysterious as the forest.

"Where have you been? I couldn't find you and I thought you were…" he asks.

Ilax just cuts him off. She's not going to relive the ambush and its aftermath right now. "I'm sorry I missed the celebrations. Congratulations on your success. I am very proud of you." She drops his hands and grins at him.

"Ilax, I have you to thank, for everything." Alkur pauses, there's so much to tell and he has to get it right. "I've seen the worst of myself. You showed me how to face my demons and be true to myself. You have showed me how to tap into my better self. Without you, I would have not..."

Before he can finish, she puts her fingers on his lips, "Hush now, dear one."

Taking his hand, she pulls him to the soft grass along the shore. "It's beautiful," she says pointing out at the magenta and purple afterglow.

After a few minutes, Ilax decides it's the right time to tell him how she was wounded and captured. She escaped her captors by shapeshifting into a hawk, then providing overflight protection for him and the natives to help them to find the camp and generator. Thoth guided her actions the whole time. She pauses, "Alkur, I asked Thoth that we be reunited for this evening."

It was not spoken, but Alkur knew this would be the last time he would see Ilax. There's silence, each immersed in their own thoughts for quite some time. Then, while holding hands, Ilax whispers, "Lie back and relax. Close your eyes, dear one, and be still."

Ilax moves next to him and allows her body to touch his. Alkur closes his eyes and is soon floating inside a tunnel of white light, surrounded by a whirlpool of vibrant colors. All his senses are alive as he feels the assuring warmth of unconditional love.

Ilax appears before him, now dressed in pure white and enveloped in a golden halo. There is an expansion of the throat centers and an exchange of light energy, as white light descends over both of them and beams of light enter each of their energy centers. This is a followed by a sudden surge of energy along the sacred paths in their spines from their lower back to the crowns of their heads. Then joined to her, he feels his body quiver in etheric orgasms that send him into sheer bliss. Ilax slowly moves closer to him until both of their bodies are touching. A whirlpool of light energy emanates from both of their crowns swirling around their bodies. Ilax then slowly steps away and kisses Alkur. It's a moment of divine union.

Wordlessly, Ilax tells Alkur how much she loves him; but despite her desire, she cannot fulfill her purpose as Alkur's lover. The greater love is now the bond between him and Hulos, his new partner for this life. Ilax tells Alkur she will continue to guide him in his many lifetimes, when he decides to return to spirit, they will be together once again. Alkur is not sure exactly when Ilax leaves, but in the gathering darkness, she's gone.

At dawn the next day, Alkur and Hulos stand on the lake's bank holding hands. They quietly take in the breathtaking view around them, capturing its beauty and energies. There is an immense sense of abundance and power around them. It's the universal power of One Mind, of divine compassion that says what they see outside is also within them.

Alkur turns to face Hulos, kisses her forehead, and says, "I love you. I'm so happy you're here." She gazes at him with love and understanding.

Alkur feels the presence of the past all around, his father, Ampero, Ilax, friends who shared his life. They are pleased for him. He knows that they paved the way. In the distance a dark speck flies above -- a condor, an omen promising another bright tomorrow.

Chapter 53

APRIL 5, 2012
1448 AVENIDA GUILLAUME

I'd carefully listed all the clues I had about Oscar's death and the skull; it wasn't much:

An old man taking pictures at the lake then giving them, unsolicited, to the newspaper reporter
Dr. Guerra, the dead diver in the cave, which may have nothing to do with anything
The green Falcon
Someone knew where Oscar lived
Oscar's guarded behavior at the lab; and his murder
My certainty that the skull was the target
The picture of the woman

What was going on?

A couple of days had passed without hearing from the police about their investigation. I met Carlos and some friends at the pub for our usual jazz night. Aware that I might be followed, I kept an eye out for anything unusual as we went.

I asked Carlos if he had any ideas about where to secure the skull. He offered to guard it for me saying that nobody notices him, he's inconspicuous he said grinning. I laughed and considered but hesitated as he made the offer. I guess I really didn't want the skull out of my reach. Carlos insisted on his trustworthiness and that he would safeguard it with his life.

In the meantime, the skull sat in a hollowed-out bread loaf on my pantry shelf. Dr. Epis had agreed that the Institute may not be secure enough but, oddly I thought, left the matter up to me although he gave me the name and number of his contact at the bank.

That evening, my fingers closed around the small skull that Don Julio had given me. I was still carrying it in my pocket. Well, it was a long shot, but the only one I could act on at the moment.

I retrieved the skull from the bread loaf and shoved it under the car seat. Since Oscar's death, I was more vigilant. Truth be known; I was terrified. I assumed that the thugs were after the skull and I'd be followed, but then again, that could be police surveillance.

Taking the back roads of the city took me through some unfamiliar neighborhoods. I briefly wondered if I should have brought Carlos or a gun with me. I was relieved when I arrived without incident.

There were no cars on the street. But the lights inside were on as I knocked on Don Julio's door.

He was expecting me and quickly ushered me in, then taking me through a courtyard along a dark path to a shack that overlooked the house. Unlocking the door, he motioned me inside. He looked over his shoulders as if to make sure he was not being seen. The quiet secrecy amplified my illusion of danger.

The room smelled of coca and alcohol. It was covered in rugs and tapestries with designs depicting tales from Andean folklore. Large baskets were stacked on shelves alongside small statues and pictures of the condor and puma. We hadn't said a word.

He turned to me and motioning toward an old carved chair said, "We're safe here for now." Waving his hand around the room, he quietly murmured, "This is where I come to do my work. Sit please."

Still silent, I handed him the bag with the skull. He carefully placed it on the table and then gently pulled it out of the bag. For a moment we both peered at it. Don Julio studied it intently and his eyes grew larger as he seemed to read the symbols under the occipital ridge. He smiled and said a few words to himself in Quechua. A part of me wanted to hear him say something, anything, as he studied the skull. Then without lifting his eyes, he said, "Yes, my friend, we will never be the same again. This is what the world has been waiting for..."

"What do you mean?" I asked. My voice sounded jarring, loud and demanding. I recovered to rephrase it more politely, "Please, tell me about the skull. Can you read the symbols?"

Don Julio raised his eyes and replied "These are bad times, not just in Bolivia, but across the planet. The dark energies are very strong now. Unfortunately, you have seen this firsthand. I am very sorry about your friend Andres. He was a good man. Oscar, is that correct?" He looked genuinely saddened.

"Yes, how did you know?"

His face relaxed slightly as he continued, "The dark energies will not stop at anything. But, it's also a time of great opportunities, like we've never seen on earth. The light is very close. Mankind has the chance to change and evolve, to make the right choices. And you have a big part to play in that."

He smiled, almost eagerly, as he looked at me. I had no clue as to what he was talking about. The scent of coca must be fuzzing my brain I thought.

"What is going on here, Don Julio?" I asked impatiently.

He closed his eyes momentarily, then opened them looking directly at me. "Andres, you have a special mission in this life, and it will affect everyone on earth."

I felt like I had walked into the wrong movie, midway through the showing. I thought to myself, I'm an archeologist for God's sake! I like my life and have no desire to take on some mysterious special mission.

As if reading my mind Don Julio's eyes grew soft as he quietly said, "It's not your career or what you've done that matters here. It's who you are that is most important -- your gift and talents. Your destiny is to bring more light into the world Andres."

Suddenly, I was not surprised. In a weird way it all fit together: our meeting, the theft at the lab, Oscar's death, the growing chaos everywhere. He was right. Strange things were unfolding and I was in somehow right in the middle of some of it.

He reminded me about how psychic I was as a child and my passion for exploring and how it turned into the quest for the cave under the lake and the crystal skull. He emphasized that there were no coincidences and that growing up fatherless gave me resilience and the courage to find a meaningful life. Don Julio also told me that my choice of archeology was a good one. That archeology required mental and emotional discipline, keen interest in history and historical artifacts and science and excellent management skills, traits he felt I had. He also felt it stretched my imagination and tapped my childlike curiosity.

Images and memories were coming back to me as I heard Don Julio's words. Time stopped and I felt as though I'd stepped into a different, foggy space.

"How do you know about me? Who are you?"

"Let's just say I am part of your life now to help you on your new path."

I stared at him. As if reading my mind, he continued, "I understand. It's vague and confusing – but it resonates with your soul. I can tell. You already know the enemy you'll face. You have seen it and have sensed their power and what they can do."

"The skull, they are after the skull. Why?" This is where I walked in. I'd have to think about the rest of the mumbo-jumbo when my head cleared.

"I know you have lots of questions. But you have the power to discover the answers. It's part of your journey – it's what you were born to do."

I took a deep breath. "Are you saying I have the ability to stop them?"

Don Julio nodded affirmatively.

"I can't believe this is happening." A hundred images flashed through my head. "Was this worth Oscar's death? Who is after the skull?

Who gave the reporter the picture? The face of the officer at the ESMA building, it's still unclear to me..."

Don Julio raised his hand to stop the flood of questions. "You are going to have to uncover the answers, Andres. It will take everything you have -- trust and discipline -- to say the course. Listen to your heart and you'll see the path. Follow it. Right now, you just need to decide to commit to this. Your intention will guide you and your journey will unfold. Trust the process, Andres."

"If they are after the skull, what should I do?" I felt like I was grappling for something solid in the fog.

"I suggest you leave it here with me, for now."

"But, they must know by now who you are and will come looking for it. You may be in grave danger."

Don Julio smiled, "I have been in worse situations before. I know how these guys think."

We talked throughout the night. Just before dawn, I left Don Julio's home confused but reassured. I was not sure what I had just accepted.

Chapter 54

APRIL 6, 2012
AVENIDA MERCEDES # 61, LA PAZ, BOLIVIA

B ack home after a brief nap, I settled into the sofa with a cold beer and took my work journal from my briefcase. The pages were covered with copies of the skull designs. I also had Oscar's notes on potentially similar patterns. The carvings on the skull were the biggest mystery. I found myself staring at the pictures almost willing them to talk to me.

I examined each symbol trying to decipher its meaning. Each was unique yet related to the others. Surely, someone wanted the skull because it had some still unexplained power. I figured that the symbols were the source of that power.

After a half hour of fruitless consideration, I set them aside. An old meditation technique came to me. If we're in the realm of psychic power, why not ask the symbols to reveal their message?

I copied each symbol on a separate sheet of paper carefully to get them just right. When I finished I closed my eyes, took a deep breath and tuned into my heart, feeling unconditional love. I have been doing this intuitively for years, but now, as the mysteries of the skull unfolded in my life, I understood the power and my meditations had become a conscious practice. Then, I sent love to each symbol. I asked for clues to help me understand the symbol and its importance.

Slipping into the quiet space of meditation, I saw myself moving through the lines and patterns of the symbols and feeling waves of color wash over me. I sensed distinct vibrations with each symbol. I slipped into a deeper still state. Then a minute later, I felt a slight shift, a soft yet powerful pulse reverberated through my body. My breathing had slowed.

Then, one by one, each symbol appeared in my awareness and with it a unique vibration that resonated in the core of my being. My eyes opened and I started writing next to each drawn symbol. I heard letters of the alphabet, A, K, M, L, R, E, K, I, B, followed by combinations AKMA, LA, AKMA-LA, AKMA-RA, AKMA-RA-LA, AKMA-RA-NA, El-KIBA, AK-EL-KIBA, and RA-MA-TI–MA. They each had a distinct, specific vibratory quality.

The pulse between my eyes intensified. I pronounced each symbol out loud as I had written it. As I did this I opened my eyes and looked at the symbol.

For each symbol I began free writing. For AKMA, I wrote divine power and will, guidance and divine truth. The words just flowed from me. It felt as if this symbol was inviting me to connect with the divine within. The information just came through me. I followed the same process for each symbol. For AKMA-LA, the words angels, divine light, and intuition came to me. As I said the syllables, I felt a subtle shift as if my energy field was being cleansed of darkness and negativity. Somehow, I realized this symbol's meaning was the Light of God. For AKMA-RA-LA, I wrote joy, spiritual growth and awareness, divine light and intuition. These emotions and realizations continued to float into my awareness as the meditation went on until I had written down something for every symbol. The last one, RA-MA-TI-MA was revealed to mean "Everything is blessed—everything is sacred."

As I pronounced the syllables again I received a vision, perhaps a cryptic message of a distant past.

I was in a cave, just a boy of eight or nine. In the middle of the room stood a low altar with a huge quartz skull centered between candles. The young me was dressed in an amethyst robe with a gold necklace and bracelets on each wrist. A woman stood nearby gowned in white with pearls. She announced her name, Ilax, and her status as a Maji, a high priestess of the Law of One. She talked about healing energy and manifestation.

The boy, the young me, was tasked to be the Keeper of the Crystal Skull. I watched as he began to chant and, as he did, the crystal skull lit up. The sounds sent energy coursing through his body; he began to emit a light that completely illuminated the cave. I understood unexpectedly that the power of my conscious thoughts caused the skull to shine. These thoughts had to be of a pure consciousness and then the skull was like a generator that senses thoughts, and acts.

I fell asleep.

Chapter 55

APRIL 9, 2012
AVENIDA MERCEDES # 61, LA PAZ
BOLIVIA

After the skull meditation, and the extraordinary revelations of the symbols, I was stunned. I just didn't know what to think. It all felt true, but how could I explain it to any one? "Oh yes, Dr. Epis, here are the symbol meanings that I dreamt last night..." I could just imagine how that conversation would go and how quickly I'd be relieved of my duties with an admonition to take a long vacation.

I missed Oscar. The lab wasn't right without him. He would have listened and perhaps found a connection between my odd notes on the symbols and some ancient culture or belief system. But Oscar was gone and there was nothing in his work journal suggesting anything unusual.

I called Don Julio but he didn't answer. I wasn't ready to tell Carlos. Thankfully, I had a weekend to reflect on this miracle – or mystery— before I had to go back to work. But it didn't quite work out that way.

I was awakened by masked men who broke into my home, wrestled me from the bed to the floor and pummeled me with blows to my body and head. Next thing I knew, I was lying somewhere, almost unconscious, bruised, in pain with my hands handcuffed in back and feet hackled. My shoulders were stretched in some awful way that ached relentlessly.

A hood was pulled down over my head; I felt like I was suffocating. I couldn't tell if it was day or night. Deep breaths dispelled my panicky anxiety. I listened carefully for anything, a voice, an engine, anything.

As I came to, I was really pissed. "Where the fuck am I?" kept running through my head. Then, I heard a door open and a deep staccato voice saying, "Levanatalo...y traiga al hijo de puta. Pick up and bring the son of a bitch!"

Unseen hands lifted me to my feet and pulled me outside to a waiting car, its engine running. The hood slipped to the side giving me a peek out. It was night and I was being loaded into an olive drab Ford Falcon. Jesus, this is the same car I saw by Oscar's home the night he was killed. I was shoved headfirst onto the floor of the back seat. The car smelled of sweat and shit as if these guys were living in it. We sped away in the darkness.

It could have been an hour later that we stopped. I was hustled down a flight of stairs and dropped on the floor of a cold, dark room. I heard the door slam and lock. There was some commotion in an adjacent room but I couldn't make it out. Sometime later, I was abruptly awakened by the door opening and a man removing my hood. My eyes flinched in the sudden brightness. A man at the doorway watched me. He wore a dark suit and tie, a very professional and clean cut appearance. He was medium height and a stocky build, rather heavyset, perhaps in his sixties, a receding hairline and a thick black mustache. The jarring note was that he carried a swagger stick in his right hand.

I know this guy, I thought. He was by the lake the day we found the underwater temple.

"Good morning, Andres." He said in a loud voice. "I hope you're comfortable with your accommodations." He was all business.

My first thought was that this asshole has a sense of humor. My second was to ask, "Who the hell are you and what do you want?" Discomfort always made me a little grouchy.

For that, I got a glancing blow to side of the head from someone behind me.

"Leave him alone for now," the man commanded. "Por ahora. For now."

The large man motioned to the man behind me and said, "Levantalo, Bring him."

I was taken to a room with no windows and yellow walls. There were a couple of dim naked bulbs hanging loosely from the ceiling. The walls were covered with stains, splattered blood, and maybe crap, it's hard to say. It was like someone tried to paint over the walls of a slaughterhouse. The air was dense; whoever did their remodeling forgot to put in any ventilation. Directly in front and staring at me was a metal table with straps.

An old tale from the junta's time in Argentina came to me. They called their torture chambers the "Quirofano." There the desaparecidos were introduced to electric shock "therapy"; a charge of 220 volts was found to encourage confessions. They called the table "Susana." "Vas a ver a Susana pronto...You are going to meet Susana soon" they would taunt their captives.

Thousands had been interrogated by the military; the torture was conducted in the most ordinary of surroundings. It could be a simple room with a bed where the person would be given a "picana" where electric shots were intensified by drenching the prisoner with water. Sessions on the "machine" as the prisoners referred to the electric cattle prod, were supplemented by beatings, waterboarding and being tied up or chained to the ceiling or wall for days.

A prisoner said that when electric shocks were applied, all one felt was their flesh ripping apart. The pain was excruciating. Afterwards, he wouldn't feel the blows. Nor did he feel them the next day, when there was no electricity but only blows.

My turn.

I was shoved onto the table and strapped in tightly. I tried to roll and push away but couldn't. At a signal from the man in the suit, a smaller fellow came up and connected cables shorn of insulation to my chest and head.

I noticed the well-dressed man walking towards me. "Allow me to introduce the maquina," he said.

Wait a minute ...this guy is not Bolivian ... he has an Argentine accent. What is this? The Quirofano, maquina, the accent ... Who are these guys?

The man in the suit, standing just inside the door said calmly, "We know what you're doing. Where is the skull?"

"What skull?"

"I see...Andres, do you like poetry?"

"Yo soy un hombre sincero, de donde crece la palma, y antes de morirme quiero, echar mis versos del alma...A sincere man am I from the land where the palm trees grow. And I want before I die my souls verse to bestow..."

"Jose Marti"

"Magnifico! Very good. I see you have been educated well."

"He visto vivir a un hombre con el punal al costado..." " I have known a man to live with a dagger at his side",

"sin decir jamas el nombre de aquella que lo ha matado..." "And never once the name give of she by whose hand he died..." I added bluntly.

"Bravo!! We must share our mutual interest at some other time." The man slowly stepped forward and looked right into my face.

"Don't fuck with us, puto !" growing annoyed.

I looked up at him surprised shaking my head as if I didn't understand and then suddenly the juice was turned on. My body writhed, jolted and arched upwards. I spit and bit down on my tongue at the same time, tasting blood in my mouth. I screamed as the electricity coursed through my body. Holy shit...stop! I smelled my flesh. It stopped. Seconds went by and then it started up again. I can't take this! I hollered, screamed. It stopped. I almost passed out.

I did not sign up for this! As soon as that thought zipped by, I thought of Don Julio's mission for me. And then, the image of my father saying

"I am always with you, Andres" through a fog appeared. It's all about the skull. It's always been about the skull.

The man in the suit half-smiled. God, what a sadist, I thought. But suit-man was saying, "This is just a taste of the hard way. Take the easy way. Tell us where it is and this matter is finished. You'll be free to go."

I caught my breath and uttered, "Who... are... you?"

There was a slight pause then my heart was jumping out of my chest as the juice was switched on for a second and then abruptly stopped. I can't take this anymore...

Suit-man actually replied to my question, "Naval Captain Julian Becerra Marti, at your service."

"How... Where...Have I ...met...know you from?" I was stuttering while my nerves jumped. The picture I saw at ESMA came to mind. It was him. The recognition must have registered on my face. There was silence.

"I saw you at ESMA," I managed to say.

Everything was abruptly awkward like I had gained some leverage somehow.

Suit-man barked, "Take him away!"

Hands unstrapped me and pushed me to my feet. My legs promptly gave way but I was caught before passing out. When I awoke sometime later, I was lying on a cool floor and the hood was back in place on my head. Feeling around me, my hands found a small plate of food. I wasn't hungry but the irony of leaving food for me while covering my head so I couldn't see what I supposed to eat seemed absurd. I just lay on the floor while my body convulsed spastically as if unspent electricity was still trapped inside me. I could hardly feel my extremities.

Sometime later, days, hours, minutes, I heard the door open and feet came near me. Without a word of warning, I was punched and kicked then pulled up and punched repeatedly in the stomach, torso and face. A blow to my chest knocked me backwards and I hit my head on cold floor.

"You fucking bastards, cowards" I cried out and tried swinging at them although my hands were bound. They're laughing and having fun with me. I rose to my knees to get up but a roundhouse kick to me head knocked me back down. I spat blood but stayed curled on the floor. Stay down! They continued to kick me. Goddammit, I vowed that they would have to pry my off this floor. Then just as it began, it's over and the men leave. I could hardly breathe, tasted blood, tried to check in. I slowly drifted away.

"We have all the time in the world, Andres." The voice booms over me as I look up. I am on the table again. How did I get here? Did I ever leave?

It's suit-man again.

"Only you can decide your fate now. All you have to do is cooperate."

"Is this what you were trying to get from Oscar, you bastard?" I was exhausted but the words came out anyway.

"Oh yes, Oscar, your friend. He interfered and then, of course, he was of no use."

"He was working for you, right." My mind was beginning to take interest, not just hide shell-shocked from the physical abuse.

"Of course, let's say he saw the writing on the wall. It's too bad he couldn't leave well enough alone." He looked almost disappointed.

"The photo – you took the photo at the lake." It still didn't make sense, but pieces were slowly connecting.

"Yes, congratulations, we didn't realize you saw us. You did our work for us by finding the skull."

"And…Dr. Guerra?"

"Very perceptive"

"Even if I told you where it is, you are destined to fail, you bastard."

He grabbed my hair, pulling my head back, and placed the tip of his commando knife at my throat. His face was inches from mine. His breath was thick with garlic. I thought, no matter, mine is worse. I breathed full in his face.

He said, "Now you listen to me, you comemierda…shithead. You are way over your fucking head. Do you read me? Do you honestly believe you are stronger than me and have a chance of succeeding in your mission?

He talked about mission. Did he know Don Julio? How is this, my mission? Maybe suit-man is right; maybe I am not strong enough. Who are these guys I asked myself for about the millionth time? I realized that Capitan Becerra Marti was not just angry, but doing a job.

Then I remembered Don Julio's message "The dark energies surround us but we can see their shadow."

I blurted out, "You worked at ESMA during the junta. I saw your face, recognized you. You're Argentine."

"Very good, bravo." He backed away releasing his grip on my head.

I saw him raise his hand to the voltage lever. Then, out of the blue, I shouted, "Naval Lieutenant Junior Grade Francisco Paredes."

He hesitates. "Who?"

"You know. You killed him; you betrayed your own kind, you … bastard."

I saw the others looking at him stolidly, interested. He dropped his hand from the lever and looked intently at me. "Yes, we knew each other. How do you know him?"

"He was my… father." I blurted.

In a moment of recognition, suit-man Naval Capitan Julian Becerra Marti stood very still staring at me. Maybe the words had hit a hidden place I should not have gone. I was not sure. But a subtle change crossed his face, too subtle and too fast for me to figure it out. I must have passed out because when I was conscious again, I was alone with the hood over my head in the room.

That night I dreamt that I was in a large room with many others, all of us tied down with chains around our ankles. A blindfold was slipped over my head and my hands were cuffed. The guards began calling out numbers and, at some point, mine must have been called. Someone pulled me up and placed my cuffed hands on the shoulder of the man in front of me. I couldn't see him, only felt his shoulder.

We were marched along a hallway, the shackles clanked as we tripped down a flight of stairs to a basement. After being pushed to the ground, someone grabbed my arm and gave me an injection. It took a while for its effects to be felt. I grew very weak, breathing hard, did not want to move. Then, with the others, I was taken outside and loaded on to a truck. We drove until I heard the idling engines of a prop plane. We were boarded and told to sit on the floor. The door closed.

The plane was airborne. I was stuffed in the back next to a woman who sat cursing and sobbing uncontrollably. After a long time, she stopped. The only sound was the droning engines. I heard her whisper my name repeatedly, "Andres, Andres..." I was startled to hear my name from this woman, and then I recognized the voice. It had to be my mother.

Voices neared us then and I heard them grab her and pull her away. She fought them screaming. The engines throttled back and a door opened. Cold air blasted through the cabin. I heard more screams. Strong hands grabbed me and pushed me to the door. I instinctively resisted trying to pull back, the cold wind blasting against my body. They were trying to kill me. I was falling, screaming.

I awakened shivering in a large dimly lit room, my hood off, unshackled, hands free. Sitting across from me was suit-man, Capitan Becerra Marti staring at me. In an almost friendly tone, he said:

"Andres, your life depends on how you answer my questions."

"I see."

"The skull. Where is it?"

I said nothing.

"You are very stubborn thinking that you can beat us."

"Us?"

"People in high places, people of money, power, and influence work."

"So ... so why do you need me, or this skull you're talking about?"

"I guess you are ignorant of the skull. You don't seem to understand that when you reactivate sacred sites, you gain power, gain energies. I want what you want. Don't you see? We can share in this power together como hermanos, no." "like bothers, you see."

What sacred sites? What energies? I tried to keep my face empty as my thoughts raced. But I knew he wouldn't kill me. He needs me, at least for the moment.

My horrible dream swarmed into my head. Taking a stab in the dark, I asked "Who was she?"

"Who?"

"The woman on the plane?"

"What do you mean?"

"The woman! She was thrown from the plane, wasn't she?"

Marti shifts uncomfortably in his chair and angrily, "She was a Montonero who refused to confess. An enemy of the State and had to be eliminated."

"Was this after you raped her?"

He looked at me angrily now, his fists tightening. Stupid, stupid me for saying such a thing. But my words kept coming, "Was that the plan? Rape them and kill them... including the pregnant ones?

His face was stone for a few minutes. Then his eyes half-closed and he said, "The pregnant ones went to a maternity ward until they delivered. Afterwards, they wrote letters to their families so that the babies could be reunited with them later."

"The letters were never delivered, were they, you bastard? Neither were the babies. It was all a lie, a show that you put on."

Silence. He still watched me with shuttered eyes. Then he said as way of explanation,

"They were enemies of the state. As far as we were concerned, they had to be dealt with."

He stopped. I continued, "Tell me, what was it like was to murder my mother and then betray and kill my father, one of your own. And now, here I am."

Silence.

"Truth and justice eventually prevailed. It happened in Argentina; it will happen everywhere. Evil is always exposed. You lost. You and your kind fucking lost! How is it that you believe you will win this struggle?"

He looked at me sadly and said "We'll see." He rose and left the room.

Later, while in my cell a man came in and untied my hands and feet and removed my hood. He left without saying a word. It took a moment but then I noticed that he had left the door to the room wide open.

After a while, even though I could barely stand I slowly got up and stood there for a minute while the blood began to recirculate in my legs. I hobbled slowly to the door. It was quiet. I was alone. I looked out the doorway expecting to see or hear someone. There was no one. Then I walked as fast as I could through a narrow unlit corridor.

Once outside I ran towards the road.

Chapter 56

APRIL 13, 2012
1448 AVENIDA GUILLAUME

A man and his daughter found me lying on the side of the road. They stopped their truck to see if I was alright. After seeing my bruises and cuts, they offered to take me to the Urgent Care in La Paz. I thanked them and asked instead to be dropped off at Don Julio's which, thankfully, was on their way to their destination. Just their kindness made me feel a little better. Riding in the truck bed, I curled up covered by old burlap potato bags. It was cold and I was banged up and tired. It had been a rough 96 hours. I was lucky to be alive.

After what seemed like forever, I climbed out and slowly walked to Don Julio's front door. It was late and I hadn't told him that I was coming. I hesitated but without options, knocked. The door was slightly ajar so I walked in.

"Don Julio, its Andres!"

There was no answer. Could he be in the back, at the hut on the hill? Looking out the window, I saw the light on in the hut. I found the back door and then could see him walking down the path to greet me. In broken Spanish again he greeted me with a slight smile and outstretched hand. As he takes in my injuries, the smile is replaced with the lowered brows of concern,

"Andres. I am glad to see you. What happened to you? Was there an accident?" He glanced toward the driveway and must have seen that my car wasn't there.

I sighed, "I was slightly inconvenienced, Don Julio. A bizarre story really – I'm not sure where to begin." I paused waiting for the right sentence to form in my head. "Let's find a place to talk."

"Okay." He led me to back up the small rise to the hut.

I could barely walk, and found myself dazed and tripping on the stones in the dark, yet feeling his strong grip as he guided me forward. I asked "Do you have the skull?"

"Yes, it is safe for now." He looked back at me, "Why do you ask?" he murmured. A serious look, almost worry, crossed his face.

"What?" I couldn't quite hear him his voice was so soft. We had reached the door to his hut where he stood to the side to let me enter first.

"I had visitors last night Andres." He motioned to the chair by the window; a small lantern was lit on the side table. His Spanish was flawless again.

You too? I thought, but only said, "What happened?"

"Two men broke in looking for the skull, I think. I was in the hut, lucky for me. They tore the closets and cabinets down. Jose, my neighbor, has been helping me put things back together since."

I looked around and sure enough the place looked a mess. Papers and books were piled around the room; some cushions may have been torn open. It looked like the stuffing had been pulled out of the edges.

Don Julio continued, "The papers were disturbed, but ..."

I interrupted. "Did they get the skull? Did they find it?"

"No, it's here. But, it was strange, curious. I had put it in the drawer by the day bed. The drawer had been pulled open, yet the skull was not taken. "

"What! They didn't see it?"

"I don't know but suddenly, there was a lot of screaming coming from the bedroom. The men ran out as if in pain and desperate to get away. When I returned, the floor was charred black as if it had been burned with a torch. Also, I noticed hand prints around the drawer, burnt into the wood. The rest of the room was not affected. It was very strange." He stopped, looked up at the ceiling, then back to me.

"Andres, I cannot explain this except, well except to say that the skull has unique powers. It must be able to disappear or become invisible. Or it must have heated itself so they couldn't pick it up. It was exactly where I left it. All I can tell you is that the men ran away afterwards."

"Disappear? As in dematerialize?"

"It's been said … well, that some crystals can vanish and then mysteriously re-appears at another place. Did it ever happen when you were a child collecting crystals?"

I shook my head; I'd never heard of this.

"Let's just say that these occurrences happen with crystal beings. They materialize into matter and can dematerialize as a result of what you call 'mind over matter'. Anyway, it's a theory."

Thinking back, I remembered…I did lose some of my crystals and found them again in places I would never have expected. And in the cave at the lake, the skull had disappeared from my vision for a few moments as if it were gauging my intentions. Was this de-materialization?

Changing the subject, I asked Don Julio "Tell me about the sacred sites…portals. And then I've got to tell you what happened to me."

"Ah, yes. The portals. But first let's take care of you." He got a small basin of water, some towels and ointments from an adjacent room. I lay down on the sofa while he quietly went to work on me.

Afterwards, Don Julio retrieved the skull and set it on the table. He motioned towards some pillows on the floor so I settled down leaning back against the stone wall. He sat down opposite me at the edge of an old rug. He passed me some coca leaves which I put in my mouth to chew and warm chicha morada, a sweet native drink made of corn.

A companionable silence filled the room with the slight warmth emanating from the lantern giving a pleasant sensation in the cool evening. The horrors of my kidnapping faded.

Don Julio leaned forward, "The portals are centers, actually gateways into higher dimensions. They were activated by the Brotherhood of Light to seed the planet for its future ascension. Some believe that the crystal skulls came to earth through the portals to help to activate and re-connect us to the portals and the dimensions beyond."

"How do you know you're at a portal; where are they and how are they recognized?" I knew I was interrupting but needed to get the practical questions answered before we took a spin through the cosmic philosophy I thought may come.

Don Julio patiently nodded and responded, "These portals are located at sacred sites around the world and conform to the magnetic grid of the planet. Some are in areas that were once the homes of the ancients. Many have a very low activity; either because they were consciously deactivated or because people have stopped connecting with them."

"Regardless, it's important, no imperative, that the portals are activated again. They have been waiting a long time for the consciousness of the planet to rise high enough for reactivation. It will be up to you to decide where they are and how they will be activated." He stopped and moved the coca leaves around in his cheek.

For once, I didn't feel compelled to push for more information. I waited. The effect of the coca flowed lightly through me as a calm thread of relaxation. What I needed to know would come, in its own time. I settled down in the cushions, my arms lighting resting on my thighs. The stillness felt right.

Don Julio went on, "The portals are ready to reactivate now. But, as the light comes, so does the darkness. The alchemists of the dark priesthood have returned to manipulate the magnetic grid. That's one reason it is so weak today. They want to control everyone with subliminal sounds and electromagnetic frequencies. Regrettably, our modern technologies make their job much easier. So, in effect, we are in a race – again the darkness and against time."

Shadows cast by the lantern crossed his face; it was peaceful and unhurried. Don Julio spoke slowly and quietly. "The portals must be opened and the grid strengthened to allow the light to express itself. This must happen for the light to prepare us, and the planet, for ascension."

A minute passed before I asked, "How do the skulls fit?"

Don Julio smiled as if approving of my question. "There were thirteen skulls manifested in early Atlantis. These were sculpted by higher beings, members of the Brotherhood of Light so that the Atlanteans could do their work on earth with direct guidance from the higher dimensions."

"The Atlanteans were much closer to the source that most of us are today. Their high priest and priestesses knew how to program their knowledge into the skulls, similar to how we program our computers. Legend says that their wisdom included the story of human origins and the mysteries of life. Amazing." He stopped talking, and then asked "Would you like some tea?"

I just shook my head no and said, "Please continue the story." I was caught up in the narrative, like a child and a fairy tale.

"The twelve skulls, one for each tribe in Atlantis, were made from quartz crystal. Each one was like an advanced computer storing all the knowledge of that tribe. All that and much more was stored so that future generations would have that wisdom when they're ready."

"What does it take to be ready? Are we there?" The questions popped out without thought. I found the idea of stored wisdom intriguing. What would I learn?

Don Julio replied, "We'll be ready when humans are sufficiently sensitive to tune into the skull's very high frequency and read the contained information."

He spoke with complete certainty. "Prior to its final destruction, and often at great risk, the temple elders and their descendants carried their skulls with them as they escaped from Atlantis. The twelve skulls are now hidden around the planet."

My mind woke up. This is what my writings about Atlantis and Alkur are telling me. Is it possible that it wasn't just a fantastic and coherent dream.

"I think I'm beginning to understand. What started this and why am I here" Now I had done it. I was asking about my mission – not questioning that it was real.

Don Julio didn't skip a beat, but he imperceptibly leaned back to tell the ancient story. "At the time there were interdimensional beings called the Annunaki. They were masters of deception and darkness. Using frequencies and sound they manipulated the priesthood to gain power and wealth. The Annunaki tried to recode the skulls to dominate the world. If it had been successful, it would have devastated the earth."

"The Brotherhood of Light decreed that this would not happen. To protect each of the twelve skulls, official "Keepers of the Crystals" were selected. These were the elders who took the skulls to secret regions of the earth to wait for the earth's readiness."

"Wait, you said thirteen skulls were made – what about the last one?"

Don Julio paused to adjust the lantern wick then continued, "The master skull, the 13th, was considered too powerful for humans. It was de-materialized and assigned to the higher dimensions for safekeeping. In the future, it will reappear when the Keepers of the Crystals, the descendants of Atlantis, join together to reopen the portals. And the portals will assist Gaia, earth, to ascend into the higher dimensions." Don Julio said this as though repeating a catechism.

He looked at me seriously. "These individuals, the Keepers, are very old souls like you. You have all been reincarnated now to perform this sacred task — that is, to reunite the thirteen skulls before the closing of the year 2012. The ceremony will make possible, and bring in, a new age of Aquarius."

My heart was pounding. It was the most direct and pure truth I'd ever known. Alkur was there to tell me the past and show me the way. The American college professor had been on to something after all!

Don Julio patiently watched as the story settled in my soul. Acceptance must have been clear in my eyes.

"Andres, what you discovered at the bottom of the lake is the 13th skull. It's materialized now for this purpose. In a brilliant stroke of genius it was hidden right in front of us waiting for the right time and right energies to materialize again."

"With the appearance of this master skull, the 12 can be brought together to reopen the portals and regain contact with other dimensions. The Light Ones of all frequencies in other worlds and universes have been waiting for this moment."

My heart rate slowed again calmed by his gentle tone. I was mesmerized and yet in full control of my senses. I felt alive as never before.

"The 13th skull brings the 12 aspects of the others into oneness, into one functional whole. It brings a new level of knowledge, insight and consciousness to our world. The number 13 was considered sacred by the ancients, Andres, because it helps us transcend this reality into something new. Jesus knew this. He was the 13th with the 12 apostles and brought us the Christ Consciousness, a glimpse of our higher self and a doorway to the Cosmic Consciousness of Source."

The hut felt warmer now, like a comfortable soft blanket lightly resting on us. Don Julio's voice suddenly sounded clearer. His accent was nearly gone or did I imagine that.

"Congratulations, Andres! You are embarking on a huge undertaking. You, the master Keeper, are here now with a specific mission. You will bring the 12 skulls together, with the 13th, and create a shift in consciousness. It's a spiritual step forward for mankind and the planet."

"In a previous life as a high priest in the Temple of One you knew the dark power of the Temple of the Sun. You saw how they exploited and controlled people with electromagnetic frequencies that distort and form fear and havoc. And yes, once again, the dark and light forces are engaged on planet earth. The memories of Atlantis will empower you, and others who have returned to earth, to assist in our renewal ascension."

I looked at Don Julio again. His face looked different in the lantern's yellow light. His eyes were deeper somehow; his voice was still gentle but now gaining in power.

"Now let's talk about the different frequencies that are at work here. You've already discovered the ancient healing symbols that clear energies, both of people and of the earth. The skull has already taught you that."

How did he know that? I nodded saying, "In a meditation, I was able to decipher specific sounds and letter combinations. I made notes of their purposes but don't know how to use them."

"Good, it's crucial that you set the intention with the skull before you try to open a portal. The skull is the key to accessing the portals and the higher dimensions of consciousness."

"To use the skull, you must become a vehicle for expressing love and compassion for yourself and all humanity. Evoking love through your heart with the skull will bring you to a state of high vibration which will then let you use the symbols to open and activate the etheric energies of the portals."

I must have frowned because he said, "Don't worry; you'll be guided on how to do this."

Don Julio paused, his face changing again, "It's all about healing yourself first. Clear your energy field first and then through harmonic resonance you'll heal the earth, Andres. These ancient symbols are activating energetic imprints of power that have lain dormant in your DNA since Atlantis. You've already been reprogrammed as a vessel of light."

He paused. "Do you understand?"

"Not really but maybe. Yes, I believe so." I couldn't have explained it through words, but in the core of my being, I understood. My next sentence surprised me. "What about Captain Marti?"

I told Don Julio about my kidnapping, incarceration and torture. I told him about the woman who had been thrown from the plane. I told him the door was left open. I told him about being found and coming to his place. He didn't look shocked, just relieved that I had made it through.

"You've done well. You can see what you're up against. I would not have wished it for you, but am glad you're here, now, my friend."

I wondered about his simple acceptance of such horrible things. I thought he had forgotten my question, but then, after a minute, he continued.

"Captain Marti carries a lot of karmic baggage in this incarnation. It's hard for you to accept this, to have him around – and I believe it has been difficult for him as well. But he motivates you to action. The opposition of darkness to the light brings struggle and creates movement. Don't worry. You see, your work is helping his soul evolve. Remember, the darkness will always show up as an uninvited guest on your journey. But it wants the same thing – that the light can be furthered."

Helping Captain Marti evolve wasn't high on my list of things to do; I was more focused on just knowing who the hell he was and why he murdered Oscar.

But Don Julio looked at me and laughed, "At the end of the day both the light and the dark will be sitting at the bar drinking Pisco Sours and talking about how they tried to out maneuver each other, always recognizing that they are serving the Creator and the evolution of the Universe. They bring the Christ Consciousness into view. It's a big stage out there, Andres, and all the actors are diligently playing their part. Get used to it, because you also are playing a big part."

"Is there anything else I should know?" Certainly there was a lot more I needed.

"Yes, the skull has awakened your higher sense perception and all your senses. It is sending you messages through your dreams and especially your writing. Pay attention to them. They are important."

I closed my eyes and tried to think of nothing.

I need to call the police.

Chapter 57

APRIL 14, 2012
POLICE STATION

I picked up the phone and pulled out Captain Bedoya's card and dialed. I had to report Captain Marti.

"This is Captain Bedoya, a la orden."

"Captain, this Andres Paredes. I may have some more information on Oscar's murder."

"It is good to hear from you again. Please continue, Senor Paredes"

"There is a man…by the name of Marti. His full name is Julian Becerra Marti, an Argentine in his 60's dark, medium height with mustache, dresses well. Former military. I believe he is involved in Oscar's death."

"And how do you know of this man?"

"Let's just say that I met him the other night. I was kidnapped from my home by him and his pendejos. Shitheads."

There was a moment of silence at the other end. "I see…are you safe now, Senor Paredes?"

"Yes, I believe so, for now."

"Where are you?"

"At home. I just got back a few moments ago. You're my first call."

"I must warn you that…I will assign an officer to watch…"

I interrupted. "That will not be necessary Captain. I will be alright."

"As you wish, you have my number"

"Why do you believe Senor Marti is involved? Tell me everything."

"Well…they are after the skull we found at the lake."

"I see, the skull that was stolen from the Institute. And this Senor Marti…was he one of the men that kidnapped you?"

"Yes."

"Senor Paredes, please elaborate and give me the details. I do not like it when people withhold information…"

"Yes, Captain, I understand, but I was not sure who I could …"

"Have you told anyone else about …the skull?"

"Well, yes, only Oscar and my friend Carlos Gutiérrez. Dr. Epis and the Institute also know about the skull. You see, I found it hidden in Oscar's car."

"Yes, yes, we know that, thanks to Dr. Epis. You should have mentioned this earlier. Tell me about the kidnapping."

"I was taken from my house by thugs and driven somewhere, some dark shabby place. Marti was there, as was equipment for electric shocks and other brutalities. They beat me trying to find out the location of the skull. Marti said that Oscar had interfered with them and had to go." Finally, they let me go."

Silence, then Bedoya asked, "Can you locate the building where you were held?"

"No."

"Did you recognize anyone other than Senor Marti?"

"It's Captain Marti, and no, I couldn't see his heavies."

"I will send a forensics group to your home to collect any evidence. Tell me, this Senor Carlos…Gutiérrez … he a friend of yours, si?"

"Yes, I have known him for a few years now. Why?"

"Senor Paredes, we must follow all leads in our inquiries. It so happens that your friend was seen on closed circuit television at the Institute prior to the break-in. A coincidence perhaps."

For a moment I was stunned. Carlos. What was he doing there? I wondered.

"Anyway, we will follow up, of course. And, expect police at your home shortly. Is there anything else we should know? Perhaps the location of the skull?"

"No, Captain, I cannot divulge that now. Except to say it is safe and will be returned to the Institute in time."

I was still thinking about Carlos.

"Thank you, Senor Paredes. If you have anything else to share let us know. It is always a pleasure to hear from you. We will be in touch Buen Dia. Good Day."

"Of course. Thank you."

Chapter 58

APRIL 16, 2012
AVENIDA MERCEDES, APT # 61,
LA PAZ, BOLIVIA

I stayed up all night writing and re-reading what I had written, trying to understand all this. I laid awake in bed, trying to make sense of it all.

In the end, Alkur confronted Saail and recognized that his shadow, or darker side self was drawing him down. He used love to make the best things possible. It seemed so right when Alkur's father appeared to bring Saail's soul into the light where it belonged. It felt as if there was closure.

In my heart, I accepted I'm Alkur returned in this lifetime. It all fit: my writing about Atlantis, the psychic experiences; the dreams about Atlantis as a child and the crystals; finding the skull at the lake; meeting Don Julio; the picture of a woman from long ago; the similarities of Alkur's loss with mine; and Captain Marti and the forces of darkness conspiring to prevent me from my purpose. I remembered all of it as if I lived it before. I did live it before. Life repeats.

I felt good, purposeful but lighter and freer. I had a renewed sense of purpose in my life. I would continue to work at the Institute as much as possible but as a secondary pursuit.

Through my writings about Alkur, my heart had opened to a completely new aspect of my being, one filled with more serenity, love, forgiveness, and self-acceptance. Out of the confusion, I gained clarity.

It's hard to believe that the two who I thought were my parents, weren't. My biological mother was killed at ESMA. Marti... my father! But I can set all that aside.

Now, I can move forward. The crystal skull has given me an incredible opportunity to learn the wisdom of the ancients and share it with the world. I am beginning to see that, like Alkur, I have a bigger destiny in this life -- one that uses all of my past and present life experiences and gifts to serve humanity.

One totally unexpected path from this is that I felt called to help the deceased souls of the "disappeared" in ways that I could never fathom. Many are still earthbound spirits caught in the secret detention camps throughout Argentina. These spirits do not know that they're dead, that they died over 40 years ago. They have not moved on. With the skull's help, I can communicate with them to help them realize they are dead and ask them to embrace the light. It will be difficult, tedious work. I think Papa, as both a perpetrator and victim, would be pleased.

There are many who aren't ready to embrace the light and move on. I've had to call in their guides, even deceased family members or loved ones to help them depart. I know it is also my calling to clear the camps and their surroundings to release the dark energies that linger. I'll do this as long as I am needed.

I was invited to address a group of spiritual seekers and talk about the skull and ancient wisdom at the United Nations. It seemed to come out of the blue, that is, until I saw Dr. Epis' name on the letterhead as a member of their leadership board. Although I had not spoken with him for a while, he was aware of my work. I'm certain that he was behind the invitation. Of course, I accepted. I would be speaking in the Fall.

PART 4: A NEW HOPE

"Put on the full armor of God, so that you will be able to stand firm against the schemes of the devil. For our struggle is not against flesh and blood, but against the rulers, against the powers, against the world forces of this darkness, against the spiritual forces of wickedness in the heavenly places. Therefore, take up the full armor of God, so that you will be able to resist in the evil day, and having done everything, to stand firm..."

EPHESIANS 6:12

Chapter 59

OCTOBER 23, 2012
UNITED NATIONS GENERAL
ASSEMBLY, NEW YORK CITY

I'm in New York to address the United Nations Assembly. I'm still astonished at how Spirit has orchestrated this terrific opportunity. It must have started with Dr. Epis' group in La Paz and spread by word of mouth. I've been speaking to spiritual groups, churches, anthropological associations, divinity schools and more the past months. At first, I wasn't sure what to say but it turns out that was a needless worry. Once I get started, Alkur takes over and I'm just a channel for his, or our, message.

I'm still at the Institute but on a part-time basis. Drs. Epis and Glasser have fully supported that move and have made Institute resources available to me. Carlos, my friend of many years, was arrested in connection with the theft of the skull and the murder of Oscar. It turns out the police had tracked Carlos as he searched my home shortly after I gave the skull to Don Julio. Carlos had quickly pointed the finger at an Argentine syndicate for the whole horrible affair. The last I heard from Captain

Bedoya, the police are still holding Carlos as their prime suspect and looking for accomplices. But that feels like truly ancient history.

New York is beautiful now, resplendent with crisp blue skies and a golden sun heralding fall. Most of the trees have already turned from red and gold to brown; fresh fallen leaves swirl around my feet as we head to the United Nations plaza. What a wild ride it's been these past few months.

It's still spreading. My address last month to the United Nations Society for Enlightenment and Transformation (SEAT), part of the United Nations Staff Recreational Council (UNSRC), was a huge success. Those aren't my words – they are right out of the newspaper article that reported on the meeting. The article went on to say that the teachings for humanity were far-reaching and profound.

Following that session, the leadership voted unanimously that I address the entire General Assembly during their next meeting. A request through the Secretariat through the President was later approved and I was given a small window on the Assembly's agenda. Once again, doors opened and the path was cleared.

We'd been briefed by the staff ahead of time on security and entry protocols. Once through the metal detectors, we were whisked past the Security Council chambers through to the anteroom of the Hall. The guards were very curious as they scanned the bag that held the skull that set off all the alarms. When I opened the bag for inspection, they gawked. But we got through.

A staffer led me to the anteroom to await my introduction. Peeking out I could see the United Nations emblem on the podium; its distinctive map of the world is flanked by olive wreaths, the symbols of peace.

The Assembly Chamber itself was magnificent. The rooms huge, seating all 191 member delegates along with limited staff. Today, they'd been invited, for the first time in the UN's history, to a program that does not conform to the usual grist of global affairs. It was billed as a talk on the wisdom of the crystal skull of Atlantis.

The uniqueness of the topic must have piqued interest. The delegates filed in, filling the aisles, chatting and talking. Slowly, they take their seats, flip through papers and finally look toward the rostrum.

I was introduced. Stepping out, I looked around the room to see representatives of the entire world's people sitting together. I am archeologist, never in my wildest dreams would I envision this. I adjust my new tie, straighten the lapel microphone they gave me and look directly at the audience. I saw Don Julio off to the left smiling. Then I took the skull from its bag placing it on the podium. I took a deep breath.

"Good afternoon. I'm honored to address you today on the most urgent subject we have, and that is peace. My name is Andres Paredes, an archeologist from Bolivia. But, that is only today's identity or more precisely, my name during this lifetime. I thank you all for being here today."

A few bewildered looks pass. "On earth, during my last incarnation, I was an Atlantean priest called Alkur. And it is from that experience that I speak to you today."

"My task is to help you gain more understanding about the energies at work in your lives. This ancient Atlantean skull that was discovered a few months ago has given us clues to the amazing transformation of this planet. It's a message to everyone as our spiritual evolution quickens and we enter the Golden Age of Aquarius this coming December 21, 2012."

The delegates look up at me in stunned silence. I see them trading glances, as in, what sort of a nut case have we got here today? Then, in my peripheral vision, I see a familiar man sitting on the left in the third row, right behind Don Julio. I look directly at him; yes, it's Captain Marti immaculately dressed. What's he doing here? It can't be. I must concentrate. I close my eyes and begin to channel.

"Greetings, dear ones. I am Alkur, a guide for Melkizadeck, of the Brotherhood of Light. I've been assigned to earth to bring continued enlightenment and peace to all and to help your planet rise to the higher dimensions of spirit. I embrace all of you, and the nations you represent, with unconditional love."

"Unconditional love will unite all the nations of your beloved earth. Yes, my dear ones, we are all together in the process of ascension. There will be more to say, but for now, it's enough to assure you that the Brotherhood of Light surrounds you with its source energy to nurture and empower you. You are each Masters on your path of Ascension. You are all sacred beings and powerful beyond measure."

"I have incarnated on earth many times, the last time I was on the island of Atlantis as it was destroyed by fire and water. Some of you are probably skeptical of what I'm saying, and believe me, I understand. Yes, Atlantis did exist. During that time, I was a high priest, communicator and healer. I have since been serving the Brotherhood of the Light bringing greater understanding, inspiration and clarity to ascended souls, like you and your people."

"Many of you are wondering what is really going to happen on December 21, 2012. The doomsday prophets are in high gear, aren't they? We've all heard predictions about the end of time, imminent collisions with comets, cataclysmic polar reversals and even economic collapse. It's even in your movies. It's wild. So let me set the record straight."

I pause and speak more slowly to make sure everyone understands. "Masters, planetary changes will occur, as the planet undergoes a cleansing or detoxification for the higher good. The regional quakes, shakes, winds, waves, storms and other phenomena are natural parts of this process. For Gaia, the earth, is a living organism like yourself and she has her ups and downs." A little laughter rippled through the Hall.

"It's not the end of the world but a new beginning. This is a planet of free will and, despite the fears that are so prevalent today, the planet will ascend. Everywhere, people are rising above fear and bringing in new energies. In other words, dear ones, a new Earth will be manifested in 2012 and beyond, because you have willed it. You will have greater access to your divine creativity and greater understanding of who you really are."

"Fear is the old energy. It is time to let go of it. Jesus, the Christ, said that love is the absence of fear. Feel into that. It is true."

"There are more truths you should know." At this point, I paused, feeling the attention of the delegates. They were listening carefully.

"Humanity has been visited by inter-dimensional beings for millennia. Your ancients knew this. Life from higher dimensions came to teach about Spirit. The ancients of your planet are emissaries of light for you, gifts that continue even now to do the work."

"As above, so below. You are all representations of the Universal power-er, created in the image of God, Yahweh, Allah, or whatever you choose to call the source of all. You are all co-creators with the divine. All the prophets have spoken of this. Love is the code for God's plan. All is love. All is one."

"Think about that for a moment. You are perfect manifestations of the divine, yet you have forgotten who you really are. Take charge of your higher energies and get on with your lives."

"The greatest force in the Universe is love; it the light that we all can radiate. Love is the highest and clearest vibration. It's the energy that separates the material from the spiritual. It is the energy that creates life."

"With more love, you would have a far more beautiful planet. Love, not greed and competition, is your life force. Love is the very nucleus of your being, your essence. You are all expressions of unconditional love."

"Life on earth balances between the good and evil, light and dark. This duality must be experienced to develop spiritually. Acknowledge your faults, reconcile and forgive. Know that the darkness serves the light; they are both the same energy and both serve the divine plan."

"As you enter 2012, your consciousness and planet's vibration will rise. You will become less influenced by the darkness and negative energies. In fact, I expect the old-energy holdouts will fight back hard as they are drawn out of the shadow and exposed for everyone to see."

"There is darkness in all of you. It's part of being human on this plane of existence. In time, you will process the darkness, not by condemning or avoiding it but by loving and accepting it. Then, nothing can touch you. Enlightenment is embracing the dark and turning it to the light. You need that flip of perception before you can access wisdom."

"The planet's energy is changing. And the old guard of political power over love cannot stand in the new paradigm. You are seeing this now as tyrants and corruption fray. Heart centeredness and love is the new energy, the new accounting, my dear ones. Get used to it, because it is here to stay."

"Embrace forgiveness and liberate yourself. It's not war and violence that makes man progress."

"Bring more serenity and peace of mind into your lives. From a serene state you can always feel the abundance that source is providing and will always provide for you. In serenity, we offer our challenges to God, for the Divine will always bring us a resolution. Develop a more visionary faith in serenity, instead of blindly following the ego. Serenity is our natural state of mind when we yield to grace."

"Be inspired. Take a deep breath and visualize your breath as a beautiful blue light filling you. Connect to the flow of the universe. It will help you find peace and create love and joy. Inspiration is a divine gift. Allow stillness to let the flow of creative ideas come into your consciousness. Let this creativity help you make decisions for peace in the world."

"You control your own energy and emotions. Accept responsibility for it and keep your vibrations high. As we bring in the higher energies of 2012, it's crucial that everyone commit to raising his or her vibration. Together, we'll lift the frequency of the planet. I promise that if you make a commitment daily to raise your vibration and make positive changes in your life you will be making the greatest contribution you can in helping the planet. We change the world by changing ourselves."

"Ancient Atlantis created crystal skulls to enable all of the different tribes to communicate with each other and to foster love, peace, harmony and unity. There were 13 skulls in Atlantis; the first 12 represented the 12 tribes. The 13th skull was the conduit for direct communication between Atlantis and the Intergalactic Council. During the final days of

Atlantis, the 13th skull was hidden for safekeeping, far away from those who lived in negative energies."

"The skulls will be reunited on December 21, 2012, when the rising sun aligns with the center of your Milky Way. On signal, they will vibrate at their programmed resonant frequencies and open a galactic portal that will raise the consciousness of the planet. It is all preparation for mankind's ascension. There will be much celebration throughout the Universe. It's your destiny."

"When all 12 skulls are brought together again, which they will be in your time, the 13th will materialize. It is already here. It is an amethyst master skull, a unique crystal that teaches humility. It teaches us that the ego, which is any belief or thought that keeps you separate from others, holds us back. It also brings balance and an integration of the whole human into a unity consciousness to realize the full potential self."

"With humility, without ego, the universe will direct and guide us. Then the Divine can fill us with wisdom and love. When you let go of ego, you are open to receive and create so much more. This is because the ego believes in separation and you are by your divine birthright One with your creator. You cannot create with ego."

"Even now, the crystal skulls are working deep within your inner being to support your healing. They will restore your freedom to love. They will help you make an evolutionary leap in consciousness, to develop an infinite consciousness. The skulls will help bring you into balance and resolve interior conflicts."

"The crystal skulls are teaching us a new way to perceive reality. They are sharpening your perceptions and awakening your creativity. They are showing you how to put aside materialistic distractions, clarify your highest intentions and expand your consciousness individually and collectively."

"The skulls remind us that all humanity has divine origins as star people. They send out coded signals to awaken your spiritual brain. Humanity and the skull are one; we all came from the stars, light formed into matter. The ancients knew this. Your science is proving this now."

"The skull energies will enhance your intuition and with it the understanding that everything happens in its own time. You will have heightened awareness and sensitivity to your surroundings. You will experience more synchronicities in daily life. You will have more empathy with others and deeper levels of compassion and heart-centered unconditional love. You will respond more positively to nature and all earth's creatures. You will honor the environment of the Earth and all her peoples."

"You will find a new encompassing sense of unity across people and nature. It goes beyond the mental polarities of good and bad. You will feel the unity as peaceful collective quantum awareness. You will discover new models of energy technologies and quantum healing modalities."

"Finally, you as human beings will be able to enter the darkness to find the light within, and reclaim your cosmic connection to illumination."

"As I conclude, allow me to say again that we are all about love. That is what exists beyond the veil. Make decisions based on heart, not ego. Choose to live free, and choose to release fear and worry. Co-create with Spirit your own well-being. Respect and nurture one another, and above all embrace LOVE."

"That's my message for today, dear ones. As you return to your homes and nations, understand that civilization is moving forward. Yes, that's right, you are moving into a new energy and a new consciousness. The old ways don't work anymore."

"I know, some of you may be thinking this isn't true. That in fact, civilization is regressing into violence and pain. Your news media would like you to believe this. Don't. And this message of love will not sit well with those of you who are invested in old teachings and tradition. Don't worry about it. Trust that you're headed in the right direction. And so it is. Thank you and bless you all. I am Alkur, in service to Melkizadeck and the Brotherhood of Light and humanity."

I finished the channeling returning to Andres and saw that Captain Marti was gone. I stayed just a moment to acknowledge the applause and then stepped quickly back into the anteroom.

Chapter 60

DECEMBER 19, 2012

I had been on whirlwind tour since returning to Bolivia from New York; requests for interviews, presentations and appearances flowed in without stop. Among them, was an e-mail from Dr. Humberto Masnor, who I had met at SEAT, telling me about a special show that CBS 60 minutes was going to run about the Mayan prophecy for December 21, 2012.

Dr. Masnor attached a link to the interview by CBS reporter Leslie Stuart with Dr. Simrah and Dr. Busam from the National Aeronautics and Space Agency (NASA) Jet Propulsion Center at the California Institute of Technology.

Curious, I clicked on the link.

Leslie: Good day gentlemen and thank you for your time. So December 21, is soon upon us. Is this a significant day for you both?

Simrah: It should be a normal day at work (laughing). A rare astronomical configuration of the planets has been unfolding recently on the Center's telescopes: an alignment of Uranus, Pluto and Neptune that happens every 26,000 years.

Leslie: So this is a big deal?

Busam: Yes.

Leslie: And, there is the Mayan prophecy. Is there any relationship here with the Mayans and this alignment?

Simrah: The Mayans were incredible astronomers. They mapped the galaxies, and predicted this alignment would occur every 26,000 years, so we are seeing now what they predicted.

Leslie: What does NASA say about this?

Simrah: Apocalyptic rumors and speculation have floated around the world based on an interpretation of Mayan prophecy that said the end of time would happen when the ancient Mayan calendar expired. NASA scientists have heard it all. The stories were so rampant at one point that the U.S. Government website posted an article reassuring everyone that the reports of earth's imminent demise on December 21, 2012 were not true. NASA went so far as to release a video explaining why the Mayan calendar does not accurately predict the day of reckoning.

Leslie: What did the video say?

Simrah: It said that the rumors of the world's end in 2012 have been commonplace on the Internet for some time involving the Mayan Calendar. It said that the world would not end in 2012 and that there would be no catastrophic cosmic strikes or a hidden planet sneaking up and colliding with us and many others."

Leslie: I did not realize that the U.S. government had an opinion on this. Did you believe what they were saying?

Busam: Of course (laughing). No...we were both beginning to wonder.

Leslie: About the end of the world? Gentlemen... will we still be here afterwards? (laughing)

Busam: Yes, of course, but as we studied the frames coming back from the Hubble Telescope, we were surprised, and yes, excited by what we were seeing.

Leslie: What were you seeing?

Simrah: As you know the new Hubble Space telescope has been the cutting edge technology in space astronomy. It was designed to peer deep into space where no one had ever been able to see before to search for small extra-solar planets orbiting distant stars. Hubble made possible more sophisticated investigations of the mysterious dark matter that causes the universe to accelerate and expand.

When we examined Hubble's picture of the center of the Sirius A globular star cluster we found the details amazing. We also saw something peculiar in the star system.

The results were so surprising and extraordinary that we focused on monitoring the Sirian globular cluster for several months using short duration microlensing events to measure its true mass and direction.

Leslie: So, you were seeing a possible new planet?

Busam: Yes, that's what we thought as we aimed Hubble through the center of the Sirian star cluster lying between Earth and the galactic bulge.

Simrah: I remember saying to him, "What's that?" as we focused the computer picture on a dark mass to the side of Hubble's frame.

Busam: I told him, "I don't know. Can you bring it in closer?" Simrah then fiddled with the software to highlight and enlarge the unusual shadow.

Simrah: We flipped the computer to a different screen to search for mass and magnitude indicators. The software just showed a whirl of numbers, something dynamic and moving in unexpected non-elliptical ways. We could not get a good resolution until we went to the camera. Then we saw it for the first time.

Leslie: The planet?

Simrah: Right. We saw a solitary mass, many times the size of the earth, orbiting the star.

Leslie: Well, what did you think? Was it a new planet or just dust or something else?"

Busam: At first we were skeptical — we thought it was either a small planet that's been gravitationally torn away from its parent stars in the cluster or a massive asteroid. We weren't sure. Simrah and I concluded that it was a very dark orphaned planet several magnitudes larger than Earth. But, it also appeared to move in a linear, not elliptical movement which we thought very strange.

Leslie: Could you tell what direction it was moving?

Simrah: Yes. We had a theory or a wild guess that it was headed our way."

Leslie: Towards earth?

Simrah: Yes.

Leslie: So, gentlemen, was this find significant in light of the doomsday scenarios and all the publicity of 21 December, 2012?

Simrah: We were not thinking of any apocalyptic scenarios, Leslie, but were excited that this was a newly discovered planet and if it was confirmed, it would be one of the most incredible discoveries of the century.

I finished reading the interview which continued to discuss the work being done at the Center and discussions about the telescope that will replace Hubble and recent information about Pluto.

I could not help but notice an anonymous commentary below the link that caught my attention:

Unknown to the astronomers, however, the planet they were seeing had been sighted before by the ancient Sumerians, over 3,500 years earlier. The Sumerians tracked it for centuries and named it Nieburu. Ancient Sumerian diagrams depict not only the sun, moon, and the nine planets in their relative positions, but they also portray this tenth planet and the extensive route it travels. The Sumerians knew that Nieburu travels throughout the galaxy and returns to earth's section of the solar system every 3,600 years.

I remember Ilax and Don Julio talking about the Nieburians and the Annanuki.
I wondered whether the Nieburians were returning to earth again on 21 December 2012?

Chapter 61

DECEMBER 21, 2012
ISLAND OF THE SUN, LAKE
TITICACA, BOLIVIA

Without doubt, Lake Titicaca's Island of the Sun is one of the most glorious places on earth. It is Titicaca's largest and most important island, rich in myth, history and natural beauty. The scenery is visually stunning, and the energies magic. For the Incas, the pear shaped island was the sacred home of the Earth and Sky. Today, it's Aymara and Quechua-speaking inhabitants proudly trace their lineage to Manco Capac and Mama Occlo, the father and mother of the Incas, who are said to have been birthed here from the Inca Sun god Viracocha at "El Roque" or the hallowed Puma Rock.

On the island, granite mountain peaks stand guard over terraced hillsides planted with wheat, quinoa, potatoes and other crops. The small fields nestle among Inca and Tiawanaku ruins. Among the ruins is a sacred rock on the highest part of the island, perfectly centered with a view on three sides of the lake below. Two temples also rise above the farms, one for Pachatata honoring Father Sky and one for Pachamama, Mother Earth.

Passing through the rock gates of the Pachamama shrine, a circular path with smaller spirals lead to a solid rock altar. It is shaped like a womb to symbolize the divine mother that perpetually receives and gives life. Elaborate carvings on the wall celebrate the virtues of openness and fertility. Close by, the Temple of Pachatata symbolizes the energy from the skies, like rain, that penetrates the earth and feeds Pachamama.

I'd gotten to the island the previous day. I woke up around at 4 a.m. to a still morning cloaked in the silence that lives between the night and the emerging day. Thousands of stars filled the inky dark sky. Not even the air was stirring.

Despite the comfortable accommodations, I'd slept very little. Today promised to be exciting. As my anticipation of the day's events quickened my pulse, it was joined by a cool breeze coming from the lake. It was a delightfully crisp and refreshing start. In the darkness, I wondered if the Incas had experienced the same thing – and had marveled at the brilliance of the stars. One shooting star was quickly followed by another. I was so thrilled to be alive and finally here.

Just before dawn, Jose, my Peruvian guide joined me outside the posada. The usual good mornings were accented with our growing sense of exhilaration. Eagerly, we walked to the main procession gathering point, the start of a winding road up to the temple on the hilltop.

Today is special; it's a once in a lifetime, or more accurately, once in many lifetimes event. Today, an ancient Incan ceremony at the "El Roque", the most sacred place of the Inca and a portal will bring in the 5th Inca Viracocha or cycle of ascension and with it a new message of hope for all humanity. It's December 21, 2012. The 12 skulls will be reunited for the first time in centuries.

Not since Atlantis has there been such a gathering. The six men and six women who serve as keepers are here. They're all extraordinary healers representing the world's native tribes. Each brings their sacred crystal skull that they have safeguarded down through the generations waiting precisely for this auspicious moment.

ROBERT R. MALDONADO PHD.

It's worth recounting their separate journeys to this moment. The first keeper, an Inca Mallku male revealed himself at Q'ollorot'I, a sacred annual festival held high in the Andes. He traveled along the ancient energetic lines, called seques, that connect the sacred sites to Cuzco, the ancient capital city of the Inca Empire.

Simultaneously, the second healer, an Aztec from Mexico, arrived from the ancient temple of Wiracocha at Raqchi. He, too, followed the seques to Cuzco. There, the two healers recognized each other as skull keepers, during the feast of Corpus Christi. This happened again and again, as the skull keepers migrated in and miraculously discovered each other.

The third, from the Maya of Mexico, was revealed at the shrine of Taytacha Temblores, the Earthquake Lord, in Cuzco. The three journeyed together to Lima where, at the sanctuary of Pachakamilla, they found the two more skull keepers, a Hopi man and a female Maori Tohuna from New Zealand. Together, the five traveled to the sanctuary of the Virgin of Chapi in Arequipa, where they met a female skull keeper from Mongolia. Then in Bolivia, the group met up with an aborigine elder from Australia at the sanctuary of the Virgin of Copacabana.

The group, now numbering seven, gained the eighth in Puno where they recognized a woman skull keeper from Tibet at the sanctuary of the Virgin of Candelaria. They all returned as a group to the Wircacocha Temple where they waited for one full day as the final four skull keepers arrived: two men and two women, who came representing tribes from Siberia, the Inuit of Canada, the Zulu of South Africa, and the Kahuna of Hawaii.

Once all twelve were united, they sailed to Amantani Island on the reed boats of the Uru tribe for the reuniting of the skulls. After the Island of the Sun ceremony, they planned to move to the ancient Inca ruins of Machu Pichu to open a dormant portal there, and other sacred sites on the continent.

For weeks, the Inca shamans of Amantani had eagerly awaited this magical moment for their prophecy to be fulfilled. They had meticulously cleansed and activated the energy vortices. The grounds around "El Roque" which were in dreadful shape were renewed and refurbished.

The shamans had positioned themselves in towns and mountains surrounding the lake and using sacred incantations and prayers had created a dome of high energy to seal the gateway to the darkness and raise the portals' vibration so only light beings could enter. They had asked the land's mountain spirits, the apus to infuse the island with their power during the sacred ceremonies. All this has happened in the previous weeks.

Now, in the early morning darkness, I saw dozens already gathered. Our procession began a slow ascent to the temple. Jose had given me sacred coca leaves to offer as blessings at specific points along the route. We stopped at the first portal, a large, stone arch doorway. He turned to partially face the followers and explain, "Each portal has a guardian spirit and its permission must be granted to proceed further." Heads nodded in understanding.

Jose continued, "The first portal belongs to the Great Serpent, which we Incas believe represents the lower world and the root energy. At this level, we are not conscious of spirit or much else and can't discriminate between our self and others. The focus is on individual survival." Jose began chanting prayers requesting permission for safe passage and blessings on our journey. The group waited patiently. A few moments later, Jose signaled us to continue the walk.

As we climbed, Jose explained that each portal activates a chakra or energy wheel of the human energy field. Passage through is a sacred ritual that purifies seekers before they arrive at the temple. Each chant prepares people to participate and receive blessings during the ceremony. He also reminded everyone that in the Inca tradition to be granted access through the doorways was a great honor, one that had to earned.

We stopped at each of the seven portals where Jose led us in sacred chants to the portal guardian. He began, "At the second portal, the Sacred Puma rests. It represents the present world or reality, self-control, strength and nurturing. It teaches us to discriminate between good and bad, and between our self and others.

At the third portal, the energy of the Condor inspires the soul to continue on its path towards enlightenment. Here, we learn to align with our innate goodness and become aware of our shared consciousness and immortality."

Finally, after what appeared to be a few hours, we arrived at the hilltop where we would find "El Roque." As I approached I immediately sensed the intensity of the energies of this place and why it had been chosen. "El Rocque" appeared to a natural half dome rock outcropping about 5 feet tall and 2 feet wide.

In the darkness I noticed the open face of the "El Rocque" surrounded by what appear to be offerings—flowers, animal parts, coca leaves, fruits, vegetables and other memorabilia that others had placed over time. Directly in front of it noticed an enormous stone table set on four smaller stones circled by 12 stone monoliths. This was the altar. There was also a larger diameter circle surrounding the Holy Rock and smaller stones. The energy was incredible. I just stood there in reverence taking it all in. Jose and others went forward to the rock and knelt in prayer, some chanting and placing coca leaves and gifts at its base.

Guided by the elder shamans, we walked in the larger diameter circle counterclockwise in silence then clockwise in the inner circle. After a while we individually stepped forward to the Atlar in reverence placing our offering on it. We each have stones or crystal skulls that we placed on the altar in a circle for the ceremony. I placed the 13th in the center.

The elders watch carefully. The moon's fading silver light seems to move counter-clockwise as each object is placed. We waited for the signal.

Chapter 62

DECEMBER 21, 2012 ISLAND OF THE SUN, LAKE TITICACA, BOLIVIA

At last, we're motioned to approach the altar. Suddenly, a familiar Inca melody calling to awaken Pachamama filled the air. The four oldest shamans sat facing the four directions invoking the spirits with beautiful sacred native chants.

In the inner circle surrounded by the 12 stones and closet to the altar sat the six women skull keepers. Jose whispered to me that they represent the divine feminine energy. Around them stood the circle of six men, holding hands, representing the divine masculine protecting the inner feminine and sealing the sacred space.

The oldest shaman turned and called me to move forward. I was the lead officiant for the ceremony. My pulse quickened with excitement. I'd prepared for this, but still felt a thrill of anticipation.

As I am about to begin I looked around the temple and then up to the sky, where a large condor, its enormous wings outstretched, is gliding, silhouetted against the starlit sky. It was a good sign.

I began chanting AKMA, AKMA-RA-LA, AK-EL-KIBA, AK-RA-NA, saying the old words of invocation and asking the blessing of the four directions. I could feel the entire area becoming filled with a sense of exultation. With the chanting I could feel a very balanced energy, neither masculine or feminine, a neutral harmonious blend vibrating through me.

Along with everyone else, I watched the altar. The skulls are activated now and generating an enormous energy throughout the circles. It felt as if each circle's energy was moving in balanced opposition to each other in a synchronistic manner creating vortex like field. Each skull was glowing. As the energy built, the skulls telepathically invited the world's people, tribes past and present, to be born again into today's world. I was about to witness a step into the higher consciousness of ascension.

Through the dawn, I saw the shadowy outlines of a long stream of beings appearing: the high priests of Atlantis and the descendants of the 12 tribes reunited as prophesied. I saw the figure of an Inca shaman appear out of the earth, and then many Inca shadows followed him weaving a loop through the entities. At first, only their heads appeared, spiraling around the circle. Then, their bodies emerged from the earth. There were hundreds, maybe thousands of them, in brightly colored robes, with elaborate designs and images painted on their faces, masks and feathers in their hair. Their energy was incredible.

Some placed etheric objects on the altar, others just marched by. Many more shapes and forms arrived, tribes from around the world, perhaps thousands in ceremonial robes and carrying sacred objects. I recognized the Hopi, Maori, and Zulus and the others. The effect was electrifying. This continued for some time.

And then, with the 12 glowing, the 13th skull lit up in the center of the gathering. It white rays illuminated the entire temple, without casting shadows. The beams gently opened the third eyes and heart centers of all those gathered. Sweet tones filled my chest, filling me with profound beauty and awe. Tears of joy and peace welled in my eyes as I contemplated the profundity of what I was seeing and doing. I felt in the presence of the divine and loved.

And then I was jolted back into reality and that this incredible moment of light held the greatest threat. The shamans were vigilant because they knew that the darkness always intrudes, trying to disrupt light-filled ceremonies. The shamans stood ready to protect the temple against any darkness that may try to destroy our force field of light.

And soon enough, the air shivered as a cold breeze blew in.

Chapter 63

DECEMBER 21, 2012 ISLAND OF THE SUN, LAKE TITICACA, BOLIVIA

The skulls still glowed but a strange ground mist unexpectedly began to rise from the earth, enveloping everyone in the inner circle. A ferocious wind, dark clouds and loud thundering booms shook the area. As the ground started shaking, a noisy rumbling sound was felt. The sky darkened as enormous lightning bolts hit the stones; the trees and bushes began to sway violently. I was buffeted by the strong wind and struggled to just stay standing.

I looked around, fearing the storm, but the shamans were neither surprised nor rattled. They countered it with their continued chanting. I heard their tones and felt it raising the vibration of unconditional love, trying to maintain the circles energetic integrity. Many of the people in the circle were, like me, surprised but somehow held their positions. The skulls continued to pour out their light which made the mist appear opaque.

Suddenly, a loud clap of thunder announced the presence of a dark swirling cloud of dust before us. Within it appeared a formidable black cloaked figure. Tall and glaring, he slowly glided to the circle's center. Swiftly, more dark cloaked figures appeared behind and around it. Then out of nowhere a huge space craft mysteriously appeared lighting the sky and emitting a low humming sound. The craft floated above, filling the sky.

Everyone was frightened. Some prostate threw themselves to the ground cowering, others frozen in fear. The sound grew louder as the seconds passed, the earth trembled. It felt as if time was suspended.

The oldest shaman passed his hand over his eyes then approached the dark figure. Speaking clearly and firmly, he said "You must be the high priest of Annunaki. We have met in dreams. You have no place here. Go! Go now!"

The large figure stared down at the shaman and with a swift swipe of its hand sent him flying into a pile of rocks, knocking him unconscious.

Behind the dark figure stood the Atlantean generations of the Dark Priesthood. As they wheeled within the circle, the dark figure continued to peer intently at those gathered and at the skulls. He was followed by all the dark priesthood throughout history. I saw the reincarnations of the sons of Belial through time: Amillius, Genghis Khan, Ivan the Terrible, Adolph Hitler, Benito Mussolini, Saddam Hussein, Osama bin Laden and more.

The magnitude of evil dwarfed anything imaginable. The dark figure then commanded the elements and a strong hurricane force wind and a tornado of dust engulfed the temple. People were flung about; some in desperation threw themselves on the skulls to keep them from flying away.

The shamans continued their chanting but then I felt an energy well up within me as if a deep channel was opening and something uncontrollable was coming through.

It was Alkur!

Immediately, the Annunaki figure shifted his stance to face me and shape-shifted into Salkuzzar, the high priest of the Temple of the Sun. He stared directly at me and sneered, "How foolish of you to imagine you could win." His face distorted with his contempt. He continued and, almost screaming, chastised me. "Do you think you can stand up to me?"

Alkur looks at Salkuzzar with no thoughts of anger or revenge. He quietly says, "Your heart gave you away long ago. We were ready for your arrival and call now upon all the angels, the Brotherhood of Light, spirits of love and light to touch your heart and those of your entourage. Even the blackest heart cannot stay closed against the power of love." His voice carried unmistakably above the sing-song intonation of the chants.

My arms lifted to the heavens. "I, Alkur, implore the Gods and spirits to send not revenge, but the vibration of unconditional love. I command the power of the light to bless these beings and all gathered, including the dark shadows."

In response a tremendous flash of light lit the sky. It hit the altar and separated into a dozen immense rays that struck the skulls and created a whirlpool of white shimmering light. Salkuzzar was thrown back out of the circle; the other dark entities slowly backed away.

Then, those of us gathered for the ceremony, and the dark priesthood beings, bowed and lay prostate on the ground as the most enormous white luminous forms materialized around the temple. They were inter-dimensional beings; emissaries of the white Brotherhood, I thought. Some had wings like the drawings of angels in times past. Columns of light scattered through the circle and surrounding land. Then the luminous forms began to sweep the dark energies from the temple, just as if they were housecleaning. I peeked up to watch in amazement as one picked up a shadow and cast it into a light column. In short order, the darkness was gone, almost literally swept away before my eyes. A shift was felt as the beings quickly dematerialized.

The oldest shaman rising slowly to his feet changed his chant to one of gratitude and praise. We all raised our heads and slowly rose to our feet, our eyes on the sky. The space ship slowly retreated and began to fade from sight. A small woman with moss-green eyes stood near me;

her head barely reached my shoulder. She whispered, "The Nieburians are leaving; they are gone forever. Earth's consciousness has shifted and they have been found out. There's no place for them here, now. They will never return again.

The ship dematerializes completely. I looked down again, but the woman was gone.

The wind stopped, the clouds vanished and the moon faded away. The sun rose, as it does every day, as we sat with the skulls in silence, our eyes closed in gratitude. The land had changed forever. We had done it.

Another portal had been opened.

Chapter 64

DECEMBER 22, 2012
ISLAND OF THE SUN, LAKE
TITICACA, BOLIVIA

This morning I climbed back up the mountain to the El Rocque site. I had spent most of the night trying to understand what had happened during the ceremony. Although tired, the climb was revitalizing. I reached the peak just as the sun rose on the horizon, the glimmer of sunlight awakening the world with its bright embrace. I just stood there in the stillness, mesmerized by the potency of its beauty. I understood now why the Incas considered the Island of the Sun sacred. The energy was magnificent.

I slipped the backpack off my shoulders and swung it softly down to the ground. Then, sitting cross-legged on a low level rock, I placed the skull in front of me. When I retrieved it after the ceremony, the oldest shaman had formally presented me with a tightly woven red cloth. I sat the skull on this mat. Closing my eyes, I began chanting the words I'd only learned a few months ago.

"AKMA, AKMA ATA, AKMA-RA-LA, AK-EL-KIBA, AK-RA-NA." The syllables lifted me into a deep, peaceful space. Effortlessly, I grew lighter and freer and soon felt surrounded in a vortex of brilliant white light. I felt so much harmony and love as I ascended into the vortex. Then, crossing a large portal I saw a golden gate and a well-traveled dirt road traversing an extraordinary field of yellow and white flowers. It was perfect. All my senses were alive.

After some time of walking along the road, I saw a lone man some distance away. I immediately recognized him.

"Papa, Papa!"

He ran to me and, pausing only for a moment, grabbed me in a huge bear hug. We held each other for a long time. Stepping back to get a better look, I saw his eyes wet with tears. He reached up to stroke my hair. He was young and handsome, just like I remembered him as a child.

"Andres, how are you? It's so good to see you. Walk with me a while and tell me, how are things now? I've missed so much."

The story of my life just flowed out of me as he listened attentively. He looked radiant and happy.

When I finally stopped talking, he just nodded. "I'm so proud of the man that you've become, Andres. The angels are also applauding!" He softly laughed.

I could only smile. I didn't want this moment to end.

He told me what happened to him and how he missed my growing up.

He shook his head at his own naivety. "How young we were. But, we grew up fast. I joined with patriotism in my heart, but I soon saw that the government's methods mirrored the evil they purportedly fought. The harsh interrogations, the kidnappings, the total absence of legal process, the murders in the detention centers..." His voice trailed off. I couldn't know what he was remembering.

"I was an interrogator at the ESMA, Andres. I hated it."

He went on to tell the story that Don Julio had told me but filling in the blanks. How he met my mother and fell in love and his betrayal and arrest. He had arranged for mother and me to find refuge in the Bolivian Embassy and be flown to a Bolivian base for our safety.

"I knew I'd never see you two again. My heart was broken. It was only days until I was caught and put through the same spiral of fear and torture that I had inflicted on others. I was sentenced to life in prison by the secret military tribunal for conspiring with the enemy of the state. Did you know your mother was a known Montenero leader? She was brilliant. None of this was ever divulged publically; it was kept quiet even in military circles. It was so long ago, Andres. So filled with darkness."

"In prison, I didn't contact your mother for fear that she too would be discovered and arrested."

"Papa, tell me about Captain Marti Becerra. Who is he?"

"Yes, of course. Marti is an old soul, Andres. But for this life, he returned to learn new lessons and pay his karmic debt from previous lifetimes, many on other planets. It's a difficult soul contract and a lot of planning went into it."

I started to ask for specifics, but he went on, "We've all had similar journeys, you included. Don't judge him harshly. Andres," he paused again, then said, "Marti is your biological father in this lifetime. All of this was presented to you in this life for knowledge and for you to gain a greater understanding of your emotions, the fear, anger and frustration that you have experienced, so that you may progress. Many of the answers can be found in the lifetime you experienced as Alkur. These are in essence opportunities, gifts, if you will, to allow you to move forward, to grow towards source."

I couldn't hide from it anymore. "Yes, I suspected that."

"Marti and I had been great friends, but fell out when we were both at ESMA. He decided to have your biological mother murdered and I just couldn't agree. She was beautiful and courageous; her name was Sarah Inez Escobedo. Marti raped her shortly after her arrest. After that we broke off our friendship."

I thought for moment, everything must come in its own time. I could now understand my mother's silence. If I had heard this as a child, or a younger man, it would have been horrible.

"She became pregnant. She didn't want you and Marti certainly didn't want anything to do with a baby. But I pushed and pushed saying that I'd adopt you. Finally, Marti relented, and let her have the baby, and I brought you home. At first Elizabeth objected, under the circumstances. You see Elizabeth could not conceive. This was by design."

"So, you knew Sarah?"

"Not well. We were acquainted but I could not help her. She knew this at the time and at the time I regretted not doing more."

"What happened to you?"

"I was killed when the junta saw that democratic change on the horizon. My sentence was changed and I was thrown from a helicopter into the sea. They just couldn't risk having witnesses to their crimes. I had long before signed up for my life to end that way. It was part of the divine plan for the growth of everyone's souls."

"I have no regrets. It was a good life and, most importantly, I did my part to help you and your mother's souls develop. There are no coincidences in the divine plan Andres. This was the contractual set-up. We've agreed to everything beforehand; it's all bringing more glory to God. I'm at peace. Just know, Andres that Sarah, Elizabeth and I are always with you."

I was both happy and sad at these words. Papa just raised his eyebrows and said, "Elizabeth and I are again planning future lives together. Like you and Hulos did before. Maybe we'll be part of new adventures together, eh?

The glow in the vortex was fading to pink. "Andres, I must go now."

"Just one more small question papa. How did I escape from Marti? I heard your voice."

"Ah, yes. Marti was going to kill you. You humiliated him, and he's always hated that. I reminded him that your murder was not part of his soul or yours contract. Although there is always free will, I was able to persuade him to change his mind. We agreed to a new 'potential' path forward Andres. Marti is not as bad as you think."

"Goodbye for now. I am always with you. Andres, don't look back now. The past is behind you. Live your life with joy. Vaya con Dios! Go with God!"

"I love you, Papa." He was gone before I finished speaking.

Another shape slowly materialized in front of me. She was a small young woman, very pretty but hesitant. Her long dark hair and green eyes were shining. She smiled and shyly said, "I'm Sarah."

Then she reached out and held me tightly, telling me how much she loved me. I was overwhelmed. I blurted out "mama" and I kissed her gently.

She recounted the story of my birth and said that although at first she wanted an abortion, she had changed her mind, wanting me to have a life, a good life. First, she had to ensure I would be cared for. She even thought that maybe she'd be freed and we'd be together, although she knew this would probably never happen. She said that my adopted mother Elizabeth loved me deeply just as she would have. She was the mother I was meant to have.

"I was resigned to my fate. I needed to learn to forgive and to let go. That was my journey. But having learned forgiveness, I know now that we are all part of one another, forever, across time."

"What do you mean that all along you were resigned to your fate?" Suddenly, this was very important to me.

Sarah spoke plainly, "After you were born, I was selected for "transfer." That was the handy euphemism meaning swift execution. They drugged me, loaded me, along with others, onto an airplane. Somewhere over the La Plata River, I was tossed alive from the plane." She stopped. "It was long ago."

"I've been afraid, Andres, that I passed along my own fears and guilt to you. The terrors of prison may have infected the innocents born there. I'm so sorry." Her sweet apology pushed aside any such memories. She was gone.

I came out of the meditation finding tears streaming down my face. There were feelings of gratitude and relief, and then a certain peace knowing that goodbyes are not forever.

Chapter 65

AVENIDA MERCEDES, APT # 61,
LA PAZ, BOLIVIA

Looking back, the winding path seems inevitable. But sitting here, having opened a new portal near Vilcabamba, I feel a renewed confidence, and courage to face myself and the future. I was moving forward to a new future.

The other day I received a letter containing a handwritten poem:

No es que oscuro, demonio peligroso de la muerte
Eso a menudo corre suelta en nuestra mente
Que grande, toro intimidante, a la vez potente y audaz
Los mejores matadores enfrentan, tal vez de sucumbir a su muerte
Con una confianza que debemos emular.

Esta confianza se llama "Llegar ver" en el ring
El matador entiende esto
Para que significa "a verlas venir"

Para plantar sus pies como el matador
Para mantener su posición y ver con calma
En cámara lenta la carga del toro
Te permites maniobrar el toro con seguridad por

Confianza reside en esta capacidad
Siendo aún es uno de los pasos en la oración
La confianza se encuentra en la quietud
Viene de muchos pases y peleas
Usted puede controlar el toro y derrotarlo
Porque has hecho antes

Nuestro toro viene cuando hemos perdido toda esperanza
O cuando la ansiedad me hace la desesperación por un problema
O cuando se me olvida el amor de Dios en mi vida
El toro viene a continuación,
Él piensa que le doy la bienvenida

Yo lo sé ahora. Yo lo puedo ver en la niebla
Le Sense antes de que se mueve
"Vamos! Yah, Toro "
Acusa
Le paso con seguridad por
Con un giro de la capa de mi confianza
La multitud ruge en mi cabeza --- OLE OLE OLE!
Luego el silencio como el toro es derrotado
Y en ese silencio que escucho la voz
"Bien hecho, mi hijo"
                    Marti

There is that dark, dangerous demon of death
That often runs loose in our mind

That large, intimidating bull, both powerful and fearless
The best matadors face it, maybe succumbing to its death
With a confidence we should emulate.

This confidence is called "ver llegar" in the ring
The matador understands this
For it means "to watch them come"
To plant your feet like the matador
To hold your ground and see calmly
In slow motion the charge of the bull
You allow yourself to maneuver the bull safely by

Confidence lies in this ability
Being still is one of the steps in prayer
Confidence lies in the stillness
It comes from many passes and fights
You can control the bull and defeat it
Because you have done it before

Our bull comes when we have given up all hope
Or when anxiety makes me despair over a problem
Or when I forget the love of God in my life
The bull comes then
He thinks I welcome him

I know him now. I can see him in the mist
Sense him before he moves
"Come on! Yah, Toro"
He charges
I pass him safely by
With a swing of the cape of my Confidence
The crowd in my head roars---OLE!

Old saints who passed their bull pulling for me...OLE! OLE! OLE!
Then silence as the bull is defeated
And in that silence I hear the voice
"WELL DONE, MY SON"

Marti

Along with the poem was a small picture creased by time. It showed young Naval Lieutenant Francisco Paredes and Lieutenant Julian Becerra Marti standing together, all smiles, with arms around each other's shoulder.

I know now that Don Julio's message, 'the dark energies surround us but we can see their shadow,' was all about recognizing our dark sides, those negative thoughts, beliefs and feelings, our toros or bulls.

The shadow will always remind us that it's there, but it also gives us a new awareness, bringing us into wholeness. We own it, consciously or unconsciously. The Marti's of the world remind us of this. Like skilled matadors, we can just let the bull go by.

I'm still working on accepting and integrating both my inner light and darkness.

Andres

Chapter 66

INTERGALACTIC COUNCIL 2012 A.D.

The Inter Galactic Council sends a flash news bulletin throughout the Universe summoning all beings to observe the changes taking place on earth, also known as the "planet of free choice."

Members of all the major star systems from the Pleiades, Arcturus, Orion, Sirius and Andromeda and others gather to witness this culminating event. They're celebrating victory as the bulletin joyfully announces that another inter-dimensional portal has reopened in the South American region of Lake Titicaca. This occasion has been eagerly awaited.

Intergalactic music and festivities take place as millions of inter-dimensional beings celebrate earth beginning her ascension. It is wonderful news for the entire universe as an enormous energetic shift occurs and aspiring souls return to the higher dimensions while others prepare for their earthbound journeys.

Greetings brothers and sisters from Planet Earth.
We greet you with the honor and respect that you deserve, for you have accomplished much.

We are the Intergalactic Council representing the ascended Pleiades, Arcturus, Cassiopeia, Alpha Centouri, Orion, Cygnus, Ursa Major, Taurus, Zeta Reticuli, Sirius and Andromeda, Central Sun of your Universe and other Universes.

We announce the opening of an Intergalactic Atlantean portal in the Lake Titicaca region of Peru.

This portal is connected to the crystalline energy of the central crystal of Atlantis, which is located at the Central Sun, the ascended Pleiades.

This portal will help align Earth with the galactic equator and strengthen its crystalline grid.

It will assist the earthly entities who, having brought back memories of their lives in Atlantis, now choose to transition to a higher frequency level dimension.

This portal transferred the energy of unconditional love through the sacred crystal skulls. It is prompting the opening and strengthening of many other intergalactic portals on Planet Earth necessary for the ascension of the Earth and humanity.

All the star systems are watching Earth now as you move forward in this cosmic-generated destiny of ascension.

We celebrate you and will continue to work through you.

The Intergalactic Council

EPILOGUE

F ollowing the final destruction of Atlantis, the survivors including the High Priests and Priestesses, each led their tribes to their new locations throughout the globe. Here, the refugees interbred with the local people and shared their knowledge and wisdom with them. This resulted in a huge advance in civilization worldwide enabling more people to carry the wisdom of Atlantis to future generations.

The tribe of Thoth migrated to South America where they became the Incas, famed for their gold work, spirituality and architecture. The Inca to this day are proud to trace their lineage to At-ach-u-chu or better known as Kon-tiki Wircacocha, a tall, red haired, bearded, fair skinned man and culture bearer who arrived by ship and was the leader of survivors from the final destruction of Atlantis.

Where they ended up...

Alkur- would live to a ripe old age following in the footsteps of his father and becoming a wise, compassionate leader and father to the Pachakutic lineage of Inca leaders.

Akaus—a princess, who used her talent in music in the Law of One to pacify conditions between humans, and their environment. She made music into a sacred art, a powerful source of communication with the divine world using combinations of powerful pentatonic tuning and soothing melodies inspiring the laying of songs and instruments during Inca religious celebrations and funerals.

Amillius — escaped Atlantis only to be allegedly murdered by survivors during a conspiracy/rebellion at sea. Rumors are that he was later sighted in Egypt.

Am-ee-lee—following initiation, became a high priest-healer and expert in native shamanism and scared ceremony. Guardian of the skull.

Asa-masa-ee—learned over 12 distinct dialects to become an expert linguist and ambassador for the native leadership and communities. She was later recognized as a high priestess and guardian of the secrets and sacred mysteries of the Inca.

AxTos—the physician became an expert in medicinal cures using local herbs and plants. He created a school to train others in alchemy, herbology and medicine practices and was beloved by all his pupils and the natives he helped.

Caphala—was best man at Alkur's wedding; became a military leader who was killed in subsequent native uprisings and by request his remains were scattered along the lake he grew to love.

Captain Julian Becerra Marti -was indicted by an Argentine Court in 2009 for the kidnap and torture of 250 men and women at ESMA during the dirty War (1976-1983). He is currently on the run from justice.

Don Julio Carasco—still lives in La Paz where he teaches young children metaphysics and the mysteries of the Universe.

Elchi—captivated the natives with his knowledge of seamanship. Lived with the Uros tribe on Lake Titicaca becoming one of their leaders and teaching them boat building. The Uros trace their lineage from the Atlanteans and Incas and today live on forty self-fashioned islands on Lake Titicaca.

Hulos—married Alkur in an elaborate ceremony and gave him two sons. She would live to see her two sons become successful leaders and fathers.

Ilax—would profess her deep love to Alkur and be called back to the astral world by Thoth to help returning soul's transitioning from earth to the higher dimensions of Spirit. She is still on the job.

Rariru—native chief who after surviving the purge of Saail became instrumental in blending newly arrived Atlanteans into prehistoric Peruvian society; he instituted worship of the Sun and Inti-rai-mi—the most sacred sun god ceremony.

Saail—Legend has it that his restless spirit can be seen wandering about in the Andes and the lower astral realms. His spirit returned later as Genghis Khan, Hitler and Saddam Hussein.

Salkuzzar—escaped the final destruction of Atlantis only to be shipwrecked and never heard from again.

Skull - the skulls are now privately owned and in museums around the world.

GLOSSARY

Akashic Record—the etheric memory of all time, place and consciousness of the universe in the DNA of all conscious beings.

Atlantis—an island state mentioned within an allegory on the hubris of nations in Plato's work Timaeus and Critias as lying in the Atlantic Ocean.

Amethyst—a violet quartz crystal quartz often used in ancient Atlantis. It teaches humility and letting go of the ego-consciousness of negative thoughts and beliefs.

Amillius—ruler in Atlantis prior to and during 3rd cataclysmic destruction of Atlantis. He rose to power when the existing council government was ineffective and under attack. The Belial Illuminati, creation of the former ruler Belial sought control over the Atlantean government in order to gain the support necessary for their agendas. They wanted the installment of the "old order" form of government, whereas the followers of the Law of One supported the continued council.

The failing and endangered high council relented and agreed to conduct a series of hearings for a cooperative reorganization of government. From these came a triad form of government—a compromise in the system consisting of three "advocates" acting as the ultimate authority over all matters of government: the people's advocate and elected representatives of the temple of the law of one and the temple of the sun. Despite this, there was further argument and division the triad government was ineffectual. This confusion was exploited by the Belial Illuminati.

The Sons of Belial of the Temple of the Sun came to influence a majority of those in high places, to support a new government. This new government would be strong and determined concerning itself first, with the growth and development of Atlantis and her people a secondary goal. They envisioned Atlantis going forth in the world, to develop a new world order of peace and prosperity. Amillius, then a high priest at the Temple of the Sun rose to prominence as leader of the Belial Illuminati. He displayed great talents of ambition, deception, and manipulation. He found a great avenue of experience in politics and furtherance of his ultimate goals for himself and Atlantis. He became obsessed by his lust for materialism and power. Like his predecessor Belial, Amillius through his political and monetary support of the sons of Belial, as well as religious support of the Temple of the Sun, would appoint himself a seat upon the triad government and an advocate for the Temple of the Sun in the triad government.

Through the maneuverings of Amillius, the triad government collapsed. He then went forth and forced a public issue on the establishment of a new order government. Amillius declared himself head of the new government and did so with the full support of the sons of Belial, the military and the industrial elements. However, the Law of One temple leaders challenged him. Having affected public opinion, and being confident of the people's support, he called for elections to take place. The elections were manipulated by the illuminati and Amillius officially became the ruler and the way was established for a new world order.

Throughout Atlantis people who resisted Amillius's election were vilified as revolutionaries and resistance grew to armed rebellion. The Temple of One led many peaceful protests against the injustices of the government in the far lands but enjoyed little success and were vilified as "resistors to progress" and "traitors". The Sons of Belial promoted, through the Temple of the Sun and media outlets, acts of violence against them. Many fled to rural areas and safe havens in far lands. Others went underground, changing their identities and hiding to escape. Other resorted to violence and attacks against government figures.

Annunaki—the ruling elite of the planet Nebiru, a planet that orbits between the Sirius system and our solar system every 3,600 years.

Atlantean Healing System–an energetic system of healing used by old Atlantean masters consisting of symbols that amplify the hidden essence of the Atlantean connection between body and spirit. Its connection with the divine is profound as well as its ability to heal all the spiritual bodies and the unconscious mind.

Ascension—the souls journey from darkness to light.

Belial Illuminati—secret organization founded by Atlantean ruler Belial of the Sons of Belial.

Children of the Law of One—focused on love, community, and practiced prayer and meditation together; hoping to promote divine knowledge. They were referred to as the Children of the Law of One because they advocated One Religion, One State, One Home, and One God.

CODEP— also known as National Commission on Disappeared Persons, appointed by Argentina's President Raul Alfonsin to inquire into the circumstances surrounding the disappearance and presumed death of thousands of people during the period of military government from March 1976 to December 1983. The report issued in 1983 was fifty thousand pages of interviews and eye-witness accounts. Its findings were that an established minimum of 8,960 people-and probably a third more not recorded by the commission, disappeared during the process of National Reorganization from 340 clandestine prisons throughout Argentina in during that period. They are still missing and presumed dead. Some experts place the total near 30,000.

Crystal Skulls: Carved crystal skulls have been unearthed in archeological digs in Peru and Bolivia, notably in 19th and 20th centuries.

They are human skull hardstone carvings made of clear or milky white quartz. No one really knows what they were for but it is clear from the sacred burial sites that they were prized ritual objects thought to contain great power. The skulls are often claimed to exhibit paranormal phenomena

Discoveries at Lake Titicaca

Lake Titicaca has long drawn fascination with various legends around it including an underwater city and another of Inca gold lost by the Spanish. The Incas also regarded the lake as the birthplace of their civilization and in their myth the Children of the Sun emerged from its waters. Many expeditions have been launched to find the lost treasure to include the famous French oceanographer Jacques Cousteau and National Geographic. The Bolivian government provided financial and technical support to preserve the ruins of an ancient pre-Incan temple complex found by international archeologists backed by the scientific group Akakaor Geographic under Lake Titicaca.

End of World Prediction: Actual Mayan calendars have been translated that predicted the year 2012 as "The End of Days." Some thought that this meant a natural disaster that destroyed the Earth, but most researchers believed that it meant a crucial spiritual turning point in Earth's civilizations."

ESMA (Escuela Superior de Mecanica de la Armada—Superior School of Naval Mechanics) located in the northern section of the city of Buenos Aires, on Libertador Avenue, deeded to the army in 1924 for the purpose of educating officers and sub-officers. During the military junta it became one of the biggest clandestine prisons used by the military Junta to torture an execute prisoners. Of the more than 5,000 prisoners held at ESMA, only a hundred survived. Also known as the "Auschwitz of Argentina." Today, the building houses the Museum of

Memory and a number of other cultural centers administered by various human rights organizations.

Gaia: Earth, the conscious being, a multidimensional diety.

Intergalactic Council-- a higher inter-dimensional forum that manages the will of the creator and provide guidance to the spiritual unfolding's and events on earth. The Intergalactic Council was responsible for seeding Atlantis and testing its commitment to Source.

Island of the Sun—island on the southern part of Lake Titicaca in Bolivia in the La Paz Department considered to be the birthplace of the original Inca dieties and civilization.

1976-1983--Argentina Oppressive Regime—the Junta-- The junta in Argentina was composed of the military commanders—Lieutenant General Videla, Admiral Massera, and Air Force Brigadier Agosti who in secret worked out the "charter" of the new government; to work together as a junta, a coalition, and that no one service would be supreme. The presidency would be rotated, to ensure disunity and internal coups would be avoided.

Between 1930 and 1976, the military had intervened six times in Argentina politics and was in power for over 21 years. No single civilian administration had lasted its full term. Before 1976, military governments had seized power with a clear-cut attitude of mind—a general feeling of superiority to inefficient civilian rule, as sense of their own spirit de corps, without a distinct ideology. From 1930 to 1972, the prevailing attitude had been to govern for a time, and then to hand over the country in better shape to the civilian politicians once again.

In 1976, by contrast the military had an ideology and this time they were in power to stay and impose that ideology on Argentina for good; as a permanent political solution. As an institution its first task was to destroy every vestige of opposition to their rule. It did not help that six years before the psychological conditions that had made such an ideology possible was the guerilla activities and attacks by both the Monteneros and ERP; attacking not just servicemen and officers, but their families and the places where they lived. This created an atmosphere for the junta to insist that only a through a strict policy of extermination would society be rid of left-wing violence and restore order. They saw it as a necessary "cleansing" process that could only be done by the men with the necessary toughness of purpose to carry it out—the military authorities. It reminded many Argentinians of the Nazi's rise to power in Germany in the 1930's and subsequent plan for racial purity and extermination.

In this nightmarish state of affairs, it became evident that complete and permissible illegal actions were permitted by the forces of "law and order." Since there were no longer any kidnappings by guerilla groups, the abductions of the "desaparecidos" (the disappeared ones) who were no longer missing persons any more, but instead victims of a strategy that would ensure they would disappear forever. The explanations occasionally produced by the authorities about them was that had faked their own abduction in order to go underground as terrorist; they had gone abroad for training; they had died in shootouts with other terrorists; or had been innocent bystanders killed in shootouts between security forces and guerillas, or had been shot while attacking a police station or a military installation. This was the nightmare that unfolded in Argentina.

Lake Titicaca—is a lake in the Andes on the border of Peru and Bolivia. It is often called the highest navigable lake in the world, with a surface elevation of 3,812 meters (12,507 ft.). Considered sacred by the Incas it was also used by the Tiawanaku culture.

Magi—a very powerful, devoted, and gifted Atlantean priest. They were highly trained teachers, scientists, alchemists, astrologers and psychics who practiced soul retrieval, prophecy and divination.

ROBERT R. MALDONADO PHD.

Mallku—is a title roughly translating as "prince" or "leader" in the Aymara language of South America.

Monteneros—Guerilla organization that pursued armed struggle between 1970 and 1979, although its roots go back to 1960, during the resistance to the government of Argentina President Juan Carlos Ongania. They came under the influence of the Movement of Priests for the Third World and the Marxist ideology of the Cuban Revolution. Following the violent suppression under the military, and fractured by dissent among their leaders, the Monteneros finally disappeared in 1979.

Neiburu—A three dimensional planet that moves in and out of the earth's solar system every 3,600 years.

Portals-- key power points or energy vortices on earth linked to the earth's magnetic grid, typically found at sacred sites, similar to the chakras on human beings. They are considered interdimensional conduits that allow for higher dimensional energies to flow within a focal planetary window.

Sons of Belial—an organization of "worthless and evil" individuals who's sole purpose was self-gratification, manipulation and control of others using technology to suit their egoic lusts. They were the opposing force to the Temple of the Law of One in Atlantis.

Temple of Pachamama—The temple in honor of the Inca fertility goddess Pachamama or earth mother who presides over planting and harvesting

Temple of Poseidon—most powerful place in Atlantis named after Poseidon who rules the sea. The temple was obolong in shape measuring 600 feet long and 300 feet wide (182 by 92 meters); built using white, black and red stones covered with orichalcum, a pink gold mountain copper. The floors and interior walls were pure white marble. In the temple was the great initiation chamber where the initiates were taught and tested.

The 13th skull-an amethyst skull of high frequency that contained the knowledge and wisdom of the 12 tribes of Atlantis.

The Violet Flame—a pure lavender and violet light that dissolves fear, anger, and negative thoughts replacing them with love and light.

Thoth—one of the dieties of Atlantis, Egyptian and Greek civilizations. In legend Thoth, the Atlantean and Master raised the people of Khem (Egypt) to a great civilization and erected the Great Pyramid where he posited his records and appointed Guards for his secrets from among the highest of his people. Thoth was deified as the God of Wisdom, the Recorder who passed on his wisdom in the Emerald Tablets, a Book of Record and Occult Wisdom.

Uros—a group of people who live on Lake Titicaca on artificial islands made of floating reeds that abounds in the shallows of the lake. These islands have become a major tourist attraction for Peru, drawing excursions from the lakeside city of Puno. Their original purpose was defensive, and they could be moved if a threat arose. Many of the islands contain watchtowers largely constructed of reeds.

Viracocha— the great creator god in the pre-Inca and Inca mythology in the Andes region of South America. Viracocha was one of the most important deities in the Inca pantheon and seen as the creator of all things, or the substance from which all things are created, and intimately associated with the sea. Viracocha created the universe, sun, moon, and stars, time (by commanding the sun to move over the sky) and civilization itself. Viracocha was worshipped as god of the Sun and of storms. He was represented as wearing the sun for a crown, with thunderbolts in his hands, and tears descending from his eyes as rain.

SELECTED BIBLIOGRAPHY

Alper, F. (1981). Exploring Atlantis. Irvine, California: Quantum Productions.

Andrews, S.(1997). Atlantis: Insights from a Lost Civilization. Woodbury, MN: Llewellyn Publishing.

Andrews, S. (1998). Lemuria and Atlantis. Woodbury, MN: Llewellyn Publishing.

Atlantean Healing System Manual: Diagnosis, Treatment, Symbols & Attunements (revised 2004)

Aribalo, M. (2007). Inka Power Places: Solar Initiation: Andean Archeo-astronomy. Peru: Shamanic Productions

Baldwin, W.(2003). Healing Lost Souls—Releasing Unwanted Spirits from Your Energy Body. Charlottesville, Virginia: Hampton Roads Publishing Company, Inc.

Bryant, A., & Galde, P.(1989). The Message of the Crystal Skull: From Atlantis to the New Age. St. Paul, MN: Llewellyn Publications.

Campbell, J.(1949). The Hero with a Thousand Faces. Princeton: Princeton University Press.

Cayce, E. (1988). Mysteries of Atlantis Revisited. San Francisco: Harper & Row.

Carrol, L. (2013). Kryon—The Recalibration of Humanity. California: The Kryon Writings.

Cayce, E.(2009). Atlantis. Virginia Beach, VA: A.R.E. Press.

Cooper, D.(2005). Discover Atlantis- A Guide to Reclaiming the Wisdom of the Ancients. Scotland: Findhorn Press.

Condron, Daniel & Barbara. (2001). Remembering Atlantis. Windyville, MO: School of Metaphysics.

Childress, D. (1996). Lost Cities of Atlantis, Ancient Europe & the Mediterranean. Stelle, Ill: Adventures Unlimited Press.

Cori. P.(2001). Atlantis Rising—The Struggle of Darkness and Light. Berkeley, CA: North Atlantic Publishing

Donda, V.(2010). My Name is Victoria-The Extraordinary Story of One Woman's Struggle to Reclaim her True Identity. New York: Other Press.

Feitlowitz, M.(1998). A Lexicon of Terror: Argentina and the Legacies of Torture. New York: Oxford University Press.

Joseph, F.(1987). The Destruction of Atlantis. Olympia Fields, Ill: Atlantis Research Publishers.

Joseph, F. (2004). The Survivors of Atlantis: Their Impact on the World. Rochester, VT: Bear & Company.

Joseph, F. (2012). Atlantis and 2012: The Science of the Lost Civilization and the Prophecies of the Maya. Rochester VT: Bear & Company.

Joseph, F. (2004). The Destruction of Atlantis: Compelling Evidence of the Sudden Fall of the Legendary Civilization. Rochester, VT: Bear & Company.

Litten, J.(2007). Crystal Skulls: Interacting With a Phenomena. Flagstaff, AZ: Light Technology Publishing.

Melchizadek, D.(1999) The Ancient Secret of the Flower of Life, Volume 1, Flagstaff, AZ: Light Technology Publishing.

Moore, T. (2015). Atlantis & Lemuria—the lost continents revealed. Flagstaff, AZ: Light Technology Publishing.

Morton, C., & Thomas, C. (2002). The Mystery of the Crystal Skulls: Unlocking the Secrets of the Past, Present, and Future. Rochester, VT: Bear & Company.

Osorio, E.(2003). My Name is Light. London: Bloomsbury Publishing.

O'Sullivan, T & N.(1999). Soul Rescuers. London: Thorsons.

Pearce, S.(2005). The Alchemy of Voice—Transform and Enrich Your Life Through the Power of Your Voice. Scotland: Findhorn Press.

Pearce, S.(2005). The Angels of Atlantis Oracle Cards. Scotland: Findhorn Press.

Simpson, J., & Bennet, J. (1985). The Disappeared and the Mothers of the Plaza—The Harrowing Account of a Military Dictatorship and its Victims. New York: St Martin's Press.

Stanish, C. (2011). Lake Titicaca: Legend, Myth and Science. World Heritage and Monument Series.

Timerman, J. (1981). Prisoner Without a Name, Cell Without a Number. Madison Wisconsin: The University of Wisconsin Press.

Tolle, E. (1999). The Power of Now. New World Library.

Tyberonn (2011). Earth-keeper: the energy & geometry of sacred sites. Phoenix AZ: Star Quest Publishers.

Verbitsky, H.(1996). Confessions of an Argentine Dirty Warrior. New York: New Press.

Webb-De Sisto, M.(2002) Crystal Skulls. Xlibris Corporation.

APPENDIX

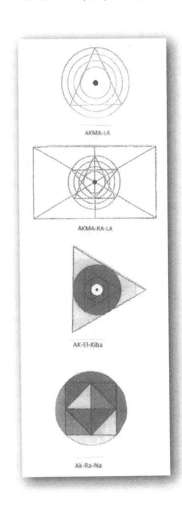

AKMA-LA

AKMA-RA-LA

AK-El-Kiba

Ak-Ra-Na

ABOUT THE AUTHOR

Robert R. Maldonado, PhD, is a healer, teacher, and retired military officer. He spent his career as a US Marine Corps helicopter pilot and with the elite Air Commandos of the Air Force Special Operations Command. Upon retirement, he taught elementary and middle school.

Maldonado holds certifications in energy medicine, healing touch, Barbara Brennan healing science, Reiki, shamanism, and is an ordained minister and Siddha in transcendental meditation. He is also a teacher of integral Chinese qigong and tai chi.

Maldonado holds a PhD in energy medicine from Akamai University where he is adjunct professor of complementary and alternative medicine. He is the author of Calling of the Heart: A journey in Self-Healing, which describes his personal experiences in transformation as a healer

He resides in Fairhope, Alabama, where he lives with his wife Ellen, cat Maggie, and dog Buddy and works as a writer, healer, and teacher.

Visit authors website at : www.authorrobertmaldonado.com

Made in the USA
Charleston, SC
22 March 2016